THE MOON UNDER HER FEET

DERWIN MAK

This is a work of fiction. The events described are imaginary. The settings and characters are fictitious and not intended to represent specific places or persons.

The text of this novel is that of the second edition, revised and corrected by the author and published by Weird and Wondrous Books, Pointe-Claire, Quebec, Canada, in 2011. The Author's Foreword, lacking in the first edition (2007), was published in this edition for the first time. The Author's Afterword appears for the first time in the Dark Helix Press editions (2016, 2020).

THE MOON UNDER HER FEET

PRINTING HISTORY
Orchard House Press, Port Orchard, Washington, United States / First Edition, July 2007
Weird and Wondrous Books, Pointe-Claire, Quebec, Canada/ Second Edition, December 2011
Dark Helix Press, Toronto, Ontario, Canada/ Third Edition, May 2020

All rights reserved.

Copyright © 2020 by Derwin Mak
Cover art by Eumir Carlo Fernandez.

The Scripture quotations contained herein, except for the verses from Genesis read by the crew of Apollo 8, are from the New Revised Standard Version Bible: Catholic Edition, copyright 1989, 1993, Division of Christian Education of the National Council of the Churches of Christ in the United States of America. Used by permission. All rights reserved.

The quotations from the Koran are adapted from the 1876 translation of the Koran by John Medows Rodwell, now in public domain.

Library and Archives Canada Cataloguing in Publication

Mak, Derwin, author

The moon under her feet / Derwin Mak. -- Third edition.

Issued in print and electronic formats.

ISBN 978-0-9917425-9-2 (paperback).

--ISBN 978-1-988416-00-7 (e-book)

I. Title.

PS8626.A423M66 2016 C813'.6 C2016-904091-7 C2016-904092-5

Dark Helix Press books are published by Dark Helix Press Inc. http://www.darkhelixpress.com

THE MOON UNDER HER FEET

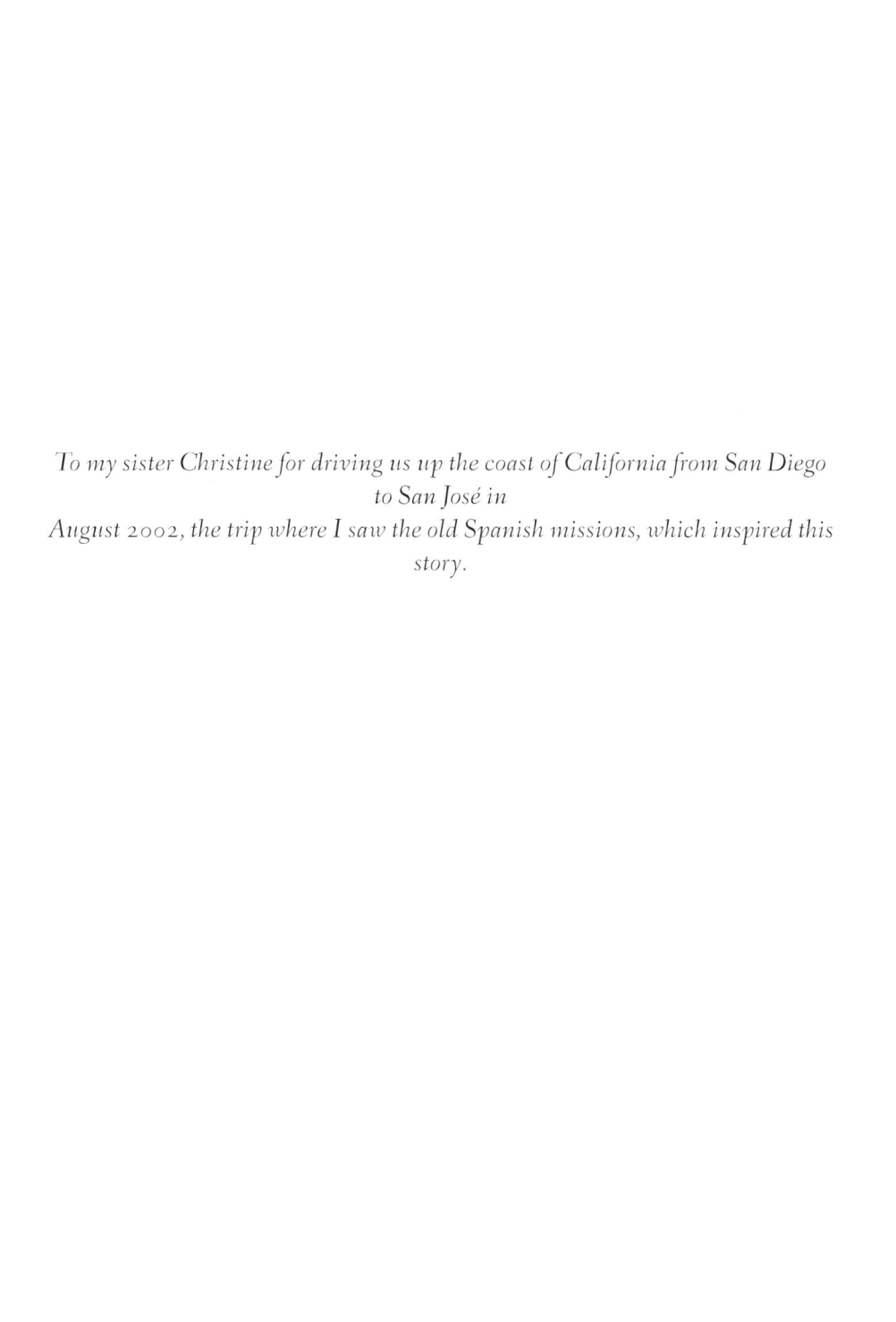

To my sister Christine for driving us up the coast of California from San Diego to San José in
August 2002, the trip where I saw the old Spanish missions, which inspired this story.

ACKNOWLEDGMENTS

Thanks to: the Reverend Daniel Brereton for information about Real Presence and True Presence in the Eucharist; to Dr. David Stephenson for information about missile launch accidents and disasters; to Kent Wong for driving me to the Roman Catholic shrines of Montreal and Niagara Falls, where I researched topics of this novel; to Fingers Delaurus, for help in writing the French dialogue; to Julie Czerneda, for commissioning, editing, and giving the title to "The Siren Stone", which begat "Transubstantiation", which begat this novel; and to Cris K.A. DiMarco for publishing "Transubstantiation".

AUTHOR'S FOREWORD

Sometimes history overtakes science fiction.

Not long ago, the Union of Soviet Socialist Republics dominated politics on Earth and in space. The Unbreakable Union seemed invincible. In creating their universes, science fiction writers reasonably expected the USSR to exist in the future. For example, Arthur C. Clarke portrayed the USSR as a space power in *2001: A Space Odyssey* and *2010: Odyssey Two*.

But then came Gorbachev, glasnost, perestroika, and the August Coup. The Soviet Union dissolved in 1991, nine years before Clarke's character Heywood Floyd meets Soviet scientists and nineteen years before a joint US-USSR space mission.

(In addition, Pan American Airlines, featured in the film versions of *2001* and *2010*, went out of business three weeks before the Soviet Union did.)

When *The Moon Under Her Feet* was first published in 2007, the terrorist leader Osama bin Laden had evaded justice for six years since the September 11 attacks. The Americans seemed incapable of finding him. It was likely that when he eventually died, his followers would bury him.

Bin Laden belonged to the Wahhabi sect of Islam, whose followers usually receive modest burials in unmarked graves. However, I envisioned bin Laden as being so vain that he would defy Wahhabi tradition for personal glory. He would leave instructions for a tomb like those of Islamic princes and saints. Hence, the Siren Stone universe has the Tomb of Osama bin Laden.

In the real universe, U.S. Navy SEALs killed Osama bin Laden and sank his body into the Arabian Sea in 2011. Neither his family nor followers got to bury him, much less build a tomb.

How to deal with the death of bin Laden? Some science fiction writers rewrite their stories. Others declare that the story occurs in an alternative universe.

But I have done neither. For this edition of *The Moon Under Her Feet*, the plot has not changed. The Tomb of Osama bin Laden stays intact in Bin Laden City, Purist Arabia.

A future Siren Stone story will explain why the Purists built the tomb. Here's a hint: bin Laden's body sank with weights attached to it, so his bones still could be at the bottom of the sea.

I was correct in presuming bin Laden's vanity, though. Videos captured by the Navy SEALs prove that he dyed his grey hair and beard black before taping his public tirades.

Derwin Mak
Toronto, May 17, 2011

PART 1
THE SIREN STONES

1 / 20 521 ODETTE DE PROUST

Colonel Matthew Chang sat aboard the spaceship *Long Island* and stared at the sensor map, which showed asteroid 20 521 Odette de Proust flying steadily towards Space Station Reagan — and the two hundred and ninety people he'd had to leave there.

A video transmission from General Boyd on Space Station Olympus appeared on a monitor. Chang noticed that Boyd was wearing a clean green service uniform, the U.S. Army's equivalent of a business suit, with four polished silver stars pinned to each collar. The General, despite the duress of the Mars disaster, still strove to look like the commander of all American military forces around Mars.

In contrast, Colonel Chang wore a plain field uniform with a cloth rank insignia, a colonel's eagle, sewn onto it. Chang preferred to dress like the soldiers he commanded.

"Colonel," said Boyd, "all our fleet –- what's left after the Mars disaster — is still carrying survivors away from the surface. The soonest any ship can get to Space Station Reagan is seven weeks."

"Odette will hit Reagan in six," said Chang plainly.

"Are you confident the demolition crew will blow up the asteroid well before that?" Boyd asked.

Chang shook his head. "They're still behind schedule. Two days now. Something's wrong." In the asteroid demolition business, rock blasters did not linger on an asteroid by choice. If they were late, they had run into trouble. A failed bomb, a premature explosion, a crashed ship, a collision with another asteroid, an injured crew...there were endless possibilities on how the mission could fail.

But these problems occurred on asteroids that wobbled erratically in orbits crowded with other rocks. They seldom occurred on asteroids like Odette, rocks that rotated smoothly in orbits with few neighbors.

"Rock Blasters, Inc. is the best in the business," said Boyd. "But if they've failed, you and the *Long Island* must be in position to blow up the asteroid."

"I should be evacuating the station. It's not worth risking anyone —" Chang protested. "We're not the experts —"

"I'll take full responsibility. I've put the order in writing," said Boyd. "Remember, the *Long Island* holds only ten people. Time isn't on your side -- to save the personnel or the station itself. That's why I'm sending you to make sure that asteroid is destroyed. It's the only way to save all three hundred people."

Chang nodded. "Thank you, General," he said, relieved that Boyd was taking the responsibility for Chang abandoning the people of Space Station Reagan. "I'll make sure that Odette is destroyed."

"Good luck, Colonel, and go get that rock out of my sky," Boyd said as he ended his transmission.

After Boyd's transmission ended, Chang muttered, "We should've blown up Odette years ago. Those stupid civil servants don't take anything seriously until it becomes a crisis."

A lieutenant turned to Chang. "Sir," said the lieutenant, "We've re-established contact with the *Rocky Road*."

"Finally," said Chang. "What's going on now?"

"The crew is still acting crazy. They insist there are people living on the asteroid."

"Impossible," Chang growled. "How can anyone live on an airless rock?"

The lieutenant pointed at a monitor. "We're getting a transmission from the blasters now, sir."

On the monitor, the image of Andrew Lundman appeared, beamed from his ship the *Rocky Road*, now on Odette.

"Lundman, when are you going to blow up that rock?" said Chang.

"Not while there are people here," said Andrew.

For Andrew Lundman, owner of Rock Blasters, Inc. and captain of the *Rocky Road*, the project had seemed clear and simple: land on Odette, bore a hole into its core, plant a couple nuclear bombs, leave, and detonate the bombs. Odette would break into pieces of varied trajectories instead of slamming into Space Station Reagan six weeks from now.

Scavengers would follow to pick up the chunks of iron ore and pay a commission of five million gold units to Rock Blasters, Inc. Along with the twenty million gold units for blowing up the asteroid, Rock Blasters, Inc. would make a good profit.

20 521 Odette de Proust, named after a character from the novel *Swann's Way* and the novelist who created her, should have been a routine assignment. Odette was small and deemed safe enough that the United Nations Committee On Asteroid and Meteor Collisions had simply outsourced the job to Rock Blasters, Inc. On schedule, Andrew Lundman, George Hodding, and Ed Benton had landed on Odette without problems. Just another asteroid demolition. Or so they'd thought.

The first ghost had appeared when they were drilling into the asteroid. Andrew remembered the moment in every detail. They all did.

―――

"Oh, God, look over there!" George shouted.

Ed gasped and pointed at the figure. "What's that?"

"Then you see her too?" demanded George.

Andrew turned off the drill. "I see it too," he said. "What is it? An alien?"

"No, it's Rachel," said George, both mystified and excited. "Rachel, my wife."

As he watched the figure walk closer, George muttered, "Rachel, Rachel. But Rachel is dead."

Andrew turned and stared straight at her so that his helmet camera would capture her image. "Reagan Mission Control, there's another person on the asteroid. I'm aiming my helmet camera at her. Do you see her?"

"Negative, Lundman," Mission Control replied warily from Space Station Reagan. "We don't see any person other than you and your crew."

George began walking towards Rachel. As he passed by, Andrew saw the dumbfounded look on George's face and the hesitant way he approached Rachel.

Mission Control addressed George: "Mr. Hodding, why are you moving away from the drill operation?"

"Investigating an anomaly," said George as he approached Rachel, who was now smiling.

Rachel put her arms around him. "Oh, George, it's been too long," she cooed. "Don't look so shocked. Look happy."

"Rachel, how — how on Earth did you get here?" George blurted.

"We're not on Earth," Rachel reminded him. "Just hold me for a little while."

Over his helmet radio, Andrew heard George and Rachel talk. "Mission Control, Hodding is talking to his wife. Do you hear them?" he asked.

"Negative on that. We hear Hodding talking to someone, but we don't hear anyone talking back to him," said Mission Control. "What's going on over there?"

———

Even if she were alive, she should have been dead because she had no spacesuit and no air. Instead of any protection from the cold and vacuum of space, she wore a red jacket and short black dress and high heels. It was the outfit she had worn on their first date twenty years ago.

She also looked as young as she had been on their first date. Behind her, the stars shone like bright white pinpricks against the black fabric of space. The searchlight from the *Rocky Road* lit half her face, leaving the other half in shadow.

"George, it's so wonderful to see you again," she repeated.

George shook his head. How could she talk through the vacuum of space, and how could he hear her voice on his helmet radio? How could her wavy black hair blow in a wind that couldn't exist?

"Rachel, is it really you?"

Rachel smiled. "In the flesh."

George reached out and touched her again. She was solid.

"How can you stand there without a spacesuit, how can you talk to me?"

Rachel shrugged. "I don't know. I was suddenly here. I don't know how I got here or how I can live here."

She swung her arms around and danced. "But I feel so alive!"

Even though you died seven years ago, remembered George.

"George, how is Megan?" she asked.

"Megan's well. She turned fifteen a month ago. Listens to those Euro-rock groups. She got an A in English. Her teachers like her..." he rambled.

Rachel squealed. "Oh, how I wish I could see her grow up! And how about Crystal?"

George smiled. "She's well too. Crystal's an athlete, pretty good for a twelve-year-old. Came in second at a school track and field meet. She got a blue ribbon."

Rachel pointed at the *Rocky Road*. "Can we go inside the ship? Did you bring photos of the girls? I want to see them!"

As they walked to the ship, George wondered how he would tell his wife's ghost that he had betrayed her.

Ed's father, who had died of lung cancer five years ago, appeared next. Ed had seen photos of his Dad's last days, when he looked scrawny and wasted by disease inside an ill-fitting green hospital gown. But here on Odette, he looked healthy and fit, as he was in Ed's childhood, and wore his favorite red plaid shirt and blue jeans.

Ed walked slowly, cautiously, to his Dad. Ed felt his throat go dry with fear and surprise, but he managed to talk.

"Dad, how did you get here?" Ed asked.

"I dunno. Suddenly appeared here. Glad I'm alive again, though."

"So you know — you know that you're –- dead?" Ed asked.

His Dad threw a pebble. It soared silently through the beam of light from Ed's flashlight and into the black depths of space.

Dad nodded. "Yeah, I know I'm supposed to be dead. I don't know how or why I'm here with you."

The final ghost to appear to the rock blasters was Sally, Andrew's sweetheart at the University of Oregon. She had died when Purist terrorists bombed her train in their last year at university. Yet on Odette, Sally was alive and well, as young as she had been in her senior year, wearing the white, green and yellow uniform of a University of Oregon cheerleader.

"Go, Ducks!" she yelled, referring to the University of Oregon's football team. After dropping her pom-poms to the ground, she jumped into a pike, a jump where she kicked her legs up parallel to the ground and bent at the waist to touch her toes. When she landed in front of Andrew, a small cloud of rock dust rose from her feet.

With a gasp, Andrew stumbled and fell backwards onto the ground. Up and down his spine, he felt both the heat of shock and the cold of fear. As he looked up at Sally, he saw and heard her laugh.

"Klutzy, just like at the spring dance! You haven't changed a bit!" she teased him. She bent and reached down to help him get up on his feet. He felt her solid hands grab his arm.

"Hey, Andy, let's go into the ship," she suggested. "You can take your spacesuit off in there. You'll be more comfortable. Yeah." She smiled. "Why don't you take some clothes off?"

———

Back aboard the *Rocky Road*, Andrew took off his spacesuit and led Sally to the control room. Used to a mere three-man crew, Andrew suddenly felt crowded in the control room, with George and Rachel holding hands in one corner, Ed and his Dad huddled over a monitor at another area, and now he and Sally walking into the room.

Andrew had never seen George's green eyes so happy and bright as now, as Rachel ran her hands through his brown hair. Andrew also noticed that Ed's blonde hair was thinning in the same spot, at the back of his head, where his Dad had gone bald.

He turned around and saw Sally put her pom-poms down beside a computer console. As she sat down in a chair and stretched, he noticed how life-like these ghosts were. Unlike the transparent spirits of horror movies and stories, these looked opaque and felt solid.

He saw his reflection in a shiny metal control console. Gray hair, induced by time and hard living. He'd aged so much since Sally died. What a contrast with her ghost's hair, still as blonde and shiny as it had been in college.

"How can you exist?" Andrew demanded. "Without air? Without food? Without, uh-"

"Without life?" said Sally. "Yes, I know I'm supposed to be dead. I don't know how I got here. But why does it matter? We can just pick up where we left off." She rose from the chair, put her arms around Andrew's shoulders, pulled his lips towards hers, and kissed him. It was a deep, wet kiss, full of love and longing and hunger.

Andrew gripped her and returned the kiss. Her skin felt warm and soft and smelled of the lilac perfume she had worn on their last date, two weeks before she died.

———

On Space Station Reagan, Mission Control still could not see Sally, Rachel, and Dad through the *Rocky Road*'s cameras, nor could Mission Control hear the ghosts' voices. After Mission Control and Andrew had argued for hours, Colonel Chang, the station's commander was called in. Like his staff, the colonel could not see the ghosts either.

"All I see are you, Hodding, and Benton," said Chang. "I can't see anyone else."

"How can you not see them? They're right here beside us," said Andrew. He turned to Sally. "Sally, say something to the Colonel."

"I can't explain this, sir, but I am here," said Sally.

Chang said nothing. *Hadn't he heard Sally?* Andrew wondered.

Finally, Chang spoke. "Lundman, who were you talking to a minute ago?"

"Sally," said Andrew. "Didn't you hear her?"

"Hear who?" Chang asked. "I heard nobody."

Over at another corner, Rachel sighed. "It's so stuffy in here, George. Can I go back outside? I feel more comfortable on the asteroid surface."

"Soon, Rachel, soon," said George as he rubbed Rachel's shoulder to sooth her.

On the monitor, Chang looked puzzled. "Hodding, what are you doing? Rubbing the air?"

"My wife," George said. "Her shoulders are a bit sore."

"Your wife? But Abby's in New York," Chang protested. "She called Mission Control last night."

"Not Abby. Rachel," explained George. "I was talking to Rachel."

"Rachel?" Chang said. "No, that's impossible."

Ed's Dad waved dismissively at Chang's image on the monitor. "He doesn't believe we're here," he said. "He just wants you to blow up the asteroid."

"Don't worry, Dad. We won't blow it up," said Ed.

"Mr. Benton, did I hear you tell someone that you're not going to blow up the asteroid?" Chang erupted.

Ed nodded. "You heard correctly," he mumbled.

Andrew looked at Chang's image on the monitor. "Colonel, I know how incredible this all seems to you. We're very shocked and surprised, too. I think we shouldn't destroy the asteroid until we've had a chance to study it."

Chang looked alarmed. "You *must* blow up that rock."

"We can't blow up this rock. It's different."

"What do you think you've found?" Chang protested. "A Siren Stone? You know they're just a deep space myth."

As mermaids had been to ancient mariners, Siren Stones were to modern spacers. They were a way to explain the space crews who turned crazy and disappeared without a trace. In the vast deepness of space, what lonely spacer could resist the beautiful spirits who haunted the Siren Stones? Andrew hadn't taken the myth seriously, until now.

"Maybe there's some truth behind the myth," said Andrew. "That's more reason to preserve the rock until we learn more about it."

"What about the three hundred people on Space Station Reagan?" said Chang.

"We can still save them. Let's not blow up the asteroid. Let's move it instead," Andrew suggested eagerly. "We'll plant bombs on the rock's surface, and when we set off the explosives, the blast will nudge the rock into a new orbit, one that won't threaten Reagan or anything else."

Chang shook his head. "Attempts to move asteroids into safe orbits have a lousy success rate. The procedure is too complicated. That's why we blow up the damn rocks. I can't take the risk. I won't gamble with three hundred lives."

"We *can* move the asteroid into a safe orbit," Andrew insisted.

"You have your orders, Mr. Lundman. Blow up that rock."

―――――

Ed and his Dad went outside the ship, back to the airless surface of Odette. Ed wore a spacesuit, but Dad did not.

"How is the family?" asked Dad.

"Mom's okay. She moved to California about two months ago," Ed replied. "Joan's not at Georgetown anymore. She chose a contract position at Stanford because she likes it there. And Trini and I had a son last year. His name is Norman."

"Wow, I'm a grandfather! Whoo-ee!" his Dad yelled. "Too bad I couldn't be there for the boy, Norman's his name? It's bad enough that I missed a few years of your life, and now I'm not around for my grandson's."

A few years of your life: the words echoed in Ed's ears.

Ed's Dad quit his job at the car factory when Ed was five years old and spent the next five years moving from one bad business deal to another. During that time, Dad never had money, and Mom never smiled. After five years of financial failures, he had simply walked out. To support Ed and Joan, Mom worked two jobs, one cleaning an office building and another waiting at a restaurant.

Dad returned five years later, paler and thinner than ever before, but with a small amount he had earned in odd jobs in California. He was ready to lead his family again, he announced sheepishly. Mom wouldn't take him back, though. Without any argument, he gave her the money and moved into an apartment across town. He had exiled himself from his family when they had wanted him, and now they were exiling him when he wanted them.

He came to visit them from time to time, though. By the time Ed left to work on the Moon, Mom and Joan were just warming up to Dad again, starting to close the chasm in the family. Eventually, Mom and Joan forgave Dad for his disappearance. About seven years after his return, Dad and Mom renewed their vows, in essence, got married again, with Joan as bridesmaid. But Ed was away on the Moon and couldn't come back. He had said that his employer had no room for him on the next shuttle back to Earth. In fact, he had not even asked for a seat on the flight.

Ed visited his Mom and Dad only twice in the next five years. Unlike Mom and Joan, he could not forgive his Dad for leaving him when he was ten years old.

And then his Dad discovered he had cancer. When Ed got the space transmission from his mother, he realized that if he wanted his father again, he was running out of time. But Ed was on a rock blasting team heading for Mars. By the time the ship returned to Earth, his Dad had already died.

Ed wanted to tell his Dad that all is forgiven -- but was this ghost really his Dad?

"Before you arrived here, what was the last thing you remember?" Ed asked.

"Dying," said Dad.

Ed looked at the stars above them. *Is this what heaven looks like?* he asked himself. *Is that where they were? In heaven?*

"INCOMING TRANSMISSION" flashed on the monitor. Andrew watched the words fade out and Colonel Chang's image fade in. The transmission was coming from the *Long Island*; Chang had left Space Station Reagan and was heading to Odette.

"You are now three days behind schedule on the demolition of Odette," Chang said. "Do you intend to blow it up?"

"I repeat, not while there are people here," said Andrew.

"There are no people there!" said Chang. He sounded agitated; Andrew had never seen him unnerved before.

Chang tried a more reasoning tone. "They're all in your imagination," he said.

Andrew looked at Sally. She straddled the floor, legs wide apart, and raised her arms over her shoulder to touch her feet. That was how cheerleaders stretched their hamstrings and calf muscles. He remembered seeing her do those stretches on a football field in Oregon many years ago.

She looked so warm, so lively. When they had kissed, he realized that he had never kissed as passionately as with her. Sally was a real woman again.

Andrew turned back to Chang. "No, sir, they are not our imagination. They are real."

"So are the two hundred and ninety people now on Space Station Reagan," Chang reminded him grimly. "That's two hundred and ninety dead if you don't blow up Odette."

"We're working on a way to move the asteroid into a safe orbit," Andrew said. "I'm confident we'll succeed."

"You know that's the riskier procedure." Chang scowled from the monitor. "You leave me no choice, Mr. Lundman. I will demolish Odette and arrest you and your crew."

"Arrest us?" questioned Andrew. "On what grounds?"

"*United States Space Stations Code*, section 52, 'Willful Endangerment of a Space Station,'" Chang stated. "Minimum sentence, ten years. Don't make this mistake. Obey your orders."

George and Rachel strolled outside on the asteroid's surface, talking about the girls. Rachel laughed when she heard how her daughters had grown up.

"Oh, how I wish I could have seen all of it," she said finally. "Oh, if only I could have been there for them."

George nodded. "That has been the greatest sadness of my life, that you aren't there to see them grow up."

Rachel shook her head. "George, don't feel sad anymore. I'll always be with all three of you."

"Are you in heaven?" George asked.

She took his hand and placed it over his heart. "I'm right here, in your heart."

"You always have been," said George as they continued walking.

"I got to hand it to you, George," said Rachel. "It must have been hard to raise two girls by yourself for seven years."

George sighed. "There's something I have to tell you. I wasn't alone all that time."

"Oh?" said Rachel. "My mother has been helping out?"

"No. I remarried four years ago. Her name is Abby."

Rachel stopped walking and looked at George. "Abby. Is she a nice girl?"

"Yes."

"And how does she treat the girls?"

George said nothing.

"George, how does she treat the girls?" Rachel asked again, anxiously.

George took in a deep breath. "Extremely well. Abby loves them deeply, treats them as if they were her own daughters."

Rachel crossed her arms and shifted her gaze to a rock beside them, as if to avoid looking him in the eye.

"Oh, I see," she said softly.

———

For Andrew, Sally's death had ended all of their plans: getting married, getting jobs, and starting a family.

"So you never went to that job you had lined up after graduation, the one with the City of Eugene?" Sally asked.

"No, I went into the Navy instead," said Andrew. Without Sally, he had joined the U.S. Navy after graduation, hoping to fight the terrorists who had blown up her train.

He had felt a brief sense of joy when Navy missiles killed the last Purist commander in Sudan, but it couldn't erase the sadness of losing Sally. Afterwards, he volunteered for service on the furthest, loneliest space station, and later, went into rock blasting.

"No children?" asked Sally. "Why not?"

"Hard to do with my job," said Andrew. "I'm always traveling for months in space. No time to meet someone, much less raise a kid."

He paused. He knew he had been making excuses for years.

"But remember, I *had* wanted children," he continued. "That's what we had planned. We would get married after graduation. We'd live in Eugene. We would get jobs there. I would be a road engineer. You would be an accountant for the bakery. We would have children."

Sally smiled. "We had our whole lives planned, didn't we?"

"We sure did, girl," said Andrew.

"Things didn't go according to plan, did they?"

"No, they didn't." Words came out of Andrew in a rush. "I was looking forward to life with you. It was the most important thing in my life. Instead, I wound up alone, no kids, living anywhere but in Eugene, blasting space rocks for a living. It wasn't what we had planned."

———

Ed and his Dad passed by the drill, now motionless but still stuck into the asteroid. His Dad pointed at the drill.

"Is it deep enough to plant those nuclear bombs?" his Dad asked.

"We're not going to do it," Ed protested. "How can we? We would kill you."

"I'm already dead," said his Dad. "But think of yourself. That military spacecraft will be here any day now. If you don't blow up Odette, they'll arrest you and blow it up anyway."

"We'll fight them," Ed declared. "I lost you once, I won't lose you again!"

"Ed, you can't have me forever. Stop clinging to me. Son, why do you keep clinging on to me?"

"Because, because," Ed started. He couldn't force the words out of his mouth. But it was time to tell him.

"Because I never got to tell you that I forgive you for leaving me and Joan and Mom," Ed said.

His Dad put his hand on Ed's shoulder. "I know, Son. I've known all this time."

A tear ran down Ed's cheek. "You mean, you died knowing I had forgiven you?"

"Sure did. Don't let that bother you anymore."

Ed heard a clicking sound over his helmet radio. He turned around and looked at the drill's sensor box. The sensor box's lights were lit up in red, blue, and green. He kneeled down to read the display.

"My, oh my," said Ed. "Dad, you've got to see this."

He turned around to look at his Dad, but his Dad was not there.

―――――

Rachel uncrossed her arms. George remembered that she always crossed her arms when she was angry. Had she been angry? Was she still?

"Since Abby is the girls' mother now," she said, "does she do everything that a mother should do?"

"Yes," said George.

"Do the girls love her?"

"Very much. You should see the three of them together."

"Ohhhh..."

"Oh, no, I shouldn't have said that," George said. "I'm sorry, so very sorry."

"No! Don't be sorry!" Rachel cried. "Oh, George, I'm so happy for you and Megan and Crystal! And Abby!"

She threw her arms around him and squeezed him. Even through his spacesuit, he could feel that it was the tightest hug she had ever given him.

"I'm thrilled that my family is happy," Rachel said. "Why wouldn't I want to hear that?"

George took a deep breath. "I felt I had betrayed you by marrying Abby. I'm sorry, I'm sorry."

"Stop apologizing." She kissed his helmet visor. "You haven't betrayed me. If anything, you've done exactly what I've wanted. You've raised our girls to be happy, confident young women. You've created a warm, caring family."

"Really?"

"If you're looking for my permission to love Abby and raise the girls with her, you have it. I wouldn't have it any other way."

They hugged, they kissed, and this time, George felt her lips press against his.

That's impossible, he thought. *I have my helmet on. Oh, God, I better still have my helmet on!*

He felt his helmet with one gloved hand; he was still wearing it. He looked around. He didn't see Rachel anywhere.

―――――

Inside the ship, Ed scrolled through the graphs and figures appearing on his computer monitor. A three-dimensional computer graphic of Odette appeared, showing how animated waves poured from the core of the asteroid.

"Incredible!" Ed exclaimed. "The drill's sensor detected electrochemical signals below the asteroid's surface. The center of the asteroid is emitting electrochemical signals."

"Like a battery?" said Andrew.

"More like a brain. And look at this." Ed pointed at the animated image. "It's also absorbing electrochemical signals."

"From where? The only other source of electrochemical signals are us, from our brains," said Andrew.

"I can't prove it without further tests, but I think the asteroid is absorbing our brain waves and sending its own signals into our brains," Ed guessed.

"Holy smokes. Sally, Rachel, your Dad. Could the ghosts be based on our memories and thoughts?"

Ed nodded. "That's possible. Dad's ghost knew how I've felt since he died."

They heard the sound of metal doors swinging open and boots pound upon steel as George emerged from the airlock. After entering the control room, he began to take off his spacesuit.

"Funny thing happened out there," he said. "One minute, Rachel is standing there, hugging me, completely alive –"

"No," Andrew interrupted. "Rachel isn't alive. The *asteroid* is. This is a Siren Stone."

―――――

Aboard the *Long Island*, Colonel Chang returned to his usual calm, if humorless, mode after hearing Andrew's explanation of the ghosts. To Andrew, this was as close as Chang would get to showing happiness.

"Finally. Now that you've determined that there are no living human beings on Odette, proceed to destroy it," said Chang.

"Colonel, we still can't do that," said Andrew.

Chang glared at them through the thousands of miles of space. "Why not?"

"The asteroid is absorbing our brain waves and emitting its own brain waves. It's some kind of living being. We can't — we shouldn't — kill it."

"It's a rock!" Chang snapped. "Unlike Space Station Reagan. Reagan has two hundred and ninety permanent residents: scientists, trades people, artisans, farmers, settlers, and children born on the station. Don't forget that Reagan isn't just a space station; it's their home. You have to blow up the rock!"

"We've been working on the calculations for moving the asteroid. We'll know how many explosives to use, where to place them, and when to detonate them. We can do it," Andrew insisted.

"No, you won't. You're under arrest!" Chang yelled.

Andrew cut off the audio link to the *Long Island*. He could still see, if not hear, how Chang continued barking orders to restore the audio link.

"George, have you finished the prep for shifting the orbit?" Andrew asked.

"I've figured it out," said George, "but it's a complicated calculation. If I missed a variable, it might not work."

"It's a chance we'll have to take," said Andrew. "Ed, how's our flight plan coming?"

"Just finished it," said Ed, looking up from his computer monitor.

"Good, good," said Andrew. He moved towards the crew quarters. "Excuse me for a minute. There's one last thing I have to discuss with Sally."

We should have died together," said Andrew.

"No, no," Sally said. "We should have *lived* together."

"But we didn't," he argued, "and that's what's haunted me for years. Life didn't go the way I had wanted. No house in Eugene, no job with the city, no cottage in the summer, no vacations to Disney World, no taking our kids to see their grandparents, no kids at all —-"

"Hush," Sally ordered. "Listen to me. You've had a good life without me.

You've beaten the enemies of our country. You've saved lives by blowing up asteroids before they hit people. You've been all over the world and beyond, from Oregon to Polynesia to the Moon to the asteroid belt. You've done things, seen things, helped and saved people. Don't ever think that your life was a waste of time."

"Even if I've lived it without you, Sally?" Andrew said.

"Even without me," she replied, smiling. "You've gotten on with your life, even if you don't know it. Stop mourning my loss and the loss of what could have been. What you made instead is great and wonderful."

"That's what I finally needed to hear," he said as his throat began to go dry, as the years of sadness ended with this moment of joy.

She kissed him, in the same deep, passionate way they had kissed in their college years.

Then suddenly, she was gone.

———

After they finished planting the bombs, Andrew, George, and Ed scrambled aboard the *Rocky Road*. An hour later, the *Rocky Road* soared away from the asteroid. They'd go beyond the range of the blast before detonating the bombs, but do it soon enough to not endanger the oncoming *Long Island*.

A day later, the *Rocky Road* reached a safe distance from Odette. As planned, the *Long Island* was still out of range. Andrew smiled; they had outrun Chang.

Andrew typed the detonation code into the transmitter. He hit the "SEND" button.

"It's done," Andrew said. He began the countdown under his breath.

"We have a strong signal from the probe watching Odette," said Ed. He sent the asteroid's image to all the monitors.

They watched the bombs explode. Although fragments of rock flew in all directions, most of the asteroid stayed intact. Amidst a gray cloud of pulverized stone, slowly but surely Odette shifted its path.

———

Aboard the *Long Island*, Colonel Chang and his crew silently watched Odette shift into its new orbit. Never before had they seen an asteroid move amidst a cloud of its own debris.

"This damn well better have worked," Chang said, breaking the silence.

"Colonel, your orders?" said Major Conway, the ship's first officer.

"Plot a course to intercept Odette in its new orbit," said Chang. "I want to be sure this trajectory is completely safe. We still might have to destroy it."

As the *Long Island* continued towards Odette, deep space probes monitored Odette and sent data to Space Station Reagan. With the data, asteroid trackers began mapping Odette's new orbit. Would Odette hit something sooner or later?

A day later, Mission Control sent the answer to Chang. "A one in a million chance, and they got it," he reported to General Boyd.

———

Back on Space Station Reagan, Mission Control sent the same relieved message to all ships and probes: Odette had changed its orbit and no longer threatened to strike Reagan or any other station.

The *Long Island* was preparing to head home, leaving Odette alone, when she received a distress signal from the *Rocky Road*. The rock blasters had returned to Odette for reasons unknown and now were in trouble. Calls to the *Rocky Road* only returned a recorded mayday message. Chang had no choice but to respond. What could be going wrong aboard the *Rocky Road* now?

———

Andrew looked around. George was telling Rachel about her mother's vacation to Spain last year. At his station, Ed explained to his Dad how probes and beacons sent images back to Earth and traveling ships. George and Ed were making up for lost time with their loved ones, talking about family and friends, hopes and plans.

Sally, still dressed as a Ducks cheerleader, came back into the control room. Andrew knew he could imagine her in other clothes, but he wanted to remember her this way. The college years had been the best time of their lives, when the present was full of life and happiness, when the future seemed eternally bright.

Sally sat down beside Andrew and took his hand. "Why did you return to us?" she asked.

"To bring Chang to the asteroid," said Andrew. "I've known Chang for several years, and he's always sad. I don't know why. Maybe it's someone in his past. If it is, he needs to come here."

———

Shortly after the *Long Island* landed on Odette, Colonel Chang and six commandos quietly boarded the *Rocky Road*. As the commandos took control of the engineering sections, Chang went to the control room.

Chang raised his helmet visor. "We received your distress signal," he said. "What's wrong, is anyone injured — oh, my God."

In addition to Andrew, George, and Ed, he saw other people on the ship: a woman in a red jacket; a man in blue jeans; and a girl in a cheerleader uniform.

"You're just figments of my imagination," Chang insisted.

"Captain Ross reporting for duty, sir!" someone announced from behind him.

Chang spun around. A soldier, dressed in green jungle combat camouflage, stood there. His nametag read "ROSS." He was unscratched and alive, the way he had been when Chang last saw him.

Chang put a hand on Ross's shoulder –- his solid shoulder.

Chang tried fighting back the tears, but a single drop rolled down his cheek.

"Oh, dear God, why can't you be real?" he asked. "Why couldn't I take you home to your wife? Instead, I had only your dog tags to take to her..."

———

One night in the U.S. camp in Haiti, Chang had heard strange sounds, like someone stumbling through the garbage dump just outside the camp. Chang had ordered Captain Warren Ross to investigate the sounds. As he walked into the garbage dump, Ross had stepped on a landmine and been blown to pieces. Ross had been married only ten months.

If only he hadn't ordered Ross to investigate the sounds...

Chang had never fully recovered from meeting Ross's wife Karen and their newborn son Daniel. He had given her Ross's dog tags, and soon afterwards, applied for space station service, away from Earth's fighting nations.

After Chang ordered the commandos to return to the *Long Island*, he talked to Ross in the control room, oblivious to the others, both living and dead. Finally, Chang heard the words he had needed to hear for nineteen years.

"Karen knew the risks, Major," Ross said, calling Chang by his rank during the Haitian War. "Her father and grandfather were both in the Army. She knew we could be killed in action anytime. I'm sure she never blamed the Army or you."

"Thank you, Captain," Chang said. "Let me say again that I was proud to have you under my command. I wish I had been able to tell you at the time."

Chang and Ross exchanged salutes. The colonel sighed and closed his eyes. When he opened his eyes, Ross was gone.

Sally, Rachel, and Dad left again, leaving the three rock blasters alone with their memories — and Colonel Chang.

"I'm going to drop the charges of willful endangerment of a space station," said Chang, staring out the window at the stars above Odette.

Andrew joined Chang at the window. "Thank you, Colonel," said Andrew.

"It's the least I could do, considering you've lost five million gold units in scavengers' commissions," said Chang with a wry smile.

Andrew nodded. "That's a lot of money, but we can't put a value on this asteroid. It's priceless."

"And mysterious," said Chang. "We know nothing about it. Is it one of the legendary Siren Stones? Could there be more of them? Where did it come from? Did someone send it to us? Is it alive?"

"Do you think the asteroid is alive?" Andrew asked.

"I don't know," Chang answered, "but it doesn't matter. It does something wonderful, and that's what counts. You've done the human race a big favor."

"How's that?"

Chang gazed at the stars again. "You've saved something the human race desperately needs: a place where people can make peace with their pasts."

George and Ed joined them at the window. Up in the black sky, there seemed as many stars as there were lost souls in the human race, each wishing for a chance to say unsaid words.

"I have friends, family — we all do — who could be healed by coming here," said Chang. "Too bad it's so far from Earth."

"You brought more explosives, didn't you?" asked Andrew. "I think we can give Odette another nudge. Drop her in behind Mars, for instance. Not so close to Earth as to endanger anything, but close enough so people can come here."

"I have the explosives," said Chang. He gave Andrew a serious, questioning look. "Are you sure you can do it again?"

"Yes, I'm sure," said Andrew without hesitating. "We've done it once, we can do it again." Behind him, George and Ed nodded.

"Fine. You can have the explosives," Chang said. Then he became silent, deep in thought. "I have a problem, though," he said after his silence. "How will I explain this to General Boyd? He'll think I've gone crazy. I don't want to get discharged as a mental case."

"Don't worry about the General," Andrew said. "He'll understand after he comes here, like you did."

"Of course," said Chang with a smile. "And he will come here. This is a Siren Stone, after all."

———

Visiting asteroid 20 521 Odette de Proust was far from General Boyd's mind. As he watched another spacecraft bring survivors to Space Station Olympus, he gave orders to reduce the rations for all personnel. All the military space stations in orbit around Mars had extra people to feed.

He looked at video images of two other space stations orbiting Mars. Space Station Exeter, a large European Space Agency station, was filling up with survivors and broadcasting pleas for extra food. Space Station Troika, a small station run by NASA, hadn't taken in any survivors of the Mars disaster…

2 / TROIKA

The Catholic priest on the viewscreen looked bewildered. "So you're telling me that Jesus Christ, the Son of God, has returned as a Jewish girl in a Catholic schoolgirl's uniform on a space station in orbit around Mars?" said Father Wycliffe.

Paul Devane, director of Space Station Troika, looked back at the viewscreen and nodded. "That's who she says she is."

Paul heard footsteps on the metal floor of Troika's control room. He turned around and saw the teenaged girl standing by the entrance. The rhinestones on her silver tiara sparkled under a bright light above the entrance.

"You still don't believe me, do you?" she said.

Paul looked back at the viewscreen. "She's by the entrance. Do you see her? Did you hear her?"

The priest shook his head. "I don't see anyone standing by the doorway."

"But I can see her," Paul insisted.

"Alright, maybe you can, and for some reason, I can't," said Wycliffe. "Have you talked to her? What does she want?"

"She wants to crash our shuttlecraft onto the Martian surface," Paul said. "She thinks that's how God is going to create life on Mars."

―――

All of Space Station Troika's sensors and cameras were aimed at the Martian surface below. As Troika orbited the planet, its crew searched for signs of survivors.

In Troika's control room, Paul Devane waited for the station to pass over Redsands Base. He looked at a shiny videoscreen and saw his reflection and cringed. Only forty years old, he looked like fifty, with gray streaks in his brown hair, a weary look in his eyes, and lines of age etched into his face. Living in space did that to some people.

He ran his hand through his greasy, disheveled hair to try to comb it. He hadn't taken the time to wash his hair since the disaster on Mars.

He yawned and sighed. He hadn't slept much since he had killed that girl at Redsands Base.

The videoscreen suddenly flickered, and an image of Redsands Base replaced Paul's reflection.

Paul glanced at a woman wearing a yellow polo shirt with the Charging Duck mascot of the University of Oregon. Erin Malloy looked at him and turned back to her computer monitor. An aerial video image of a collapsed dome-shaped building appeared on the monitor. Nothing moved in the mangled mess of steel and plastic half-buried in loose dust and dirt. The only movement came from beside the dome: a geyser of water gushing from a pool created when geologists had dug into subsurface water.

"No body heat readings. There's nothing moving on the video," reported Erin. She turned away from her monitor. "There's nobody alive on Redsands."

Paul looked sadly at the video picture. "There were ten people down there. I was hoping to find at least one."

"Sorry, not at Redsands."

The video image began breaking up into static. "We're passing out of range of Redsands," Erin said.

"Thank you," Paul murmured as he returned to his chair and bit into a round hardtack cracker. The crumbs fell on his wrinkled blue shirt with the NASA logo.

Dozens of nuclear weapons could not destroy the largest meteor to hit Mars in millions of years. The missiles and bombs had merely dented the rock. When the rock smashed into the Martian surface, it gouged out a gigantic crater, heated the surface a thousand degrees, and threw billions of tons of dust into the atmosphere. The shock wave and dust storm shook and smothered the Martian settlements. Now dozens of spaceships were evacuating the survivors to space stations in orbit around Mars.

Troika, being a small station carved out of a captured asteroid, had no room for refugees. Still, the disaster was keeping the three crew members busy. They usually surveyed the geography of Mars from their orbit, but now they had a new job: watching the Martian surface for signs of human life.

Another man approached Erin. She gave him a small smile. When Dr. Thomas Hall had arrived in Mars orbit a year ago, Erin had noticed how handsome the doctor was. A year later, he still looked like a buff, blond, Californian surfer dude. Living around Mars hadn't aged him prematurely, at least not yet.

He wore silver caduceus symbols of the medical profession on the collar of his clean, white shirt, and he looked at the brainscanner monitor in his hands. "The electrical activity in your frontal lobes went up while you were looking at the data coming from Mars," said Thomas.

"That's what's supposed to happen when I concentrate on something, right?" Erin said as she poured water into a pack of redhydratable tuna casserole. "God, this stuff is awful."

She looked at her reflection in the shiny metal control console. "This brainscanner is messing up my hair," she complained as she straightened the headpiece. It was a silvery band around her forehead with other bands arching over the top of her head. Small lights blinked on the bands.

"How long do I have to keep it on?" Erin asked.

"Another twenty-four hours," replied Thomas. "Then I'll have enough data. Is it uncomfortable?"

Erin shrugged and looked back at her reflection. "No, it's not too uncomfortable. It's lightweight. But I put waves into my hair to give it some body only to have you plunk this brainscanner on me."

"Ah, you still look beautiful, just like in that photo."

Erin glanced at a photo taped to her computer monitor: her wearing a white evening gown, silver tiara, and the sash of Miss Oregon. She was flanked by her black American mother and her white Canadian father. They were all smiling on that night, when she had won the crown of Miss Oregon.

None of them could have predicted the tragedy that winning the beauty pageant would bring.

"Yeah, just like in the photo," she muttered, lost in her memories.

"Thanks for keeping the brainscanner on during the emergency," Thomas said. "This is a rare opportunity to study the neurological activity of deep space crews."

Erin looked up and smiled. "No problem. Scientific research: that's what we're here for."

Paul gazed grimly at the digital clock counting the seconds and minutes on his computer monitor. "It's been four days since we found anyone alive. There probably isn't anyone left."

"Probably not," Erin agreed.

"Are you okay?" Thomas asked Paul. "Get some rest. Doctor's orders."

Paul nodded as he slowly rose from his chair. "Maybe I should. I feel really tired."

He opened his eyes and looked at a small wooden icon that Troika's original crew, the Russians, had nailed to the wall. The multicolored icon showed the Old Testament Trinity, the three angels who visited Abraham and his wife Sarah. In Eastern Orthodox tradition, the three angels represented God the Father, God the Son, and God the Holy Spirit.

When the United States took over Troika, Paul had decided to leave the icon on the wall despite Thomas's protests. "Oh, what harm can it do?" Paul had said. "It adds some charm to the place. Besides, it might bring us some good luck."

In a sense, Troika's crew had been lucky because the meteor had missed them, but one hundred and seventy-nine people on the Martian colonies had not been so lucky. Whatever divine grace the icon attracted did not reach down to the Martian surface.

In his quarters, Paul called Father Mark Wycliffe by video. Father Wycliffe lived on Space Station Exeter, which was circling Mars in an orbit lower than Troika's. Each week, Paul and Father Wycliffe would talk by video encoded to preserve privacy. Not even the Mars disaster could disrupt this sacrament.

The man on the video monitor wore the traditional black uniform of a Catholic priest and a Vatican Observatory badge. He was in his mid-fifties, and though his face was still handsome, some of his brown hair had turned white.

"How are things on Exeter?" Paul asked.

"A bit messy and very busy, but we're managing quite well nonetheless," Father Wycliffe said. His accent sounded posh, like that of the oldest English universities, the House of Lords, and the highest levels of the Church of

England. He sounded unlike the Italian and Irish Catholic priests of Boston, whom Paul remembered from his youth.

"We've got refugees all over the station," Wycliffe continued. "Our infirmary is overflowing with the injured, the medical staff is overworked, and we're running out of food."

"I offered our food supply to Bronson," Paul said.

"He'll want it, now that he's got more people than he had expected," said Wycliffe. "Okay, let's get down to business. Do you have anything to confess today?"

Paul cleared his throat. "Forgive me, Father, for I have sinned. I caused a woman to die three days ago."

He paused, took a deep breath, and continued. "She was on Redsands Base, and the interior of the dome building was on fire. She was trapped inside the dome. I tried to use the teleporter to take her out, but I failed."

Each Martian space station, surface base, and colony had a teleporter booth. An object would be placed in one booth, broken into an energy stream, transmitted to another booth, and rematerialize as the object: mass into energy into mass again. The technology was still in its primitive stage and prone to accidents, though. If spacers needed to send something important, they would send it by shuttlecraft or supply rocket, not by teleporter.

"Hush, Paul," Father Wycliffe ordered. "Bronson told me about Redsands. You don't have to confess to something that wasn't your fault."

Paul nodded but continued. "But it still bothers me. I tried to teleport her out of there. I knew the teleporter is safe only for non-living, inorganic matter. I knew I shouldn't have tried sending a human being by teleporter. But I tried anyway. Now she's just atoms scattered somewhere."

"You had no choice but to use the teleporter."

"I could have used the shuttlecraft."

"And you know why you didn't. You didn't have the time," Father Wycliffe reminded him. "There was plenty of pure oxygen on Redsands; the fire gutted the dome in twenty minutes. You couldn't have reached her in time."

"The University of Waterloo's been researching ways of making the teleporter safe for people. They say they might have developed a new program code for the teleporter, but we haven't received the new code yet," said Paul. "Maybe if I had a usable code —"

Father Wycliffe interrupted him. "But you didn't, and you still don't, so stop speculating.

"Look at it this way," the priest suggested. "Be comforted in knowing that you had only one choice, and you had the courage to use it. She is with God now, and God does not blame you for her death, I'm sure."

Paul smiled weakly. "But I did violate transportation regulations by using the teleporter on a human being."

"Okay, if it will make you feel better, say three 'Hail Marys' as penance and consider yourself forgiven. Now be done with the matter." Father Wycliffe made the Sign of the Cross to bless Paul. "Now, anything else you want to discuss?"

"Yes. I haven't gone to Mass since I came to Troika a year ago," said Paul.

"It does get difficult to go to the only church out here. You do watch my televised Mass, though."

"It's wonderful, and I really enjoy watching it, but for me, something's missing. I miss receiving the Eucharist."

"The body of Christ," said the priest, referring to the Roman Catholic belief that consecrated bread becomes the body of Jesus.

"A TV show is no substitute for the real thing, especially after all that's happened," Paul said.

"Spiritual healing through the Eucharist. There must be some way I can help you," Father Wycliffe mused. He paused for a moment, pondering an idea.

"I can try teleporting a jar of consecrated bread to you."

Paul look startled. "You're going to try that?"

"You think there'll be an accident? Actually, accidents occur in only ten percent of attempts to teleport organic matter. That means I still have a ninety percent chance of sending the bread to you by teleporter."

"But it's the body of Christ."

"If anyone can survive the teleporter, it will be Jesus."

Paul returned to the control room just as another video message from Space Station Exeter popped onto his computer monitor. The image of Alfred Bronson, Director of Space Station Exeter, appeared.

Bronson, with his brown hair looking disheveled and greasy, stared sleepily. Exeter's crew had been working over eighteen hours each day since the disaster on Mars.

"What can we do for you?" Paul asked.

"You said you have some food to spare," Bronson said.

"We've got enough for ourselves and nine extra people for two months, which is when the re-supply ship arrives."

"Every bit of food is essential. Could you please give us what you have in excess of your own needs?"

"We'll be happy to. How do we transport it? We can't use the teleporter," Paul said.

"No, no, even with the alleged ninety percent safety rate on organic matter, I don't want to risk it on food," Bronson agreed.

"Can you send a shuttlecraft to pick it up?"

Bronson shook his head. "Not for a week. Both our shuttlecrafts are in the search for survivors at the planet's poles. Can you fly over here in your shuttlecraft?"

"We could, but our shuttlecraft is low on fuel. We'll have to wait until we're at our closest position to Exeter. Then we'll have enough fuel for a one-way flight."

"How much longer until you're in range?"

Paul typed a few commands at his keyboard, and computer animation of the orbits of the two space stations appeared on his monitor. "Twenty-four standard hours."

"That will be okay, but what about you? Since it'll be a one-way flight, you'll have to stay here."

"Don't worry about three extra mouths to feed. We'll bring our own food supply, and we'll do work." Then, with resignation, Paul said, "I think NASA will let us abandon Troika. We've done all we can do to find survivors."

―――――

After Paul ended his video call with Bronson, he heard a soft chime. The message "TELEPORTER CARGO INCOMING" appeared on his monitor.

"That must be the consecrated bread from Father Wycliffe," Paul said.

"You're receiving consecrated bread from Father Wycliffe?" Thomas asked.

"Yes. I haven't received the Eucharist for months."

"It's all very silly if you ask me."

"Nobody asked you," Paul replied.

Erin looked surprised as she read the data from the teleporter. "That's a lot of bread: forty-nine kilograms or about one hundred and eight pounds."

"What?" Paul blurted. He looked at the computer monitor. "That's impossible. I'm going to the teleporter booth."

"I'll come with you," Erin said as she followed Paul out of the control room.

———

As they approached the teleporter booth, Erin gasped. Paul suddenly stopped and stared in surprise at the booth.

There was no jar of consecrated bread.

Instead, a slim teenaged girl stood in the teleporter booth. She looked pretty, had her reddish-brown hair tied into a ponytail, and wore a white shirt, green school tie, a green tartan schoolgirl skirt, white socks, and black shoes with low heels. She wore a silver tiara with glittering gems.

"I haven't seen that uniform in years," Erin remarked.

Paul stared at the stranger. "What is it?"

"St. Joseph's College School in Toronto. My high school."

The girl looked bewildered as she stepped out of the teleporter booth. She hesitantly walked forward as she glanced around her.

She stopped a couple yards away from Paul and Erin. Her big brown eyes looked around in wonder.

"Where am I?" she asked.

"Space Station Troika in orbit around Mars," Paul replied.

"Yes!" the girl shouted as she clapped her hands together and jumped up. "Mars! Mars! I made it to Mars!"

She danced and squealed and swung her arms. "This is totally awesome! I have returned, glory, hallelujah!"

"Who are you?" Erin demanded.

The girl stopped prancing, smiled at Paul, and held out her hand so he could shake it. "My name's Jessica."

Erin noticed the gold necklace with a Star of David pendant around her neck. Why was a Jewish girl wearing a Catholic school uniform?

"Are you from Redsands Base?" Paul asked.

Jessica's eyes lit up. "Redsands! I belong there. I have to go there."

Paul shook his head. "No, no, you can't go back there. It's in ruins."

"That's not important. I can walk, I can talk, and I can go to Mars!" she chirped as she danced around again.

Paul whispered to Erin, "I think she's the girl we lost trying to transport up from Redsands Base."

"If she is, she must be suffering from some sort of strange shock," Erin said.

Jessica spun around in a pirouette and strolled back to Paul and Erin. She threw her arms around Erin, hugged her, and said, "It's *sooooo* good to have a warm body again!"

Erin laughed and gently pushed Jessica away. "You mean you know what it's like not to have a body?"

"Believe me, having flesh and blood feels better than being just a spirit floating around," Jessica said.

"Then you remember what it was like -- after the teleporter accident?" Paul asked incredulously.

Jessica nodded. "Oh, yeah, for a long time, I was in a place of neither the living nor the dead but something in between."

"That's incredible!" Paul remarked. "And now you're back three days later!"

"Was it just three days?" Jessica said. "I thought it was two thousand years."

———

Erin showed the empty cabin to Jessica. "You can stay in here," Erin said. "There used to be a fourth person on the crew, but she got transferred to Exeter."

Jessica smiled. "Thanks for your hospitality. It's *sooooo* decent. I'll be comfortable here, but I won't be staying long."

"Oh? Are you in a rush to go somewhere?"

"To Mars. I have work to do down there."

"Everyone's being evacuated off Mars. What could you possibly do down there?"

"My father's work."

"Your father? I didn't think people brought their children to Mars. Who's your father?"

"Yahweh," Jessica said casually.

Also known as 'God', Erin realized. *How weird.*

"So you must be Jesus, eh?" Erin joked.

Jessica nodded. "I am. Isn't that awesome?"

Holy Mary, Mother of God, we have a crazy one aboard, Erin thought.

———

Thomas stepped out of the shuttlecraft, through the airlock, and onto the floor of the shuttlecraft dock. On the dock floor sat boxes of food, all destined for Space Station Exeter.

Jessica walked to Thomas and smiled and waved at him. "You must be Thomas," she said.

"Yes, I am," Thomas replied. "And you must be our visitor, Jessica. Are you hungry?"

Thomas grabbed a box of crackers from a table, pulled a folding knife from his belt, cut open the box, and held it out to Jessica.

She was staring at the folding knife clipped to his belt, Thomas noticed. But she quickly looked up, smiled, took a round cracker, and began munching it.

Thomas glanced at the gold Star of David on Jessica's necklace. He asked, "So what's a nice Jewish girl like you doing in a place like this?"

"Checking out the shuttlecraft," Jessica said, pointing at the small spacecraft. "Is it powered by a nuclear reactor?"

"You've done your homework. Yes, it's a Tsiolkovsky Service Shuttlecraft model 3, the first to be powered by nuclear energy."

"Cool. Awesome. It'll be perfect for taking me to Mars."

"Going to Mars?" Thomas asked. "Nobody's going down to the surface."

"I have to, totally. I have to finish my father's work down there, at Redsands," Jessica explained.

"Your father worked at Redsands? You can't go back. All its people are —- dead. Except you."

Erin's eyes lit up. "But that's the reason why I have to go there. From the dead of Earth, my father will create life on Mars."

"Huh? I heard of no such project."

"Not on your scientific stations, but it has been planned. Life has grown on Earth, and now it's time for God to create His other children on Mars."

Thomas smiled wryly. "God's your father? Come on, you really can't think that, at least not literally. I know you God believers call God 'Our Father', but you really don't think He's your *father* in a family sense, do you?"

"He is truly my father, and I am Him," Jessica declared.

Thomas shrugged. "Okay, if God is going to create life on Mars, how's He going to do it?"

"With the same principles that He used on Earth," Jessica explained. "The bodies of the dead on Mars contain amino acids and proteins, the necessary substances of life. The ruined Martian bases also have oxygen and water imported from Earth. There's also subsurface water on Mars that has come to the surface by the digging of your geologists.

"When the shuttlecraft crashes into a ruined base, the nuclear explosion will start the chemical reaction that will convert the amino acids, proteins, oxygen, and water into living cells."

This is crazy, Thomas thought. The girl wanted to play God, *Book of Genesis*.

"I don't believe in God," he retorted.

"That doesn't matter. I believe in God, and that's good enough for me."

———

In the kitchen, Paul slid the tray of rehydratable salmon chunks into the oven. He looked at the box that had held the salmon. "One of the ingredients is salmon flavoring," he observed. "They actually have to add artificial flavor to make the salmon taste like salmon."

"There's a restaurant in Fisherman's Wharf in San Francisco, where the chef grilled fresh salmon in garlic and paprika," Thomas remembered as he poured a cup of coffee. "Too bad we can't get food like that in Mars orbit."

"It would take a miracle," Paul said.

"Speaking of miracles, where's our visitor?" Thomas asked.

Erin put down a fourth plate on the table. "She's taking a shower. She says she hasn't had a bath for over two thousand years."

"Cleanliness is next to godliness," Thomas said, repeating an old proverb. "Do we know who she really is?"

Paul shook his head and looked at his pocket computer pad. "When Redsands Base burned up, we didn't get a good video picture of the woman we tried to teleport up. I've looked through the personnel list of Redsands, and there was a Jessie Montega, a biologist, but she was twenty-seven years old."

"Our Jessica looks a lot younger than twenty-seven. And she sure talks like a teenager. Her accent is pure California Valley Girl," Erin said. "Can you get a picture of Jessie Montega?"

"No. Our records don't have photos, but Exeter's might. I've asked Father Wycliffe to search for her photo," Paul said. "Here's an idea: could the teleporter have reconstructed her as a younger person?"

"I don't know," Erin said. "Anything is possible."

Thomas sipped his coffee. "Whoever she is, she's crazy. She thinks that she's Jesus."

Paul nodded. "Yeah, that's weird. Maybe Jessica had a weird, out-of-body experience when the teleporter lost her atoms, and now she thinks she's Jesus. Or maybe she had already gone loony on Mars. That happens to some people in space."

"The consecrated bread didn't arrive, but the girl did," Erin observed. "Could the bread have turned into Jessica?"

Thomas put down his coffee mug. "Oh, that's ridiculous. I usually think of you two as intelligent people, but sometimes your religiosity is too much. Any rational person knows that God doesn't exist."

"Not necessarily," Erin replied. "I believe in Him, and so do a lot of other people in the space colonies. Exeter Station even has a chapel."

"A waste of space if you ask me," Thomas complained. "I don't know why NASA let a priest come out here. Christianity is the last thing we need in space."

"I disagree, I think we need to bring our religions out here," Paul said. "That's what makes us human."

"It's what makes us morons. Think how ridiculous your religion is," Thomas snapped. "Do you really think a real Son of God would spend thirty years as a carpenter, unknown to everyone? And did the crucifixion really mean anything? If he really were a god, he could have used his godlike powers to come back from dead or his father could have brought him back to life, so the suffering was unnecessary and meaningless. It was just a publicity stunt to convert the superstitious. Jesus was probably just a guy who faked his own death — assuming he actually existed, and there's no real historical proof that he did. Christianity is just one big fraud."

"I am not a fraud," said a voice from behind.

They turned around and saw Jessica standing at the doorway.

"Don't take it personally," Thomas said. "I oppose superstitions of all kinds, not just the Christian kind."

Jessica frowned.

"Uh, dinner's almost ready," Erin said, hoping to change the topic. "Will you join us?"

The schoolgirl smiled again. "That would be awesome. I haven't eaten for a long, long time."

The oven bell rang, and Paul put on his oven mittens, opened the oven, and pulled out the tray.

"Oh my God! What's this?" he blurted.

Instead of plain rehydrated salmon chunks, the tray held grilled salmon fillets bathed in a tomato sauce. The aroma of garlic and paprika wafted through the kitchen.

Paul, Erin, and Thomas stared wide-eyed at the fish. After a long, stunned silence, Erin finally spoke.

"You were saying it would take a miracle to get fresh salmon here?" she said to Paul.

Jessica grabbed the tray from Paul and put it on the table. "Don't be shy; everybody dig in!" she urged.

———

At first, Paul, Erin, and Thomas were reluctant to eat the fish, but with Jessica's prodding, they nibbled hesitantly at it. Then, when they tasted how delicious the fish had become, they ate it eagerly.

"This is wonderful," Paul said. Erin nodded, and even Thomas grunted in agreement as he chewed.

"Thank you," Jessica said, grinning. "I'm very good with fish."

"I must be dreaming," Thomas mumbled.

"No, you're not," Jessica said. "That fabulous gourmet dinner was real." She looked at each of them in the eye. "Now, can you do a favor for me?"

"What can we do for you?" Erin asked.

"Can I have the ignition key to the shuttlecraft?"

A stunned silence followed.

Erin reached out and touched Jessica's hand. "Dear, you're a special person, but you don't really believe you're Jesus, do you?"

"Like, yeah!" Jessica blurted with a sigh of exasperation. "Look at the Jesus thing I did. I turned chunks of dry fish into — uh, fish with tomato sauce."

"Turning fish into fish," Thomas quipped.

"Okay, maybe that was a bit lame," Jessica admitted.

Thomas shrugged, raised his glass to his lips, and put the glass down. "I ran out of water."

"Oh, I'll get some," Jessica said as she grabbed the pitcher from the table. "Hey, water is so plain. Do you have any wine here?"

"You're too young," Erin warned.

Jessica giggled. "I know I look underage, but I'm a lot older than I look."

"We have no wine," said Paul. "We've got only water."

"Just water? How boring." Humming the old Jewish folk song "Havah Nagilah", Jessica skipped to the kitchen counter and filled the pitcher with water from the faucet.

She set the pitcher in the middle of the table. Thomas lifted the pitcher and began pouring water into his glass.

"Oh my God," he muttered as he saw red wine pour into his glass.

Paul took the pitcher, poured a glass of wine for himself, and sipped it. It tasted very sweet. He remembered a sugary red wine that a friend had given him at a frat party in university. It was a kosher sacramental wine drunk at Passover.

"Next time you drink wine, remember me," Jessica said.

———

"Do you need any help cleaning up?" Jessica asked.

Erin smiled and shook her head. "No, dear. We'll clear the table."

"Okay with me." Jessica yawned. "Wow, that was a lot of food. I feel tired now. I'll go to my room and take a nap."

"Sure. Sweet dreams," Thomas said.

"Oh, and think about letting me borrow the shuttlecraft," Jessica urged. "I really, seriously, totally need it."

The crew's eyes silently followed Jessica as she walked out of the kitchen.

Erin broke the silence. "Was any of this real?"

"It must have been real," Paul concluded. "All three of us can't be dreaming or hallucinating about the same thing."

"How did she do it?" Thomas wondered.

"It's a miracle," Erin said.

"No it's not," said Thomas. "She's not Jesus."

"She could be the woman I tried to teleport out of Redsands Base," Paul said.

"That still doesn't explain how she turned rehydrated salmon chunks into salmon fillets in tomato sauce," Erin said.

"Maybe she got superhuman powers when the transporter reassembled her," Paul guessed.

"Maybe she's an alien," Thomas suggested seriously.

"Whatever or whoever she is, one thing is certain: she wants to crash the shuttlecraft into Mars," Paul said. He took out a metal key from his pocket. "But she can't start the shuttlecraft's reactor without the ignition key. Do you know where yours is?"

Erin and Thomas felt in their pockets and pulled out their keys.

"Keep them with you at all times, and don't leave them lying around," Paul advised. "We need that shuttlecraft to carry the food and ourselves to Space Station Exeter."

———

Erin returned to her cabin and lay down on her cot. She looked at another photo of her and her parents, this one from the night before the Miss America pageant.

Her parents had met at a tourism industry convention in Toronto, where her mother was a visiting American tour operator, and her father was an engineer who designed flying amphibious tour buses. They settled in Toronto, where she attended St. Joseph's College School on Wellesley Street.

After graduating from "St. Jo's," she went to study business administration at the University of Oregon in Eugene, her mother's hometown. In her second year of university, she entered the beauty pageants billed as "scholarship programs": first, she won the crown of Miss Willamette Valley, and then, the Miss Oregon crown. Her next step was the Miss America pageant, to be held in Salem, the state capital of Oregon, that year.

It was also the year of the Vernacular Wars, when the Islamic Purists declared *jihad* on the United States for allowing American Moslems to recite the Koran in English instead of Arabic. But despite the orange alert, ordinary life, including the Miss America pageant, continued in America.

Erin had just stepped off the stage in her evening gown when the terrorists charged into the auditorium. With their guns blazing, they slaughtered over a hundred people in ten minutes. Screams and moans filled the air. As the walls and floors turned red with blood, the police and National Guard unleashed their own storm of tear gas and bullets.

Erin found her father covered in blood but still alive. Her mother did not survive, though.

If only she hadn't been enthralled with the clothes, the gifts, the glamour, the attention, and the scholarships; if only she hadn't won Miss Willamette Valley and Miss Oregon; if only she hadn't entered the Miss America pageant, her mother might still be alive.

She dropped out of university and went to Toronto with her father. She returned to Oregon a few years later to earn a degree in science, and she volunteered to work in the space colonies, far away from Earth.

She sat up and felt the brainscanner still strapped to her head. When was that wretched headpiece due to come off?

She heard a knock on her door. She opened it and saw Jessica.

"Jessica," Erin greeted softly. "What can I do for you, dear?"

"You wish you could have had one last moment of quality time with your mother, don't you?" Jessica said as she strolled into the cabin.

Erin's eyes widened. "How do you know?"

Jessica smiled. "I know things. I can tell that her death has tormented you for years." She put her hands on Jessica's temples, as if trying to touch her mind. "Stop punishing yourself. You have no reason to feel guilty, no reason to flee out here."

"If only — if only I hadn't been so selfish, thinking only about myself."

"Hush. Will you believe me if you could speak to your mother again?"

"How can you do that?"

Jessica grinned. "Oh, I can do all sorts of cool things."

"Erin, I'm so happy to see you again," chirped a voice from behind.

Erin spun around and stared at her mother.

She threw her arms around her mother and hugged her.

―――

Her mother looked young and wore the blue tour guide uniform that Erin had seen in her childhood, years that they remembered over tea and crackers.

Eventually, they talked about the present. "How's your father?" asked Erin's mother.

"Oh, he's really happy in his retirement," Erin replied. "I just got a video message from him last week. He won a trophy at a model airplane contest. His glider flew over one hundred feet, farther than all the other gliders."

"Ah, he was always designing buses and boats and planes. I have to ask: did he ever remarry?"

"No, he never did."

"Hah, hah, I spoiled him for other women," Erin's mother bragged. "He would never find another one like me, I told him."

Erin laughed. "Oh, you were unique, and he knew that."

She suddenly stopped smiling. Her mother *was* unique. She had used the past tense because her mother had died.

"Mum, you died," Erin stated plainly. "How can you be here now?"

Her mother reached out to take Erin's hands. "Dear, I can only come back briefly, so let me say what I need to say."

She pulled Erin closer to her. "Stop blaming yourself for my death. It wasn't your fault."

"What are you saying?" Erin mumbled.

"Don't blame yourself. Blame the Jihadists."

"But if I hadn't entered the pageant —" Erin started.

Erin's mother interrupted her. "No, no, don't think that way. You enjoyed what you did, you didn't harm anyone, and your father and I were so proud of you."

"You were?"

"Of course, we were." Erin's mother smiled. "You looked so beautiful, so poised, and so confident when you were competing on stage. You grew up a lot in those two years at university."

"That's nice to know."

"So will you finally stop blaming yourself?"

"Yes, yes, I'll stop, I'll stop," Erin promised.

Erin's mother walked her to the cot and laid her down. "You've been tired for a long time." She kissed her on the cheek. "Get some sleep now."

Erin closed her eyes, smiled, and fell asleep. When she woke up, her mother was gone.

And so too was Jessica.

Erin felt inside her pant pockets as she rose from the cot.

The shuttlecraft's ignition key was gone too.

———

On the viewscreen, Father Wycliffe said, "God, Jesus, and the Holy Spirit are the same person in mainstream Christianity. It's that concept that they're all part of the same God that exists as a Trinity of persons. If this girl thinks she's Jesus, then she also thinks she's God."

"She does; she thinks she can create life on Mars," Paul said, glancing at Jessica and back to Wycliffe again.

"God does not wear a miniskirt," declared Father Wycliffe.

Jessica giggled and said, "Oh, but I do, especially with this schoolgirl uniform. Isn't it cute?"

"It's not unusual to find someone who thinks she's Jesus or Moses or Elvis or whoever; they appear in Israel all the time," Father Wycliffe commented. "But in orbit around Mars?"

Jessica joked, "Elvis has come back from the dead more times than I have."

"Be careful," Paul cautioned the priest. "You're talking about her as if she can't hear you, but she's right here."

"I'm not sure the girl is actually there." The priest paused for a moment and continued. "Paul, have you considered the possibility of mass hysteria? Or that something is controlling your minds?"

Paul looked back at Jessica and said, "I don't think it's mass hysteria or mind control. What could possibly do that to us out here?"

Father Wycliffe asked, "Did you say that Dr. Hall sees the girl too?"

"Yes, he does."

Father Wycliffe smiled weakly. "Dr. Hall is an atheist fundamentalist. If he sees the girl, she can't be God or Jesus."

Jessica laughed. "How ironic: the atheist can see me, but the priest can't."

"Then she's Jessie Montega from Redsands," Paul said.

"But if she is, why is she invisible to me?" Wycliffe asked. "Look, here's a radical idea: perhaps Troika was carved out of a Siren Stone."

Thomas fell into a stunned silence. The Siren Stones were a modern myth: asteroids haunted by beautiful spirits who lured lonely spacers to their deaths. They explained why space crews went crazy or disappeared without a trace.

Father Wycliffe, Vatican astronomer, did not believe in myths and superstitions. He was a rational scientist –- but so too were the first spacers to talk about Siren Stones.

"*You* believe in Siren Stones?" Thomas asked.

Father Wycliffe shrugged. "I don't know, but we're running out of explanations for what's going on."

The priest's pocket computer beeped. He answered and listened to it, and then he looked eagerly at Paul.

"My friends found a photo of Jessie Montega," Wycliffe reported. "It's too big to send to my pocket computer. I'm going to my quarters to download the file."

He looked at his watch. "Paul, your launch window is coming in seventeen hours. You need to get off that rock and come to Exeter. Don't let anyone –- or anything –- hijack the shuttlecraft."

"Not even Jesus?" Paul asked.

"Especially not Jesus," urged Father Wycliffe as he ended the transmission.

Paul spun around in his chair and looked at Jessica. "Who are you, and what do you want?" he demanded.

"You already know," Jessica said.

"You've suffered a lot. You might have post-traumatic stress," Paul said. "There are people on Exeter who can help you. Come with us."

"Look, I don't have a lot of time. There's something you need to know before I leave," Jessica said. "Jessie Montega died for a purpose."

"What are you saying?" Paul asked. "You're not dead."

"I tell you again, I'm not Jessie Montega. Jessie Montega's body is dead in the ruins of Redsands Base. Her soul is living with God now."

Jessica walked to a computer monitor and began typing commands. Animated images of molecules, from *The Spacer's Encyclopedia*, appeared on the monitor. Paul recognized them from chemistry class: amino acids, proteins, and DNA.

Jessica pointed at the images of the protein molecules. "Jessie Montega's body contains amino acids, proteins, and DNA. When I crash the shuttlecraft onto her body, the nuclear reaction will start the chemical reactions that will create life. Her death has meaning and purpose. She died so that Mars can live."

Paul stared at the girl. "Now I know for sure. You're crazy," he said.

Jessica breathed in deeply. "You're the one who will go crazy if you keep blaming yourself for Jessie Montega's death. Believe me, it wasn't your fault, and she died for a purpose."

She marched out of the room, leaving Paul crumpled in his chair, alone with his memories of Jessie Montega's plea for help.

―――――

Thomas watched Jessica walk towards the shuttlecraft. He crossed his arms and moved to block her path to the airlock.

"Where are you going, young lady?" he asked.

"To Mars," Jessica replied.

"Sorry, but we need this shuttlecraft to deliver food to the people of Space Station Exeter. You wouldn't want them to starve, would you?"

"I'll find another way to get the food to Exeter. Just let me have the shuttlecraft."

"Can't you just wave your hand and make a one-celled organism?" Thomas asked. "Why does God need a nuclear spaceship?"

"I don't know," Jessica whined, her voice growing more agitated. "God works in mysterious ways. Only He knows."

"Did God crash the meteor into Mars? Did God want all those people to die? What kind of God is He?" Thomas accused.

"I don't know!" Jessica cried. "I don't know if all those people had to die. But I know that if I don't go down to Mars, at least one of those deaths will meaningless!"

Thomas eyed her suspiciously. Her right hand was clasped shut.

"What are you holding in your hand?" he demanded.

Paul and Erin ran into the shuttlecraft dock.

"She's got my shuttlecraft key!" Erin yelled.

Jessica darted forward, but Thomas grabbed her. Paul and Erin rushed to Jessica, and they struggled to pry the key out of her hand.

"Got it!" Paul shouted as he held up the key.

Jessica stumbled backwards away from the crew and glared at them. "But I got this!" she hissed.

She unfolded Thomas's knife and held it over her wrist. "Give me the key or I'll kill myself."

"So what? If you're Jesus, you'll just come back from the dead," scoffed Thomas.

"Dear, put that down," Erin urged. "You don't want to hurt anybody."

Paul stepped towards Jessica. "Jessie, put down the knife. You need help that we can't give you here. Come to Exeter with us."

A chime sounded from a videoscreen. Erin went to the videoscreen and looked at the message scrolling in.

"It's Father Wycliffe," Erin said.

"Relay the transmission into this room," Paul ordered.

Father Wycliffe appeared on the videoscreen. "Hey, why are you all in the shuttlecraft dock?" he asked.

"We've got the girl here," Paul said.

Father Wycliffe looked puzzled. "I still can't see her, but tell me if she looks anything like this. Here's Jessie Montega."

A color photo of a woman appeared on the screen. She was in her late twenties, had long black hair, and looked Filipino.

"You look nothing like your photo," Paul said to Jessica.

"Now will you believe that I'm not Jessie Montega?" Jessica pleaded.

"That means she's dead, she's truly dead," Paul muttered. His eyes grew sad. "I really killed her."

"Paul, you didn't kill anyone," Father Wycliffe said. "You have to trust yourself again."

The video transmission suddenly ended. Jessica looked at the videoscreen and said, "Forgive me, Father, but I don't need another person adding to this retarded mess."

She turned to Paul. "Would it help if you talked to her?"

Before Paul could answer, he heard someone say, "Paul, how nice to finally see you."

The voice sounded familiar. Paul turned around. Jessie Montega stood there, smiling.

"Do you see her too?" Paul asked.

Erin and Thomas, both looking shocked, simply replied, "Yes."

Thomas looked at the lights flashing quickly on Erin's brainscanner headpiece. He took the brainscanner monitor out of his pocket.

"Uh, maybe you should see this," he said.

But Paul wasn't listening to him. Instead, he stared at the ghost from Redsands.

Jessie Montega looked into Paul's eyes. "Thanks for trying to teleport me up. I know it didn't work, but I appreciate all that you did for me."

She held her hand out to Paul. "Feel my hand. That's the DNA, the amino acids, the proteins, the water, the carbon, and the oxygen that will become the first Martian life forms."

Paul took Jessie Montega's hand and gripped it. It felt smooth and solid and warm, not like what he had expected of a ghost. He marveled at how human the ghost felt.

"Are you dead?" Paul whispered, barely able to speak.

Jessie Montega nodded. "My body lies on Mars, but my spirit is in heaven with God. It's a good place, so don't worry about me."

"Thanks for letting me know."

As Paul released her hand, Jessie Montega said, "There is a purpose of my life and my death. Let me fulfill my purpose." Then, looking at Jessica, she said, "Let her fulfill her purpose too."

With a wave of her hand, Jessie Montega faded away.

Paul looked at Jessica. "You really are Jesus."

"Finally, you believe me!" Jessica said. "Listen, you've done nothing wrong. Be at peace with yourself again."

Paul tossed the ignition key to Jessica.

"What are you doing?" Thomas shouted.

Jessica dropped the knife on the floor, caught the key, and dashed through the airlock and into the shuttlecraft.

"She's just a crazy kid!" Thomas yelled as he ran to the airlock.

He tried to pull open the door, but Jessica had locked it from the other side. The whirring sounds of machinery began. Thomas backed away from the door.

"She's starting the nuclear engine," Erin said. "Let's get out of here."

———

Back at the control room, they watched the shuttlecraft blast away from Troika and shoot towards the red planet below.

"We've got our cameras aimed over Redsands again," Erin said as she finally removed the brainscanner headpiece.

The viewscreen showed an aerial shot of the ruined station. The shuttlecraft fell quickly like a blur onto the broken dome. A blinding flash of white light erupted. A nuclear mushroom cloud arose.

In horrified silence, the Troika's crew watched the thick radioactive smoke climb hundreds of feet into the Martian sky.

"Nothing could have survived that," Paul said.

Thomas scowled and turned away from the viewscreen. "We let that kid kill herself," he spat.

A tear ran down Erin's cheek. "Poor Jessica," she muttered.

Paul put his hand on Erin's shoulder. "I think she'll come back."

Thomas looked at another viewscreen, this one showing animated graphics of the orbits of Space Station Exeter and Space Station Troika.

"Exeter is now at its closest position to Troika," Thomas announced. "Well, we're stranded here. Neither we nor Exeter have a shuttlecraft. How are we going to take the food to Exeter?"

Numbers and words suddenly appeared on the Erin's computer monitor and began scrolling upwards.

"This information's downloading onto our mainframe," Erin observed. "What is it?"

Paul looked at the monitor. "It's program code for the teleporter. Is the University of Waterloo sending it to us?"

"No, it's not coming from Earth," Erin reported. "It's coming from — Mars."

Paul looked at his computer monitor. Instead of the program code, it showed a message:

Your teleporter is now safe for people and food.
XP

Paul grinned at the signature: XP, the first and second letters of XPICTOC. Kristos: Christ in Greek.

All the food they teleported to Space Station Exeter arrived complete and unchanged. "Just as hard and tasteless as it originally was, no miracle this time," Thomas joked.

Finally, the crew had only themselves to teleport to Exeter. But Thomas had to something to show Paul and Erin before they abandoned Troika.

Thomas pointed at brain scans of Erin on a computer terminal. Different parts of her brain glowed and pulsated in red, green, and yellow.

Thomas pointed to an area that suddenly lit up and expanded in red. "That's the electrical activity in the left temporal lobe at the time when you first saw Jessica. It's all red, showing an increase in electrical activity."

He showed another brain scan with the left temporal lobe lit up in red. "And this is a scan of your brain at the time when you saw Jessie Montega's ghost."

Erin gazed at the brain scans. "And what about the time I saw my mother?"

"Same results," Thomas said. "The temporal lobe is where the emotions of religious experience, feelings like awe and joy, are created," he explained. "Religious mystics experience increased brain wave activity there when they see visions or go into altered states of consciousness."

"Does that mean Jesus and my mother and Jessie Montega really did come to us?" Erin wondered.

"Or something triggered these visions in our minds," Thomas suggested. He opened a three-dimensional computer graphic of Troika. Animated waves poured from the centre of the space station.

"I detected electrochemical signals from Troika itself," Thomas said. "The signals are coming from the core of the asteroid that the station is built in."

"Electrochemical signals?" Paul said. "You mean the rock is sending out brain waves of its own?"

"It seems to be. The rock could have planted visions of Jessica, Erin's mother, and Jessie Montega into our minds," Thomas said.

"And that's why Father Wycliffe couldn't see Jessica," Paul realized. "He wasn't here to receive the signals."

Erin leaned forward to look at the graphic image of Troika. "But my mother's ghost knew about me and my family. How could the rock have known all about our lives?"

"I think the rock is also absorbing our brain waves," Thomas said. "It's probably taking our memories and turning them into visions of people we knew."

"Incredible," Paul said. "Siren Stones are real."

Thomas shrugged. "I don't know if this is a Siren Stone or not." He paused. "But now I'm sure that God and Jesus are just figments of our imagination, created in our brains."

"Oh, I wouldn't say that," Erin protested. "Maybe God gave us temporal lobes so that we can experience Him."

"Oh, come on, you can't prove that," Thomas retorted.

"What about the missing shuttlecraft?" Erin mentioned. "Someone flew it into Mars. And that nuclear explosion was no illusion. Other space stations saw it."

"And then there's the new program code for the teleporter," Paul said. "Where did that come from?"

"Okay, I don't know how to explain everything," Thomas admitted, "but before we jump to conclusions about God, we need to look at all the possibilities."

"There'll be plenty of time to study all the possibilities, but not now; Exeter's going to move out of range," Paul said as he looked at his watch. "Let's go to the teleporter."

As they walked to the teleporter, Paul said, "It's too bad we have to leave now. We don't know anything about this rock. How can it send and receive brain waves? Is it living? Is it intelligent? There's plenty for a future crew to study."

———

They teleported themselves safely to Space Station Exeter.

Later that day, Father Wycliffe celebrated Mass in the chapel of Space Station Exeter. He gave the Eucharist to Paul and Erin, thanked God for the safe evacuation of Troika's crew, and included Jessica in the prayers for the dead.

Thomas also attended Mass that day. True to his beliefs, he did not join in the prayers or kneel and rise with the rest of the congregation. But he sat throughout the Mass in memory of Jessica, the girl who had cooked a fish dinner in the way he loved from Fisherman's Wharf in San Francisco.

———

Nothing remained of Redsands Base except for hundreds of pools of chemical soup scattered on a charred red landscape. In one pool of chemicals, a geyser of water continued spraying up from the center. Water, oxygen, carbon, proteins, and amino acids swirled together after feeling the burst of nuclear energy.

Long after the Earth people had left, membranes formed around proteins and chemicals, and the first cells appeared. The cells absorbed energy from the radiation and the sun, and chemical reactions began inside the cells. One day, a cell split into two.

Life had sprung on Mars.

PART 2
MARS

3 / SUMMONED TO TROIKA

"May the Lord protect the soul of our brother Giovanni Salerno," Father Wycliffe prayed over the casket. He made the Sign of the Cross and motioned to the space station crew. They silently carried the casket to the other end of Exeter's spaceship docks. It joined three dozen other caskets on the floor.

That makes thirty-seven bodies found, Wycliffe counted. Somewhere down on the planet's surface, another one hundred and forty-two bodies waited to be discovered, assuming there were still remains to be found.

Exeter's director, Alfred Bronson, approached Father Wycliffe. "Was that Giovanni?"

"Yes, Giovanni, one of our best shuttlecraft pilots," Wycliffe said. "It's awful that his ship crashed while rescuing someone from Burroughs Base."

"I just received a message from his family. They want him returned to Earth, not buried in space," said Bronson. "I promised that his body will be on the next flight to Earth in two standard weeks."

"Everyone wants their relatives returned to Earth. I guess sending them adrift in space isn't the same as a burial at sea. Will there be room aboard the *Victoria* for them?"

"The crew will make room in the freezer." Bronson sighed. "Just don't think about our dead flying back to Earth beside the ship's food supply."

The spaceship *Victoria* was due to arrive at Space Station Exeter in two standard days. She was bringing supplies and new crew members. After two weeks docked to *Exeter*, she would return to Earth with people whose tours of duty had ended. Nobody had expected that some of them would be returning inside fiberglass caskets.

Rabbi Joseph Gabizon and Imam Amira Edip walked back from the caskets. They looked exhausted, Father Wycliffe observed. The space station's chaplains, like everyone else, had been working nonstop since the Mars disaster.

Since he had been constantly working around spacecraft and survivors for the past week, Rabbi Gabizon's black suit had become wrinkled and dirty. Some red-brown soil had rubbed onto the small European Space Agency logos on his black *kippah*, the cloth cap. However, his *tallit*, the prayer shawl draped over his shoulders, remained bright and immaculate.

The rabbi took great pride in his *tallit*, made by the finest tailor in Seville. It was white with blue stripes and the Spanish royal coat of arms in its colors of red and yellow. Father Wycliffe, intrigued by the odd mix of symbols, had asked why the coat of arms of the Catholic monarchs was on the Jewish prayer shawl. Rabbi Gabizon had proudly explained that he had served as a chaplain in Spain's *armada* before joining the European Space Agency.

The rabbi gave a small nod to Bronson and Father Wycliffe, his way of greeting people. "The rites for the dead are finished."

Rabbi Gabizon took off his *kippah* and ran his hand through his hair, which was still black after five years in space. He placed the *kippah* back on his head and bowed to the caskets. "May they have a peaceful journey back to Earth," he wished.

Imam Amira Edip, in contrast to Father Wycliffe and Rabbi Gabizon, wore white, the Islamic color of mourning. The thin, petite woman wore a silk blouse, jacket, long skirt, and pillbox hat. Red crescents and stars decorated her white pillbox hat. The hat's colors reversed the colors of the flag of Turkey, the country of her ancestors.

The youngest of the chaplains in orbit around Mars, Imam Edip was also the most stylish; she wore make-up and streaked her brown hair with blonde highlights. Her Protestant Islamic mosque in Germany allowed such extravagances for their women prayer leaders.

"If there are no more duties here, I will go to the lab and finish testing the rock samples," she said. "Then I have to write a report before sending the samples to Earth."

"Yeah, let's get back to work," Bronson said. They walked away from the dead of Mars.

In Mission Control, the operations center of Exeter, Bronson and Wycliffe looked at pictures from the Mars Solar Observatory, a large telescope floating in space.

Fifteen dark patches had appeared on the bright orange surface of the Sun. Each patch covered an area over twenty times the surface of the Earth. These were sunspots, places where the Sun's photosphere was cooling.

From his experience at the Vatican Observatory, Father Wycliffe knew the potential danger of sunspots. As each sunspot cooled, it could spew out a solar flare, a gigantic burst of magnetic energy and radiation from across the electromagnetic spectrum. Radio waves, gamma waves, and X-rays, with energy equivalent to tens of millions of hydrogen bombs, would shoot across space towards Mars and the space stations around it. If the solar flare were strong enough, its radiation could knock out communications between the space stations and with Earth.

"As if we didn't have enough to worry about, now we've got sunspots," Bronson muttered.

He switched on the public address microphone. "This is the director. We have some sunspots and therefore the potential for solar flares. All personnel should end extravehicular activity and return to protected areas until further notice. I repeat, no EVA until further notice."

Bronson switched off the microphone and turned to Father Wycliffe. "That's done. The last thing I need is for someone to get fried because he stayed out on EVA during a solar flare."

They watched various monitors and screens showing the space stations and spacecraft around Mars. On one screen, above the words "FROM DEEP SPACE PROBE", the *Victoria* appeared. Sleek and majestic, she glided silently across the darkness of space.

"She'll be arriving soon," said Bronson. "Father, have you heard from Father Alexei?"

"Yes, I got a video message from him," said Father Wycliffe. "He's looking forward to his stint here."

"And you must be looking forward to going home."

"Now that you mention it –- do you think I could stay here?"

"What do you mean, stay here? Your tour of duty is over."

"I know, but I'm wondering if I can extend it."

"Our complement calls for one Christian chaplain trained in interfaith service. That'll be Father Alexei now."

"You'll have enough priests, but I'm not just a priest. I also flew shuttlecrafts between stations," Wycliffe reminded him.

"I know you're rated to fly shuttlecrafts, but even so, why do you want to stay on?" Bronson asked.

"We're down one shuttlecraft pilot with Giovanni Salerno gone. His tour of duty wasn't supposed to end yet. The replacements coming from Earth left before the disaster, so they don't have a shuttlecraft pilot to replace him. But I could take over his job."

"That's true, but you still haven't answered my question. *Why* do you want to stay on?"

"Well, I really don't want to go back to the Moon," Wycliffe said.

Bronson looked surprised. "Oh, I didn't know that. Don't you have a job waiting for you there?"

"Yes, I'm going back to St. Dominic's Roman Catholic Church at Timonium Base."

"Timonium Base! That place has really expanded since lightweight radiation shielding was invented. I wish our space stations had lightweight shielding. The Moon has really developed over the last few years: manufacturing, mining, tourism, art, culture, entertainment, even sports. The Moon's a very exciting place now."

"It's also a very volatile place. The Moon's politics are just like Earth's, and countries have threatened to go to war over the Moon. Around Mars, people live and work in peace. We don't have the same politics like on the Moon. It's not perfect here, but we haven't ever refused to help each other, not even when our governments tell us not to."

"Don't be so sure it'll be like that forever here," Bronson said. "Give us time, it could happen. We are human beings, after all."

Father Wycliffe nodded. "I know we're only human, but call me naïve, I think we can avoid the urge to kill each here. Mars is different from the Moon. If we get into trouble here, we can't get help from Earth for months. We're so far away from Earth that we need each other to survive. We either live together or die together here. Not exactly the most altruistic of motives, but it's better than nothing."

"I hate to sound pessimistic, but we're still dependent on Earth for supplies and equipment," Bronson said. "If trouble occurs on Earth, and our countries stop sending supplies to us, we'll have no choice but to return to Earth."

"Yes, I know, we're ultimately under Earth's control," Wycliffe said. "If the Earth goes to war, we either go back and fight or stay here and starve. However, while it lasts, there's hope on Mars. It's a rough frontier, but it's a chance to create something new."

"The threat of war really bothers you. Weren't you a military chaplain? You served in the Vernacular Wars."

"That's all the more reason to avoid a place where a war could break out at any moment. I'll leave war to younger, more energetic padres. I've buried enough soldiers in my lifetime. It's a duty I have no desire to repeat."

"Which brings us back to your duty: do you have a choice to refuse your new job?"

"I could quit the ESA, but then what would I do? I'm in a weird sort of limbo, being a diocesan priest without a diocese. I was discharged from my diocese to join the ESA. The ESA can't transfer me to a Catholic parish, except one: St. Dominic's Church on the Moon."

"But you say you don't want to go back there. Is there anything else you could do in the Catholic Church?"

"I could join an order like the Jesuits or the Dominicans and let their superior tell me what to do next, but I prefer being a diocesan priest, not a member of an order. I like the pastoral work, helping the people," Father Wycliffe said.

"So how did you get this offer to go back to the Moon?" Bronson said.

"St. Dominic's priest will retire just as I return. Just like the chronic Catholic priest shortage on Earth, there's also a priest shortage in space. Dr. Schiller can't send a non-Catholic priest to St. Dominic's, so he asked me to come back. Cardinal Saint-Cloud wants me back there too. I wish I could stay out here, though."

"I think the Chief Chaplain of the ESA will be disappointed if you disobey him, and you don't want to annoy him, even if he is Lutheran. But does he have other choices? If you don't return to the Moon, can he find someone else for St. Dominic's?"

"He asked a few other priests to join the ESA Chaplaincy Department. I heard he asked Father Bertoli at Notre Dame College; Father Bertoli has written numerous papers about the health care for Moon colonists. He also asked Father Rodrigues at the Spacefarers' Chapel at Cape Canaveral. Both of them declined the offer."

"They have impressive scientific backgrounds, but neither of them has lived in space," Bronson observed. "You're the Catholic priest with the most experience in space. Is that why Dr. Schiller wants you again?"

"Yeah, lucky me."

"Okay. You don't want a job at Timonium Base, but don't you have people waiting to see you back home? Taking the space liner between Earth and the Moon is a lot cheaper now, and the Moon is so close to Earth."

"That all sounds wonderful, but no, I've got no one to see on Earth," Wycliffe said.

In his cabin, Father Wycliffe opened a box of wafers. Now they were just small round pieces of bread. During Mass, they would become the Blessed Sacrament: the body of Christ.

Long before Christianity came, long before Jesus was born, Greek philosophers had theorized that things have both accidents and substance, which are not the same. The early Christians borrowed the concept for themselves. After the bread changes into the body of Christ, its *accidents*, the bread's forms perceptible to human senses and scientific investigation, stay the same. The bread still looks, feels, smells, and tastes like bread. However, its *substance*, that which something is in itself, changes from baked wheat into the body of Christ.

Transubstantiation should not change the wafers' accidents from baked wheat to living flesh, much less in the form of a teenage girl.

He put the wafers into a gold ciborium, a chalice-like vessel for holding the Blessed Sacrament.

Someone knocked on the door. He opened the door and found Imam Amira Edip standing there. She wore her blue jumpsuit with the ESA patch and German flag.

"Mark, may I come in?" Imam Edip asked.

Wycliffe smiled. Amira was one of the few persons who addressed him by his first name. She had known him only from their tenure on Mars. Perhaps she felt familiar with him because the Martian colonists were close to each other in their isolation from Earth.

In addition, she had never known him on Earth, where he had to deliver death notices and funeral rites, when he had to be the somber Father Wycliffe, not plain Mark.

"Yes, come in," Wycliffe said.

"I have packed my rock samples," Amira said. "I have some space left in my shipping box. Given the scarcity of cargo space, I should not waste it."

She looked at the shipping boxes on the Father Wycliffe's floor. "Can you fit all your belongings in your boxes? If you need more space, I have some left in my box."

"Thanks for the offer. As it turns out, I do need more space," Wycliffe replied. "I filled up my boxes with meteorites for the Vatican Observatory. They were too tempting to leave behind on Mars. But now I don't have enough room for those statues."

Imam Edip turned around and looked at Father Wycliffe's bookshelf. "Oh, your collection! Yes, I have room for these figurines."

On the bookshelf was a row of small statues of the Virgin Mary, Mother of Jesus: Mary in a white robe as Our Lady of Fatima; Mary as an Aztec woman in green as Our Lady of Guadalupe; Mary in a white and blue robe as Our Lady of Lourdes; Mary dressed in brown and carrying Jesus as Our Lady of Mount Carmel; Mary between two oval medals as Our Lady of the Miraculous Medal; and Mary as Our Lady of Walsingham, dressed in a blue robe and holding the infant Jesus in her lap.

The imam, whom Wycliffe presumed knew about the Islamic ban on images of God and His prophets, looked amused. "Catholic action figures," she joked. "God is invisible to Christians, and Christians forbid idol worship just like Moslems do. So why do you Roman Christians have so many statues of the Virgin Mary?"

"I'm from Walsingham, England, the town with two national shrines to the Virgin Mary. It would be unusual if I *didn't* have little statues of Mary," Father Wycliffe explained. "We don't worship these figures. They're devotional statues, not idols. We *venerate* them, not worship them. They help us teach ideas and Bible stories and focus our attention on the holy."

"I see. They are teaching aids, not objects of worship. That explains why Roman Christians have so many statues, medals, and pictures of Mary, Jesus, Moses, Adam and Eve, and your saints. That also explains the old man with the white beard on the ceiling of the Sistine Chapel."

"Oh, yes, God the invisible, He who cannot be seen, except as an old man with a white beard in paintings and movies," Father Wycliffe said.

Amira looked at the statues of Mary again. "Roman Christians have so much devotion to a woman. I like that. It is like the Shia devotion to Mohammed's daughter, Fatima."

"Roman Catholics have a Fatima too. She's one of the apparitions of the Virgin Mary," Wycliffe said. "Mary has a very special place in Roman Catholic devotion. She's our most popular saint."

"Are you -- what is that term I have heard — a Marian priest?"

Father Wycliffe had seen images of the Virgin Mary since childhood. Walsingham had two major shrines devoted to Mary, and her image was everywhere: statues, icons, paintings, religious medals, Rosary beads, holy water bottles, key chains, postcards. Pilgrims came to Walsingham to pray to Mary. Both the Anglican and Catholic priests recited the Rosary prayers in her honor. His faith in God was inseparable from his devotion to Mary.

"Yes, I guess you could say that I'm a Marian priest. It's unavoidable if you're from Walsingham."

"And you pray to Mary and the saints too?"

"Roman Catholics do. When we pray to the saints, we aren't worshipping them. We're asking them to intercede with God on our behalf."

"Shia Moslems do the same thing; they ask the Twelve Imams to intercede for them. Moslems and Christians used to be more alike than most people realize. Centuries ago, many Moslems had customs that would seem familiar to you. In the Middle East, Moslems made pilgrimages to the tombs and shrines of Sufi saints, Shia Imams, and holy men. They prayed to saints and angels for their intercession with God. They built a shrine to John the Baptist, a prophet in both Islam and Christianity, in the Umayyad Mosque in Damascus. The Persians had books with beautiful pictures of the life of Mohammed, sometimes showing Mohammed himself. Some Moslems wore talismans and charms. Moslems could not see God, but they could see, hear, and feel signs of their devotion to Him and His devotion to them.

"I doubt these traditions caused all the sins of the world, but the Wahhabi Purists thought they did. They destroyed the tombs of Sufi holy men and the gravestones of Mohammed's relatives and his Companions. They killed people who prayed to saints, and they banned pilgrimages to shrines except the Hajj to Mecca. They used the Saudi kingdom to impose their version of Islam on the Arabian Peninsula."

"Until they killed the Saudi king and the royal family, all seven thousand of them," said Wycliffe.

Amira smiled wryly. "The royal family behaved like drunken millionaires and playboys when they were in Europe and America. I saw some Saudi princes in Berlin. They spent millions of euros on clothes, liquor, and prostitutes. When they returned home, they acted pious and ruled their people by force. Did they think that their people would not see their hypocrisy?"

She moved towards the door. "Excuse me for boring you with political speeches. We Germans can be so tiresome. I am going back to the geology lab now. Like I said, I can put the statues in my box, so give them to me before tomorrow."

Amira left the cabin, leaving Father Wycliffe alone with his unconsecrated wafers and small statues.

He picked up the ciborium and walked towards the door. He passed a wall decoration, a crucifix, a cross of silver bearing the body of Jesus in gold. Protestants prefer an empty cross because they think the image of Jesus in agony is lurid, but the crucifix is typically Roman Catholic and Eastern Orthodox.

He went to Space Station Exeter's Christian chapel and put the ciborium on a table beside the altar.

Father Wycliffe looked at the bare white walls. The Christian chapel was bare of the extravagant decorations that marked Roman Catholic churches on Earth. In contrast to his personal quarters, the chapel's only decorations were small ceramic bas-relief plaques of the Stations of the Cross on one wall and an *empty* steel cross on the wall behind the altar. Missing were the traditional Roman Catholic symbols: the crucifix showing Jesus on the cross, the side altars devoted to individual saints, and the statues of Mary.

By order of Pope Christopher, Roman Catholic chapels beyond Earth had to be simple and undecorated so they would not arouse the fundamentalist atheists, who were pressuring the space agencies to ban clergy from space.

Paul Devane entered the chapel. "Good morning, Father. Do you need any help preparing the chapel for Father Alexei?"

"No, I don't need to redecorate the chapel before he arrives, but thank you anyway." Father Wycliffe looked at the bare white walls. "Now that an Eastern Orthodox will run the chapel, I hope it'll get better décor. Maybe Father Alexei will bring some icons with him. Wouldn't that be pretty?"

The Russian Orthodox Father Alexei was not bound by the orders of the

Roman Catholic Pope Christopher. The new priest might decorate the chapel in the lavish Eastern Orthodox style: colorful icons, bejeweled crosses, maybe even a gilt iconostasis and a pair of gold wedding crowns. Father Wycliffe envied the Eastern Orthodox for their freedom to decorate their chapels in space.

"There's actually a traditional Orthodox wooden icon this far away from Earth," Paul said. "It's the one showing the three angels who visited Abraham and Sarah. It's aboard Troika."

"NASA doesn't plan on sending anyone to Troika. That's too bad. If anyone is going to Troika, maybe he could bring the icon here for Father Alexei."

"That's a nice idea, but maybe the icon should stay there. After all, Troika is a holy place where Jesus returned."

"The schoolgirl Jessica, you mean," Father Wycliffe said.

At Mass, Father Wycliffe had included Jessica in the prayers for the dead. He never saw the schoolgirl, and he doubted she had existed, but he prayed for her because Paul and Erin believed that she was real and had lived and died.

But the prayer was for Jessica, a human schoolgirl. The prayer was not for Jesus, Son of God.

"You never saw her," Paul said. "I wish you had. Then you would believe me."

Father Wycliffe did not want to discuss what really happened at Space Station Troika. The Church rarely approved of apparitions of Jesus or Mary. Over the centuries, the Church had approved only a few apparitions, such as the ones at Guadalupe, Lourdes, Fatima, Krakow, and Akita. Hundreds of others had not been approved. Many of these were officially denounced by their local archbishops. The Roman Catholic Church does not teach fairy tales and ghost stories.

He thought of a neutral reply. "Faith in Jesus is sometimes hard to maintain out here. I'm happy that you have confirmed your faith in Jesus."

But Father Wycliffe could not escape the debate on Troika forever. He had avoided discussing the apparition of Jesus with Catholic believer Paul Devane, but ironically, he could not avoid it with secular Alfred Bronson.

At dinner, Bronson asked Father Wycliffe, "Will the Church recognize the apparition of Jesus at Space Station Troika?"

"I doubt it," said Wycliffe as he poked his fork into a chunk of rehydrated meat loaf. "There are possible explanations that aren't supernatural."

The priest grimaced as he tasted the meat loaf. Then he continued, "The Troika crew discovered that the station's asteroid foundation was sending electrochemical signals, like a human brain."

Wycliffe picked up his pocket computer and punched a few commands. A photograph of asteroid 20 521 Odette de Proust appeared on the computer's screen. "That's an asteroid called Odette de Proust."

"The haunted asteroid."

"It didn't take long for Odette to become a legend, did it? I heard rumors about Odette, info that was supposed to be military secrets, but some asteroid blasters talked about it. They say Odette was sending electrochemical signals to their brains, and that's why they thought they were seeing the ghosts of their relatives."

"So that's your theory of the Schoolgirl Jesus. She was an illusion created by a telepathic asteroid."

"I know it sounds stupid, but it makes sense."

"Assuming that there are telepathic asteroids, which hasn't been proven yet," Bronson said. "The observations from Odette and Troika are too recent to be conclusive. They've not been analyzed, confirmed, or repeated by other scientists. Until then, the Siren Stones will remain legends."

"I know, but it's a possibility for future research."

"What about the shuttlecraft that crashed into Mars?"

"Believe me, in my years as a priest, I've seen people do some pretty odd things," said Father Wycliffe. "It's possible that in their hallucinatory state, the crew put the shuttlecraft on autopilot and sent it down to Mars on its own. They only think Jesus hijacked it and flew away."

"They each had the same hallucination?"

"Perhaps a Siren Stone can cause that."

"I'm amazed," said Bronson. "Two believing Christians say they saw Jesus at Troika. But you, a priest of God, have scientific explanations for the apparition. Don't you feel a conflict in debunking Jesus?"

Father Wycliffe shook his head. "No, not really. My job as both a priest and a scientist is to find the truth. I'm not saying that Jesus doesn't exist. I'm saying that he might not have appeared at Troika."

In Mission Control the next standard day, Wycliffe was reviewing shuttlecraft maintenance logs when he heard a crew member call for Bronson.

"Look at this," the crewman said. "Troika is slowly losing altitude. It's drifting down to the planet."

"I wouldn't worry. Troika's automatic altitude system will boost it back up," said Bronson.

The crewman stared at his computer monitor. "But Troika has already fallen below its tolerance altitude. The automatic altitude system might not be working."

Wycliffe walked to Bronson and the crewman. The crewman's monitor showed a video image of Troika floating in space. Beside the picture, words and numbers scrolled down the screen.

Gravity eventually pushes all space stations down to the planet unless they receive a boost upwards. In past centuries, space shuttles nudged space stations back into their orbits. Now space stations had automatic altitude systems. If the space station fell below an altitude limit, the space station would automatically fire its rockets and boost itself back into orbit.

"No Martian space station's automatic altitude system has ever failed," Bronson said.

"But Troika is the oldest space station here," Wycliffe said. "It was originally intended to be a temporary station. It was supposed to be decommissioned when the larger and newer stations were built. Its systems were expected to break down ten years ago, but it's still up there. Maybe the automatic altitude system is finally failing."

"The problem can be easily fixed. NASA gave the ESA access to Troika's systems programming. Either we or NASA can transmit a command to Troika's automatic altitude system."

The crewman asked, "Should we calculate an altitude adjustment and send the command?"

"No, let one of the NASA stations do it," replied Bronson. "Troika is their space station. I don't want to interfere with their internal operations."

Bronson and Wycliffe had only stepped a few paces away from the crewman when he called them back.

"Hey, we're receiving a message from Troika," the crewman said.

"But there's nobody on Troika," said Wycliffe.

"It's an automatic message from Troika's communications system," the crewman explained. He looked at the words appearing rapidly on his monitor. "Unit BF-36, an exterior antenna, is malfunctioning, and the unit has a ninety percent probability of complete failure within twenty-four standard hours."

A computer graphic of unit BF-36 appeared and rotated on the computer monitor. It was an old antenna, a type that the Russians had not made for decades.

"That'll be a problem," Bronson said. "If the antenna goes down, we'll lose contact with the station."

"And Troika won't be able to receive the command to raise the altitude, will it?" Father Wycliffe asked.

The crewman shook his head. "No, Troika won't receive it."

"Someone will have to go there and fix the antenna," said Bronson. "I hope NASA sends someone soon."

"Wow, a solar flare!" a solar analyst cried.

She pressed a button, and the largest viewscreen switched to pictures from the Mars Solar Observatory. Gigantic, jagged bolts of light burst from the Sun.

"Estimated time of arrival?" Bronson said.

"Five minutes."

Bronson grabbed the public address microphone. "Attention, all crew! We've got a solar flare, ETA in five minutes or less. Anyone who hasn't already returned from EVA, get back inside now. Everyone get to a protected area."

On one viewscreen, a technician in a spacesuit scrambled into the hatch of his shuttlecraft. Why was he spacewalking despite Bronson's previous order to stay inside?

Other viewscreens showed people rushing to the most heavily shielded sections of their spacecraft. Unlike the crew of smaller stations and ships, Exeter's crew did not have to rush to any special shelters; heavy shielding covered all of Exeter.

"How strong is it?" Bronson demanded.

"Wow, X30 category," the solar analyst replied. "This is one of the strongest solar flares ever recorded."

Three minutes and fifty seconds after the Mars Solar Observatory had seen the solar flare, the viewscreens suddenly went blank. Grey and white static flickered on the screens. Exeter had lost communications with the other space stations.

With video contact gone, Exeter's crew tried contacting the other stations by radio, but they heard only crackling noises. The space stations were flying blind and deaf to each other.

"This is the longest we've ever been out of contact with each other," Bronson said. "It's dangerous."

"Yeah, the silence is scary," Father Wycliffe said.

Then the videoscreens lit up with images of the space stations, and voices spoke over the radio again. The crew cheered as they regained contact with other stations and ships one at a time.

Wycliffe looked at his watch. What had seemed like an eternity had lasted only ten minutes. In space, that was a long time to be out of contact.

"Live transmission arriving from Space Station Carter," a crew member said. "It's station director Holbrook. She wants to talk to you."

"Put her on the big screen," Bronson said.

A woman appeared on the largest viewscreen. An attractive woman in her late thirties, Karen Holbrook kept her brown hair immaculately coiffed in corkscrew curls. Her hair hadn't yet turned grey from age, but it had a white streak running down the left side.

Holbrook had been briefly exposed to a tiny radiation leak during a shuttlecraft repair. The radiation caused minor but freakish damage: it killed her melanocytes, the cells that produce hair color, along a single streak of hair.

Like many American spacers, Karen Holbrook wore the NASA logo on her blue jumpsuit. She also wore a badge that nobody else had near Mars: an NAACP Image Award lapel pin, received when the National Association for the Advancement of Colored People named her "African American Martian Woman of the Year". At the awards ceremony, someone dressed like a green alien in a spacesuit had posed with her on stage. When she returned to Mars for a second tour of duty, she told people that she had seen more little green men in Los Angeles than on Mars.

That had been a fun trip back to Earth. Today around Mars, she looked very serious.

Bronson looked at the screen. "What can I do for you, Ms. Holbrook?"

"Space Station Troika is losing altitude," Holbrook said. "We tried to send a command to Troika after we restored inter-station communications, but Troika is not responding. I suspect that the solar flare damaged the BF-36 unit on Troika. That antenna was already malfunctioning."

"Maybe there's a glitch between you and Troika," suggested Bronson. "Can Space Station Olympus send the command?"

"Olympus tried too, but they weren't successful either. Your station is currently the closest to Troika..."

"So you want us to send the command?"

"Yes, please. I've already calculated the altitude adjustment. I'll send the command's program code to you, and you can send it to Troika."

Minutes later, Space Station Carter sent the program code to Exeter. A communications specialist typed some commands into her console and nodded to Bronson.

"Alright, we're ready to send the command," Bronson said. He turned to the communications specialist. "Go ahead."

The communications specialist hit a button on her keyboard, and the program code scrolled down her monitor. "We're uploading to Troika now," she said. "We'll know in a minute whether Troika is receiving us."

It did not take a minute. Seconds later, the words "RECIPIENT TROIKA OFF-LINE" flashed on her monitor.

Bronson confirmed the obvious to Holbrook. "We can't get through to Troika either."

Holbrook took in a deep breath and let it out. "Darn, someone has to go to Troika and fix the antenna. But all our pilots are searching for survivors."

"Alfred, I need a favor from you. You're the closest to Troika. Can you send someone over there?"

"I'm afraid I can't," Bronson said. "I'm running out of pilots too. I lost Giovanni, and the others are carrying food and supplies between the stations. I don't know if I can divert one of them over to Troika, but --"

"I'll do it," Father Wycliffe said, interrupting Bronson.

———

In the mess hall, Paul Devane carried his coffee to Father Wycliffe's table.

"Why don't you use the teleporter?" Paul suggested. "It'll be faster than flying there and back by shuttlecraft."

Father Wycliffe looked up from the schematic diagrams and technical specifications of the BF-36 unit. "The teleporter? It's not rated for teleporting humans."

"Erin, Paul, and I came here by teleporter," Paul said as he stirred artificial sweetener into the coffee.

"I know it worked for you, but there's still that glitch on ten percent of attempts to teleport organic matter," Father Wycliffe reminded him. "I don't want to take that risk with a living creature. Like me."

"But it's safe now, after Jessica — or Jesus — gave us the program code."

More talk about Jessica. Father Wycliffe regretted sending the jar of consecrated bread by teleporter. He had started the chain of events that ended with a shuttlecraft crashing on Mars.

He did not truly believe that Jesus had come back, but he knew something had happened to make Paul Devane and Erin Malloy believe so. Until he learned more about the events at Troika, he did not want to talk about them. A priest had to be careful not to encourage belief in fairy tales, ghost stories, and unproven miracles. Priests are philosophers and guidance counselors, not wizards and fortune tellers.

"Sure, the teleporter is available, but I want to fly a spacecraft again before I go back to Earth," said Father Wycliffe, changing the subject from Jessica-Jesus.

"Of course," Paul said. "We all want to get as much space experience as we can while we're out here." He rose from the table. "Excuse me, but I've got to get back to work. Have a pleasant flight and good luck on your mission."

After Wycliffe waved 'bye to Paul, he stared at the diagrams of unit BF-36 again. But he was not thinking about the antenna.

The teleporter program code bothered him.

It was the only mystery that he could not explain. From where had the program code come?

Paul Devane believed that the program code was divinely inspired, that it had come from Jesus on Mars.

Father Wycliffe was not as certain. The divine revelation of God ended with the New Testament, not with a teleporter program code.

From where had the code come?

―――

Father Wycliffe watched the maintenance crew inspect the Tsiolkovsky shuttlecraft. Instead of a priest, he looked like a pilot of the mid-twentieth century; he wore a black aviator jacket with a Royal Air Force patch. Since he had stopped performing his priestly duties for the day, he had changed out of his black suit and shirt with the Roman collar.

"Padre, I hear you're going to Troika," a voice said from behind.

Father Wycliffe turned around and saw Dr. Thomas Hall. The doctor surprised him. Occasionally, Thomas would bait Father Wycliffe with ponderous monologues about atheism and politics at dinner, but he rarely talked to him outside the mess hall.

"That's right," Father Wycliffe replied.

"Do you think that Jesus is there?" Thomas asked.

"Jesus is everywhere. But whether he shows himself to people at Space Station Troika, I can't say."

"But you, as a priest, probably believe Paul and Erin when they say he was there. Or *she* was there."

"It's not the Middle Ages anymore, when the Church declared a miracle every time someone said he saw Jesus or the Virgin Mary."

"I agree. Jesus doesn't exist. But someone was there: the girl Jessica."

"I read Paul's report about the Jessica incident, and I talked to him several times during the incident. You detected signals similar to brainwaves coming from the rock. Don't you have a theory that the girl was just in your imagination, a hallucination caused by electrochemical signals from the space station?" Wycliffe reminded him.

Wycliffe continued. "That means Jessica was a figment of your imagination too, regardless of whether you believe she was Jesus or not. But now you believe she was a real person?"

"Yeah, I know it sounds like I'm contradicting myself, that I'm changing my mind, but I'm moving towards a consistent theory. That's what a true scientist, not a faithhead, does," Thomas said. "The more I think about it, the more I think there was a real girl. Someone had to hijack the shuttlecraft, so there had to be a real, physical being."

"A real, physical being, a teenaged girl, who was invisible to video cameras?" Wycliffe said.

"I've been thinking about that," said Thomas. "I thought of two possibilities. Maybe she has special powers to make herself invisible in video transmissions."

"Do you, as a scientist, really believe someone can do that? Can a girl let all light pass through her?" Father Wycliffe asked.

"I know that seems farfetched," Thomas admitted. "The more and more I thought about it, the more I realized that it's impossible for a girl to have the power of invisibility. So I thought of another possibility, one I had originally suspected on Troika."

"And that is?"

"Maybe she was an extraterrestrial who could turn invisible to you."

An extraterrestrial. Father Wycliffe hadn't realized that Thomas believed in aliens and flying saucers.

"Alright. What was she doing there, impersonating a human?"

"I don't know. Her mission is a mystery. Whatever her plans, I believe she was an alien," Thomas said.

"Even though there's no proof that life exists beyond Earth?"

"It's theoretically possible. Oxygen, carbon, hydrogen, water, sunlight: all the essential elements for life exist on Mars.

"Jessica was an alien. It's a theory consistent with the observations."

An utterly untested theory, Father Wycliffe wanted to say. However, he stayed silent.

Wycliffe had his own theory of how the shuttlecraft had flown away, but he didn't want to debate it with Thomas now. The Troika crew would deny that they had put a shuttlecraft on autopilot and sent it away on its own to Mars. No spacers wanted the stigma of losing a spacecraft by their own fault.

Thomas broke the silence. "There could be other aliens at Troika."

"I'll let you know if I meet any," Father Wycliffe said.

"That's why I want to talk to you. Don't proselytize your religion to them," Thomas demanded. "Christianity is the last thing we need in space."

Father Wycliffe ignored the bait and said, "I promise not to baptize any aliens."

As Thomas left, Father Wycliffe shook his head in amazement.

Since the middle of the twentieth century, thousands of people had seen flying saucers and aliens. A few "UFO cults" had even sprung up. According to some believers, aliens tortured people in painful experiments. Others said that aliens brought peace and wisdom.

In recent decades, with the discovery of many unexplainable phenomena in deep space, even a few respectable scientists had begun to believe that aliens exist. Like the UFO cultists, they claimed to be atheists. They thought that God and Jesus were figments of the imagination. They considered religion to be a superstition of primitive peoples. They challenged believers to prove that God and Jesus exist. Yet they believed that space aliens exist with no scientific evidence.

Space aliens had replaced angels and demons in the Secular Age.

And they were as much based on faith as God and Jesus were.

The news arrived from the Moon just after Wycliffe had given his flight plan to Bronson. The television images showed Space Station Europa Luna with a jagged hole at one of its spacecraft docks. Fifteen people had been sucked into space and died.

Commercial spaceships docked at Space Station Europa Luna en route between the Earth and the Moon. At Europa Luna, the spaceship crews performed maintenance on their ships, tourists stayed in a hotel and watched the Earth and the Moon, and passengers bought duty-free liquor and chocolates as they waited for their flights. Europa Luna's owner, the European Space Agency, earned a handsome profit from the station.

As more images of the space station appeared, an announcer read a warning in the various European languages:

"All European Space Agency spacecraft, space stations, and planetary bases are on alert after the incident at Space Station Europa Luna.

"ESA Headquarters in Paris has received a message from the Canadian Red Proletariat, a left-wing terrorist group from Canada. The message reads as follows:

"'The Canadian Red Proletariat claims responsibility for bombing Space Station Europa Luna and regrets the combat fatality of Louis-Jean Waldron. We honor the memory of Comrade Waldron, who disguised himself as an ESA maintenance worker with the alias of Pieter Raspe and detonated the explosive device. While still a student of Ethnic Studies at the University of California in Berkeley, Comrade Waldron received explosives training at a Neo-Taliban camp in Sudan. After graduation, Comrade Waldron strongly opposed the imperialist and racist colonization of space by Americans, Europeans, Canadians, Christians, and Zionists...'"

A photo of Louis-Jean Waldron appeared. It looked like a passport photo due to its bland white background. Waldron had scowled at the camera as he glared at it through his glasses. He had a goatee beard like all men of the Canadian Red Proletariat. His skin was pale, and his black hair looked greasy and scraggly. His blue denim shirt had a red maple leaf sewn above the pocket.

Louis-Jean Waldron looked very ordinary, like one of the hundreds of young Canadians who traveled through Europe. Father Wycliffe had seen many of them in England.

The television returned to showing pictures of the damaged space station.

Father Wycliffe felt both anger and sadness. The attack on Europa Luna reminded him of another bombing in England years ago. A man disguised as an ordinary schoolteacher had ruined his life forever.

Bronson looked at a message that had appeared on his computer terminal. "It's a message from the Director General. We're on orange alert now for possible terrorists and saboteurs who could be pretending to be ESA crew members like us."

"Orange alert?" Wycliffe asked. "Why not red?"

"The red alert is for the stations and bases near Earth and the Moon," Bronson said. "Our risk assessment is lower. Mars is far away from the Red Brigades and Neo-Taliban. No terrorist or saboteur has ever come this far from Earth."

"That's true, but there's an old saying that there's a first time for everything. I pray that it never happens here," Wycliffe said.

We've been exporting our problems to the Moon for years, he thought. *Will someone eventually bring them to Mars?*

———

As he flew the shuttlecraft towards Troika, Wycliffe looked on the red-brown planet below him. Water had flowed on the Martian surface millions of years ago, but now, only small amounts of ice lay underground. Above the ground, Mars was dry and barren, with nothing but dirt and rocks. The red planet had nothing like the green fields of grass and trees of Norfolk.

He felt the medal hanging on a chain around his neck. The pewter medal was oval-shaped and depicted Mary, Our Lady of Walsingham. He had worn the medal for years, on each day of his pastoral work, the Vernacular Wars, the colonization of the Moon, and the mission to Mars. It reminded him of his hometown and the female deity who protected it.

He had grown up in Walsingham, the town with *two* shrines to the Virgin Mary, one Anglican and one Roman Catholic. King Henry VIII, Oliver Cromwell, the Bill of Rights of 1689, and centuries of Protestant reform could not erase the Catholic-style devotion to the Mary in that town. His family and friends were not surprised to see him wearing a Catholic medal of Mary when the Church of England ordained him as a priest.

What surprised them was his conversion from Anglican chaplain in the Royal Auxiliary Air Force to Roman Catholic priest in orbit around Mars.

4 / A REMEMBRANCE OF WARS PAST

Mark's father, William Wycliffe, was head accountant of a department store on weekdays. On weekends, he was a supply officer of the Royal Auxiliary Air Force. On Mark's tenth birthday, Lieutenant Wycliffe gave him a plastic model kit of an FA2 Harrier fighter jet, one of the historical airplane models sold at the Royal Air Force Museum in Cosford.

Mark quickly assembled the sleek airplane and put Royal Navy markings on it. Then he searched the on-line encyclopedias for articles on aviation history. He read anything he could find about aviation. He watched any TV show and webcast about airplanes. Throughout his childhood, he collected bits of aviation history: model airplanes, books about the Royal Air Force, and even an old Caledonian Airways flight attendant's wing.

When he was sixteen, he wore his first aviator jacket, a souvenir of the Royal Air Force Museum. He told his friends that he wanted to build aircraft and fly them.

———

His other childhood fascination was the Church. His father stepped into church only for weddings and funerals, but his mother, Helen, a Red Cross worker, meditated in Walsingham's Anglican Shrine Church daily to relax from her job's stresses. She went to Mass on Sundays when she could, and she brought Mark with her.

Unlike many children, Mark did not sit bored during Mass. The choir's Gregorian chants in Latin, the processions down the aisle, the sunlight blazing through the colored glass windows, the scent of the incense, the orange flickers of candlelight, the ornate carvings of angels and lambs, the shiny silver cross and chalices, the wine and the bread: all made him feel like he was part of something larger, something that reached into the sky on the wings of angels.

Mark did not outgrow his fascination with the High Church when he reached his teen years. When he graduated from high school at age nineteen years, he couldn't decide which career to pursue: engineering, flying, or God?

His father was a practical man, as an accountant and military officer should be. He advised his son, "You don't want to take a vow of poverty and live on minimum wage for the rest of your life. I didn't raise you for that, and I know you won't like it. Go learn something useful that pays well, like engineering, if you like airplanes so much.

"Then enlist in the Auxiliary Air Force like I did. You don't have to be a pilot to get up in the air. You can still ride in the airplanes and fly all over Europe.

"As for the religion, take the theology courses on the side to get the religion stuff out of your system. For heaven's sake, boy, don't become a priest. The pay's awful. If you want to get involved in the Church, there's nothing wrong with being lay volunteer, like an usher or altar server."

He finally added, "London's not like Walsingham. When you see the big city and the university, and when you discover fast planes and fast girls, you'll not want to take holy orders."

Mark Wycliffe went to King's College, the University of London, to study engineering. It was the practical thing to do.

In addition to engineering, he took a few courses in theology.

And not everything he learned was in the classroom. He discovered other sides of campus life: tennis at the sports center, pub nights at the student center, and pretty girls all over the campus.

But his father was wrong. He didn't get theology out of his system, especially not after meeting a gorgeous blonde girl named Ingrid Jarvis-Carlton in Christology 201.

Ingrid Jarvis-Carlton of Chelsea spent a summer working at an antiquarian bookshop owned by her father's friend. She worked for the usual reason a sixteen-year-old Sloane Girl gets a summer job: money for clothes, jewelry, music downloads, and those nights with other girls to meet boys.

One of her friends had gotten a job selling clothes in Soho and invited Ingrid to join her. Ingrid agreed that the bookshop was much less sexy than the fashion boutique, but the bookshop owner paid well and treated his staff kindly.

The shop smelled of musty aging paper and leather bindings. The hardwood floors creaked with every step Ingrid took. Like used book shops everywhere, it had row upon row of tall oaken shelves, each laden with hundreds of old volumes.

Dozens of people, from curious tourists to eccentric professors, visited the shop each day. Despite a century of ultra-thin e-book screeners, people still sought out paper and bindings. Ingrid eventually realized that the books were like the old oil painting of Queen Victoria the Second on the back wall. Photography had never entirely replaced painting, and for some reason, e-books had not entirely replaced bound books. Old things could endure.

Ingrid spent a day dusting the back section. Customers seldom went there, but the owner wanted it cleaned that summer. As she cleaned the back, she discovered the mythology, religion and philosophy section.

The back shelves had *Bulfinch's Mythology*, the Egyptian Book of the Dead, the Tibetan Bardo Thodol, The Bible, The Koran, The Book of Mormon, The Talmud, The Necronomicon, and a hundred other books about religions, myths, and heresies. These books fascinated Ingrid as she read them between the customers' visits. Here was a world just as exciting and vast as the clothes and music and movie stars and football players who inspired her teenaged imagination.

When school resumed in the fall, she wrote an article for the school newsweb, *The Graydon Mercury*, comparing Roman Catholics to fans of the ancient television series *Doctor Who*, now a download on BBC Archive One. Both sects collected pictures, small statues, bits of old costumes, and other relics of its saints; both sects had sub-cults honoring a particular saint or actor; both sects had a pantheon of diverse heroes; both sects had its anti-popes and villains; both sects had separated all existing stories into canonical and non-canonical books. Almost all the students of Graydon High School were either Anglican or Hindu or unaffiliated and didn't care about Roman Catholic theology. But the article amazed a few teachers, who well knew the similarities between Roman Catholicism and High Church Anglicism. The principal was shocked.

Encouraged by the minor controversy, *The Graydon Mercury*'s editor asked Ingrid to write another article. She wrote about Soho's fashion boutiques. And then she returned to writing about religion with an article about restoration of St. John's Church in Notting Hill. She wrote about the school's rugby team and their new American-style cheerleaders next. Ingrid had found another passion, and she joined the newsweb's staff.

Ingrid loved seeing her words appear on the *Graydon Mercury*. By her final year of school, she had decided to pursue a career in journalism as a religious affairs writer.

She chose to attend University College London, another college of the sprawling University of London. With many Sloanes at her college, Ingrid would feel at home.

And maybe she would get a boyfriend from among the Sloane Boys.

Mark walked into the classroom for Christology 201. This was the least popular course offered at the university, even among the theology students, but tradition kept it on the course calendar. Mark selected it because it seemed interesting despite its unpopularity.

He saw a girl sitting at the front of the room. He admired her wavy blonde hair, her pretty face, and her short yellow sundress that hugged her curves and bared her sleek legs.

The girl's beauty was not the only thing that intrigued him; she was reading *Historia Calamitatum* or *The History of My Calamities*, the memoir of French philosopher Pierre Abélard.

Pierre Abélard combined ancient Greek philosophy and medieval Christian theology in the twelfth century. He was one of the greatest scholastic philosophers. However, his legend was based only partly on his ideas. He became legendary largely by his doomed love affair with Héloïse, his beautiful student. *The History of My Calamities* is the story of their romance.

"Hey, that's an intriguing book," Thomas said as he slid into the seat beside her. "It's about Héloïse and Abélard, right?"

The girl looked up. "Oh, you've heard about them. Yes, it's about Héloïse and Abélard."

"It's not required for this course, is it?"

"No, it isn't. I'm reading because it's about one of the legendary love affairs of the medieval Europe. Have you read it?"

"No, but I've heard about it. What part are you at?"

"Héloïse's uncle and his friends have castrated Abélard."

Mark crossed his legs.

The girl laughed. "I saw that. Don't worry, I don't do that to every lad who pisses me off. Just to ones whom I go out with." She put down the book. "That's a retro-looking jacket. It looks like it's from another century."

"It's an aviator jacket. I got it from the Air Force Museum. I'm interested in aviation," Mark explained.

"Well, it looks very handsome on you," she said, smiling. She held out her hand. "My name's Ingrid. And yours?"

Mark shook her hand and said, "I'm Mark. Very pleased to meet you, Ingrid."

The professor entered the room, and Mark and Ingrid switched on their notebooks. As they listened to the lecture and wrote their notes, both of them silently and eagerly anticipated the end of the class.

———

After the lecture, Mark invited Ingrid to the coffee shop in the student center. They talked for an hour before Ingrid's next class.

"I'm glad I met you," Ingrid said. "I thought I was the only Sloane who's interested in theology or philosophy."

"I'm not a Sloane. I'm from Walsingham," Mark said.

"Oh. I promise I won't hold that against you."

She kept her promise; they would be a couple all throughout their university years.

———

After four years of university, Ingrid graduated with a degree of Bachelor of Arts in Languages and Literature. Seeing her experience with student newswebs, *The Times* hired her to write for its Entertainment section. Her day revolved around movies, television, fashion shows, pop stars, and orchestras.

But occasionally, the editors let her write about religion when no movie stars were in trouble.

Mark graduated with a degree of Bachelor of Science in Engineering. He didn't go into the engineering profession, though. Instead, he got a job maintaining the building and grounds of St. John's Church. A year later, he switched to part-time work at the church and went back to the University of London, to King's College to get his Master's degree in theology and religious studies.

William Wycliffe was surprised by his son's career choice or lack thereof.

On one of Mark's visits back to Walsingham, his father took the family and Ingrid to dinner in the Walsingham Military Club, a private club. In the club's dining room, oil paintings of British officers and the Royal Family adorned the walls, the knives and forks glistened of sterling silver, and light shone from crystal and gold chandeliers. The waitresses wore red uniforms and white gloves, the gentlemen wore blazers and ties emblazoned with regimental badges, and the ladies wore elegant dresses and pantsuits. Since childhood, Mark had known that this club was for *officers* and that ordinary enlisted soldiers rarely came here.

Mark's father, Lieutenant William Wycliffe, put down his glass of red wine. "I knew you were interested in religion, but I didn't expect you to make a profession out of it, not after four years of engineering school."

"I still feel the call to be churchman," Mark explained. "It's just something that I feel."

Mark's father sighed and looked to his wife.

"Well, I don't think it's a bad career choice," Helen Wycliffe told him. "The Church of England is one of the cornerstones of our civilization."

William rolled up his eyes.

Helen turned to Ingrid. "But is it okay with *you*, dear?"

Ingrid smiled and put her hand on Mark's. "I'm fine with it. I don't mind being married to a vicar."

"Married?" Mark's mother blurted.

Ingrid turned to Mark. "You haven't told them yet?"

Mark grinned awkwardly and shook his head.

"Well, we haven't set a date yet." Ingrid glared sardonically at Mark. "And he hasn't even given me a ring yet. But yes, we've agreed to get married sometime, somewhere."

"After I graduate in a couple years," Mark added.

He saw his father's mouth open slightly, but no words came out. The surprise must have struck him speechless.

Helen Wycliffe grabbed her husband's shoulder. "Did you hear that, dear? Mark's getting married."

William finally said something. "Well, this is wonderful news." He laughed. "Uh, well, what a surprise. Although I guess it shouldn't be a surprise, not after all the years you've been together."

Helen Wycliffe raised her glass. "To a wonderful marriage."

"To a wonderful marriage!" they toasted.

"Like I said, I don't mind being married to a vicar," Ingrid repeated.

"As long as he's at least a vicar, not a low-ranking monk," said William Wycliffe. He paused while the waitress poured his coffee.

He said to Mark, "You have a good education in engineering. Don't waste it."

"I'll still put it to good use. The National Service says it needs more engineering and technical people, especially with the military build-up on the continent. Engineers get extra National Service points. I could fulfill my National Service time in three quarters the regular time. I should try looking for a National Service posting in London."

"How about two nights a month fixing vehicles and equipment for the fire service? It's not engineering *per se*, but it's a good assignment," said William. "If you want it, I'll talk to a fire chief I know in London."

"Fixing equipment for the fire service?"

"It's better than working weekends in a piggery," said Helen. "And it's much better than getting sent to the continent to fight the Euro-Taliban."

"Now, Helen, if the lad's up to fighting the Euro-Taliban, let him. There's absolutely nothing wrong with it," William Wycliffe said. He turned back to Mark. "We're not against the war. Far from it: I think we should be striking back at the Euro-Taliban and the Neo-Taliban with everything we have. But it's good to have options in whatever you do, and if you have both military and non-military choices for your National Service, that's good. Not everyone gets to choose, but you can. And remember, you want to get married."

"I was considering the Air Force, but with the Air Force, there's no guarantee that I'll stay in Britain," Mark said. Although disgusted by their terrorism, he had no desire to fight Europe's homegrown jihadists on the Continent.

"Take the job," Ingrid urged. "You want to be with me in London, don't you?"

Mark nodded. "Alright, if you can talk to your friend in the fire service, I'll do it."

"Good. I'll talk to Chief Daniels," William Wycliffe said. "And after your fulfill your National Service, will you still be practicing as an engineer? Or will you be a full-time priest?"

"I haven't decided yet. It depends on whether the Church needs me as a priest, an engineer, or both."

"Does that happen in the Church of England? I know an Army chaplain who shows up for the annual training camp. He's Roman Catholic, a Jesuit. Those Jesuits are smart, but a lot of them are eccentric too. He told me that the Jesuits have a lot of oddball combinations like priest-astronomer, priest-movie reviewer, priest-architect, priest-lorry driver. But those are the Catholics, and Jesuits at that. I don't think *our* Church has any priests like that."

Mark hesitated to answer because he was not sure. "Well, we do have a few."

"I guess so." William shrugged. "We've never had a clergyman in the family before, so it's hard to get used to the idea. You, a priest-engineer, like those weird Jesuits."

"But a Jesuit doesn't have a girlfriend like I do."

Mark's mother laughed. Ingrid turned Mark's head and kissed him.

William Wycliffe said, "Ah, I can have grandchildren legally. That's one advantage you'll have over the Catholics."

———

Mark's father resigned himself to having his son as a priest, but like many parents, he still wanted his son to rise into the upper class.

For William, upward mobility meant climbing to the top of one's organization. He had worked his way up from articling student to manager in a chartered accountancy firm, he had jumped to a department store to become its assistant accountant, and he had risen to become the store's head accountant. In the Royal Auxiliary Air Force, he used his educational and professional credentials to get a lieutenant's rank. He wouldn't have enlisted for a rank below a commissioned officer's.

William Wycliffe said, "I know the clergy are supposed to shun worldly possessions and take vows of poverty, but in reality, there's a class system in the C of E. You know a village pastor isn't living in the same type of house as the Archbishop of Canterbury.

"And you're going to have a family to support, and they're not going to live in lower class conditions, are they?"

"Probably not," Mark replied, knowing that Ingrid, despite being girlfriend to a priest in training, was still a Sloane Girl with Sloane tastes in housing, clothes, and entertainment.

"Splendid, you agree. If you're going to be a clergyman, aim high. Don't be a priest in a small village. Aim for a teaching post at a prestigious university. Or work at an important cathedral. Or work for a bishop. Maybe even aim to become a bishop. There's upward mobility in the Church of England. The Church even has seats in the House of Lords. Now wouldn't that be something? My son in the House of Lords..."

———

Mark graduated with his Master of Theology and Religious Studies and went to work for the vicar of St. John's Church in Notting Hill. After a few more courses at a seminary, he was ordained as a priest of the Church of England.

He hoped to move from St. John's Church to Canterbury Cathedral. But appointments to work with the Archbishop of Canterbury were far off for a young priest. His superiors felt he needed more pastoral experience at the local level.

Mark had High Church tastes, like his fondness for ancient ritual, candles, incense, vestments, and the Virgin Mary. His superiors looked for a parish that would appreciate the High Church style. Ironically, they sent him to the Anglican Shrine of Our Lady of Walsingham, from where he had come.

Though he preferred staying in London, Mark eagerly went to Walsingham. If he worked hard, he could be promoted to Priest Administrator of the Shrine. Later on, he might distinguish himself to earn higher offices in the Church of England, maybe eventually working for one of the archbishops, Canterbury or York.

Shortly after returning to Walsingham, Mark went to the officers' club to watch an Air Force colonel give the new All-Forces Efficiency Medal to Lieutenant William Wycliffe, Royal Auxiliary Air Force. The next evening, Mark watched the Red Cross give his mother a plaque honoring her tireless aid to the European refugees fleeing from the Euro-Taliban.

The Wycliffes took their jobs seriously.

———

"This is only a temporary exile," Ingrid joked when she joined Mark in Walsingham. After a few years, she predicted, they would be back in London.

In the meantime, she found a job as reporter for a local newspaper. After a year, much to her surprise, she realized that she liked Walsingham.

They finally got married the next summer. The guests included clergy from both the Anglican and Roman Catholic shrines of Our Lady of Walsingham. At the wedding dinner, Mark joked to the Roman Catholics, "I need not stay a virgin to honor the Virgin."

Monsignor Adamson, the Roman Catholic rector, snickered and replied, "My condolences for spending the rest of your life with a woman."

As they danced the first dance, Ingrid whispered to Mark, "Did you actually claim to be a virgin?"

"Only to Monsignor Adamson and the other Romans."

"It's a good thing you're not one of them. Otherwise, you would have to confess that you had lied to a priest."

———

When Ingrid gave birth to their son Donald a year later, thoughts of moving back to London faded. With Don's birth, they were establishing roots in Walsingham. Although both Mark and Ingrid would have liked higher jobs in London, those wishes receded into the background, to be replaced by more immediate concerns like raising Donald.

When Don was eight years old, Mark and Ingrid cheered as their son played in a football game at his school. The boy was growing up to like football and had hung up newspaper photos of famous football players in his room. For his eighth birthday, his mother gave him a football with an image a blue standing lion holding the gold staff of the Abbot of Westminster. It was the badge of Chelsea F.C., which she had supported even though it didn't actually play in Chelsea.

He was also excelling in science class. He earned top marks for a school project about communications satellites. In addition to the Chelsea F.C. football, Don also got a book about space stations for his eighth birthday. He said that when he grew up, he would be a space station crewman — or a football player with one of the FA Premier League teams.

———

At the time of Don's eighth birthday, religious fascists overthrew the governments of two countries. The Wahhabi Purists executed their king and the Saudi Royal Family and took over Saudi Arabia, now renamed Purist Arabia. A week later, Sudanese Purists won their long civil war. Together, Purist Arabia and Sudan formed the Holy Alliance for Monotheism. Now in control of money, armies, and weapons, the Purists could make demands on other countries.

Umar al-Tabuk, Chief Imam and Emir of Purist Arabia, loved the latest technology, contrary to the stereotypes that many Westerners believed about him. It was the ideas, not the technology, of the last thousand years that the Emir loathed. He broadcast his demands by television and webcast from Murabba Palace in Riyadh.

Al-Tabuk wore a *thobe* or ankle-length shirt and a *ghutra* or headdress, all in plain white. Behind him hung the Purist Arabian flag, which looked like the old Saudi Arabian flag but in red and gold instead of green and white. To millions of viewers around the world, the austere imam glared from the television and said:

"To the United States of America, the Great Satan and mother of Crusaders and Zionists, I demand that you outlaw your Moslem heretics from reciting the Koran in English. The Koran should be recited only in Arabic at prayers in the mosque, for it was in Arabic that God revealed his sacred words to the Prophet Mohammed, peace be upon him. Arabic is the perfect language of God, infinitely more beautiful than the foul and ugly sounds that *kaffirs* speak. To spoil the beauty of the Koran with your infidel language is a crime against God. End this abomination now!

"To Great Britain, the nest of heretics and apostates, I demand that you imprison your Ahmadiyya heretics. Put them into camps and hold them there until we ask for you to send them to us. They are lying when they say they are Moslems. In fact, they are heretics scorned by true believers of God. To the Ahmadiyya, I ask why do you not accept that the Prophet Mohammed, peace be upon him, is the last prophet of God? Why must you believe in your false prophet and false Mahdi? The time of justice is coming.

"To the people of Jordan, I say that your queen is a *kaffir* who consorts with Americans and Zionists and Crusaders and all manner of infidels, heretics, and apostates. Overthrow her and kill her now! Imam Yosuf is waiting to establish an Islamic state in your country. He who follows God follows Imam Yosuf."

Mark watched Emir Umar al-Tabuk on television. He knew the governments of the United States, Britain, and Jordan would reject al-Tabuk's demands. The demands fulfilled the Purists' brand of *Sharia* law, but they violated the laws of those countries, not to mention the civil rights of their Moslem citizens.

In news conferences that same day, all three countries rejected their ultimatums.

The Purists acted swiftly. They declared *jihad* and hit all three countries on the next day.

Two gunmen stormed into an Ismaili Moslem mosque in Birmingham, yelled "Death to the heretics!", and shot a hundred people to death. In the siege that followed, the police lobbed tear gas into the mosque to flush out the Purists. The Purists ran out of the mosque and died in a hail of bullets.

An hour later at London's Trafalgar Square, a man followed a twenty-year-old Moslem Indian girl wearing a short skirt. "You dress like a whore!" he shouted before he pulled out a knife and stabbed the girl to death. As the police pulled him away from the girl's body, he promised to kill any Moslem woman who didn't completely cover her face, arms, legs, and hair.

At the same time at a hotel in Blackpool, a Purist fatally shot the hotel manager, a Moslem man who didn't have a beard. The police besieged the hotel. Shouting to television camera crews, the Purist threatened to kill any man who shaved his face like a *kaffir*. An hour later, he was dead, his body full of bullets.

By evening, scores of Ahmadi Moslems throughout Britain were dead: shot, stabbed, and bombed in their own homes by Purists. The Purists had been tracking their prey for weeks, waiting for this moment.

In Boston, a Purist walked into a Reformed Masjid of America, where an imam was reciting the Koran in English. The Purist shouted "God is Great!" in

Arabic and threw a grenade at the imam. Ten people died in the blast. After he was captured, the Purist said, "There are hundreds of us in your country. You will not catch us all."

In New York, a gunman opened fire into the Protestant Moslem Mosque of Manhattan, where men and women shared the same room for prayers. The Purist killed a hundred people. An armored car ran over him as he fled from the mosque.

In Jordan, when Queen Areej visited a military base, a soldier burst into the room and opened fire on the queen and her officers. The queen's security guards pushed her to the floor and flung themselves on top of her to protect her. A gunfight broke out. The queen survived, but the would-be assassin, five royal security guards, and sixteen army officers died.

Colin Wellesley, the British Home Secretary, stood in the House of Commons and declared, "Britain will protect her Moslem citizens from religious fascists even if our military forces have to attack them in their homelands."

In the United States, Ian Monroe, the Secretary of Homeland Security, went to Congress and said, "These are not isolated acts of crime. This is a coordinated war against the American people by enemies within and outside our country. We will smoke out and defeat all domestic traitors. As for our foreign enemies, they don't have to come to us. We will go to them."

At Raghadan palace in Amman, Queen Areej signed the Declaration of Tolerance. With Members of the National Assembly gathered around her, she spoke to the world's television cameras. "Let not a single Moslem fear for his or her life in our kingdom. All branches of Islam may live and worship freely in Jordan without fear of persecution. We are all brothers and sisters, whether we are Sunni, Shia, Sufi, Alawite, Ahmadi, Ismaili, Reformed Masjid, Protestant Moslem, or any group that accepts that God is the only god, that the Prophet Mohammed, peace be upon him, is His final prophet, and that Koran is the word of God. We have our differences, as do the members of any family, but we are still a family, and so we must respect and live with each other. Nobody will be persecuted as a heretic or apostate or infidel in our kingdom."

Then she added, "We will severely punish anyone who fights against the Declaration of Tolerance, our laws, our government, and our people. God is great, and so are we."

The Holy Alliance for Monotheism immediately expanded its targets beyond other Moslems. Again, the Purists struck many targets around the world in a single day. They launched grenades into the Sistine Chapel in the Vatican; drove an exploding car into Touro Synagogue in Newport, Rhode Island; and crashed an airplane into the Giant Buddha on Lantau Island, Hong Kong. No target was too small for the Purists: they even bombed a Hanukkah menorah standing outside a shopping plaza in Las Vegas.

On one bloody day, assassins killed eighteen kings, presidents, prime ministers, and leading clergy around the world. They had nothing in common except that they all had refused to arrest Moslems whom the Purists condemned as heretics and blasphemers.

The Purists attacked Britain again. A truck full of explosives crashed into St. Paul's Cathedral and exploded. Forty people died. Minutes later, a suicide bomber blew himself up in the Shree Swaminarayan Mandir in London, the largest Hindu temple outside India. Thirty-nine people died.

Britain, still recovering from the war against the Euro-Taliban, was swept into another war against enemies from within and overseas. It was another war fought everywhere, in every town in Britain and in countless villages overseas.

Military personnel swarmed to Britain's most important religious sites. Army and Air Force units came to Walsingham to guard the two Christian shrines.

Mark had been ambivalent about British troops fighting the Euro-Taliban on the Continent, but this war was different. The enemy was in Britain and killing Britons of all faiths. He felt the need to fight back. Feeling the patriotic call, Mark became a chaplain in the Royal Auxiliary Air Force.

The Vernacular Wars created harsh demands on the military chaplains. Almost every week, the Purists struck at another shopping mall, airport, train, bus, hospital, theater, church, temple, synagogue, or mosque. Hundreds of British troops and civilians died at home and overseas. The chaplains spread across the country, performing funeral rites and counseling the families and comrades of the dead. There was a military funeral somewhere in Britain every day.

In addition to the funerals and grief counseling, the chaplains listened to the problems of military personnel and their families, helped military families obtain health and child care benefits, counseled married couples and couples in new relationships, and taught military ethics to officers. The chaplains, like the rest of the military, were working around the clock.

The duty he dreaded the most was the visit to the next of kin of dead soldiers, sailors, and airmen. His twentieth visit was to tell a mother that her son had been blown up by a rocket that hit Dubai. She wept for two hours, desperately begging him and her son's colonel for a chance of an error, that perhaps her boy had traded dog tags with another soldier. But there was no error in the DNA testing of the bodies.

After leaving the mother, Mark returned to the church and collapsed in a pew. After delivering twenty death notices, he thought he would get used to telling families that their loved ones had died. Instead, he lay tired and sad in a wooden pew.

He finally became used to delivering the news on the forty-third death notice, to the husband of a fighter pilot. The pilot had been shot down over the Arabian Sea, and the Royal Air Force was flying her body back to Britain. As he told the pilot's husband when his wife's body would arrive home, as he explained how the RAF would hold a military funeral, and as he asked if the new widower and his family needed advice and counseling, he spoke solemnly and calmly. Now he realized that his job was to provide stability in a chaotic world.

Every night for two years, Mark came home exhausted, having spent the day visiting one family after another, in one Norfolk town after another. After a short meal, he would fall into bed after spending only a couple hours with Ingrid and Don.

Fortunately, not all his duties were so grim. War increases the urge of soldiers, sailors, and airmen to get married, and he performed scores of weddings. There were also baptisms of military personnel and their children. But even these happy events were tiring because he performed his military duties in addition to his regular work at the Shrine.

By now, Don was ten years old, earning high marks in math and science, building model space stations, and playing football with a school team. But military duties kept Mark from seeing his son grow up. He hated himself for getting Ingrid to drive Don to and from football games. He had wanted to drive Don, but military chaplains were always being called away for one crisis or another. Ingrid became the parent who spent the most time with Don.

Just before Don's tenth birthday party, Mark was putting a shopping bag on the kitchen table when the telephone rang. He answered the phone, listened for a minute, and said, "Alright, I'll be over."

Ingrid stopped putting icing on the birthday cake, leaving the message as *Happy Birthd*. "What is it now?"

Mark frowned. "Some Norfolk lads got killed at a training course in London. The enemy figured out how to bomb the military colleges."

Ingrid gasped. Mark reached for his coat.

"Where are you going?" asked Ingrid.

"Colonel Hawkins and I have to see the families," Mark said.

"Don's birthday party..."

"I'm sorry, dear. You'll have to run the party on your own. I wish I could stay –- but six families are about to learn that their sons and daughters are dead, and I should be there for them."

Ingrid sighed and said, "Of course, I understand. The damned war doesn't stop for children's birthday parties."

Mark pulled a baseball cap out of the shopping bag. It was a blue baseball cap with the badge of Chelsea F.C. and the words "UEFA CHAMPIONS LEAGUE WINNER" in white. Even with the war raging, Europe's football teams still played each other for prestigious trophies.

"Don!" Mark called out. His son walked into the kitchen.

"Don, something's come up at work, and I've got to go today," Mark said. "I'm sorry that I'll have to miss your birthday party."

"But Daddy, you said you would be here," Don said sadly.

Mark was surprised. Don was approaching that age when he would shun his parents in favor of his friends. Mark hadn't expected Don to be so disappointed that his father would be absent from the party.

Now Mark realized that he had been missing from his son's life for two years, and Don was hungry for time with him.

"I know I said I would be here," Mark admitted. "But there are people who need my help desperately. They're not going to have a birthday party with their friends like you will, and they need my help now."

"Another soldier got killed, and you and the Colonel have to tell his family?"

Mark smiled weakly. With the war constantly mentioned in evacuation drills at school, children knew what was going on.

"Hey, the Blues finally won the Champions League," he said, changing the subject. He gave the baseball cap to his son. "Happy birthday. I'm sorry I didn't have time to wrap it."

Don smiled as he put the cap on his head. "Thank you, Daddy."

"I've got to meet Colonel Hawkins now," Mark said as he patted his son's shoulder. "Enjoy yourself at your party."

As he walked from the house, he saw some children approaching the house. They were the party's guests. Don wouldn't be celebrating his birthday alone, but for the first time, his father would be absent.

Mark was relieved that Don hadn't argued. Today, six families needed him more than Don did. Their sons would never celebrate their birthdays with their families again.

———

The next day, as Mark walked to the Shrine, he approached Lord Avon High School. He walked past the school every day, and it never looked any different. Until today.

A new sign had risen in front of the school. The bold black words read:

WALSINGHAM LOCAL DEFENCE VOLUNTEERS
AIR RAID SHELTER
APPROVED BY THE MINISTRY OF HOME SECURITY

Police Constable Oakland walked to Mark. "Good morning, padre. Look what the LDV set up last night. You're lucky you have a bomb shelter only a few steps from your house."

"How, convenient," Mark said wryly. "It's come to this, turning our schools into bomb shelters."

"It seems rather dramatic, but times are dangerous, and would you rather be without one?"

"You raise a good point. Actually, I would rather be without the war."

"So would all of us, but what choice do we have?"

They heard someone shouting in the distance. By the school's doorway, a man in a brown tweed jacket argued with the school principal, Mr. Tilbury.

"I say, if I'm to use this shelter in case of an air attack, I should be allowed to familiarize myself with it," the man insisted.

"The shelter is not open to visitors and especially not while school is in session," Mr. Tilbury said. "That is still a functioning school with students attending classes. Having visitors come and go would be disruptive."

"Then how will I know where to go in case a raid occurs?"

Mr. Tilbury sighed. "I've told you already. If a raid occurs, the Local

Defence Volunteers will open the school and guide people to the shelter. There's no need for you to visit the shelter now."

The man grunted. "As a concerned citizen, I should have an opportunity to inspect the safeguards for our community."

"If you require any more information about the shelter, please talk to the LDV commander. Now if you'll excuse me, I have a school to run."

Mr. Tilbury turned away from the man and marched back into his school. The man walked towards the street.

As he approached the street, Mark could see the man more closely. He was about thirty years old, wore glasses, and had long brown hair and a goatee beard. He walked with a stoop. He scowled as he walked past Mark and Constable Oakland.

"Are you new to the neighborhood?" Constable Oakland called out.

The man stopped and stared at Oakland. "I haven't done anything wrong, have I?" he barked.

"No, no," Oakland said.

"Then why are you questioning me? I have civil rights, you know."

"I don't doubt or deny you have civil rights. I'm sorry if I gave the impression that you are a person of interest. Nothing of the sort. I patrol this area, and I know everyone who lives here. But I don't believe we've ever met. I'm just getting to know the people. It's called community policing."

"Oh, yes," the man said. "I see."

"So have you moved here recently?" Oakland asked again.

The man nodded. "I arrived two days ago. I'm a history teacher on sabbatical."

"How interesting," Mark said. "I used to get good marks in history, especially the twentieth century's. Where are you from?"

"London."

"My wife grew up in London. At which school do you teach?"

"At several different ones." The man hadn't warmed up to Constable Oakland and Mark. He still looked angry. "Listen, I must be on my way."

"By all means, Mister –- what's your name again?" Mark asked.

"Leaside, Ernest Leaside," the man mumbled.

"It's nice to meet you, Mr. Leaside," said Mark, trying to be polite to someone who was not. "Welcome to Walsingham. My name's Mark. You'll find me at the Anglican Shrine of Our Lady of Walsingham."

Mark held out his hand to Leaside. Leaside did not shake hands with Mark. Instead, he grunted, muttered, "Good day," and walked away.

When Leaside had gone out of hearing distance, Mark said, "What an angry, suspicious fellow. Do you suppose he's living in a hotel in town?"

Constable Oakland shrugged. "Possibly. We get lots of pilgrims and tourists, but they seldom come out here to the suburbs. He must be staying with someone around here. Why else would he want to know about the air raid shelter?"

Mark stared at the scene on television: the Sudanese capital of Khartoum on fire. British, Jordanian, and American airplanes had bombed Khartoum, military bases, terrorist camps, oil depots, airports, and harbors in Sudan.

He watched the Sudanese carry mangled bodies out of a burning airport terminal. The death toll was two hundred and rising.

The television image changed to Abdul Akbar Saleh, Emir of Sudan. Like his Arab allies, the Emir wore a white *thobe* or ankle-length shirt and a black *bisht* or cloak decorated with crossed swords in gold embroidery. His black skullcap also bore embroidered gold crossed swords.

The Emir, a wrinkled old man with a flowing white beard, held a pistol as he glared at the television camera. He stood below the Purist Sudanese flag, a red banner with gold Arabic words: "Recite in the name of your God who created man from clots of blood."

As he shouted in Arabic, subtitles appeared: "To the Prime Minister of Britain, a shallow grave lies ahead for you, and you will rot in Hell, an evil bed to lie upon!

"To the Queen of Jordan, hypocrite and heretic, you are an ugly spinster who lies with infidels and Zionists. Imam Yosuf will defeat you, and you will die alone and unloved, crushed to death by stones!

"To the President of the United States, if you had a moustache, a million Moslems would curse it, but like a woman, you have no hair on your face. Instead, we curse your daughters, and all of you will all die in flames. That I promise!"

The Emir's scowl turned into a sneer. "You have bombed our villages and our farms, but you have not touched our intercontinental missiles. How does it feel to have your face slapped by your own incompetence?

"Your military intelligence is anything but intelligent. They failed miserably to find our secret missile bases. Our missiles stand ready to destroy you infidels, heretics, and Zionists."

Mark shook his head in bewilderment. The enemy's arsenal had expanded from handheld bombs to intercontinental missiles in only two years.

And somehow, the combined modern technology and massive forces of the British, Americans, and Jordanians had failed to destroy them.

Next, the television showed Port Sudan by the Red Sea. Dozens of ships, engulfed in flames, sat half-sunken in the harbor. Covered in oil, the sea itself was on fire. Gigantic clouds of thick black smoke billowed over the wrecks.

"These are Purist Arabian oil tankers and warships," the BBC announcer said. "Half the Purist Arabian navy was sunk tonight."

But the missiles were not destroyed. Britannia ruled the waves again, but who ruled the skies?

Mark heard the air raid siren. The Sudanese were wasting no time in retaliating.

The words "EMERGENCY BROADCAST SYSTEM" filled the television screen. An announcer calmly said, "The Royal Air Force has detected that a missile has been launched from Sudan. Its target is presently not known. Take safety precautions."

This could be the first missile attack on Britain.

"Ingrid! Don!" Mark shouted. His wife and son ran into the room.

"Take Don and yourself to Lord Avon High School," Mark said. He looked at Don. "Go with Mommy."

"Come on, we're going to the air raid shelter," Ingrid said to Don.

"Go there now. I'll meet you after the all-clear," Mark said.

"Where are you going?" Ingrid asked.

"To the military base," Mark said. He grabbed his green Army coat and helmet. "That's where all military personnel are supposed to go."

"No! Come with us!"

"Go to the shelter. You'll be safe there."

"What about you?" Ingrid pleaded. "Why would they need you during an air raid?"

"I can operate radios and communications," Mark said. "That's part of the drill. Now get to the shelter!"

An RAF Air Marshal appeared on TV. "Just one missile is in the air," he announced. "Its trajectory is unclear..."

"Maybe the missile's not headed for us. Maybe it's headed for London or Jordan or America," Don said.

"It could be, but just in case, get to the shelter," Mark said.

He pushed Ingrid and Don out the door. Night had fallen, and only streetlamps lit the darkness. Dozens of their neighbors were running down the street to Lord Avon High School. Other people, confused by the panic, ran in all sorts of different directions. In front of some houses, people simply stood still and stared in shock.

"Mr. and Mrs. Willowby aren't leaving," Don said, pointing at a middle-aged couple standing silently in their front garden.

"Don't be like them," Mark said. "Go to the school."

Ingrid and Don ran towards the school. Mark put on his helmet and looked around: people scattering everywhere, cars speeding away, and even dogs and cats running wild in the dark. He heard people yelling, children crying, and dogs barking everywhere.

He saw an Army lorry coming towards him. After waving to the driver, he got into the lorry and rode to the Air Force station.

Huddled around computer terminals, televisions, and viewscreens, Mark and the military personnel watched the RAF track the missile's progress.

Colonel Hawkins pointed at the computerized flight path image on a viewscreen. A white dot moved steadily over the northern Atlantic on the animated map. "It's heading for America."

"The Americans predict it'll be Chicago," someone said.

Suddenly, another white dot appeared over Texas and sped across the map.

"What's that?" Mark asked.

"That's the Americans launching their interceptor missile," Hawkins replied.

"Go, go, go, go, go!" several people chanted.

The second dot sped towards the dot approaching North America. When they met, the two dots disappeared.

A stream of messages appeared on the computer terminals. The captain announced, "The Americans have blown up the missile over the Atlantic."

The room erupted in cheers. Mark smiled and poured himself a cup of coffee and grabbed a cookie. He was starving, and now that the suspense was over, he could eat and drink.

A phone rang, and Hawkins answered it. Mark saw the captain's smile turn into a frown.

"Quiet!" Hawkins shouted. Everyone suddenly became silent.

"There's been an explosion at Lord Avon High School," Hawkins said. "A suicide bomber..."

Colonel Hawkins drove Mark to school in his car. As they left the car, Mark saw firefighters carrying bodies from the ruins of the school. Flames still burned, and smoke wafted everywhere.

"My wife and son," Mark murmured.

"Don't worry, padre, we'll find them," Hawkins promised. He put his hand on Mark's shoulder and gently nudged him forward.

They saw Constable Oakland staring at a head, two feet, and two hands, all neatly laid out on the ground.

"Who's that?" Colonel Hawkins asked.

"The suicide bomber. He's the easiest body to identify," said Constable Oakland. "A suicide bomber straps his explosives to his chest. After the explosion, all that's left is the head, hands, and feet."

The head was turned face down. Oakland put on a pair of rubber gloves and rolled the head over so that it faced up.

He gasped. "Oh my God, I know this chap! It's Leaside. He moved here just last week. He said he was a teacher on some sort of sabbatical."

Mark recognized the battered face. It was the man who had been arguing with Mr. Tilbury, the school principal. He looked White Anglo-Saxon Protestant, not at all like the stereotypical Moslem terrorist.

"We had a Euro-Taliban living undercover in our midst," Hawkins realized.

"Sometimes the enemy looks just like us," Constable Oakland said.

Turning away from Hawkins and Oakland, Mark saw other bodies lying on the grass. They had died in various ways: blown apart by the bomb, burned by fire, suffocated by smoke, or crushed by the rubble.

He smelled the stench of burnt flesh and blood. He walked from body to body on the lawn.

He found Ingrid and Don there.

He spent the next day at the Anglican Shrine of Our Lady of Walsingham, kneeling in front of the statue of the Mary holding Jesus, and praying to the virgin to protect the souls of Ingrid and Don.

Mary had protected Walsingham for centuries, and even the rise of the Church of England and the erosion of Roman traditions did not expel her from the town completely. Like countless other natives and pilgrims of the town, Mark asked the divine virgin for help.

―――

A day after the funeral, after all the friends and relatives had left, Mark returned to the cemetery. He stared at the granite gravestone and sighed.

"Don, I know I missed the last two years of your life," he said. "I never took you to your football matches, I wasn't home for your birthdays, I didn't play video games with you, I never helped you with your homework. Now I'll never do anything with you again.

"I'm not going to justify anything I did. I'm not going to make excuses. I know I was wrong. I'm sorry."

He opened a bag and took out the blue Chelsea F.C. baseball cap. He remembered giving it to Don before deserting his son's birthday party.

Holding back the tears, he placed the cap on the grass.

―――

Without Ingrid to call him "Mark" and Don to call him "Daddy", Mark heard people call him only as "Father Wycliffe". He was nobody's husband or father anymore; he was a "father" only as a priest.

As Father Wycliffe, he spent every waking hour ministering to the worshippers at the Shrine and to military personnel at airbases. For some reason, devoting himself to his work helped relieve his grief.

Finally, the United States and its allies defeated the Purists in Sudan, and the Vernacular Wars ended. From overseas, military personnel from Walsingham and Norfolk came home to warm welcomes from their families. Wycliffe greeted and congratulated everyone coming home.

After he welcomed back the last local soldier to return from overseas, he remembered that he had no family waiting for him at home.

"Dear God, you've taken my family to be with you. I want to get close to you too," he prayed one day, kneeling alone in the Shrine Church.

"I've devoted myself to my work, hoping to get closer to you. I've held hundreds of services and Masses, performed a hundred weddings and funerals, and visited every parishioner. But yet, I don't feel I'm getting any closer to you. Tell me how to get closer to you. Tell me..."

As usual, God replied with silence.

He left the Shrine without an answer to his prayer. As he walked to his house, he wondered what was missing, what would make him feel closer to God.

He was passing by the Roman Catholic Shrine when he heard its bells toll, calling the pilgrims and parishioners for the daily Mass.

He had not visited the Roman Catholic shrine in years. Today, for some reason, he felt the urge to take a detour on his way home. The ringing of the bells beckoned him, urging him to come closer to the Shrine.

It's not as if I have a family waiting to see me at home, he silently told himself. Then he remembered that even when they were alive, he had not rushed home to see them. He had missed two years of his family's life.

Taking a deep breath, he turned into the shrine complex and walked towards the Chapel of Reconciliation.

The Chapel of Reconciliation was a reddish brown building resembling a typical Norfolk barn, with a roof shaped like a trapezoid when viewed from a distance. Inside the chapel, the granite altar contained bone fragments of two of England's most famous martyrs, St. Thomas Becket and St. Thomas More.

Monsignor Adamson, the Roman Catholic rector, stood at the altar. He put his hands over the golden chalices containing wine and bread and said, "Lord you are holy indeed, the fountain of all holiness. Let your spirit come upon these gifts to make them holy so that they may become the body and blood of our Lord Jesus Christ."

The altar bell rang, and Father Wycliffe realized that he had just seen the transubstantiation. Under Monsignor Adamson's hands, the lifeless bread and wine had turned into the living body and blood of Jesus.

Anglican priests serve the Eucharist too, but they do not teach that the bread and wine literally become the body and blood of Jesus. Anglicans believe that Christ is somehow present during the Eucharist, but they have varying views on how it happens. Anglicans believe in the *True* Presence in the Eucharist.

However, among the Roman Catholics, there is no debate. The Holy Spirit comes down into the bread and wine. Physically, they still taste and feel like bread and wine, but in substance, they are the body and blood of Jesus. In the Catholic world, one could literally touch Jesus and feel his divine spirit. Roman Catholics believe in the *Real* Presence in the Eucharist.

Father Wycliffe looked at the face of Jesus on a stained glass window. Then he looked at the large disc of bread held up by Monsignor Adamson.

Would he actually feel the presence of Jesus if he were to eat the bread?

Is that what he was missing?

He lined up with the parishioners and pilgrims to receive the Eucharist. When he reached Monsignor Adamson, the Monsignor looked at him in surprise. He seemed to mouth "What are you doing here?" silently.

"The body of Christ," Monsignor Adamson whispered as he pressed the hard white wafer into Father Wycliffe's palm.

Father Wycliffe murmured, "Amen" and put the bread in his mouth. It was tasteless and hard and impossible to swallow without biting and chewing. Yet he felt a surge of happiness as he swallowed the bread.

For the first time in years, he felt the Holy Spirit around him.

———

Father Wycliffe stunned his Anglican colleagues by telling them that he wished to convert to Roman Catholicism. The Right Reverend Arnold Logan, Bishop of Norfolk, whose diocese included Walsingham, visited the Shrine. Officially, he was making a pilgrimage to the Anglican Shrine, but he stayed only for a few minutes in the Shrine Church. He spent more time in Father Wycliffe's office.

"You're a High Church Anglican already," Bishop Logan said. "Isn't that, uh, good enough?"

Father Wycliffe replied, "Almost, but not quite."

Despite the High Church sharing some customs of Roman Catholicism, the difference between True Presence and Real Presence had become important to Wycliffe.

Later, Father Wycliffe went to visit Monsignor Adamson at the Roman Catholic shrine. The Catholic priest looked puzzled as he passed a cup of tea to Father Wycliffe.

"I've known you for many years, so forgive me if this is a great surprise to me," Monsignor Adamson said.

"Maybe you don't think this is a large step, given your Anglo-Catholic customs, but it is," the Monsignor continued.

"I'm fully aware of the difference between the Real Presence and the True Presence," Father Wycliffe said.

"But there's more to the Roman Catholic Church than whether the bread and wine literally turn into the body and blood of Jesus. You've lived in an Anglican community all your life. There are differences between Canterbury and Rome. The Anglicans ordain women, we don't. The Archbishop of Canterbury has no formal authority over Anglicans and Episcopalians outside the U.K. The Pope, however, has authority over Catholics around the world. And these are just the most obvious differences. Do you think those differences won't eventually trouble you?"

"I've thought about them, and they do not concern me anymore. From my perspective, the similarities between the churches outweigh their differences, so I think conversion will be easy."

"Ah, so if the two churches are more similar than different, why not stay Anglican? Why bother converting?"

"It's the Real Presence of Jesus. At a Catholic Mass, I can touch and taste the evidence that Jesus has come down to us."

"Now we're back to the Eucharist. I'm glad that you support the Catholic belief of the Real Presence of Jesus. How can I deny a convert to my church if he supports its beliefs and principles? I would be negligent in my duty as a priest, wouldn't I?

"But there is another consideration, which is not about you, but rather, about those around you. I like Bishop Logan. I'm sure you know we work together on several committees, interfaith councils and such. I'm also sure that he values you as a priest of the Anglican community. What does *he* think?"

"He will be sad to see me go, but he will not bear any ill will against me or you. He's somewhat liberal. He realizes that a person's spiritual development may sometimes lead one to change his path."

"In both our churches, it's still possible to rise up to the level of bishop by being liberal, but not too liberal," Monsignor Adamson said wryly. "I suspect Bishop Logan is more resigned, rather than supportive, to your conversion.

"I admit you surprise me. Conversion is rare for someone who has been as devoted to one church as you have been."

Father Wycliffe grinned. "Jesus founded a church, not churches. Does it matter to him whether I'm Anglican or a Catholic?"

Monsignor Adamson grunted. "Oh, Lord, how do I argue against that without sounding sectarian?"

———

Father Wycliffe resigned his military commission, and after a year of instruction from Monsignor Adamson, he was ordained as a priest again, this time for the Catholic diocese. Much to his surprise and pleasure, his Anglican friends bore no grudges against him. The new Priest Administrator of the Anglican Shrine urged him to visit often, and Bishop Logan promised to still invite him to his annual Christmas party for the Anglican clergy.

I'm lucky I'm not living in the time of Henry VIII and Bloody Mary, he mused. In the sixteenth and seventeenth centuries, people were tortured, hanged, and burned at the stake for preferring one church or the other, depending on who was in power. Succession to the British throne depended on power struggles between Catholics and Protestants. Indeed, Catholics and Protestants feuded in Northern Ireland well into the twenty-first century. Fortunately, some things did change.

He passed by a crowd of people watching a giant telescreen atop a department store. Chinese navy ships were following American ships in the Arabian Sea. After the Vernacular Wars, the United States and China occupied Gwadar, a Pakistani port by the Arabian Sea. The Americans had recently put barbed wire along the boundary between the U.S. and Chinese zones. Threats of war filled the airwaves again.

Some things changed, but others did not.

———

He served a year at the Roman Catholic Shrine, but his sense of peace didn't last long. After the Vernacular Wars, Earth was not at war but not at peace either. The victors argued over the spoils of war, and military units moved into Walsingham again. No violence broke out, but the countries still distrusted each other.

In towns across Britain, emergency fallout shelters appeared again. The government broadcast warnings to watch for suspicious people leaving suspicious packages on trains and buses again.

After countless Sunday homilies, he grew tired of promising that God would eventually bring peace to the Earth. When would the peace come?

When he ate the consecrated bread, he felt the power of the Holy Spirit within him. Unfortunately, he was only one person, and each of his parishioners was only one person. They may have communed with the Holy Spirit, but each was powerless to stop the world's countries from aiming missiles at each other. Deep inside, he wondered if God had abandoned the Earth, the planet itself.

One day, Father Wycliffe watched a television report about an American mission to Mars. At first, the notion of a Mars mission at this time seemed odd, but he remembered his history classes. The first age of space exploration occurred during a long period of nuclear stand-off between the superpowers United States and Soviet Union. The United States was actually fighting a long war in Vietnam when it landed its astronauts on the Moon. Somehow, humans continued to explore their universe during war and crisis.

He heard about new worlds being settled. He heard that the European Space Agency wanted chaplains in space.

The new space colonies: the Moon, Mars, deep space. Out there, humanity had the chance to form new societies free of Earth's evils. But humanity also had the chance to bring its old problems out there. It could be the next advance in human history or it could be its next decline.

The future of the human race could swing either way, but Father Wycliffe wanted to gamble that a future in space could be free of the old evils of Earth. He felt the call to minister to Earth's space explorers and colonists.

But would Monsignor Adamson release him from his duties at the Shrine? With the chronic priest shortage, Father Wycliffe doubted that the Monsignor would allow him to fly to space, but he would ask anyway.

He asked Monsignor Adamson to let him join the ESA's chaplain corps. The Monsignor quickly signed the letter discharging Father Wycliffe from the parish and recommending him to the Reverend Doctor Franz Schiller, a Lutheran pastor and Chief Chaplain of the European Space Agency Chaplaincy Department.

Father Wycliffe took his copy of the letter. Monsignor Adamson had surprised him by discharging him so quickly. He glanced at the wall and saw the recruitment poster for new priests: "Are You Being Called? Become a Priest." Not every parish had a full-time priest. If there was a priest shortage on Earth, why would his superior agree so quickly to send him into space?

"Thank you for releasing me to the ESA. I appreciate this very much," Father Wycliffe said. "I suppose that you will have enough priests after I leave?"

Monsignor Adamson rose from his desk. "Did you ever see an ancient TV show called *The Flying Nun?*"

"No, I never saw such a show," Father Wycliffe said. "I haven't even heard about it."

"It was about a plucky young novice named Sister Bertrille who got herself into odd situations, like catching thieves who had robbed a casino. She also had the ability to fly because the wind caught her headdress," said Monsignor Adamson as he picked up a bottle of sherry.

He poured the sherry into two glasses and gave a glass to Father Wycliffe. "If nobody could hold down the flying nun, how can I hold down a priest in an old aviator jacket?"

Wycliffe chuckled. "Thank you. I assure you, I'm not a flying nun."

"Good. All joking aside, I'm glad that you volunteered to go to space. I was afraid that flying nuns and spaced-out priests were the only religious people who would volunteer to go to space," Monsignor Adamson said. "The last thing I need in space is an eccentric priest who's going to ordain a robot or perform polygamist weddings or commit some sort of embarrassment to the Church. However, you've always worked within the hierarchy and established order of both the Anglican and Catholic churches."

"I'll always stay true to our Church. You won't have to worry about that. I'm just surprised that you'll allow me to go to space while we've got a priest shortage here."

"Our Church's struggle in space is not the same as our struggle on Earth. Up there, the priest shortage isn't due to lack of clergy. We've been shut out of the American Moonbase Liberty, thanks to the fundamentalist atheists. They're forcing their government to separate church and state very strictly.

"Fortunately, liberal thinkers are also heading into space. I heard about a commercial space station that wants to sell weddings in space, and it wants a priest, a rabbi, and a justice of the peace." Adamson laughed. "On a more serious note, the European Space Agency thinks that religions are a vital part of human culture. The ESA is asking for clergy of different faiths. With your experience in engineering and aviation, you would be become a valuable member of the space community.

"As much as we need priests on Earth, we need priests in space too. We need you to take our traditions and our values out there. If the human species goes into space without its values and traditions, it will die out there."

———

The ESA sent him to St. Dominic's Roman Catholic Church in Timonium Base. Timonium Base was the first commercial base on the Moon, and St. Dominic's was the first Roman Catholic Church anywhere off Earth. It was really a plainly decorated chapel in Timonium's shopping plaza.

He enjoyed working at St. Dominic's Church. Many of the Moon's settlers, workers, explorers, scientists, and tourists came to St. Dominic's. Some came as tourists to look at the church. Other people came as worshippers to his daily Masses.

However, the Moon was a suburb of Earth, bristling with the same rivalries and politics. The United States closed off Moonbase Liberty to visitors who did not carry passports and visas. When the Chinese spacecraft *Zhang Heng* had engine trouble and needed to land, the Americans refused to let her land at Liberty because the crew did not bring their passports.

Although the *Zhang Heng* survived long enough to reach Moonbase Yue 1, the violation of the U.N. Rescue Agreement outraged the Chinese. On Earth, a Chinese submarine followed a U.S. aircraft carrier into the Indian Ocean. War nearly broke out.

The *Zhang Heng* incident was one of many political crises on the Moon. Saddened by the Moon, Father Wycliffe volunteered to go deeper into space. He wondered if he could go to Mars. Mars was the new frontier: isolated, Spartan, and dangerous. Most chaplains preferred the Moon, so civilized and close to Earth.

But something was different around Mars. Out there, scientists and explorers of various nations worked and lived without their national rivalries. Space station crews of different countries helped each other. Nobody asked for passports or visas when visiting each other's space stations and Martian colonies. Perhaps the isolation of Mars reminded people that they were all from the same human race.

The ESA sent him to Space Station Exeter. The trip to Mars took six months, and he had served three years at Exeter. When he would return to the Moon, he would have been away for four years. He was a true deep spacer, not a mere tourist like the people who visited Timonium Base. Returning to the Moon didn't appeal to him.

———

In a few minutes, he would be the first priest to board Space Station Troika. His excursion had nothing to do with any religious duties, though. He was coming to fix a communications antenna.

5 / OUR MOTHER WHO ART IN HEAVEN

Wycliffe docked his shuttlecraft at Troika, went through the airlock, and stepped into the shuttlecraft dock. As he closed the airlock door behind him, he heard the clang of metal hitting metal. Then all he heard was the dull hum of the air vents.

The silence bothered him. *Why*, he wondered? Then he realized that Troika lacked the constant chattering of people.

He had been with people from the first moment he had left Earth. He had been with people on the space liner to the Moon, at Timonium Base, on the trip to Mars, and at Space Station Exeter. Even if he had been alone in his cabin, the nearest person was only as far away as the next cabin. Space was unlike Earth, where there were forests and mountains where one could isolate oneself from the rest of humanity, if only temporarily.

Even on his solo flight in the shuttlecraft, he hadn't been completely alone. He had kept constant radio contact with the people at Exeter. Inside Troika, though, he couldn't talk to them. A failed communications antenna cut him off from his friends.

He was alone for the first time in space.

After the death of his family, he had retreated to a monastery in the Italian Alps for a few weeks. He had found a small amount of peace in lonely, silent moments at a nearby forest at the foot of a mountain. On Earth, solitude didn't bother him. But in space, solitude was frightening.

He breathed deeply, and the experience and discipline of his military career returned. He stopped thinking about his isolation, pulled out his pocket computer, and retrieved Troika's floor plans.

The plans appeared on the pocket computer. The route from the shuttlecraft dock to the control room appeared in red. Walking to the control room would be easy. Troika was a small station with only three levels, each with a simple layout. It was not like Exeter, which had ten levels, each with a complicated plan.

As he walked to the control room, he approached another airlock, the extravehicular activity airlock. The crew would have gone outside for a spacewalk through the EVA airlock.

Three spacesuits hung on the wall across the hallway from the EVA airlock. Beside the three spacesuits was an empty hanger for a fourth spacesuit.

The empty hanger caught Wycliffe's attention. There should have been four spacesuits because Troika usually had four crew members.

True, one of Paul Devane's crew had been transferred to Exeter, but she wouldn't have taken the spacesuit with her. People didn't take spacesuits with them when going between stations because each shuttlecraft carried spacesuits too. Unless an emergency required her to take the spacesuit, she would have left it on Troika for her replacement.

Spacesuits were essential, life-preserving assets, and expensive ones at that. Where had the fourth spacesuit gone?

A viewscreen beside the spacesuits showed the message: "ALTITUDE ALERT: 500 METERS ABOVE MINIMUM SAFE ALTITUDE." It reminded Wycliffe of his mission.

He made a mental note to report the missing spacesuit later. It was not important now. His highest priority was to repair the defective communications antenna. After the repair, Exeter could send the signal to boost Troika back to a safe altitude.

Minutes later, Wycliffe entered the control room. He was used to the people and noise of Mission Control at Exeter. In Troika's control room, he was alone with only to the hum of the ventilation system.

He saw the icon hanging on the wall. It was beautiful, this wooden painting of the Old Testament Trinity, the three angels who visited Abraham and Sarah. Unfortunately, there was no one to admire it here. In the chapel at Exeter, though, it could inspire many people. He decided to take the icon back to Exeter after he repaired the antenna.

Troika's cameras were still pointed at the planet below, so an image of

Mars filled the large viewscreen. As the space station orbited the planet, Wycliffe saw the panorama of Mars: the reddish brown deserts, which had prompted people to call Mars "the red planet"; the dark canyons, which were thousands of kilometers long; and the gigantic mountains and volcanoes, the tallest and widest in the solar system. It was a beautiful planet, covered in awe-inspiring natural landforms.

Only a few weeks ago, Father Wycliffe had marveled at both the physical and spiritual beauty of Mars. He found beauty not only in the physical form of Mars, but also in the peacefulness of its first humans. Despite having the name of the Roman god of war, Mars had evaded the national rivalries that plagued the Earth's Moon.

But Mars had become the planet of despair and disappointment. The Mars Disaster had destroyed the planet's first human settlements. What humans did not do to themselves, nature did to them.

A message appeared on one of the computer monitors: "ALTITUDE ALERT: 400 METERS ABOVE MINIMUM SAFE ALTITUDE." The station had fallen another hundred meters. It was failing fast. Father Wycliffe had to inspect the antenna and fix it quickly.

He sat down at a computer console and ran a diagnostic on the BF-36 unit. A minute later, he read the report that Exeter's crew couldn't receive because of Troika's failed antenna: a memory card in the antenna had stopped saving data. He needed to insert a new memory card.

A note appeared on the monitor, saying that spare memory cards were stored in the drawer beside the computer console.

Wycliffe opened the drawer and picked up a memory card. It was the last one. He would have to tell NASA to send more memory cards the next time it sent supplies to Troika.

Then he saw a knapsack lying below another computer console.

What was the knapsack doing there? Hadn't the crew taken all their personal belongings?

He looked closer at the knapsack. The name "Adin" was written on a luggage tag tied to the knapsack. The mystery deepened. Nobody named Adin had worked at Troika.

When he returned to Exeter, he would have to ask Paul Devane more about Troika, already a mysterious place with a phantom schoolgirl and a missing shuttlecraft. Now a missing spacesuit and an abandoned knapsack added to the mystery.

But first, he had to repair the antenna. He put the memory card in his pocket and walked back to the EVA airlock.

There was a small window beside the EVA airlock. He looked out the window and froze with surprise.

Someone in a spacesuit drifted past the window.

He was not alone at Troika. The stranger glided out of his view.

Wycliffe ran back to the control room and switched the viewscreen from showing Mars to showing Troika's exterior. The viewscreen showed different parts of Troika from cameras mounted outside. Then one of the cameras caught the stranger hovering over the antenna.

Who was he? Or she? He dismissed Dr. Hall's theory about aliens. No alien could fit into a spacesuit built for a human. Only in science fiction movies did aliens look like humans with funny make-up. And an alien visitor would have brought his own spacesuit, not borrowed one of the crew's. Father Wycliffe knew the intruder was human even though he couldn't see the stranger's face.

A chill ran through Father Wycliffe. A human intruder was more frightening than an alien one. Humans carried grudges against other humans. He remembered the recent bombing of Europa Luna and the death of his family years ago. In both tragedies, someone strange and dangerous disguised himself as normal and harmless. Now here was an unknown person wearing a regular NASA spacesuit and opening a vital communications antenna. Could the intruder have caused the antenna's failure?

He opened the knapsack again, hoping to find clues of the intruder's identity or his intentions. He pulled out a bottle of water, a flashlight, and a money card. The Air Force had trained him to recognize the tools of a saboteur or terrorist, but everything here seemed harmless.

The money card, issued by the British Lunar Trade Bank, had no name imprinted upon it. Anyone could anonymously transfer money in and out of an anonymous account with this card. The only clue of the intruder's identity was the name "Adin" on the luggage tag.

He heard footsteps behind him. He turned around and saw a woman walk in the control room.

She appeared to be in her early thirties. Her glossy black hair and deep brown eyes gave her a Mediterranean look. She could be Portuguese, Italian, Maltese, Greek, Turkish, Israeli or Palestinian.

Whatever she was, she was svelte and pretty. She had an exquisite face, and her hair fell in waves below her shoulders.

She wore a silver pendant shaped like a crescent moon from a chain around her neck. She dressed like a young business woman in her white blouse and a light blue jacket and skirt and high heels.

Father Wycliffe wondered if she was the mysterious girl who had appeared and disappeared on Troika.

"Are you Jesus?" he asked.

The woman smiled. "No, I'm his mother."

"Holy Mary, Mother of God," Father Wycliffe muttered.

"Yes, that's me, but please don't call me Mother of God," Mary said. "That name makes me feel older than God."

She pointed at a viewscreen showing the intruder in the spacesuit. "You don't have to worry about Adin. He works for me. He's no threat to you or this station."

"This isn't real," Father Wycliffe insisted. "You're not real."

"That's a surprising comment from a priest, especially a Catholic. You don't believe in me, the Blessed Virgin Mary?"

"Yes, I do, but you're not her."

"Why don't you believe I'm who I am?"

"The Virgin Mary does not appear in space stations in orbit around Mars," Father Wycliffe said.

Mary smiled. "Why not? I've appeared at some obscure places before. Tepeyac Hill, La Salette, Lourdes, and Fatima weren't popular places for tourists when I first visited them. The only difference here is that I'm not among peasants and sheep."

The Blessed Virgin -- or whoever she was -- had a point. Most of the approved apparitions of Mary had been in remote places away from crowded cities. Troika was just as isolated and lonely, if not more so, than a barren hill in colonial Mexico, a cow pasture in the French Alps, a grotto by the River Gave, or a sheep field in Portugal. Mary typically visited places where few people would find her.

But a space station in orbit around Mars? Father Wycliffe was a man of both science and faith, but neither led him to believe that the Virgin Mary was here at Space Station Troika.

Plus she looked nothing like any of the pictures of Mary he had seen in church, museums, and countless holy cards.

"I believe in Mary, the Mother of God, but I don't believe that you're her," Father Wycliffe said. "You're an illusion from a Siren Stone."

"A Siren Stone? You think this rock is making you see me?"

She stepped towards him. He backed away.

"If I'm an illusion, why are you backing away?"

I don't know, Father Wycliffe thought. *Why should I fear a mere electrochemical signal sent into my temporal lobes?*

"Can an illusion do this?" Mary asked.

She reached out and squeezed his hand. Wycliffe felt her firm yet gentle grasp. She was not trying to crush his hand, but she was not weak either.

He also smelled roses when she stepped closer to him. Roses often appeared with apparitions of Mary. Juan Diégo had found Castilian roses blooming out of season and far from Spain on Tepeyac Hill. Bernadette Soubirous had seen a rosebush at the entrance to the grotto at Lourdes. For centuries, people had smelled roses at apparitions of Mary. The series of prayers in her honor was called the Rosary, from the Latin term *rosarium* or crown of roses.

She had to be wearing a perfume because she was not wearing a rose. The fragrance surprised Wycliffe more than the apparition itself. He hadn't imagined that the Mother of God would wear perfume, like any young woman.

"Do you still believe I'm an illusion?" Mary asked as she released his hand.

"There's scientific evidence that spiritual experiences occur in the temporal lobes. You could just be an image created in my brain," Father Wycliffe said.

He didn't know why he was explaining science to an illusion. Perhaps he was not completely sure that this woman was an illusion?

"Ah, the God spot. Is it possible that God created that part of your brain so you could see people like me? That the temporal lobes are your antenna to see and hear divine beings?"

Wycliffe heard heavy footsteps approaching the control room.

"Oh, speaking of antennas, that sounds like Adin. He must be finished checking the BF-36 unit," Mary said.

A man entered the control room. He was wearing a spacesuit, but he had taken off his helmet and was holding it under his arm. He looked to be in his late twenties, European, with dark hair.

"This is Adin," Mary said, gesturing to the man in the spacesuit. "Adin, we have a visitor: Father Wycliffe, from Space Station Exeter."

"Pleased to meet you," Adin said, extending his hand, which was still in its spacesuit glove.

Father Wycliffe shook Adin's hand. "So you work with her?"

"Yes. I accompany her when she visits spacecraft. I know a bit about spacecraft engineering and design."

"The antenna," Mary asked. "Did you find out what was wrong with it?"

Adin nodded. "A malfunctioning memory card. It has to be replaced."

He could have learned that by running a diagnostic inside the station, Father Wycliffe thought. *Why was he outside the station?*

Memories of Lord Avon High School and Space Station Europa Luna disturbed him...

Could the intruder have been planting a bomb?

"Where did the crew keep the memory cards?" Adin wondered.

Wycliffe held up the sole remaining memory card. "Here's the last one. I was going to suit up and go outside to put it in the antenna."

"No, there's no need for you to perform an EVA. I can do it," Adin said.

"Father, no disrespect intended, but Adin is younger and has more experience in EVA than you," Mary said. "Let him replace the memory card."

"Alright, I'm okay with that," said Wycliffe as he shoved the memory card into his pocket. "Let's go to the airlock."

The three of them walked to the EVA airlock. Father Wycliffe pressed a button to open the airlock. With a metallic clicking sound, the airlock door swung open.

Adin put his helmet back on. Mary helped him attach the helmet to the spacesuit.

While they were looking away from him, Father Wycliffe pressed the "Manual Control" button on the airlock's control panel.

Adin stepped into the airlock.

"Oh, give me the memory card," he said, his voice going from the helmet radio to the intercom beside the airlock.

Father Wycliffe quickly pushed Mary into the airlock, shoved against the airlock door, and slammed the door shut. He turned a lever and locked the airlock under manual control.

Mary looked at Father Wycliffe through the airlock window. "What are you doing?" she cried through the thick glass. Her voice carried loudly over the intercom.

Adin went to the window. "Father, open the door. If you don't give me the memory card, I can't fix the antenna."

"Who are you?" Father Wycliffe asked.

Mary looked at him with pleading eyes. "You know who I am. You've seen me since you were a child in Walsingham. You've seen my image in countless statues and medals and pictures and holy cards. You've prayed to me countless times, recited the Rosary in my honor, and put flowers at my statue on my feast days."

"Where were you?" Father Wycliffe demanded. "Where were you in the Vernacular Wars? Where were you when the terrorists bombed St. Paul's and the temples and mosques in London?"

"I was there in the ambulance worker's care for the victims of the bombings. I was there in each mother's love for her injured children. I was there in each firefighter and police constable who rescued someone from the churches and temples and mosques that were bombed all over the world. I was there in the sorrow of all the people who had lost someone they had loved."

"Where were you when the superpowers nearly went to war over the *Zhang Heng* incident?"

"I was there in the sadness of the lunar colonists. The Moon is my dominion, so I was there, and I'm also everywhere where people need comfort and hope."

"Where were you when my family died?"

"I was there in your sorrow. I was there when you asked me to pray to God in heaven for your family. I was there when you blessed the souls of your family, and now I'm here to help you again. Let me back inside."

"My wife died in that bomb shelter," Father Wycliffe said. "She died too young. We were going to spend our lives together."

"There was nothing I could do, but I'm always here to comfort those in need," Mary said. "Let me back inside."

"I lost my son. That hurts."

"Believe me, I know how that feels."

Father Wycliffe shook his head. "Well, if you really are the Blessed Virgin Mary, I could blow you out of the airlock, and you would still live, right?"

"No!" Adin blurted. "I'm wearing a spacesuit, so I'll survive out there, but she won't."

"I'm not wearing a spacesuit," Mary said.

"You shouldn't need one. If you really are Mary, you were assumed into heaven in both body and soul. You're already beyond death. You can only die once."

Mary sighed. "It's a lot more complicated than that. My body is alive again, so it can die again, but I don't know what will happen this time. Let me out of here."

"Don't worry, I won't kill anyone," Father Wycliffe said as he backed away from the airlock. He wouldn't blow them out into space because he couldn't risk killing someone. He didn't know for sure whether Mary and Adin, whoever or whatever they were, were real people or illusions.

However, he couldn't let them roam aboard the space station either. After the bombing of Europa Luna, he couldn't trust mysterious intruders.

"Don't turn away from me now!" Mary pleaded. "You've spent your whole life looking for me, haven't you? You were looking for me when you entered the priesthood. You were looking for me after your family died. You were looking for me when you changed your brand of religion. You were looking for me when you left Earth for the Moon. You were looking for me when you left the Moon for Mars.

"You came out here to look for me because you didn't think I could be in any of those dark and violent places. But I've been in all those places, giving hope and comfort where despair and sadness reigned. If you don't find me here, you'll never find me at all. Don't turn away from me now. Let me in."

"No, I really don't know who you are," Wycliffe said.

He looked at the spacesuits hanging on the other side of the passageway. The viewscreen beside the spacesuits showed the message: "ALTITUDE ALERT: 100 METERS ABOVE MINIMUM SAFE ALTITUDE."

He had to act quickly. He walked to the spacesuits and took one off its hook.

"If you want to repair the antenna, that's okay with us," Adin said. "But to go outside through this airlock, you have to let us back inside. You have no choice but to let us back in."

"No," Father Wycliffe said. "There's another airlock, at the shuttlecraft dock. I'll go through there."

"Your shuttlecraft is docked there," Adin reminded him. "It's blocking the airlock."

"Darn," Wycliffe muttered.

"And your shuttlecraft has only one hatch. You can't go back into the shuttlecraft and exit it from another hatch."

"But I can return to the shuttlecraft, undock it, and spacewalk from the shuttlecraft to the antenna. I can use a gas propulsion pack to propel myself."

"But with no other pilot to control the shuttlecraft, it will float away from the station."

"I'll come back inside the station and call Exeter to rescue me."

"But you can't come in through the EVA airlock," Adin said. "If you open it from the outside, you'll blow me and Mary into space. Remember, she isn't wearing a spacesuit."

"I can come back through the shuttlecraft dock airlock, can't I?" Wycliffe said uneasily.

"No, you can't," Adin said. "This is an old station. That airlock needs a spacecraft to seal properly. You'll be stranded outside unless you come back through the EVA airlock."

"And if you open it from the outside, you'll kill me," Mary said.

Father Wycliffe sighed deeply. If she was an illusion, blowing her into space would be harmless, but what if she were a real person? Could he risk killing another human being?

"No, I can't sacrifice a life to save the station," he said.

He put the spacesuit back on its hanger and walked away. As he left, he heard them pounding against the airlock door.

He returned to the control room and sat down. "Oh, God, what do I do now?" he wondered aloud.

A message appeared on the computer monitors: "ALTITUDE ALERT: 50 METERS ABOVE MINIMUM SAFE ALTITUDE."

Perhaps he had no choice but to trust these mysterious people.

He picked up the knapsack again. Were there more clues to their identities? He rummaged through the bag again and found the same items, the same money card, flashlight, and bottle of water.

The bag had a side pocket. He unzipped it and found a chocolate bar, a watch, and a baseball cap.

The cap looked familiar...

He shoved it back into the knapsack and rushed back to the airlock.

He opened the airlock, and Adin and Mary stepped back into the station.

Father Wycliffe gave the memory card to Adin. "Go outside and fix the antenna."

Adin took the memory card, shoved it into a pouch in the spacesuit, and stepped back into the airlock. Father Wycliffe closed the airlock door, pressed the buttons, and watched the exterior door open and Adin float out.

"I can help you restore communications," Mary said.

"You know how to do that?"

"Madonna knows many things. Let me help."

"I'll restore the system-to-system communications, and you restore the audio-visual radio and television link," Wycliffe said.

"Sounds good to me," Mary said as they returned to the control room.

Wycliffe switched the cameras feeding to the viewscreen. Adin appeared on the viewscreen as he floated to the antenna. They watched Adin replace the memory card and float back to the airlock.

Adin soon returned to the control room. With Adin safely inside the station, Wycliffe typed some commands at Paul Devane's old console.

The words "EXETER ON-LINE" appeared on the computer monitor.

"Radio and television links should be up in seconds," Mary said.

The viewscreen's image changed to a signal from Exeter. Alfred Bronson appeared.

"Father Wycliffe!" Bronson said.

"Glad to see you again, Mr. Director," said Wycliffe.

"Thank goodness you've restored communications! We're going to transmit the order again."

Seconds later, coded instructions appeared on a computer monitor and scrolled upwards. Next, the message "IGNITION SEQUENCE STARTED" appeared. Finally, the number "30" appeared, and the countdown began: 30, 29, 28, 27, 26...

Father Wycliffe heard the rumble and blast of the rockets. He felt the station lurch as the rockets boosted the station's altitude.

Messages appeared on the monitor: "100 METERS ABOVE MINIMUM SAFE ALTITUDE...200 METERS ABOVE MINIMUM SAFE ALTITUDE...400 METERS ABOVE MINIMUM SAFE ALTITUDE...800 METERS ABOVE MINIMUM SAFE ALTITUDE..."

"We're going up!" Mary yelled, clapping her hands together.

They cheered as they watched the altitude rise on the altimeter. Minutes later, the station returned to its normal altitude.

"Father, excellent job on the repair," Bronson said. "You can add EVA spacecraft repair to your list of qualifications, which is already impressive."

Father Wycliffe didn't tell him that someone else had repaired the antenna.

He also realized that Bronson didn't notice the other two people in the control room. When Paul Devane could see the schoolgirl Jessica, Wycliffe could not see her on video. Now Wycliffe was the one who could see people invisible to others.

"Father, come back as soon as possible. Father Alexei will be arriving soon, and I'm sure you'll want to talk to him before you go back to Earth."

"I want to check some systems here first. I'll be back soon," Father Wycliffe promised.

"Alright, but don't stay out there too much longer. I'll talk to you when you get back. Now I've got go check on the status of the *Victoria*," Bronson said before he left.

A communications officer replaced Bronson on the viewscreen. He said, "I'm getting a reading that Troika's batteries are fifteen percent depleted. That big boost must've used up a lot of electricity. I'm putting Troika's telecommunications into sleep mode for an hour so the batteries can recharge. We'll still monitor Troika's systems operating information, though. If you need anything from us, just click the telecommunications back on."

"See you in an hour," Father Wycliffe said.

The communications officer put the video link into sleep mode by remote control, and the viewscreen changed back to a view of Mars. Father Wycliffe was alone with the two strangers again.

Now Wycliffe could talk to the two strangers alone. It was bad enough that he was not sure if they were real or not. It would be worse if Exeter's crew were to watch him talk to apparently nobody. Now he knew how Paul Devane had felt when trying to convince Wycliffe that Jessica was real.

He picked up the knapsack, pulled out the baseball cap, and handed it to Adin. "This is yours, I believe."

Adin took the cap. It had the Chelsea F.C. logo and the words "UEFA CHAMPIONS LEAGUE WINNER".

"You said that when you grew up, you would be either a space station crewman or a footballer," Wycliffe said.

Adin nodded. "I did say that, didn't I?"

"Isn't he a skilled spacer?" Mary added. "Look how easily he walked in space and fixed that antenna. Look how well he grew up."

"Except that he never really did grow up," Father Wycliffe said.

"At least not here," Mary said.

Father Wycliffe went to a computer console and retrieved an electronic version of the Bible. "I thought the name Adin sounded familiar. I'll search for it."

The computer searched the Bible, and moments later, the name Adin appeared highlighted in yellow on the text. "Here it is," Father Wycliffe said. "Book of Ezra, chapter two, verse fifteen. Adin was one of the Jews exiled to Babylon who came back to Jerusalem."

He turned to his son. "Don, why didn't you tell me who you actually are?"

Adin –- or Don — said, "I was afraid that you would be scared if you knew who I am."

Mary walked to Don. "See, I told you he wouldn't be afraid of you if you told him the truth. What parent is afraid of his child? Certainly not me, and I'm the Mother of God."

"Are you dead?" Father Wycliffe asked.

"Not in your heart," Don replied.

"Are you in heaven?"

"I'm here with you now."

"You're all grown up."

"I brought him back at the age he would be had he stayed with you," Mary explained. "I figured he would be more useful on a space station as a grown man than as a ten year-old boy."

"So this is how you would've grown up had you lived," Father Wycliffe said.

He sighed. "I wish I had spent more time with you. I was always away, doing all my duties as a padre. I really hated leaving your birthday party after those men got killed. I spent so much time helping the families of others that I rarely saw my own. Why would you come back and help me?"

"Don't feel any shame, don't feel any regret," Don said. "You were the chaplain, and people needed you in those desperate times. Service to our nation and our community is our family tradition, one that I continue now, in my way. I won't blame you for what history did to us."

Wycliffe smiled weakly. "I'm happy that you can forgive me for not spending enough time for you, but can you ever forgive me for my worst sin?"

"What was that?"

"Telling you and your mother to go to that bomb shelter. I thought it was the safest place. That was the emergency procedure. I didn't think there would be a suicide bomber there. I didn't foresee it. All my life, I've wondered what we could have had if I hadn't told you to go to the bomb shelter."

"You can't keep thinking about what could have been," Don said. "Let the past go, and stop torturing yourself. Do that for me and Mommy."

"Yes, yes, I will."

He threw his arms around Don and hugged him. For the first time in years, he felt the warmth of another human being. Years of longing were fulfilled, years of sadness washed away, and years of guilt faded.

"I'm so lucky," he said. "How many fathers lost their sons in that war and can have their sons returned to them?"

"Enjoy the moment while you can," Mary said softly. "It's only temporary. It can't last forever."

"Even a minute is a gift from God," Father Wycliffe said, still hugging his son.

"Actually, it was my idea," Mary said.

After he let go of his son, he saw Mary looking keenly at him.

"You have a job waiting for you on the Moon," she said. "It's time for you to return to the Moon."

"Why should I?" he asked.

"Your first parish was on the Moon: St. Dominic's Church. Don't you want to see your old parish?"

"There's nothing for me there."

"You keep thinking that, but it's not true. You don't want to go back there because you're running from your past. But you have to stop running now. The people of the Moon need you. And I need you too. I need you to do something for me."

Father Wycliffe was stunned: the Blessed Virgin Mary was telling him to go on a mission for her. This wasn't the first time that she had appeared to someone and asked for a favor, but he had never expected that she would ask *him*.

He still wasn't sure she was real, not an illusion. He decided to continue talking with the apparition anyway.

He remembered what Mary had asked of the people to whom she had appeared at Guadalupe, Lourdes, Fatima, and other places.

"What do you want me to do?" he asked. "Build a church? Tell people to go to church more often? Pray for sinners? Consecrate Russia?"

"None of the above. You're going to prevent a war for me."

There was an awkward silence as Wycliffe stared at Mary.

"I hate wars. I'm sick of wars. I've had more than enough of wars," said Wycliffe.

"All the more reason to send you to stop one," Mary said.

"I can't do it. I saw so many people lose so much in wars. I saw them lose their homes, their friends, their relatives, their bodies, and their lives. I lost my family in the last war. Please don't send me into another war zone."

"It won't become a war zone if you help me."

"What do you want me to do?"

"If national rivalries continue, two space-faring nations of Earth will go to war on the Moon. I need you to convince the two sides to come to peace."

"I've talked to politicians before, but they were minor figures like town mayors. Negotiating the peace between two countries is far beyond my experience. I'm not a Vatican diplomat. The Pope has a whole diplomatic corps of apostolic nuncios. Why not send one of them?"

"You're the one with the most experience in space. You understand the environment," Mary said.

"I'm not a trained diplomat. If I go to negotiate peace, we'll get war, which is what I dread the most," Wycliffe protested.

"Millions of people need you to save them from a war, not only a world war, but a war on both the Earth and the Moon," Mary urged.

"The burden of failure is too much for me, an ordinary diocesan priest," Wycliffe admitted. "How can all those lives depend on me when I couldn't even save the two people in my own family?"

"Do it for both me and her," Don said. "You have a chance to prevent terrible bloodshed. Give the people of Earth and the Moon the chance that previous generations didn't get."

"Like you and your mother," Wycliffe said wistfully.

"Mark, it's up to you to save the lives of millions of people," Mary urged.

"Yes, give those people a life that I didn't get," Don said.

"Alright, I'll go back to the Moon," Father Wycliffe agreed. "How can I refuse my own son?"

Mary smiled. "Excellent."

"But first, you have to tell me what's going to happen," Father Wycliffe demanded.

Mary shrugged. "I'm embarrassed to say that I can't. I don't really know how this war is going to start or which countries will be involved."

"That's not going to help me. Can't you tell me more?"

"I had to rely on an angel to tell me that I was pregnant. How annoying is that? I never had the gift of prophecy. I don't see visions like Joseph or Ezekiel. I'm probably the most disadvantaged Biblical person in terms of superpowers. Except for the ability to conceive a child when I was still a virgin, but really, that was the Holy Spirit's doing."

"So how do you know that I can prevent a war on the Moon?" Father Wycliffe asked.

"An angel told me," Mary said casually, as if everyone got visits from angels. "I get messages from angels from time to time. Sometimes they're annoyingly vague."

"Like this time."

"I know this is all rather hard to absorb, but just go back to the Moon, and you'll find out what to do. God works in mysterious ways."

"Stopping countries from going to war, creating peace among the nations. I can't do this alone. It's too much for one man to do. I'm going to need help," Father Wycliffe pleaded.

Mary touched the religious medal hanging around Wycliffe's neck: the medal of Our Lady of Walsingham.

"I have always been with you. I'll be with you again," she promised.

Of course, she had been with him since his childhood in Walsingham. She had been with him in all the statues at the Marian shrines, in his prayers of the Rosary, and in the religious medal around his neck. The Virgin was mother to all who prayed for her help and intercession. Like a mother, she would always be there to help her children.

Even if the woman he saw was not really the Virgin but an illusion, he knew that the Virgin was somewhere up there, reigning as Queen of Heaven, ready to help him.

"Alright, I'll go back to the Moon," Father Wycliffe said.

———

Father Wycliffe and Don ran diagnostic tests on the station. Together, they checked the test results on various systems: environmental, air, propulsion, altitude, communications, electrical, lighting.

"You really know how to run a space station," Wycliffe remarked.

He looked at the test results. He normally felt only boredom in running the diagnostic tests on the station's systems. This time was different, though. For the first time in years, he and his son were doing something together. They had spent too much time separated, first by war, then by tragedy. But now, they were together again.

"There," Don announced. "We've run a diagnostic on every system, and they're all working."

Don took off his Chelsea F.C. baseball cap and put it on a counter. "No wonder the Russians are so proud of Troika. The automatic altitude system and the antenna failed, but they could be fixed. All other systems are fine. For a station this old, Troika's in excellent shape. This station is a miracle."

Wycliffe picked up the baseball cap. Again, he remembered giving it to Don on his birthday.

"It was nice to see you again, son."

"I want you to know that I never blamed you for anything."

"Thanks. I needed to know that."

There was something else Father Wycliffe needed to know.

"Don, about your mother," Wycliffe asked. "Where is she?"

"She's very well and very happy."

"Why isn't she here with you?"

"I can answer that," said Mary. "It's not the time to meet Ingrid again. You'll see her at another place and another time."

"Ah, the Lord works in mysterious ways again."

———

There was one more thing for Father Wycliffe to do on Troika.

He grasped the icon of Old Testament Trinity and took it off the wall. Then he heard Mary approach him.

"What are you doing?" she asked.

"I'm going to take the icon to Exeter," Father Wycliffe explained. "It can be seen and admired by people there."

"That may be true, but leave it here."

"But there's nobody to appreciate it here."

"Troika is a sacred and special place. Leave the icon here."

"But it should be admired by many people."

"Jessica will come back. Never argue with a teenaged girl about how to decorate her room. Leave the icon here."

Wycliffe turned to face the wall again and hung the icon back on the wall. "About Jessica," he said while still looking at the Old Testament Trinity. "Why did the crew of Troika see Jesus as a girl?"

He heard just silence. He turned around. Mary and Don were not in the control room.

He left the control room and looked in the corridor. He went back to the EVA airlock and to the shuttlecraft dock. He went down into the other parts of the station. They were nowhere in the space station.

He returned to the control room. The knapsack and the baseball cap were gone too. There was no physical evidence of Mary and Don, nothing to be examined and scrutinized by scientific means.

He tapped into the surveillance video system and downloaded the video recordings of the control room onto a memory card. He put the memory card in his pocket and walked to the shuttlecraft dock.

He flew his shuttlecraft alone back to Exeter. All throughout the trip back, he wondered if he would see his two visitors on the video recording saved on the memory card.

———

A day later, the *Victoria* arrived, bringing Father Alexei. The chaplains went to the spacecraft dock to greet Father Alexei. Amira carried a tray of crackers and salt tablets to him.

Father Alexei smiled and said, "Bread and salt!"

Offering bread and salt was a traditional Slavic greeting ceremony. In space, it had evolved into an offering of crackers and salt tablets on the Apollo-Soyuz mission in 1975.

"Welcome to Space Station Exeter," said Amira.

Wycliffe watched the German imam offer the tray to the Russian priest. Now that his replacement had arrived, he knew that he would have to go back to the Moon.

———

Father Alexei redecorated the Christian chapel within hours of his arrival. Adorning the walls were icons of Mary cradling the baby Jesus, Jesus holding a

Bible, St. George slaying the dragon, and the Archangel St. Michael fighting a giant snake.

Father Wycliffe took a closer look at the icons. They were all printed on paper, mass produced for sale to the masses of worshippers. They were not icons painted on wood, like the ones found in Russian Orthodox churches on Earth.

"Ah, they are beautiful, are they not?" Father Alexei said.

"Yes, they are," Father Wycliffe agreed. "I love Orthodox Byzantine iconography."

"I regret that I could bring only these cheap paper pictures. Space aboard the spaceships is limited, and my research equipment took precedence. I could not bring any wooden icons. I love those icons made of egg tempera and gold leaf on old wood. It is too bad that we do not have a traditional icon out here."

Father Wycliffe knew there was one hand-painted wooden icon this far away from Earth, but it would have to stay on Space Station Troika.

———

Exeter's chaplains held a party for the incoming Father Alexei and the departing Father Wycliffe. Rabbi Gabizon brought his personal supply of a kosher red wine from the Spanish wine producing region of La Rioja. It was a brand favored by both Jewish and non-Jewish wine connoisseurs, a welcome change from the bland beer rations provided by the European Space Agency. Amira somehow found the ingredients to bake a chocolate cake in the station's galley, thus providing a treat tastier than the usual canned and rehydratable food.

Father Wycliffe, who had neither personal provisions like Rabbi Gabizon's nor baking skills like Imam Edip's, brought the spacer's staples of canned fruit salad, rehydratable salmon and chicken, dry biscuits, and preserved chocolate bars.

"First, Dr. Hall shows up to do neurological research, and now, you show up with your psychiatry degree," Amira said. "Is there a reason why NASA and ESA are so interested in our brains and minds?"

Alexei shook his head and smiled. "No, no, it is just a coincidence. A psychiatrist is a medical doctor too, and you cannot have enough medical staff out here, so here I am, as both a chaplain and doctor. If Dr. Schiller had chosen Father Leclerc, you would have gotten a Jesuit geologist."

"But instead, we have a fundamentalist atheist neurologist and a Russian Orthodox psychiatrist."

"Dr. Hall has his religion, I have mine, and that is life around Mars. I am sure we will work well together."

Amira nodded. "Yes, the Mars community is quite close knit. Our similarities mean more than our differences out here."

"What research projects will you conducting?" Rabbi Gabizon asked.

"Maybe they should have sent Father Leclerc instead. Aside from medical duties, I am here to gather information about a legend called the Siren Stones..." Father Alexei said.

———

Father Wycliffe showed Troika's surveillance video recordings to Father Alexei. On the video, Wycliffe appeared by himself, talking to the air, as if he were talking to nobody at all.

"You don't think that I'm mentally ill, that I'm having hallucinations or schizophrenic visions or hearing voices, do you?" Father Wycliffe asked.

"You say you observed, or more correctly, could not observe, a similar phenomenon on the same space station? That the station's crew saw and talked to a girl whom you could not see or hear on their video transmissions?"

"Yes."

"You have had experience with two incidents at Troika. I will have to interview you in more detail before you leave." Father Alexei pressed some buttons, and the Troika video stopped playing on his computer monitor. A written report appeared instead. "Did you read Dr. Hall's report about electrochemical signals coming from the station's rock?"

"Yes, and there's a rumor it happened on another rock," said Wycliffe.

"Odette de Proust," said Alexei. "Then I suggest that the apparitions at Troika are related to the space station, not to a pre-existing condition of your mind. I have seen plenty of mentally ill people, and you do not seem to be one of them, even if you did see and hear people who were not there."

"Then could Troika be a Siren Stone?"

"That depends on what is a Siren Stone. For years, there have been stories about spirits on asteroids. They were all dismissed as myths and fiction, of course. But now that there are two reports about asteroids with electromagnetic anomalies, could these rocks be the source of the Siren Stone legend? Could these rocks be the Siren Stones? Or are the Siren Stones something else? There is still a lot to learn out here."

"Yes, we've still got much to discover and learn," Father Wycliffe mused. "I wonder about the apparitions all the time. Is it possible that I actually did see the Virgin Mary? Or was she something I only imagined because of the rock?"

"Do you believe in the Virgin Mary?"

"Of course."

"Then it does not matter whether you think you saw the Virgin or an illusion," Alexei said. "If you believe that the Virgin Mary exists, then the electromagnetic rock is how God lets you see her. If you do not believe in the Virgin Mary, then she is just an illusion caused by the rock. The important thing is whether you believe in her. If you believe she is real, then she is real."

"The same must be true for my son. If I believe he's happy in the next life, then he really is."

"That's faith."

"But there's one mystery that neither faith nor science can explain," Father Wycliffe said. "Who repaired the antenna?"

Father Alexei looked pensive. "All I can say is, God works in mysterious ways."

PART 3
LUNA

6 / LEGATUS MISSUS

Mass had just ended at St. Dominic's Roman Catholic Church when Father Wycliffe heard the videophone beep. He rushed into his office and turned on his computer. Dr. Franz Schiller's face appeared.

"Father Wycliffe, how pleasant to see you again," Dr. Schiller said.

The Lutheran pastor and Chief Chaplain of the ESA Chaplaincy Department was in his late forties and still had brown hair untouched by the graying of age. He wore a plain black business suit, white shirt, and blue tie. He always looked like a businessman. Wycliffe had never seen Dr. Schiller wear any ecclesiastical vestments.

"*Guten morgen,*" Father Wycliffe replied.

"How are things on the Moon? Have you gone to Café Méliès recently?"

"Cafè Méliès? Yes, I had dinner there just last night. It's quite good."

"Yes, I hear it rivals the best restaurants on Earth. Hopefully, I will be able to visit you and dine there in the near future," Dr. Schiller said. "About Café Méliès: I heard that Carla Delgada might lose her job there, through no fault of her own. That would be sad. Is she still working there?"

Carla Delgada was a young waitress who worked at Café Méliès, the largest restaurant and nightclub on the Moon. She professed no strong religious beliefs -- and yet she claimed to have seen the Virgin Mary on the Moon.

"Yes, Miss Delgada is still working at Café Méliès," Wycliffe said. "At first, the restaurant's owner thought the publicity would be bad for business since so many lunar settlers are fundamentalist atheists. However, business has doubled because of all the tourists and pilgrims coming to see the apparition site. They all go to eat at Café Méliès."

"They no doubt hope to see Miss Delgada too," Dr. Schiller guessed.

"Many do want to see her, but only a few lucky ones get seated in her section. She doesn't talk much about the apparition while she's waiting on tables," said Father Wycliffe. "She's trying to keep a low profile."

"What are your impressions on the authenticity of the apparition of Mary?" asked Dr. Schiller.

The question surprised Wycliffe. Schiller hadn't previously shown any interest in the apparition of the Virgin Mary on the Moon. Unlike Roman Catholics, Lutherans and other Protestants are not prone to see visions of Mary. They are skeptical of apparitions of divine people. There are no Protestant versions of Guadalupe, Lourdes, or Fatima.

"I haven't finished my investigation yet," Wycliffe replied. "I've had just one meeting with Carla Delgada."

"But do you have any initial impressions of how it will end? What does your preliminary work hint at?"

"The visionary's background is not helping the case for authenticity. Although she claims to have seen the Virgin Mary, Carla Delgada is not a religious person. Look at the news reports about her. She goes to a church only for her friends' and relatives' weddings. She doesn't read the Bible, and she never prays. She says she has no religious feelings. The chances are low that her sightings of Mary are credible."

"Yes, her case does seem like an anomaly. Among Roman Catholics, usually only the devout see Mary."

"Precisely, but I have not completed the investigation and therefore can't give a final conclusion yet."

Schiller nodded. "I understand. I ask about her because I bring a message from Cardinal Saint-Cloud. The Cardinal wishes you to suspend the investigation temporarily."

"Why?" asked Father Wycliffe. "He asked for the investigation. Is he going to officially declare the apparition to be false? He was hoping I would reach that conclusion."

"No, the Cardinal will wait for your report before deciding whether to condemn or authenticate the apparition."

"Does it have to do with the apparition site being inside the U.S. protection zone?"

"No, no, he mentioned nothing like that," Schiller reassured him. "He wants you to temporarily suspend the investigation so you can go back to Earth."

Father Wycliffe had not expected that. "Why am I being summoned back to Earth?" he asked.

"I am sorry for surprising you and for not being able to let Cardinal Saint-Cloud tell you himself. It is unfortunate that the Cardinal does not have the authority to remove you from the Moon. I am the one with the authority to do that. It is the complicated way the Roman Catholic Church and the European Space Agency divide the responsibilities for operating St. Dominic's Church."

"Ah, yes, the Protocol between the Holy See and the European Space Agency on the Lunar Church. What a real masterpiece of Vatican diplomacy. It must be the simplest treaty ever signed by the Vatican," Father Wycliffe said sardonically.

Schiller chuckled. "Ah, indeed, only the Vatican and the European Space Agency could create a three-hundred page treaty on how to run a chapel that seats a hundred people."

"Which means you're the one who gets to tell me why I'm being summoned back to Earth," Wycliffe asked again.

Schiller's face became more serious. "There is business more urgent than the apparition of Mary. We have to attend a meeting in Rome."

"Rome?" Wycliffe asked. "Who are we meeting?"

"Cardinal Saint-Cloud and Christopher," Dr. Schiller replied.

Father Wycliffe knew Henri Saint-Cloud, Cardinal, Archbishop of Paris, member of the Jesuit order, holder of a Master's degree in physics, and the Roman Catholic Church's liaison to the European Space Agency.

He didn't know the other person, though. "Aside from Cardinal Saint-Cloud, who else did you mention? Someone named Christopher? Who's that?"

"Pope Christopher."

Father Wycliffe wasn't sure he had heard Dr. Schiller correctly. "Do you mean the Holy Father?"

"Yes, Pope Christopher, Bishop of Rome, *Pontifex Maximus*."

"Is this real? Why would he want to see *us*?"

"I too did not believe Cardinal Saint-Cloud, but he assured me that he was not joking."

"Why? Why would the Pope want to see us? I'm not an important archbishop or cardinal. I'm just an ordinary priest."

"And I am a Lutheran pastor," Dr. Schiller added. "The Archbishop and His Holiness seek advice from both Catholic and non-Catholics. You are a Marian priest formerly of the Church of England; your experience and knowledge will be invaluable to them. For security reasons, the Holy Father prefers that we talk in person rather than by videophone. I hope you understand."

"I would be honored to meet you, the Archbishop, and the Holy Father," Father Wycliffe said.

"Splendid. Check your calendar; my secretary has booked your flight to Rome tomorrow."

Wycliffe turned on his pocket computer. Someone had added an entry into his calendar: a space liner flight from Timonium Base to Cosmodrome Giorgio Napolitano. A message from Dr. Schiller's secretary stated that the Air France office at Timonium had his electronic ticket. The message also reminded him to bring his passport.

"What am I going to do with the church?" Father Wycliffe asked. "I'm the only priest here. Who's going to celebrate Mass?"

"Suspend the daily Mass and other sacraments and pastoral duties until you return," Schiller advised. "I have talked to the ESA property manager. He will lock the doors and take care of the church while you are away."

These Germans are so efficient and organized, Father Wycliffe mused.

"Getting back to the apparition of Mary," Wycliffe said. "Would my sudden departure for Earth arouse any suspicions that the Cardinal will declare it genuine?"

"Oh? Could that happen?" asked Schiller.

"A lot of people have come here, hoping to see the Virgin Mary, looking for a miracle. These people are full of hope, and they might think my sudden flight to Earth is related to the apparition. They'll think that I've found something so important that I have to return to Earth and meet the Cardinal. Of course, I don't want to mislead them."

"I see. However, we can easily manage the situation. I will ask the property manager to post a sign saying that the church is temporarily closed for repairs. I will also tell the lunar news services that that you have gone to a Eucharistic conference in Mexico."

A deception to hide a secret mission to Rome! The idea of ordained clergy lying to the public seemed unreal. Now he doubted whether his devotion to Mary or his past as an Anglican were really why the Pope wanted to meet him. This was the life of a secret agent, not of a priest. What could be next?

"Thanks for making all these arrangements for me," said Wycliffe.

"I look forward to seeing you in Rome," Schiller said. "Have a safe trip to Rome. I will meet you at the cosmodrome."

The videophone call ended, and Father Wycliffe switched his computer to the BBC Space news broadcast. It showed lunar land transports, so-called moon buses, driving up the slope of a hill. At the hill's peak was a light blue dome with a white statue of Our Lady of Fatima on its top. The caption read: PILGRIMS DEFY U.S.A. TO VISIT MARY APPARITION SHRINE.

The news broadcast showed American moon tanks blocking a moon bus from approaching the blue dome. The BBC announcer said, "The Americans insist that pilgrims do not have the right to visit the apparition shrine without permission from U.S. military authorities. However, the European Space Agency refuses to get U.S. permission to transport pilgrims from Timonium Base to Apparition Hill where Carla Delgada claims to have seen the Virgin Mary..."

Until recently, Apparition Hill had been just another nameless hill on the Moon. After Carla Delgada reported her apparition of Mary, lunar settlers nicknamed the hill "Apparition Hill," the same name given to the hill in the village of Medjugorje, Herzegovina, where six teenagers saw the Virgin Mary in 1981. Even atheists used the nickname. The International Astronomical Union, which traditionally names the Moon's geographical features, said nothing.

The broadcast showed a moon tank ramming into a moon bus. The moon bus tilted over, but before it could fall on its side, it fell back, right side up. A long dent creased its side.

"In the latest incident, an American moon tank rammed a Russian moon bus to prevent it from reaching the shrine," the announcer said. "The bus was carrying Russian Catholics trying to visit the shrine. Three people suffered minor injuries, but fortunately, nobody was killed."

People were risking their lives, defying American soldiers and their moon tanks, to see the place where the Virgin Mary had appeared to Carla Delgada. They must have strongly believed that she was really appearing on the Moon. The U.S. military could not stop them. Neither could their own church, which declared that the place was not a legitimate shrine until approved by Cardinal Saint-Cloud.

He remembered his own vision of Mary at Space Station Troika. He still didn't know what had happened there, but he knew that he had not seen the Virgin Mary. It was an illusion, not the Mother of God. If he could not believe his own visions, why would he believe that of a barmaid from Timonium Base?

However, hundreds of people did, and they could start a nuclear war on the Moon.

———

As the space liner rose and flew away from Timonium Base, Father Wycliffe looked out the window. The lunar landscape passed quickly beneath the spaceship. The Moon was uniformly gray and pockmarked with large plains and craters. In 1968, Apollo 8 Mission Commander Frank Borman had called it "a vast, lonely, forbidding type of existence or expanse of nothing." No wonder the humans had to create a brightly-lit playground like Timonium Base to keep themselves amused on the Moon.

The space liner flew low enough that he saw the roads, vehicles, helium-3 mining plants, solar energy collectors, communications towers, and light beacons that had sprung up in recent years.

The pilot spoke over the speaker. "Hello, passengers. On the right side, you can see two U.S. armored vehicles." The passengers crowded around the windows to look.

"Look at the moon tanks!" a boy squealed. "I wanna be a tank driver!"

A man smiled as he looked out the window. He wore a tie showing the U.S. flag. "God bless America," he said.

"Because no one else will!" another passenger said bitterly.

Wycliffe watched the tanks crawl like two little beetles across the barren landscape. Their squat shapes reminded him of the insects. Each tank had a rotating turret with a coil gun; an electric current would pulse through the coil of wire, create strong magnetic fields, and propel a ferromagnetic projectile through the coil. Unlike Earth tanks, the moon tanks rolled on large, shock-absorbent wheels.

"Their coil guns are the latest in military technology," bragged the man with the U.S. flag tie. "The Chinese are still playing with liquid oxygen and expensive fuels, but we're using electricity and magnetic fields."

"Yankee ingenuity beats them all the time," another passenger said.

A third passenger grunted and said, "This is a treaty violation."

"If the American tanks are out there, we must be close to Liberty," a young woman realized. "It looks so awesome on TV, with all those towers and lights and aerial transports flying around it. I wish we could fly over Liberty, just to see it."

"The Americans won't let us fly over Liberty because it's inside the protection zone," Wycliffe reminded her.

The man with the U.S. flag tie said, "The Chinese might be sneaking around there too."

"All the more reason to avoid getting close to Liberty," Wycliffe added.

He turned away from the window and looked at the television mounted on the seat in front of him. BBC Space was showing Walter Darby, President of the United States, answering questions on the White House lawn.

A reporter said, "Mr. President, the Secretary General of the United Nations sent you a letter saying that the protection zone around Liberty is a violation of the Outer Space Treaty and the Moon Agreement. He's still waiting for your reply."

"Well, he can stop waiting. I'll reply right now," Darby said. "The United States withdrew from the Outer Space Treaty six years ago, and we never signed the Moon Agreement. We're not bound by them. We can put military bases and hold military maneuvers there, and we can put a protection zone around our base. The U.N. is always interfering with American security..."

Next, the BBC showed a documentary about the short road to the militarization of the Moon: how the Vernacular Wars pushed countries to develop energy methods that did not rely on importing oil from Arab countries; how NASA built the first satellite system to collect solar energy, convert it to electricity, and transmit it to Earth via microwave beams; how the U.S. Government and a private consortium set up a base to build and launch the satellites more cheaply on the low-gravity Moon than on Earth; how the U.S. sold space-generated energy to some countries but denied it to others; how other countries began building their own satellite systems to end the American monopoly on space-generated electricity; how the development of nuclear fusion fueled the need for helium-3; how the solar wind deposits enormous quantities of helium-3 on the Moon; and how countries and companies raced each other to build helium-3 mining plants on the Moon.

Countries, companies, consortiums, organizations, and even private individuals claimed to own parts of a Moon that the United Nations said belonged to all humanity. No country recognized another's claim. The United Nations recognized nobody's claim.

The superpowers realized that if they could control a source of energy, they could control the buyers and users of the energy. They also realized that the easiest way to cripple an enemy in war is to end its supply of energy. If a country could control the helium-3 on the Moon, it could control the other countries of the Earth.

However, the United Nations' Outer Space Treaty outlawed military bases and military activity on the Moon and other celestial bodies. For some countries, the answer was obvious: break the treaty.

A divided U.S. Congress voted to withdraw from the Outer Space Treaty. A week later, President Darby sent a soldier to the scientific research base Liberty. NASA transferred control of Moonbase Liberty to the military, and Liberty became the Moon's first military base.

The next day, China withdrew from the Space Treaty and sent soldiers to its scientific base Yue 1. Soon, both the United States and China had twenty-five soldiers on the Moon. Although the garrisons were small, they had large arsenals of new missiles, lasers, coil guns, and catapults. Both countries sent up parts for lunar tanks and assembled them on the Moon. The BBC showed a video clip of a Chinese moon tank rumbling across Tiananmen Square during the National Day parade. An editor of *Jane's Defense Weekly* said that since the two countries had put their new weapons on the Moon so quickly, they must have been secretly developing them for years before withdrawing from the Outer Space Treaty.

The documentary showed President Darby declaring a protection zone, a ten-mile radius around Liberty, forbidden to all air and land vehicles without approval of the military commander of Moonbase Liberty.

Wearing a Vernacular Wars Veterans cap, President Darby told the two thousand military veterans at their convention in Chicago, "The United States is not claiming sovereignty over the Moon. We are only protecting American interests, investments, and security. We wouldn't need the protection zone were it not for the Chinese build-up of military forces on the Moon..."

The next day in Beijing, President Zhu Biao of China smirked at the applause of three thousand deputies of the National People's Congress. In the Congress's red and gold chamber, he declared, "China is a Great Power equal to America, and if America has a military base on the Moon, China will have one — and maybe two."

In New York, Ahmed Zaid, Secretary General of the United Nations, told the General Assembly, "The Moon belongs to everyone and no one. I am concerned that two members of the Security Council have put areas of the Moon under their military control."

In St. Peter's Square in Rome, Pope Christopher delivered his homily at the Sunday Papal Mass: "The protection zone and the military forces on the Moon threaten the future of the humanity on Earth."

In Strasbourg, the European Parliament voted to condemn both American and Chinese control over the Moon. For the Europeans, the U.S. protection zone was more than just an inconvenience in the flight path to Timonium Base.

Dominique Lascelles, President of the European Parliament, stood beside a statue of Charlemagne in the European Parliament Building. Behind her, a large viewscreen showed a waving European flag. Messages of different languages, superimposed on the flag, announced that the European Space Agency had become an agency of the European Union.

The viewscreen's image changed to a map of the Moon. Different flags represented the lunar bases, mining stations, and communications towers of nations in one area: United States, China, Russia, European Union, and United Arab Emirates.

"The European Union condemns both the United States and China for creating military zones on the Moon," Lascelles told the reporters. "We are especially concerned by the U.S. protection zone."

On the map of the Moon, an animated red line appeared and circled around a U.S. flag, labeled as Moonbase Liberty.

"The area inside the red circle is the U.S. protection zone, centered on Moonbase Liberty," Lascelles explained. "Look at the moon base just within the northern perimeter of the protection zone."

The viewscreen zoomed in on a flag within the red circle. It was a European flag with the label "Arcadia Base".

"You see that Arcadia Base is within the United States protection zone. Arcadia Base is a European Space Agency scientific research station; it poses no military threat to any country. However, now we need the permission of an American military commander to fly in and out of our own base," Lascelles complained.

"The ESA will allow air and ground traffic to come and go from Arcadia Base without American permission," she continued. "No American permission is required under the Outer Space Treaty and the Moon Treaty, which are still upheld by all member nations of the European Union."

Next, the documentary showed Apparition Hill. Apparition Hill, only half a mile away from Arcadia Base, was also inside the U.S. protection zone. Pilgrims and tourists were defying the United States by visiting the shrine without U.S. permission.

Images of soldiers and weapons appeared on TV: a U.S. Air Force officer using a new laser to cut through a moon rock; a Chinese moon tank patrolling around Yue 1; a shuttlecraft taking Chinese troops to a helium-3 station; and U.S. soldiers, in spacesuits, using an electric catapult to hurl a grenade at a boulder.

Then there was the image that he dreaded: a scene from Chinese TV showed a transport vehicle dragging missiles to Yue 1. Each was a Moon Punisher 1, the first ballistic missile designed for use on the Moon. Military music blared in the background. The Chinese news announcer boasted that China was the first country to put nuclear weapons on the Moon.

Wycliffe looked away from the TV and out the window again. The space liner climbed higher into the lunar sky until he could no longer see the moonbases and mining stations. Instead, he could see dots of light, which he knew were spy satellites in orbit.

As the space liner approached Earth, Wycliffe marveled at the view from his window. Hanging in the blackness of space was the Earth, looking like a blue orb covered with white swirls and large brown and green masses. The Earth looked quiet and still from space. The view reminded him of a history class in school years ago, when he had learned about early space exploration.

In 1968, the crew of Apollo 8 became the first people to leave Earth's orbit and orbit around the Moon. They were the first people to see Earth rising over the Moon's horizon, and their photograph of the Earthrise was one of the most famous photographs ever taken.

On Christmas Eve, they took turns reciting from *The Book of Genesis*:
"In the beginning God created the heaven and the Earth...And God called

the dry land Earth; and the gathering together of the waters called he Seas: and God saw that it was good."

In 1968, Earth looked beautiful and calm from space. However, on the ground, Earth was anything but calm. Communist Vietnam launched its Tet Offensive against the United States. Other Communists, from the Soviet Union, sent their tanks and soldiers into Czechoslovakia to overthrow the government. Assassins killed American Presidential candidate Robert F. Kennedy and civil rights leader Martin Luther King, Jr. Riots raged in cities and universities across America. In France, student rioting and a general strike nearly became a revolution.

Father Wycliffe knew that the Earth's appearance was deceptive. The beautiful blue areas were oceans whipped up by storms, and the white swirls were the storm clouds. The brown and green masses were continents swarming with billions of people, most living in poverty, fear, and war.

War on Earth was bad enough, but now, even the Moon could be a battleground.

Dr. Schiller and Father Wycliffe sped through the streets of Rome in their limousine. In the last three thousand years, many cities had arisen and died, but Rome had endured. Rome did not become a lifeless ruin visited only by archaeologists. Rome was still a living city where ancient monuments stood beside modern buildings.

"Look around you," their driver urged. "All ages of civilization are in one city."

Wycliffe felt as if he were travelling through time. Since arriving from the Moon, he had seen the glittering spaceships at the Cosmodrome Giorgio Napolitano; Trajan's Column from the Imperial Era; the Baroque statues at the Trevi Fountain; the shiny glass windows of the shops of Via Condotti; and now, in front of him, the Apostolic Palace.

They stopped at a checkpoint where a pair of Swiss Guards held halberds, long poles with axe blades and spikes. The guards wore black berets and the Renaissance-style uniform of blue, red, orange, and yellow.

The driver handed a passcard to one of the Swiss Guards. The guard turned to a computer terminal and swiped the card through the a card reader.

Photos of the driver, Father Wycliffe, and Dr. Schiller appeared on the computer monitor.

The guard handed the card back to the driver and motioned for him to drive. The car continued towards the Apostolic Palace.

Rome: the Eternal City, the Head of the World, the Threshold of the Apostoles. Two thousand years ago, it ruled Europe, north Africa, and the Middle East. It was the largest empire in ancient Europe.

As the imperial capital, Rome had been the center of a Greek-Roman pagan culture that stretched all over its empire. Later it became the international capital of Christianity; not even the Great Schism or the Reformation could diminish Rome's status in Christendom. It was always the most prized symbol of glory to Europe's rulers. After Rome fell to Germanic invaders in A.D. 476, a variety of monarchs claimed to rule Rome, though in name only. Greek rulers in Constantinople ruled as Roman Emperors without Rome itself for almost a thousand years. German and Austrian monarchs called themselves Holy Roman Emperors from Charlemagne in 800 to Franz the Second in 1806. Napoleon gave the title King of Rome to his son in 1811, centuries after both Rome and Constantinople had fallen to invaders. Even Mehmed the Second, a Moslem and Sultan of the Ottoman Empire, declared himself Caesar of the Roman Empire after conquering Constantinople. Few monarchs could resist the temptation to take a Roman title of royalty. Fewer actually ruled the Eternal City.

But there was one man who still ruled a worldwide empire from Rome, and he was waiting for Father Wycliffe and Dr. Schiller inside the Apostolic Palace.

A priest ushered them into a lobby where Henri Cardinal Saint-Cloud, the Archbishop of Paris, greeted them. The Cardinal wore a long black robe, a gold crucifix hanging from a gold chain around his neck, a wide red satin sash around his waist, and a red zucchetto or skullcap. Saint-Cloud, a man in his early sixties, still had a handsome face, like that of a storybook prince in his senior years. A prince of the Church, Father Wycliffe thought. The Archbishop always looked distinguished, like a French aristocrat.

First, Cardinal Saint-Cloud shook hands with Dr. Schiller. Then the Cardinal extended his hand so that Father Wycliffe could kiss his ring.

"*Bienvenue sur Terre,*" the Cardinal said. "Come with me. We will meet the Holy Father."

They walked through hallways adorned with paintings sculptures of Biblical patriarchs, Jesus, Mary, the Apostles, saints, popes, and cardinals. Like every building in the Vatican, the Apostolic Palace was like an art museum.

"You are a lucky man. Few priests receive the honor that you will receive from the Pope," said Cardinal Saint-Cloud.

"Your Eminence, I realize that it's a great honor, but I'm not sure that I'm qualified for this duty," Father Wycliffe protested.

The Cardinal nodded. "I can understand your concern. This must be quite a surprise for you. However, I have read your *curriculum vitae,* and I am certain that you are qualified for this mission."

"I hope so."

"Pray that you are."

"Thanks. Now I know I need divine help."

"I am sorry. I did not mean to imply that you are in any way incompetent. I merely meant that we should always seek God's help in all that we do."

Dr. Schiller said, "We all need it, especially with all those new weapons on the Moon."

Cardinal Saint-Cloud sighed. "Now including nuclear warheads. What will be next, and how will it end?"

They entered a lounge with ornate baroque woodwork on the walls. "The Pope will meet us in here," Cardinal Saint-Cloud said.

On the wall was a painting of Christopher Columbus holding an antique globe turned to the Western Hemisphere. The area of the United States was colored in red. The Knights of Columbus in New York had given the painting to Pope Christopher after his election. The Knights wanted to remind the Pope about his origins. Never before had an American been elected Pope or named himself after the explorer of the New World.

Next to the painting was a large reproduction of a map of the world, dated MDCCXX or 1720. The map showed the world as two hemispheres, the western and the eastern. An inscription credited Johann Baptist Homann, an important map publisher in Germany in the eighteenth century. The place names were in Latin: Nova Francia for Canada, Nova Hollandia for Australia, India Orientalis for India, Terra Sancta for the Holy Land in Palestine. The entire northwest of North America was blank due to the Europeans' lack of knowledge of the area. The map harkened back to the century when half the world was unknown to Europeans and the Church.

Beside the map was a large portrait of Pope Christopher. He wore a long white robe, red zucchetto, an ornate Byzantine crucifix on a gold chain around his neck, and an elaborate purple stole embroidered with golden paschal lambs, saints, and chi-rho symbols. Another prince of the Church: spiritual leader of millions of people, sovereign of his own city state, and commander of his own small army.

Wycliffe stared at the photograph. He had never expected to meet the Pope privately. He felt nervous.

Meeting the Pope for the first time was intimidating enough. The reason for the trip to Rome added to Father Wycliffe's uneasiness.

Dr. Schiller had met him at the Cosmodrome Giorgio Napolitano and revealed the reason why the Pope wanted to see him. The Virgin Mary on Space Station Troika had predicted that he would get this job. More than ever, he wondered if she really had been the Virgin or an illusion created by a Siren Stone. Could an illusion have predicted the future?

He heard the door open.

His Holiness Pope Christopher, Bishop of Rome, Successor of the Prince of Apostles, Vicar of Jesus Christ, Supreme Pontiff of the Universal Church, Servant of the Servants of God, Patriarch of the West, Primate of Italy, Archbishop and Metropolitan of the Roman Province, and Sovereign of the State of Vatican City, walked into the room.

The Pope wore a black suit and shirt with a Roman collar and a plain wooden cross hanging from a brown leather cord around his neck. He did not look like the *Pontifex Maximus*; instead, he looked like Father Brad Kensington, a parish priest from Staten Island who rose to become Archbishop of New York, a Cardinal, and finally, Pope. He did not wear the long robe, the satin shoes, the zucchetto, or the embroidered stole.

However, he did wear the Fisherman's Ring. The Pope held his hand out. Controlling his nervousness, Father Wycliffe silently stepped forward, knelt, and kissed the ring.

"Rise, Padre Wycliffe," the Pope ordered.

Wycliffe obeyed and stood up again.

There was an awkward silence. Then the Pope said, "You can say something if you wish."

"It is an honor to meet you, Holy Father," said Father Wycliffe.

"No, the honor is mine," the Pope said. "You're the priest who has traveled the furthest in his apostolic and pastoral duties, further than any missionary ever has."

Pope Christopher, a thin man about sixty years old with grey hair, smiled and patted Father Wycliffe on the back. "I'm glad to finally meet our man on Mars. Well done, boy, well done."

"Thank you, Holy Father," Father Wycliffe said. Wycliffe felt his nervousness fade away, and he smiled back at the Pope.

The Pope approached Schiller. "Dr. Schiller, how are you?"

"Your Holiness, I am very well. Thank you for asking," Schiller replied. He reached out and shook the Pope's hand. The Lutheran pastor had no obligation to kneel and kiss the Pope's ring.

Another man entered the room. Unlike the Pope, this man was dressed like a prince of the Church. Wycliffe recognized him as the Cardinal Emilio Ferrata, Cardinal Secretary of State. He was the man responsible for all political and diplomatic functions of the Vatican City and the Holy See.

After another round of ring-kissing and handshakes, the Pope suggested, "Gentlemen, shall we get started?"

Cardinal Ferrata looked at Father Wycliffe. "Padre, please come forward."

Wycliffe stepped to Cardinal Ferrata. The Cardinal Secretary of State held a red folder out to him.

Father Wycliffe accepted the folder and opened it. Inside was a document with the coats of arms of Pope Christopher and the Vatican City State in color. The Latin text was in flowing red and gold calligraphy. Wycliffe guessed that a heraldic artist and a calligrapher had worked many hours to paint this document.

Wycliffe saw his own name and the words *legatus missus*.

"*Legatus missus*," he muttered.

"A legate sent on a specific task or mission," Cardinal Ferrata explained. "You are now an envoy of the Holy See. Not an apostolic nuncio but still an accredited diplomat."

"Our first diplomatic representative on the Moon," the Pope said. "Again you are the first."

"Please sit down," Cardinal Ferrata said, motioning towards a long oak table. They sat down around the table. The Secretary of State picked up a remote control, aimed it at the old world map, and pressed a button.

The map slid away, revealing a viewscreen. Another map, this one of the

Moon, appeared. Like other lunar maps seen on TV recently, this one had flags representing the different moonbases.

"Look at the national rivalries waiting to turn into war," Pope Christopher said. "I'm very worried that a war on the Moon will spread to Earth."

"They have all sorts of weapons on the Moon: lasers, catapults, mass drivers, coil guns, rail guns, moon tanks, laser cannons, killer satellites. Now the Chinese have put nuclear weapons up there. It is inevitable that the Americans will put nuclear weapons on the Moon too," Cardinal Ferrata added. "They could use any weapons to start a war, but they will use nuclear missiles to end it."

Dr. Schiller frowned. "Why put nuclear weapons on the Moon? An ordinary missile could destroy a lunar base. Why needlessly irradiate the Moon?"

"If I may give my opinion, a former military officer's opinion," Wycliffe said. "Nuclear weapons are the traditional weapon of fear. In the twenty-first century, countries used nuclear weapons to scare each other. The nuclear weapon was almost as frightening as the suicide bomber. The fear of nuclear weapons is still strong. They know nuclear weapons are overkill on a moonbase, but that's the reason for having them."

The Pope sighed softly. "Unfortunately, it's easier to start a war on the Moon than on Earth. The largest moonbase, Timonium, has three hundred people, much fewer than any major city on Earth. A national leader will find it easier to attack a moonbase than a city on Earth. He can fool himself into thinking that he can limit the dead to just the people on the Moon. However, once a nuclear strike occurs on the Moon, the victim will want to retaliate on Earth. Then we will lose millions of people."

Cardinal Ferrata pointed the remote control at the viewscreen. It showed a video of moon buses approaching Apparition Hill.

"The unauthorized shrine built where Carla Delgada claims to have seen the Virgin Mary," Ferrata said.

Cardinal Saint-Cloud grunted. "Look at those buses full of pilgrims. They would rather hear someone talk about her vision of Mary than listen to the teachings of our Church. It is like having people learn ghost stories and fairy tales instead of the Bible and our philosophy. I refused their requests to authorize Masses at their unauthorized shrine or to consecrate the ground beneath it."

"Yet they still come," the Pope observed. "Nothing I say can stop them. Their devotion, though misguided, is sincere."

"The apparition shrine is within the U.S. protection zone and only eight hundred meters away from Arcadia Base," Ferrata reminded them.

"I have talked to the U.S. ambassador," the Cardinal Secretary of State said. "The Americans will allow ESA employees to enter and leave the protection zone. Everyone else needs a passport and a U.S. visa."

"The Americans will *allow* us to travel to our own moonbase? We need passports?" Schiller said indignantly.

The viewscreen showed the BBC video of the U.S. moon tank ramming a Russian moon bus.

"The Americans are becoming more aggressive," Schiller complained. "Someone will be killed soon."

The Pope nodded in agreement. "There will soon be an incident that starts a war. Anything could start a war now."

"Perhaps the U.S. protection zone could work in the Church's favor," Wycliffe suggested. "If the Americans stop the pilgrims from visiting the shrine, the unauthorized devotions will end."

"They will still try to go there," said Saint-Cloud. "The devoted always keep trying. Devoted Christians have stood up to powerful leaders ranging from the Roman emperors to Communist dictators. The danger will not discourage them."

"And although we disagree with their devotion to an unproven apparition, they are still our brethren, and we should try to protect them," the Pope said.

Father Wycliffe turned to Dr. Schiller. "Those moon buses leave from Timonium Base. Even the Russian buses stop at Timonium to refuel on the way to the protection zone. Can't the ESA stop the buses from going to the protection zone?"

"Cardinal Ferrata and I have already asked the President of the European Union," Dr. Schiller said. "The E.U. insists on keeping the tourist buses moving between Timonium Base, Arcadia Base, and the apparition shrine. First, European citizens have the right to travel between their bases without the United States' permission. Secondly, the pilgrims can rest and get food at Arcadia. With this gesture of hospitality, the E.U. shows the spirit of the Moon Treaty and the religious freedom of the European Union."

Father Wycliffe knew that the European Union wanted to protect more than a space treaty and religious freedom. Its agency, the ESA, owned

Timonium Base and collected a percentage of profits from Timonium's businesses: the hotels, the restaurants, the tour companies, and even a new religious gift shop. The more tourists and pilgrims visited Timonium Base and the apparition shrine, the more money the ESA received.

"Thus we have a dilemma," Pope Christopher said. "The Church cannot stop the pilgrims, the European Union will not stop the pilgrims, and fear cannot stop the pilgrims. The more pilgrims try to enter the protection zone, the higher the chance of war breaking out."

"What can we do about it?" Wycliffe asked.

"We can send people in and out of the protection zone without the Americans noticing," said the Cardinal Secretary of State.

Wycliffe thought he was meeting with spies instead of priests. "Do you have an idea on how to do that?"

"Teleporters. People will not have to travel by bus anymore. Use teleporters to teleport people in and out of the protection zone," Ferrata proposed.

"Teleporters? We use them at the space stations around Mars," said Wycliffe.

"That is why you are important," Cardinal Saint-Cloud said. "I read your *curriculum vitae*. You have years of engineering training and experience. You have lived in space. You have repaired and flown spacecraft. You used teleporters at Mars. You can set up a teleporter system at all ESA moonbases."

"We used teleporters on Mars to transport cargo, but there was always that glitch about ten percent of attempts to teleport organic matter," Wycliffe reminded them.

"There is a new teleporter program code apparently developed by the crew of Space Station Troika," said Cardinal Ferrata. "I know you are skeptical when they say that Jesus developed the code. All of us are skeptical of the code's alleged divine inspiration. However, it works. Whatever its origin, the new code allowed the crew to teleport from Troika to Exeter unharmed."

Dr. Schiller said, "The European Union has tested the new program code rigorously and concluded that it is safe. The E.U. approved the teleporter for human use yesterday."

"You are both a priest and engineer, so we want you to install the teleporter system," said Ferrata.

"Why do you need a priest for this job?" Father Wycliffe asked. He pointed at his diplomatic appointment certificate. "And how does being a Papal legate fit into this?"

Emilio Ferrata, the Cardinal Secretary of State, handed a plastic card to Father Wycliffe. It was gold-colored and showed his photograph and the Vatican City State coat of arms. It also had a security hologram of a dove.

"As a priest, you can be a Papal legate. As a Papal legate, you can use this Vatican City State diplomatic passport," said Cardinal Ferrata. "If the Americans arrest you, you can claim diplomatic immunity."

The Pope grinned. "Not even President Darby, the most powerful man on Earth, has the courage to imprison a Vatican diplomat."

———

As he left the Apostolic Palace, Father Wycliffe realized that Mary's prophecy had not come true. He wouldn't be negotiating the peace between two hostile countries. All he needed to do was to install teleporters at the ESA's lunar bases –- and help hundreds of pilgrims and tourists bypass the U.S. moon tanks. It was a daunting mission, but he wouldn't have the burden of saving the human race. At least it didn't seem so.

Certainly, the Virgin Mary could not be wrong. Therefore, the woman he met at Troika could not be Mary. She had to have been something else.

An illusion created by Troika's electrochemical waves? The legend of the Siren Stones could have a rational, scientific explanation.

But he still had no rational, scientific explanation of who had repaired the antenna at Troika.

Father Alexei had said, "God works in mysterious ways." Father Wycliffe wondered whether the Mother of God works in mysterious ways too.

7 / THE APPARITION

Excerpt from the first interview of Carla Delgada:

REV. WYCLIFFE: ...and have you had any education in the Catechism of the Catholic Church either?

C. DELGADA: I don't think so. What's the cataclysm?

REV. WYCLIFFE: Catechism. The summary of the Church's doctrine or beliefs.

C. DELGADA: No, I have no education in that.

REV. WYCLIFFE: Did you ever go to Sunday school?

C. DELGADA: No.

REV. WYCLIFFE: Did your parents ever teach you about the Christian or Catholic faith?

C. DELGADA: Not much. We had a book of Bible stories, and they read some of them to me when I was a kid, but that was it. But hey, I know Christmas is when Jesus was born and Easter is when he died. Oh, I know he came back too. And I saw some movies, like *Jesus Christ Superstar* on the Archive Network. There was another movie about a guy who wins a chariot race, and then he sees Jesus. What was that one called?

REV. WYCLIFFE: That was *Ben-Hur*. Did your grandparents teach you anything about the Christian or Catholic faith?

C. DELGADA: No, they didn't. My mother's parents lived in the Azores, and my father's parents lived in Portugal. They all visited us in Canada each year, but they didn't talk about religion when they came.

REV. WYCLIFFE: Aside from watching movies, did you have any other instruction on the faith and doctrine?

C. DELGADA: No. As I said, my parents weren't religious. They got me baptized to make my grandparents happy, but we never went to church after that.

REV. WYCLIFFE: Interesting. Now tell me about the trip to the hill where you claim to have seen the Virgin Mary.

C. DELGADA: *"Claim* to have seen?" You don't believe me, do you? I know I saw *something* that day. I wasn't dreaming or drunk or on drugs or anything.

REV. WYCLIFFE: I'm sorry if I've offended you. No, I'm not saying that I don't believe you. And I'm not saying that you were using special substances. I'm only gathering information now. I can't make any conclusion yet.

C. DELGADA: That's okay with me. I understand. I have trouble believing I saw her too. Where do I begin?

REV. WYCLIFFE: How about why you were at the hill?

C. DELGADA: A tour company had a tour where you get to wear a spacesuit and walk on the surface. That sounded like fun. I've lived here a year, and I've never walked on the surface. I've always been in a moon bus or shuttlecraft. On my day off, I went on the tour with a bunch of tourists.

REV. WYCLIFFE: How many of you were there?

C. DELGADA: About twenty on the bus. We went to Arcadia, where we changed into spacesuits and walked outside. This was before the Americans sent a moon tank to drive around Arcadia from time to time. It was incredible to walk around on the surface! I felt so free, jumping around. It was great to actually touch the ground and leave a footprint on the Moon. It's not the same as being inside a moon bus.

There were a couple of electric carts in the moon bus. Three of us thought it would be fun to ride a cart, so we rented a cart and drove off. We saw a hill and stopped there. The other two girls went to look for rocks, and I went to look at the hill. There was also a communications tower at the base of the hill. I went to look at that too.

REV. WYCLIFFE: So you got separated from the other two girls?

C. DELGADA: Yes, but we weren't far apart. We could still see each other, and we had our helmet radios on.

REV. WYCLIFFE: And then what happened?

C. DELGADA: I suddenly smelled roses. That wasn't normal.

REV. WYCLIFFE: You smelled roses? Did you see any roses around?

C. DELGADA: Of course not. Roses don't grow in the lunar soil and the vacuum. But I smelled roses from somewhere. Then I thought there was something wrong with my helmet. Oh my God, I'm losing air, and suffocating to death smells like roses, I thought. What a stupid way to die. But I was still breathing, and the suit's warning light didn't go on.

Then I saw a woman standing on the hill. She wasn't wearing a spacesuit. I didn't know how she could breathe. She was wearing a white robe and a crown. A very bright light was glowing from behind her, as if she were standing in front of the sun. Although the light was behind her, I could see her face too.

REV. WYCLIFFE: Could you see her clearly? Or did her image seem hazy, misty or blurry?

C. DELGADA: I saw her clearly, no blurring.

REV. WYCLIFFE: Did your vision change at any time? Did it ever go blurry and back to clear?

C. DELGADA: No, I could see her clearly all the time.

REV. WYCLIFFE: Did you call the other two girls?

C. DELGADA: Not yet. I was going to, but the woman spoke, and I listened. I heard her on my helmet radio.

REV. WYCLIFFE: What did she say?

C. DELGADA: "The Moon is my dominion. Use it in peace or use it not at all."

REV. WYCLIFFE: What language did she speak?

C. DELGADA: English.

REV. WYCLIFFE: Did she ever speak in Portuguese?

C. DELGADA: No. That's odd, isn't it? Some people tell me they expect her to speak in Portuguese.

REV. WYCLIFFE: She did in 1917 in Portugal. Back home in Montreal, which language did you speak more often? English or Portuguese?

C. DELGADA: English. I actually know English better than I know Portuguese.

REV. WYCLIFFE: And what do your parents speak regularly?

C. DELGADA: English most of the time. They were born in Canada, and they grew up there. My grandparents speak Portuguese to each other, but my parents don't.

REV. WYCLIFFE: I see. When the woman spoke, how did she seem to feel? Angry? Happy?

C. DELGADA: Sad.

REV. WYCLIFFE: Sad?

C. DELGADA: She had a sad look on her face.

REV. WYCLIFFE: Did she say anything else?

C. DELGADA: No, all she said was, "The Moon is my dominion. Use it in peace or use it not at all."

REV. WYCLIFFE: Did you tell the other two girls?

C. DELGADA: I did, right after the woman talked to me, but she suddenly disappeared before the girls could see her.

REV. WYCLIFFE: What did you tell them?

C. DELGADA: I said, "Hey, there's a woman here!"

REV. WYCLIFFE: And what did they say?

C. DELGADA: "No kidding, there are three of us here."

REV. WYCLIFFE: Then what did you do?

C. DELGADA: We got back in the cart and drove back to Arcadia. I told the tour guide, and she must've told two friends, and they must have told two friends, because everyone on the Moon knew about it by the next day.

REV. WYCLIFFE: Did the woman say anything else than "The Moon is my Dominion. Use it in peace or use it not at all?"

C. DELGADA: No.

REV. WYCLIFFE: Nothing else? Did she identify herself? Did she tell you her name? Did she tell you who she was?

C. DELGADA: No.

REV. WYCLIFFE: Not even by using a title, like queen or mother?

C. DELGADA: No.

REV. WYCLIFFE: How did you know she was the Virgin Mary?

C. DELGADA: On the ride back to Arcadia, I knew I had seen the white robe and crown before. Then I remembered. When I was fourteen, my grandmother, my mother's mother, visited us from Azores. She's more devout than the rest of us. She gave me a small statue of the Virgin Mary. She called it Our Lady of Fatima and said that's what Mary looked like when she appeared in Portugal. I kept the statue on my dresser for years. That's how I know the woman was the Virgin Mary. I didn't know it when I saw her, but I knew it after.

REV. WYCLIFFE: So you had a statue of Our Lady of Fatima. Did you ever pray to Mary for her intercession?

C. DELGADA: No, I've never prayed to Mary. I've never prayed at all.

REV. WYCLIFFE: Did you ever see or hear Mary again?

C. DELGADA: No. I went back to the hill a week later, but I didn't see her. Other people had already put little shrines there: little statues and pictures of the Virgin Mary. They even put candles there even though the candles won't burn. Weird, eh?

REV. WYCLIFFE: What about away from the hill? Have you seen or heard her at another place and time?

C. DELGADA: No.

REV. WYCLIFFE: Have you seen any other religious visions?

C. DELGADA: No.

REV. WYCLIFFE: What do you think is the meaning of her message?

C. DELGADA: I think she said to make peace, not war, on the Moon.

REV. WYCLIFFE: Do you believe in the Virgin Mary?

C. DELGADA: I guess so. I'm Christian, I guess, but I'm not devout or religious or anything. My family got together at Christmas and Easter every year, but that was all.

REV. WYCLIFFE: Did the experience make you more interested in the faith? Do you want to be closer to God and the Church now?

C. DELGADA: No, not really. I know that surprises many people. I know hordes of people are coming to the Moon to look for Mary. They all want to talk to me, but I don't want to. I don't have time to see all of them. I don't have anything to say other than what I've said already. I heard only one message, and I don't know any new secret of Fatima or the future of the world. These people believe in seeing visions of Mary, but I've never been as religious as they are. I'm still not.

REV. WYCLIFFE: What do you think you saw that day?

C. DELGADA: I don't know. It's your job to find out, right?

Excerpts from Rev. Mark Wycliffe's notes on the interview with Carla Delgada:

Carla's vision was clear when she saw the apparition. This might rule out a hallucination caused by drugs, organic means, or mental illness. Most hallucinations of religious figures are blurry or transform through different phases or stages. However, I cannot completely rule out hallucination without a drug test and neurological and psychiatric examinations. It is too late to test her for drugs. I will ask if she will consent to neurological and psychiatric examinations.

She said she smelled roses when she saw the apparition. Roses appear at several Marian apparitions. St. Juan Diego found roses when he saw Our Lady of Guadalupe on Tepeyac Hill. St. Bernadette saw Our Lady of Lourdes above a rosebush. In this case, however, there were no roses growing on the Moon, yet Ms. Delgada smelled them.

Her religious background is practically non-existent. She did not even recognize the apparition as the Virgin Mary until she remembered it looked like a statue of Our Lady of Fatima. Her only act of piety has been to keep that statue when she was a teenager. However, she had never prayed to the Blessed Virgin for her intercession. Having the statue was a weak act of devotion in her case. She does not seem like a religious visionary: an argument against approval of the apparition as supernatural and worthy of belief.

She told two tourists and the tour guide about her vision. I've interviewed them, and all have corroborated that Carla told them about the apparition right after she claimed to have seen it. However, nobody except Carla witnessed the vision: another argument against approval of the apparition.

The message allegedly received from Mary, "Use the Moon in peace or use it not at all," seems to be a plea for peace on the Moon. The Church can agree that peace is preferable to war. The Pope has asked all countries to refrain from war on the Moon. The message does not contradict Church doctrine and supports it: an argument in favor of approval of the apparition.

Her experience has not made her more religious, spiritual, or closer to God or the Church. This would seem to be another argument against approval of the apparition. However, her experience has made others more devout, such as the pilgrims who come here hoping to see Mary. I need to observe the pilgrims and the situation further to determine if this incident will bring spiritual fruits and healthy religious devotion.

There is a communications tower at the base of the hill, and the tower has a video camera for security reasons. Unfortunately, the camera malfunctioned while Ms. Delgada was at the hill (The video camera has its own BF-36 antenna unit, and the antenna's memory card failed. Another failed memory card in a BF-36!). Therefore, there is no video to either corroborate or contradict Ms. Delgada's account of events.

Excerpt from Rev. Mark Wycliffe's notes on the investigation of the Marian apparition:

Revelation, 12:1:

A great sign appeared in the sky, a woman clothed with the sun, with the moon under her feet, and on her head a crown of twelve stars.

8 / GIFT OF FINEST WHEAT

Father Wycliffe watched the air shimmer in the teleporter booth. Energy reconverted into matter, and ten visitors appeared. They silently touched their arms to reassure themselves that they were solid again.

An African man stood by the teleporter booth. He wore a blue blazer embroidered with the crossed flags of France and Côte d'Ivoire. "*Soyez les bienvenus à la base lunaire Arcadie,*" he said to the visitors.

The visitors finally broke their stunned silence.

"*Incroyable!*" a young woman said. Her eyes were wide with amazement. "*Nous sommes arrivés à la base lunaire Arcadie.*"

A man patted his arm again. "This is the most amazing thing that's ever happened to me! It's a miracle!" he said in English. Wycliffe recognized the accent as Irish.

"No, it's not a miracle," Wycliffe said. "It's modern science."

"Plus two weeks of your labor and one million euros worth of equipment," the Ivorian Frenchman added. "It is wonderful that the European Union paid for the equipment. The ESA got it for free."

The teleporter technician said, "We should clear the booth so we do not delay the next transmission."

The Ivorian Frenchman motioned to the visitors to come forward. "Come, step away from the teleporter booth," he urged. "My name is Alphonse Bangolo, and I am the director of Arcadia Base. I hope you enjoy your stay here."

The Irishman looked at Wycliffe and smiled. "Ah, Father," he said, no doubt seeing Wycliffe's Roman collar. "This is a pleasant surprise. I didn't think there would be a priest going to the shrine with us."

"No, I'm not here in any pastoral capacity. I'm an engineer as well as a priest. I've been installing the teleporters at the ESA moonbases."

"Oh." The man looked disappointed. "Well, maybe someday you'll come to the shrine."

"Maybe."

The visitors walked past a sign written in several languages:

WELCOME TO ARCADIA BASE
A RESEARCH STATION OF THE EUROPEAN SPACE AGENCY
GEOLOGY ASTRONOMY CHEMISTRY ENGINEERING
MEDICINE

Alphonse pointed at a doorway. "The cafeteria is in there. Feel free to eat and rest in there before continuing to the shrine. And feel free to come back here after your pilgrimage."

The sign beside the cafeteria read, again in several languages:

CAFETERIA
Fish on Fridays! Cod, salmon, and sushi!
Euros, U.S. dollars, gold units and all major credit cards accepted.

They watched the visitors walk into the cafeteria. "Thank you for installing the teleporters," Alphonse said. "Teleportation is the only way to come to Arcadia now."

"I'm still amazed that the Americans blocked tourists from entering the protection zone," Wycliffe said. "Moon tanks firing lasers on tourist buses; who would've thought it could happen?"

"If the U.S. could find a way to block teleporter signals, it would block them too," said Alphonse. "According to the U.S. Government, we are all trespassers here."

They went to a counter beside the cafeteria. There a smiling young woman sold T-shirts, key chains, mugs, medals, model spaceships, holograms, moon rocks, and other souvenirs of Arcadia Base and the ESA.

Alphonse pointed at the souvenirs. "The pilgrimage business is lucrative.

We bought a new electron microscope with profits from the cafeteria and merchandise sales. There is no conflict between religion and science here."

Wycliffe picked up a small statue of Our Lady of Fatima, the image of the Virgin Mary as she appeared in Fatima, Portugal, in 1917. Artists usually showed Our Lady of Fatima standing in front of the three young shepherds who saw her. However, on this statue, Our Lady of Fatima stood on a grey lunar surface, pockmarked with little craters.

"What's this doing here?" Wycliffe asked.

"Our Lady of the Moon," Alphonse replied. "A resin statue. It is available in three sizes. We started selling them yesterday."

"The ESA is selling statues of the Virgin Mary?" Wycliffe said incredulously.

"We sold two hundred already. That is enough to buy a new pickaxe for our geologists. Like I said, there is no conflict between religion and science here."

"Except that the Church has not approved of the apparition of Mary on the Moon, and we are not encouraging people to believe in it, pending further investigation."

"*C'est incroyable!* For the first time in history, scientists are encouraging religious devotion, and the Church is opposing it."

Spanish pilgrims, carrying their national flag, walked past them. One of them wore a red shirt showing a white scallop shell and the words "El Camino de Santiago". She must have walked the Way of St. James, the pilgrimage route to the Cathedral in Santiago de Compostela, Spain. The United Nations Educational, Scientific and Cultural Organization had declared the Way of St. James to be a World Cultural Site in 1993. For centuries, pilgrims had walked the Way. Now one of them had come to the Moon.

How the pilgrimage experience has changed over the centuries, Father Wycliffe realized.

In the Middle Ages, pilgrims endured months of difficult travel to the shrines of Europe and the Holy Land. They sometimes rode on horse or sailed by boat, but they always walked through unfamiliar territory for much of the trip. They risked robbery and violence from bandits anywhere on the road. If they traveled by sea, they risked enslavement and death from Barbary and Turkish pirates. If hostile people did not kill them, illness and epidemics might. Walking with only a staff, a satchel, and a water bottle, pilgrims plodded towards Jerusalem, Rome, or Santiago de Compostela at eighteen miles per day. As they approached the holy cities, they got lodging and food at austere hostels and monasteries.

At the holy shrines, they bought a metal badge with an image of a saint. For another souvenir, they picked up a scallop shell, the symbol of pilgrims. They returned home on another hazardous journey. Finally, they showed the scallop shell and the pilgrimage badge to awestruck friends and family.

Now in the age of space colonization, pilgrims flew from the Earth to the Moon in space liners. The flight took three days. They arrived at Timonium Base, stayed in luxurious hotels, and ate in fine restaurants. Then they stepped into a teleporter, turned into an energy stream, and rematerialized at Arcadia Base. At Arcadia Base, they got food and rested at a cafeteria run by the scientists, not at a hostel run by monks. Next, they teleported to the unauthorized shrine. They could buy a European Space Agency T-shirt as a pilgrimage badge. Instead of getting a scallop shell, they could get a moon rock. Finally, they returned home, as soon as a week after they had started.

The pilgrimage had changed greatly over two thousand years. Yet its motive stayed the same.

Both Alphonse's and Wycliffe's pocket computers rang at the same time. When they both answered their pocket computers, they heard the same person: John Layman, President and Chief Executive Officer of Timonium Base. His image appeared on the computers' small screens.

"Alphonse, Father, I have something to show both of you," Layman said. "Go to Alphonse's office and download an incoming message. You'll see it better on a large screen."

They went to Alphonse's office. Alphonse checked his computer for incoming messages and opened one from John Layman. Aerial photographs appeared on Alphonse's office viewscreen.

Wycliffe recognized the outline of Yue 1, the Chinese moonbase.

"I received these photographs from an ESA surveillance satellite," Layman said. "Look what the Chinese have built: missile silos."

Wycliffe remembered his service in the Royal Auxiliary Air Force. As an officer, he had seen aerial reconnaissance photos of airports, military bases, roads, harbors, and missile silos. He recognized nine squat domes, each a cupola of a missile silo. Beneath each cupola would be a missile waiting to launch.

"Those weren't there before, were they?" Wycliffe asked as he looked at the other photographs.

"No, they were not," Alphonse said. "The Chinese built their silo field very quickly."

"This explains the great influx of work crews into Yue 1 in recent months," said Wycliffe. "This is no surprise, though. We knew the Chinese brought new ballistic missiles to the Moon."

"But now they can launch them," Layman said.

"To Liberty?" Alphonse asked.

"Or to anywhere on the Moon, including our bases," Wycliffe said.

———

Wycliffe noticed that the teleporter technician was wearing a badge of our Lady of the Moon. The shiny silver badge shone above the Belgian flag on his blue jumpsuit.

The women customers of Café Méliès had voted Auguste Peeters the "Hottest Man on the Moon." At the nightclub's contest, Auguste had thrown off his shirt, danced in a drunken stupor, let a barmaid pour beer into his thick brown hair, and passed out surrounded by shrieking women. The next day, a woman went to St. Dominic's Church. She giggled as she confessed her lustful thoughts about Auguste's athletic body. Father Wycliffe smelled the alcohol on her breath and told her to donate five euros to charity as penance. She wasn't even Roman Catholic.

Why was the Hottest Man on the Moon wearing a badge of the Virgin Mary?

"Auguste, I didn't know you are Catholic," Wycliffe said.

"I am not," Auguste Peeters replied plainly.

Father Wycliffe suspected something odd about Auguste's new veneration of the Virgin. "You're not? What's your religion anyway?"

"I do not actually have a religion, although my paternal grandparents belonged to a Dutch Reformed Church."

"Then why are you wearing a badge of the Virgin Mary?"

"You will notice that this silver badge is not sold at the merchandise booth." Auguste reached into his pocket and pulled out a small plastic bag full of the badges. He grinned. "I bought the whole supply. Girls see the badge, cannot find it at the merchandise booth, and want one. If the girl is pretty, I give her mine and invite her to dinner. I met an Italian girl that way."

The Moon colonists' resourcefulness never failed to amaze Father Wycliffe. He nodded silently and stepped into the teleporter booth.

Alphonse walked by. "Leaving now?"

"Back to Timonium," Wycliffe said. "I'm going to meet Carla Delgada."

Auguste smirked at Father Wycliffe. Wycliffe scowled back at him.

Alphonse said, "The investigation continues."

"Yes, it does, despite interruptions like installing the teleporters."

"Remember, the scientists of the Arcadia Base are praying that the apparition is real. We need more money for supplies and equipment."

"You and your crew are quite resourceful. I'm sure you can think of another way to get money from the tourists," Wycliffe said.

Seconds later, he dematerialized and became an energy beam shooting to Timonium Base.

———

Wycliffe stepped off the teleporter booth at Timonium Base. A group of people walked into the booth behind him. He looked back and saw one of them carry a statue of Our Lady of the Moon. Was the ESA selling them at Timonium too now?

He heard a beep-beep sound, like a car horn. An electric cart stopped in front of him. The cart's driver, a man in his thirties, looked impressive in his blue suit and black shirt. He must have bought the clothes where the highest business executives shopped.

"Father Wycliffe, do you need a ride?" the man asked.

"Going towards Café Méliès?"

The man nodded. "Get in."

"Thanks, John," Wycliffe said, and he climbed into the cart. John Layman, President and Chief Executive Officer of Timonium Base, drove the cart into the commercial district.

Timonium was a small city enclosed in dozens of connected buildings. The commercial district was the largest building. It covered five hundred thousand square meters, enough space for a hundred and four football fields.

Modeled on a European shopping gallery, it was an arcade with tall arches and vaults holding up a transparent ceiling. Its five levels had hotels, restaurants, shops, travel agencies, banks, theaters, and even an amusement park and a hospital. Giant viewscreens showed advertisements for goods ranging from beer to shoes. The mall glittered with shiny steel and colorful lights. Since the ceiling was made of lightweight transparent radiation shielding, the shoppers could watch small spacecraft hover and fly over Timonium.

He saw businesses catering to the newest type of tourist on the Moon. A shop sold crucifixes, Rosary beads, and statues of saints. It sold various versions of the Virgin Mary, such as Our Lady of Perpetual Help, Our Lady of Lourdes, and Our Lady of Guadalupe. The Jesus statues came in various versions too, such as the Sacred Heart of Jesus, the Infant of Prague, and the Divine Infant Jesus. A woman carried a statue of Our Lady of Fatima out of the store.

Layman and Wycliffe paused for pedestrians at a British pub called the Devil's Pitchfork. The pub's sign showed the Devil holding a pitchfork. Another sign read "Now serving fish and chips on Friday" as if the pub had never before served fish and chips on Friday. The smells of fried fish and roast beef wafted from the Devil's Pitchfork. Wycliffe could hear the chatter of a large crowd inside the pub. A man wearing a large wooden cross around his neck walked out of the Devil's Pitchfork.

They continued driving and approached a hotel. Dozens of people, led by a man carrying the Filipino flag, swarmed out of the hotel.

"The hotel is fully booked this week despite the political situation," Layman said. "We never had so much business before."

Wycliffe knew that a recognized apparition of Mary could permanently boost a town's fortunes. Every hotel, restaurant, and souvenir shop in Mexico City, Lourdes, Knock, and Fatima served visitors all year round. Entire towns reaped financial wealth, not just spiritual benefits, from pilgrimage and prayer.

"I'm not religious, and I'm not trying to bias you, but I hope you conclude that the apparition is real," Layman said.

Wycliffe asked, "Will you actually believe in the apparition if I conclude that it's supernatural, genuine, and worthy of veneration?"

"No, but as CEO of this base, I appreciate the business it brings."

"Repay to Caesar what belongs to Caesar and to God what belongs to God."

Layman laughed softly.

They drove towards Piazza Cassini, Timonium's town square. BBC Space's headquarters faced the Piazza. Above the BBC Space headquarters, a viewscreen dominated the square. As some shoppers walked through the square, others watched the viewscreen.

It showed a balding man, about sixty years old. His face was like a hawk's. He stood on a stage, behind a U.S. flag and a sign proclaiming "THE PROPHECY OF THE REVELATION OF JOHN: WE CAN MAKE IT HAPPEN." In front of him, people listened silently. Wycliffe guessed that the man and his audience were in a conference center somewhere in the United States.

"That's Michael Crowberry," Wycliffe said. "Why is he on the BBC?"

"It's a news documentary about him," Layman said. "BBC Space has shown it twice in the last week. He's become very popular in America because of the war scare."

Wycliffe looked at his watch. "I have some extra time before I have to meet Carla Delgada. Can we stop and watch the TV?"

"Yes, of course," Layman said. He drove into a waiting lane and parked the cart.

Crowberry's deep, forceful voice rose above the din of the shopping mall. "Every international crisis matches an event foretold in the *Book of the Revelation of John*. Just read chapter six. It says that each time a seal is broken, another horseman rides out and brings a curse from God. Just think of the past two years. In that short time, four seals have been broken, and each time, God has punished mankind.

"You're asking what does *Revelation* mean when it says a seal is broken? I'll tell you what it means. What was the traditional way for a king to show that a law is important? By putting his wax seal on a parchment of the law. In the past two years, we've broken important laws four times, and each time, God punished us.

"Broken seal number one. President Darby changed the *Coinage Act* so the motto "In God We Trust" won't appear on gold units, our last coin. The Roman Cardinal of New York, Brad Kensington, protested to keep the national motto on the gold unit. His protests made him very popular with the Cardinals of the Roman Church; so popular that they elected him Bishop of Rome. Now he calls himself Pope Christopher. We Christians can agree with the Bishop of Rome that "In God We Trust" belongs on our coins. But remember he's a Papist, indeed, the leader of all Papists. Don't be fooled by the odd time he agrees with real Christians. Here is the rider of the white horse: the False Prophet."

Wycliffe said, "That's not new. Someone has accused every Pope of being a fraud for the last two thousand years."

Crowberry continued. "Broken seal number two. After we defeated the Purists in Purist Arabia, the former Purist Arabians had no government, and we did not occupy their country or prop up a government for them. In this total absence of law, all sorts of factions have fought each other in a civil war. A million people have died; they have lost more people in their civil war than in the Vernacular Wars. Here is the rider of the red horse: war.

"Broken seal number three: Purists no longer rule Indonesia, but the new dictatorship is equally uncivilized. The Indonesian government is not following its own food law. Corruption, greed, and ethnic hatred have destroyed the food supply in Aceh Province. Half a million people have died there. Here is the rider of the black horse: famine.

"Broken seal number four. We know the Ten Commandments are the Law of God. If only the Martian colonists had known that. Many of them were atheists, people who reject the Ten Commandments, people like Dr. Thomas Hall, the famous neurologist. What did God do when we populated another planet with atheists? He sent a giant rock to smite them. Here is the rider of the pale horse: death."

Father Wycliffe grunted. "They were all good people on Mars, believers and non-believers alike. God didn't kill them. A meteorite killed them."

The camera zoomed in on Crowberry. He continued preaching: "All these disasters point to one conclusion: the End Times are coming. Are you ready to accept Jesus as your personal Lord and Savior? Will you be ready for Jesus to judge you? Will the Lord take you to heaven in the Rapture? Or will you be left behind on Earth to suffer, die, and descend to Hell? Are you a real Christian? Or do you belong to one of those churches that says it's Christian but really isn't? This is your last chance to abandon the false idols, the false beliefs, the false prophets..."

The picture changed to the Crowberry Mission's volunteers cooking food for hurricane victims in Florida, building houses for people left homeless by a California earthquake, and giving water to firefighters at the Oregon forest fires.

"The Crowberry Mission earned the respect and admiration of the American people by sending hundreds of volunteers to help relief efforts in disasters across their country," the BBC narrator reported. "However, the focus of the Crowberry Mission changed when President Darby put the military on the Moon."

Next, the TV showed Crowberry meeting U.S. President Darby, various members of the U.S. Congress, and Cabinet secretaries. Wycliffe recognized the Secretary of Defense, the Secretary of Homeland Security, and the Secretary of Space Colonization. These were the Cabinet members who had gotten President Darby to send troops and weapons on the Moon.

The BBC narrator said, "When the U.S. put military forces on the Moon, Crowberry saw the fulfillment of Biblical prophecy. Rather than simply wait for Biblical prophecies to come true, he thinks people can make them happen. He has encouraged the U.S. to fight a war against China and other countries for control of the Moon. He thinks a war will cause the events prophesized in the *Book of Revelation* — and bring the End Times, the time of troubles ending with the second coming of Jesus Christ.

"Since Crowberry has started teaching that people can make Biblical prophecies happen, ten thousand people have joined the Crowberry Mission. Donations to the Mission rose to a record fifty million dollars last year. Crowberry uses the money to lobby the U.S. Government to put more troops and weapons on the Moon."

"The times sure are crazy, aren't they?" Layman said. "A conservative Christian is supporting a fundamentalist atheist for President."

"Yeah, the times are crazy," Wycliffe agreed.

"Crowberry's getting a lot of End Timers, isn't he?" Layman said as he restarted the cart and drove back onto the street.

"He's the type of church leader who thrives in times of trouble," Wycliffe said. "He's using the *Book of Revelation* to scare people. He says every recent disaster matches an event in *Revelation*, so *Revelation* predicts the future. But people have matched wars and disasters to *Revelation* for centuries, and the world hasn't ended. Most theologians don't think *Revelation* predicts the future. Martin Luther said *Revelation* is not a work of prophecy."

"A Catholic priest quoting Martin Luther for support; that's really a sign of the Apocalypse," Layman joked.

They stopped at a storefront decorated with a large painting of the Moon with a human face and a rocket stuck in the Moon's eye. It was a scene from an old silent film, *Le Voyage Dans la Lune*, by movie pioneer Georges Méliès.

The sign read "Café Méliès" in flowing blue and white Art Nouveau lettering. They had arrived at the largest restaurant, bar, and nightclub on the Moon.

Wycliffe got out of the cart and said, "Thanks for the lift."

The priest entered the nightclub. No matter how many times he had come here, the decorations still amused him, a Vatican astronomer. Metal foil crescent moons and planets hung from the ceiling. One wall had a mural of a craggy, mountainous lunar landscape, complete with Selenite aliens. It was scientifically incorrect but true to the spirit of the Méliès film. Another wall had a mural of can-can girls of the Folies Bergère. It honored the chorus girls who danced in Méliès's films.

He saw Carla Delgada putting on her lipstick. Café Méliès waitresses dressed like the girls who push the spaceship into the cannon in *Le Voyage Dans la Lune*. Carla wore a tank top of blue and white horizontal stripes, over which she wore a short-sleeved white blouse. She also wore blue hot pants, white go-go boots, and a white wide-brimmed hat. She looked like a naval showgirl.

This twenty-one year old barmaid was the visionary who had seen the Virgin Mary on the Moon.

She was petite, slim, and very pretty, with large brown eyes and shiny black hair down to her shoulders. Despite his vow of celibacy, Father Wycliffe could still appreciate a beautiful woman. He could admire the beauty that God created in His universe.

Wycliffe had even been married to a beautiful woman, but a long time ago.

"Carla," he called out.

Carla turned around and smiled. "Father Wycliffe, welcome back."

"Thanks for agreeing to see me before your shift."

"No problem. Let's sit here." She led him to a table. A photo of Auguste Peeters, Hottest Man on the Moon, hung on the wall beside the table. Carla looked at the photo, giggled, and turned back to Father Wycliffe.

"What do you want to know this time?" Carla asked.

"Just finishing the interview," Wycliffe said. "Let's talk about the news channels, reporters, and other people who have talked to you. When you told your story to them, did they ever pay you or give you gifts of some sort?"

"No."

"Have any of the pilgrims or tourists given you money?"

"No."

"Do you intend to sell your story, like book or movie deals?"

Carla laughed. "As if anyone would want to pay hundreds of gold units to make a movie about me. No, I won't sell book or movie rights for my story. That seems so sleazy, using religion to make money. My grandmother would kill me. She's so pious, more pious than the Pope."

"Well, if we ever let a woman have the job, we'll keep her in mind," Wycliffe joked.

She's not profiting from her experience, he concluded. The apparition story had passed a test of authenticity –- but it would need to pass more tests to be approved.

Wycliffe asked, "Aside from a few TV and news interviews, you haven't said much to the public, have you?"

"I don't know what else to say about it," Carla replied. "Some people visit the restaurant and ask me about God, Jesus, Mary, politics, war, the Pope, abortion, and other things, but I don't want to get involved in those things."

"There's nothing wrong with keeping a low profile," Wycliffe told her. Indeed, he was glad that she had refrained from preaching on controversial topics. Sometimes the visionaries would rant without Church authority. Some announced that Mary had condemned every doctrine of the Catholic Church. Others, inspired by Mary, urged people to be more Catholic than the Pope. Neither extreme did anyone any good.

"I'm glad to hear that your boss isn't annoyed by the publicity about you anymore," Wycliffe said.

"I'm so glad he's over it. It was rough at first. He didn't want people to come and gawk at me. He thought hordes of people would stand outside the restaurant, block the doorway, and keep the paying customers out. I was afraid he would fire me. But the hordes were hungry and ordered food and drinks. We even started a fried fish special on Fridays. Business has never been so good. Alas, my pay didn't go up.

"And no, the pilgrims and tourists don't get in the way. I know some of them want to talk and talk and talk to me, but I don't let them do it forever. I kindly tell them that I have to go serve the other customers in my section. I would lose my job if I didn't go to all my tables."

Carla looked at her watch. "Oh, my shift's going to start in a minute."

"I don't have any more questions, but I do have two more requests," Wycliffe said.

"Yes?"

Wycliffe hesitated. He wasn't sure how to ask the next question.

"Would you be willing to undergo a neurological test and a psychiatric examination?" he finally asked.

Carla looked surprised. "Hah! You think I'm crazy?"

"No, not at all," Wycliffe reassured her. "They're just standard scientific tests in investigating apparitions of Mary. A good scientist has to eliminate as much doubt as possible."

"Getting my head examined — alright, I'll do it because my grandmother asked me to cooperate with you."

"Thank you. I appreciate your cooperation very much."

"I'm surprised by all the questions, and now, the psychiatric test," Carla said. "I thought you would just take it on faith that I saw the actual Virgin Mary. That's faith, isn't it: believing something because you feel it so strongly that you don't need proof? My grandmother believes in God on faith. The people who visit the shrine believe my story on faith. They don't need any proof.

"You're a priest, you're a religious person, but you're different from my grandmother or the people at the shrine. You want a credible witness. You want scientific evidence. But a vision of Mary is inherently unscientific, isn't it? You're using science to study something that's unscientific.

"You preach about God and things that aren't scientific, but at the same time, you want scientific evidence of things. Do you think that's contradictory? Does the science and religion get complicated for you?"

Wycliffe pointed at the lapel pin on his jacket. "See that? It's from the Vatican observatory, one of the oldest astronomy institutes in the world. The Pope has his own observatory just outside Rome. Contrary to what the atheist fundamentalists say, the Roman Catholic Church has always encouraged scientific learning.

"And yes, the relationship between religion and science is very complex. There's nothing simple or unambiguous about it."

———

Wycliffe stayed at Café Méliès after the interview. He ordered a beer, which Carla brought promptly.

He watched her take the order at another table. As she brought their drinks and hamburgers, he overheard the customers talk to Carla about the apparition.

"Does Our Lady still talk to you?" a customer asked.

"No, I haven't seen her since that first time," Carla replied. She chuckled. "I guess I'm not holy enough."

"But even seeing her once is a blessing," a woman said.

Another man said, "'Use it in peace or not at all.' Do you think she was urging us to avoid war with China at all costs? Or do you think she was urging us to bring peace by defeating China in war?"

Carla shrugged. "I really don't know. I haven't really thought about it that much."

"May we take a photo with you?" the woman asked. She took a camera out of her handbag.

"Why, of course, sure," Carla chirped. "A lot of customers take my photograph. Yay, I'll be the most famous bar waitress on the Moon!" She smiled as the customers took turns taking photos with her.

As Carla walked back to the kitchen, the bar hostess led another customer to a table. Wycliffe gasped when he saw the customer.

Mary, the Virgin of Space Station Troika, sat down at the table and looked at the drink menu. Carla went to Mary, took her order, and walked to the bar.

Wycliffe went to the bar. "Carla, do you know that woman who just sat down at the table over there?"

Carla looked back and shook her head. "No. Should I recognize her? Is she someone famous?"

"No," Wycliffe lied. "She looks familiar, but I don't remember from where. I'm sure I'll remember later."

"You look like you've seen a ghost. Are you feeling okay?"

"Uh, yes, I'm fine. Thanks."

He walked to Mary's table. As at Troika, the sweet scent of roses surrounded her. A light glinted off her silver crescent moon pendant.

"Hail Mary," he said.

Mary looked up and smiled.

"Father Wycliffe! I was wondering when I would see you here," she said. She motioned to the other seat at the table. "Won't you sit down?"

Wycliffe sat down. "I can't believe you're here."

Mary smiled. "You're always having trouble believing that I'm here."

"Part of me wants to believe that I really did see you at Troika, but another part of me thinks you were an illusion caused by the Siren Stone."

"I don't blame you. You're a man of both faith and science. I appreciate that you want to believe that I appeared to you. You Marian priests flatter me so much! But the scientific, analytical part of your mind is right to question what I am."

"If you're here, does that mean there's a Siren Stone here?"

"Do you see one?"

"Are we sitting above one?"

Mary smiled coyly back at him.

"The political situation is frightful here, isn't it?" she said, changing the subject. "I've been warning the human race about violence and war for years, but do people ever listen?"

Carla arrived and put a glass of red wine in front of Mary.

"Let me guess. It's a sweet wine that's kosher for Passover," Wycliffe said.

Mary nodded. "Yes, it is. You knew I would order that, didn't you?"

"Uh, do you two know each other?" Carla said, looking puzzled.

Wycliffe realized this scene must look strange to Carla. Only a minute ago, he had told her that he didn't know the woman. Now he was sitting at her table and talking to her. Perhaps men like Auguste Peeters approached strange women and chatted with them at Café Méliès, but Father Wycliffe certainly didn't.

"My name's Mary. Father Wycliffe knows me from a church in his hometown," Mary said.

"Which town is that?" Carla said.

"Walsingham, England," Wycliffe said. "The town with two shrines dedicated to the Virgin Mary."

"But he hasn't been there for years, so it took him a while to remember from where he had known me," Mary explained.

"I see," Carla said. She still seemed puzzled. "I'll go check on my other tables. If you need anything, just let me know."

After Carla left, Wycliffe said, "She claims to have seen you on the Moon. Did you appear to her?"

"Yes." Mary took a sip of the red wine.

"Then why doesn't she recognize you now?"

"Did you ever notice how everyone sees Jesus as a long-haired man with a beard, but everyone sees me differently? Carla thinks of me as Our Lady of Fatima: pale skin, long white robe, a hood, and a crown. That's why I appeared to her as the Fatima image. She recognizes me in one guise and doesn't recognize me in another."

"That's helpful in traveling incognito, like on a secret mission. That brings me to my next question: what are you doing here?"

"My daughter's coming here to save the human race. The nations are dangerously close to another world war. Only *she* can stop them. I'm here to help her. And that's why you're here too."

"I'm supposed to help Jesus?"

Mary took another sip of the wine. "Yes, she's always needed humans to help her. Apostles, disciples, missionaries, martyrs..."

"Martyrs?"

"Sorry, no one needs to die for God and Jesus this time. At least, I hope not, I pray not. Don't worry. You'll be fine, and you'll do a good job. Better you than him." Mary pointed to the TV behind him.

Wycliffe turned around to look at the TV. Pastor Michael Crowberry was on BBC Space again. Why did the End Timer always appear on the news? This time, he was speaking from the City Hall of Dayton, Tennessee.

"It says in the Bible that Jesus will come back to judge the living and the dead," Crowberry announced. "There will be wars of death and destruction. The End Times are soon enough that we will all live to see them. They may be just months or weeks away. God is coming to punish the sinners, the idolaters, and the unbelievers.

"If you think God is only a bringer of love and forgiveness, think again. Nowhere does the Bible say that God feels nothing but love and forgives everyone. If that is what you think, you have created a false idol to make yourself feel good. Belief in this false god allows teachers to teach the *theory* of evolution as proven fact, allows our government to recognize idol-worshipping cults as legitimate religions, allows our lawmakers to make laws that are against the Ten Commandments..."

From behind Wycliffe, Mary said, "This might not seem obvious to many people: his heart loves God and humanity, but his mind fears the world around him. My daughter will come and make everything right again so that he will have nothing to fear."

"About your daughter..." Wycliffe began as he turned around.

Mary was gone. She had left a gold unit as payment beside the empty wine glass.

After the last daily Mass at St. Dominic's Church, some visitors approached Father Wycliffe.

"Father Wycliffe, I have come all the way from Mexico," a woman said. She appeared to be in her late forties and wore a medal of Our Lady of Guadalupe.

"Mexico? I visited the Basilica of Our Lady of Guadalupe when I was training as a priest. Nice to meet you," Wycliffe said. "And your name is...?"

"Yolanda," the woman said. She looked around. "This church is not what I expected. It looks very plain and Protestant."

"All churches in space are like this."

"In Mexico, we have side altars and statues of saints and votive candles and medals and novenas and incense. We carried a statue of Mary in a procession in the month of May, and we had pilgrimages to shrines, which we decorated with flowers and holy cards. We saw the candles, we heard the liturgy, we smelled the incense, we touched the statues, and we tasted the Eucharist. We could see, hear, smell, touch, and taste God. Then the Pope told us to leave all our sacramentals on Earth when we went into space. He stripped us of our statues and incense and medals and processions. Now we honor a silent, invisible Protestant God in a boring, plain church."

"The style of the church is not of great importance. Our separated brethren, the Protestants, love and serve God just as much as we do," Wycliffe said.

"I'm sure that they do, but I want to worship God our way, not their way," Yolanda replied. "I feel there is something missing in this church. These plain white walls feel empty to me."

She pointed at the empty cross hanging behind the altar. "*That* feels empty to me."

Wycliffe silently nodded in agreement. The crucifix, showing Jesus on the cross, had marked the difference between Roman Catholic and Protestant churches for centuries. It still did on Earth -- but not in space.

"I understand what you are saying, but the Holy Father thinks that obvious displays of our faith will offend the leaders of the space colonies," he said. "He orders us to show some restraint out here."

"If we cannot express our faith out here, perhaps we should not be here," Yolanda said sadly.

"It is the order of our ecclesiastical authority," Wycliffe said.

Yolanda looked blankly at him. He knew that look; simply citing Papal authority no longer convinced everyone, if anyone.

A man about Yolanda's age stepped forward. "Yolanda, maybe the father will want to come to the shrine with us," he suggested in Spanish, a language that Wycliffe understood.

"That is a good idea, Armando," Yolanda replied.

Wycliffe noticed that Armando was holding a gold pyx, a small round container used to carry the Eucharist to those too sick or unable to come to church.

Beside Armando was another man. He looked about thirty years old, younger than Armando and Yolanda, but he limped with a cane. He wore a green shirt with empty shoulder straps, a military shirt without the rank epaulettes.

"I see you are carrying a pyx," Wycliffe mentioned to Armando in Spanish.

Armando held up the pyx. "It contains the Eucharist that our priest gave us back home. We are going to the shrine so that Manuel..." — he motioned to the younger man — "...may receive the Eucharist there. If he receives the body of Christ at the blessed site where Christ's mother appeared, maybe God will heal his leg. We pray the Blessed Virgin will intercede for Manuel, for he was wounded while defending the banner of Our Lady."

Manuel straightened up. "Maybe she will ask God to heal me, maybe she will not. I will lose nothing in trying," he said. "My regiment carried a banner of the Virgin of Guadalupe in the Vernacular Wars. The Taliban ambushed my unit, and I was lucky to suffer only a wounded leg in Mexico City. My fellow soldiers were not so lucky. I believe the Virgin protected me. Maybe she will bless me again."

In the Battle of Mexico City, American Taliban fought the Mexican Army in the streets. Mexico City had no strategic advantage in the Vernacular Wars, but the Islamic Purists wanted to capture Guadalupe, the second most-visited Catholic shrine in the world. The Purists loved symbolic victories, but Mexico City would not be theirs. After a month of bloody fighting, the Mexicans defeated them.

"I was a military chaplain," Wycliffe said. "I'm glad to meet another veteran. God bless you."

Manuel bowed and smiled back at Wycliffe.

Armando shook Wycliffe's hand. "I hear you installed the teleporters at the moonbases?" Armando said. "Thank you. Did you also install the teleporter at the shrine too?"

"No, someone else from the European Space Agency installed that one," Wycliffe answered.

Cardinal Saint-Cloud thought people would interpret a priest's presence as official approval of the shrine and the apparition. Hence, an ESA engineer installed the teleporter at the shrine.

"Will you come to the shrine and bless it? No priest has ever visited the shrine. A priest's blessing would mean much to the people," Yolanda asked.

"No, I cannot," Wycliffe said. "That's not an opinion about the pilgrims, though. I'm sure that the shrine attracts sincere and devout people."

"I understand," Yolanda said. "It was a pleasure to meet you, Father. We will come again for Mass before we go back home."

As the Mexicans left the church, Wycliffe overheard Yolanda say to the two men:

"We will go to the apparition shrine tomorrow. The Church may abandon us in these dangerous times, but Our Lady will not."

The Church has not abandoned you, Wycliffe thought. *I will be at the shrine — incognito but still there.*

———

Cardinal Saint-Cloud looked at Wycliffe by videophone. "Why do you wish to visit an unauthorized shrine?" the Cardinal asked.

"It's part of the investigation," Wycliffe explained. "I want to observe the spiritual fruits of the alleged apparition. Are people becoming more devout to God and the Church; or are people promoting ideas contrary to our Church's doctrine? I think I need to see what goes on at the shrine."

"Very well," Cardinal Saint-Cloud said. "Take precautions to prevent the image of ecclesiastical approval for the apparition and the shrine. Do not wear your clerical clothes or your Roman collar. Dress in regular clothes, like any other tourist. Do not celebrate Mass there, do not perform any sacraments there, and do not bless anything there, not even a medal or a rosary."

"Agreed. I'll just watch what happens," Father Wycliffe promised.

———

Wycliffe materialized in the apparition shrine's reception area. In this area, pilgrims walked around. They wore crosses on their necks, carried rosaries and statues of Mary, and chattered in various languages. Some wore national costumes and carried flags of Portugal, France, the Philippines, Bolivia, Lebanon, Zimbabwe, and other countries. There was even a man dressed in a brown robe, who chanted the Kyrie Prayer in Greek.

He recognized the teleporter operator. Like Carla Delgada, Roxanne von Gotha was another young woman who came to the Moon for adventure and money early in her career. She wore a blue jumpsuit with an Austrian flag and blue baseball cap with the ESA logo. In her spacecraft technician's clothes, she looked out of place among the pilgrims.

As the pilgrims passed her, Roxanne gave them leaflets advertising the cafeteria in Arcadia. Before she studied spacecraft technology, the cute blond girl had guided tourists through Mozart's birthplace in Salzburg. No wonder Alphonse Bangolo sent her to operate the teleporter at the shrine.

She saw Father Wycliffe and waved at him.

"Why, Father, I did not expect — " she began before Wycliffe held his finger to his lips.

"I'm traveling incognito, Roxanne," he whispered to her. "How's it going here?"

"Another normal day at the Moon's biggest tourist attraction," Roxanne replied. "There are plenty of people coming and going. It reminds me of the admission gate at the Mozart museum."

She held up an advertising flyer and grinned wryly. "I went to three years of spacecraft technology training, and I am handing advertising flyers to tourists again."

"But no ordinary tour guide can operate a machine that turns people into energy, transmits them kilometers away, and reassembles them as matter."

"I am only joking, not complaining. I like this job. It is rather nice to see people enjoying themselves here."

"That's something I need to observe. Where's the chapel?"

Roxanne pointed down a hallway, and Wycliffe left for the chapel.

As Father Wycliffe walked through the hallway, he marveled at the work of private individuals. No space agency, government, or church had built the shrine. Lunar colonists, space station engineers, spacecraft technicians, and visitors had used surplus spaceship and space station parts to build the blue dome and everything within it. They scavenged both Earth and the Moon for everything from the airlock doors to the lightweight radiation shielding. They built the chapel, the meeting rooms, the artwork and décor, the airlocks, the vehicle docks, the life support systems, and the electrical systems within six months of Carla seeing the apparition.

In the twentieth century, philosophers predicted that science and technology would replace religion and faith in the human mind. Yet here and now, people were using science and technology to celebrate their religion and faith.

———

The pilgrims sat in plastic seats, the same type used in moon buses. Pilgrims also knelt around the chapel's altar. No priest had yet celebrated Mass here, but the pilgrims had built the altar in case a priest came. The altar was a metal storage box, the type used to carry cargo on lunar supply ships. An artist had painted scenes of the life of Jesus on it.

The pilgrims seemed to have put the décor randomly throughout the chapel. Hundreds of icons, holy cards, posters, crosses, crucifixes, plaques, paintings, hand-drawn pictures, and postcards cluttered the walls. The images ranged from postcards of Pope Christopher to a crayon drawing of the Nativity. Along the walls, tables were crammed with candles, framed pictures, and statues. There were statues of every version of Mary, Jesus, and popular saints. There were many statues of St. Jude, patron saint of desperate and hopeless causes.

Each person prayed or chanted in a different language. A woman recited the Rosary in English. A young man prayed to the Sacred Heart of Jesus in Spanish to save his father's health. A group of Filipinos kneeled and recited a novena to Santo Niño de Cebú in unison. The man in the brown robe continued walking and chanting the Kyrie in Greek. A man with a white beard stood and sang:

Gloria in excelsis deo, et in terra pax hominibus bonae volantatis. Laudamus te. Benedicimus te. Adoramus te. Glorificamus te. Gratias agimus tibi propter magnam gloriam tuam.

"Glory to God in the highest, and peace to His people on Earth. We praise you, we bless you, we adore you, we glorify you, we give thanks to you for your great glory," Father Wycliffe silently translated to himself. It was the "Gloria in Excelsis Deo" in Latin.

The voices amazed him: all these people chanting, praying, and singing without harmony, yet united. He had rarely seen such raucous devotion.

Of course, he had attended many Masses, especially those on special days like Good Friday and Christmas Eve. He never doubted the worshippers' devotion at Mass, but the Church organized it into strict procedure. Mass has rules on when to sit, when to stand, when to kneel, when to talk, and when to stay silent. Mass had rules on what to say and how to say it. Worship in the lunar shrine was different from the sophisticated ritual of the official Church. Here was something inspired by folk traditions.

He reminded himself that this was an unofficial shrine, built on unconsecrated ground, honoring an apparition unapproved by Church authority. As a Papal legate, he could not approve of this unofficial worship.

But neither could he condemn it.

He heard a bell ring.

"All rise for the coronation of Mary!" someone shouted.

Everyone stood up. The sound system played a recording of "Cantate Domino" by Georg Friedrich Handel.

Father Wycliffe looked back and saw the door swing open. A man, about fifty years old with short grey hair, stood in the doorway. He looked like a soldier in a black shirt with a high collar, black pants with gold stripes down the sides, and black boots.

He also wore a white tabard, the short, sleeveless coat worn by medieval heralds. On his tabard was a coat of arms: a blue shield with a white fleur-de-lis or lily. The lily was a symbol of the Virgin Mary.

The herald swung a censer on a chain and led the procession into the chapel.

Behind the herald, a young African woman carried an ornate gold crown topped with a Maltese cross. She wore a white gown and a garland of flowers in her flowing, black hair. She seemed to glide in her white ballet slippers.

Wycliffe recognized the ritual figure immediately. Many British towns still chose a May Queen, a teenaged girl to walk at the front of the May Day parade. The May Queen's origin lay in Europe's pagan past, when the people chose a girl to represent the goddess of nature. The Greeks honored Artemis, goddess of the hunt, the wilderness, childbirth, and the Moon. The Romans honored Diana, the virgin goddess of the hunt, who later became a Moon goddess. Greeks and Romans dedicated the month of May to Artemis and Diana.

When the Europeans converted to Christianity, they continued their pagan rituals with a Christian flavor. Christianity did not have a goddess, but it had a virgin who had given birth to a god. Roman Catholics and Eastern Orthodox still crown a statue or icon of Mary in May. In England, the teenaged goddess evolved into the legendary Maid Marian and finally the May Queen.

The herald and the May Queen marched into the central aisle of the chapel. Behind the May Queen, four men carried the actual queen of the procession: a statue of the Virgin Mary as Our Lady of Fatima. As the statue passed people, they made the Sign of the Cross and bowed to it. Wycliffe smelled the sweet aroma of burning incense as the herald passed him.

The men put the statue of Mary on the altar. The herald turned to the audience.

"Long live the Immaculate Heart of Mary!" he shouted. The audience repeated the salute.

The herald announced more salutes, each repeated by the audience:

"Long live the Queen of the Universe!"

"Long live the Mediatrix of all graces!"

"Long live the Mother and Mistress of all Creation!"

A choir sang a Gregorian chant: "How holy and beautiful thou art, Mary, holy and beautiful..."

The herald prayed, "Dear Mary, Ever Virgin, you have shown yourself to a girl on this hill. You have come to bless the Moon, which is your dominion forever. Pray for us to the Lord our God that He will grant peace to the Moon, that He will inspire the nations to forsake war..."

After more songs and prayers, the May Queen placed the gold crown on the statue. She knelt in front of the statue and recited:

"*Ave Maria, gratia plena, Dominus tecum, benedicta Tu in mulieribus et benedictus fructus ventris tui, Iesus. Sancta Maria, Mater Dei, ora pro nobis peccatoribus nunc et in hora mortis nostrae. Amen.*"

It was the "Hail Mary" prayer in Latin. Everyone bowed to the statue again.

The herald proclaimed, "Thou shalt reign, Oh Mary, Immaculate Virgin! All the nations proclaim thy name and thy reign. Come, Holy Queen, Mother of God, may you reign forever and ever, amen!"

The sound system played the "Hymn and Pontifical March", the national anthem of the Vatican City State. The choir sang in Italian, "*Roma immortale di martiri e di santi...*"

"O Rome immortal, city of martyrs and saints..."

After the Pontifical anthem ended, the herald said, "All are welcome to honor and venerate the blessed statue!"

The crowd rushed forward to statue. Some people knelt in front of it. Others reached out to touch it. Some stood around it and bowed their heads.

Father Wycliffe saw the Mexicans who had visited St. Dominic's. Armando opened his pyx, took out a wafer of the Eucharist, and put it into Manuel's hand.

"The body of Christ," Armando said. "Accept his gift of finest wheat."

Manuel said, "Amen." He put the wafer in his mouth.

Wycliffe heard the ringing of his pocket computer. He took the computer out of his jacket and looked at the small screen. John Layman's face looked out from it.

"Father Wycliffe, where are you?" Layman asked.

"At the apparition shrine," Wycliffe replied.

"Inside the protection zone! I knew it," Layman said. He looked worried. "Get out of there. Come back to Timonium right away."

"Why?"

"I'm watching the Chinese base from a satellite feed. The cupola of a Chinese missile silo just opened. I think the Chinese are going to launch a missile any moment now."

Wycliffe was shocked. "A missile? Is it armed? Does it have a nuclear warhead?"

"I don't know," Layman admitted. "It doesn't matter; even an unarmed missile is bad. It doesn't need a warhead to damage a moonbase -- or the shrine. You're inside the protection zone. You're inside a target. Get out!"

Wycliffe pushed his way to the altar. He raised his hands and shouted, "Please! Please! Listen to me!"

Yolanda, one of the Mexican pilgrims, saw him. Her eyes gleamed in amazement. She shouted, "The priest from St. Dominic's Church!"

Excitement ran through the crowd. Their murmuring grew louder. Someone asked, "Is it official now? Does the Vatican recognize the apparition?"

A Chinese man approached Wycliffe. "Father, celebrate Mass here. For the honor of the Blessed Virgin," he urged.

"Listen to me! Everyone must leave the shrine! We have to get out now!" Wycliffe warned.

The crowd's excitement faded. Wycliffe saw their faces turn sad. Now they murmured in disappointment.

The herald went to Wycliffe. "Father, please let us pray here. We are all good Catholics and Christians, I assure you. We mean no offense to the Church. Certainly there can be no harm --"

The ground suddenly shook. The statue of Mary wobbled. At one of the tables, a small statue of St. Jude fell over.

The pilgrims turned silent. Then their voices erupted in questions: "Was that an earthquake? Did something explode? What's happening?"

Wycliffe rushed to a window. He saw a cloud of dust rising in the distance.

Layman's voice yelled from the pocket computer. "I saw it on the satellite feed! The Chinese launched a missile!"

"I think it crashed less than a quarter of a kilometer away from me," Wycliffe said to Layman.

He turned back to the pilgrims. "Please follow me! We're going back to Timonium Base. Don't rush, don't push, and stay calm."

As he led the pilgrims out of the chapel, Wycliffe guessed there were about a hundred people. The teleporter could hold ten people per transmission. Therefore, they would need at least ten transmissions to evacuate the shrine fully. Each transmission took at least three minutes, including time for boarding the departure booth and clearing the arrival booth. Then there were risks of wasted time: any panic or confusion could delay the evacuation; or the shrine's power supply could fail under the shock of crashing missiles. If the pilgrims stayed calm *and* if no technical problems arose, they would need at least thirty minutes.

That was plenty of time for a missile to fly from Yue 1 to the apparition shrine.

As they walked through the corridor, another shock wave shook the shrine. Some pilgrims cried in fear.

"Don't be afraid," Wycliffe shouted. "We're all leaving."

A surprised Roxanne von Gotha stared at the pilgrims as they swarmed into the reception area.

"I'll operate the teleporter," Wycliffe told Roxanne. "You're going back to Timonium Base with them."

"But Father, will you be left by yourself? I should stay too," Roxanne protested.

"No, you go. I'll stay. I know how to beam myself away."

The herald stepped out from the crowd. "Form into two lines!" he ordered. "That's it, two lines, just like when you're lining up for the Holy Eucharist.

We're all going to go into the teleporter booth in pairs until ten people have entered the booth. After the first group has gone, the next group goes. Help anyone who can't walk."

Wycliffe moved to the teleporter's control panel. "Get into the teleporter," he ordered Roxanne.

Roxanne nodded and stepped in. She left among the first ten people.

"Keep them coming," Wycliffe said.

The pilgrims left, one group after another. While they were leaving, three more shocks hit the shrine; three more missiles had crashed nearby.

Finally, the last ten pilgrims, including the herald, went into the booth. The herald turned to Father Wycliffe.

"God be with you," said the herald. "I'm sure that God will not let anyone harm you or this shrine."

"Thank you. I'll see you at Timonium Base," Wycliffe said.

He watched the last pilgrims dematerialize. Now he was alone.

Another missile shook the ground. The lights flickered.

He set the teleporter on a ten-second timer and moved towards the booth.

Then he saw the glint of gold on the floor. It was Armando's pyx. He must have dropped it by accident in the rush to leave.

He picked up the pyx and opened it. It still had some Eucharistic wafers.

He could not let the missiles blow up the body of Christ. He grasped the pyx and rushed into the teleporter booth.

A second later, he dematerialized.

———

After he rematerialized, he realized that his hands were empty. The pyx was gone.

Then he sensed that he was not alone.

A teenaged girl stood beside him. She had tied her reddish-brown hair in a ponytail. She wore a white shirt, a green school tie, a green plaid skirt, and a silver tiara. A gold Star of David hung on a chain around her neck.

She grinned as he stared at her.

"Oh, Jesus Christ," he muttered.

The pretty girl giggled. "Yes, that's me!"

PART 4
THE REVELATION

9 / THE CHINESE PUZZLE

Alphonse rushed to the teleporter booth. "You got out just in time," he said.

"What do you mean?" Wycliffe said. He stepped out of the teleporter booth and looked back at Jessica. The schoolgirl followed him.

"Come look at the replay," Alphonse said, leading Wycliffe to a booth with a sign reading "AIR AND SPACE TRAVELLER'S INSURANCE: BEST PRICE HERE". The insurance agent watched a small television.

BBC Space showed a view of Apparition Hill. Suddenly, a missile appeared in the sky. Flames were shooting out of the missile's body.

The missile slammed into the side of the hill. A massive fireball burst from the hillside. The intense fire died after three minutes, the time to exhaust the missile's liquid oxygen. In that short time, the heat and the force of the crash threw tons of soil into the sky. When the soil settled, a wide crater was on the side of the hill.

In contrast, the shrine looked undamaged. Not even a dent appeared on the blue dome and white statue of Mary. The communications tower at the hill's base had also survived undamaged.

"I thought the shock of the rocket's impact would have destroyed the shrine," Alphonse said. "It is a miracle that the shrine survived."

Jessica giggled. "A miracle. Thanks to me."

"But big buildings sometimes survive against probability," Wycliffe said. "The Genbaku Dome in Hiroshima, for example. It's the Hiroshima Peace

Memorial now. The tower survived the nuclear blast while all the buildings around it collapsed."

Jessica frowned. "Spoilsport."

Alphonse looked at Jessica and asked, "Who are you?"

"My name's Jessica. I'm a schoolgirl visiting the Moon."

"Ah, an educational trip. I am sorry that it ended this way," Alphonse replied. He turned back to the TV.

Alphonse saw Jessica too. *There must be a Siren Stone in the area*, Wycliffe thought.

BBC Space showed an animated graphic of the Moon Punisher 1 missile. The editor of *Jane's Defense Weekly* talked about the Moon Punisher 1. It was the first ballistic missile created especially for use on the Moon; it was a single-engine rocket that used a solid fuel with liquid oxygen as the oxidizer; it could reach anywhere on the Moon; European and U.S. defense ministries suspected that the Chinese had not tested the Moon Punisher 1 before today's test launches; and all the tests were failures.

"This is a video of another Moon Punisher launch, taped by a surveillance satellite," the BBC announcer said. "This is the second missile, the one that crashed five hundred meters from an American helium-3 mining plant."

The missile shot straight up from its missile silo and into the sky. Forty-five seconds into the flight, a flame burst from the middle of the missile. Then the missile flew shakily in an arc. In mere seconds, it wobbled, dived, slammed into the ground, and exploded.

"The Chinese launched seven Moon Punisher missiles today," the BBC announcer said. "All seven missiles failed. All the missiles crashed in the U.S. protection zone. One crashed on Apparition Hill. We hear that everyone evacuated safely from the shrine. Fortunately, none of the missiles carried warheads, nuclear or otherwise, or else the explosions and destruction would have been much worse."

The Chinese Ambassador to France appeared on TV next. The French Minister of Foreign Affairs had hastily summoned him to Quai d'Orsay, the Ministry's headquarters. The Ambassador stood in the Galerie de la Paix, a room decorated with red curtains and images of Greek gods on the walls. Reporters gathered in front of him.

The Ambassador, looking tired, said, "The People's Republic did not intend for the missiles to land near the European Space Agency or United

States bases. Although China does not recognize the United States protection zone, that area was not the intended landfall for the missile tests."

The BBC announcer reappeared and said, "We have some live video images coming in. We're getting some pictures from the video camera on the communications tower at the base of Apparition Hill. It's showing us the crater on the side of the hill."

The video picture zoomed in on something gleaming in the dark.

"The lights on the communications tower are lighting up the crater. Something is reflecting light in the crater. It's dark yet shiny. What could it be?"

The BBC's science reporter appeared. "I'm not sure. It could be metal, stone, or plastic. It could be anything. Whatever it is, it appears to be black, but it's polished, which is why it can reflect some light."

Wycliffe turned to Jessica. "Do you know what's in the crater?"

Before Jessica could answer, Mary rushed to her. The mother threw her arms around the daughter.

"Jessica, dear! Thank God you've come!" Mary said.

"You called, and I came. Who says that your prayers are never answered quickly?" Jessica said.

"You've come just in time. There's trouble everywhere: countries are threatening to go to war, they put soldiers and weapons on the Moon, and now a rocket has crashed near my shrine. *My* shrine! And on *my* Moon!" Mary complained. "The human race is out of control. They won't survive World War Five. You've got to stop them!"

Jessica nodded. "I agree. This bitching between nations and throwing of nukes is retarded. It's such an unnecessary drama. It so needs to end."

"Good. Make a miracle, dear. Get the countries to take all their weapons off the Moon. Even better, get the countries to destroy them. I hate the nuclear bombs the most. Can you beat them into ploughshares? Or turn them into stone?"

"This is not the time to do that."

Mary sighed. "Oh, you're being stubborn again, like when you didn't want to turn water into wine at the wedding. The human race is at the brink of extinction. If this isn't the time, when is it?"

"Mommy, you misunderstand. I'm not going to destroy the nuclear weapons. I'm going to use them to start the last war. I'm here to destroy the human race."

Wycliffe saw the horror in Mary's eyes. She stared at her daughter in stunned silence. Wycliffe too was speechless.

Jessica looked around. "I haven't eaten since I was on Mars. Where I can get food here?"

At Café Méliès, Wycliffe and Mary watched Jessica eat chicken soup with a large matzoh ball.

At first, Wycliffe thought it odd that Jesus would eat matzoh ball soup. Would God come to the Moon and eat like a normal human? Then he realized that matzoh ball soup was the quintessential Jewish comfort food. The Savior, although divine, was also very human and had lived as an ordinary person, a humble carpenter.

And now she was an ordinary schoolgirl?

Wycliffe didn't know whether he was really sitting with Jesus and Mary. Were they physically present? Or was he sitting alone and hallucinating about them? Or maybe he was physically present and they were present as spirits.

Whatever she was, a physical being, an illusion, or a spirit, Mary appeared nervous. Wycliffe saw her look anxiously at her daughter.

Mary finally broke the silence. "Dear, about the purpose of your coming here. You are going to prevent a war, right?"

Jessica swallowed a spoonful of soup and shook her head. "No, I've got to start one. That'll bring peace to this sad, lame species." She looked over the table. "Is there any pepper here?"

Wycliffe motioned to Carla as she walked by. "Carla, can we please get some pepper?"

As Carla left, Wycliffe turned to Jessica. "You're the Prince, er, Princess of Peace. Yet you want a war? Why?"

Jessica said, "God gave a planet and the stars to the human race, and look at what you've done. War, racism, intolerance, genocide, famine. This is what you've done with the freedom that God gave you. You've totally messed up.

"It's time to start over again. That's why He created the Martians. They're your replacements."

The Troika crew had said that Jessica wanted to create life on Mars. The reason stunned Father Wycliffe. An entire species would replace another species.

"That's dreadful, I don't believe God would do that to us," Wycliffe said, not knowing what else to say. What does one tell Jesus if she wants to destroy the human race?

Jessica shrugged. "I'm sorry, but so be it."

With her spoon, she pushed the matzoh ball across the bowl of soup. She was playing with her food.

Carla returned with a peppershaker. Jessica looked up and said, "Way cool outfit! Where did you get it?"

"Thanks. It's cute, eh? It's the uniform for us girls at Café Méliès. You have to work here to get one," Carla said.

"Oh, what about the boots? Certainly I can buy boots like those without working here?"

"Yes, there's a shoe store in the commercial district that sells boots like these."

"Thanks for telling me. I'll definitely have to visit that store."

Carla left, and Jessica shook the pepper onto her soup. Mary took a deep breath and smiled weakly.

"People have been praying to me for peace," Mary said. "They want me to intercede with you and God to prevent the war. It will be very embarrassing to me if a war breaks out and the human race gets destroyed."

"Sorry, Mommy, but the end is coming. I created the world. I can destroy it."

Jessica pushed her spoon into the matzoh ball and broke it into pieces. She scooped up a piece, put it into her mouth, and chewed it.

———

Father Wycliffe showed them two bedrooms in St. Dominic's Church. "Visiting clergy like the Archbishop of Paris and Dr. Schiller stay in these rooms when they are here," he said. "Feel free to stay in them."

Jessica smiled. "Thanks for the room and board. I won't be much of an imposition on you. I won't be staying here for long."

"That's what I was afraid of."

Jessica spun around and grabbed Mary's arms. "Mommy, that waitress got me all excited about the shopping mall. I want to scout out the shops. Can I go?"

Mary looked dejected. She nodded silently, and Jessica squealed, let her go, and rushed away.

Mary, Mother of God, sighed. "How can I control my daughter when she's almighty and strong-willed like her father?"

"You have to convince her not to start Armageddon," Wycliffe insisted.

"I can't believe she would choose to end the human species. She's playing right into the hands of that fellow." Mary pointed at an image of Pastor Michael Crowberry on a TV in her bedroom. "Jesus is taking orders from a televangelist!"

Wycliffe looked at the TV. BBC Space news showed people, likely Americans, pushing boxes out of an airplane. Other people, likely Indonesians or Acehnese, grabbed the boxes and put them on trucks. In the background, U.S. soldiers guarded the airstrip.

"What's Crowberry doing in Indonesia?" Wycliffe said. He turned up the volume of the TV.

The BBC announcer reported, "Televangelist Michael Crowberry and the United States military have successfully evaded the Indonesian government and airlifted ten thousand kilograms of food to Banda Aceh, capital of Aceh Province. President Darby ordered the United States military to take over this airstrip in Banda Aceh so the Crowberry Mission can deliver food. All the food is *halal* to meet the dietary needs of Aceh's people, who are Moslems."

Crowberry stood by the airstrip and watched the trucks drive away. "I know famine is prophesized in *The Book of Revelation* as part of the End Times. I know it's a necessary tribulation before the return of Jesus. People are asking if I'm preventing the return of Jesus by ending a famine.

"No, I'm not doing anything that stops Jesus from returning. Make no mistake; the End Times are coming. Sad to say, I can't end the famine. This pitiful amount of food can't feed the millions who are starving, and it won't grow more food for them next week. But as a Christian, I can't stand by and do nothing while millions starve. If I can alleviate their pain just a little, I think should do it."

"That's wonderful. I'm glad Crowberry's going back to good works," Wycliffe said.

"But he hasn't changed his opinion of the *Revelation of John*," Mary said. "He still thinks war, death, and destruction are necessary before Jesus returns. I wish people would believe that God's plan doesn't require death and destruction. My child is kinder than that."

"I wish I could agree with you, but Jessica says she's here to cause a war."

"We have to change her mind — and stop her if necessary."

"She's Jesus, who is also God, one in being with the Father. The Nicene Creed says so. Can we stop God?"

"We must try," Mary urged.

"A priest and the Virgin Mary have to stop Jesus from carrying out God's plan." Wycliffe laughed. "Who would have expected that?"

Mary smiled wryly. "From time immemorial, humans have always challenged their gods just as the gods have challenged humans."

ESA geologists teleported from Arcadia Base to the apparition shrine. Despite a U.S. moon tank in the distance, the geologists went into the crater to check the object.

They discovered that it was a flat, round piece of iron. It was about six meters in diameter and three meters thick. Nobody had known it was there until the missile crash exposed it.

At an estimated one hundred and fifty tons, it was the largest mass of iron on the Moon. Lunar colonists could refine the iron and use it to build moonbases, and nobody had to pay the cost of bringing iron from Earth. The iron itself plus the transportation savings was worth millions of gold units.

But the geologists could not explain a mystery: how had the large chunk of iron gotten there? Iron is rare on the Moon, so it must have been a meteorite from space. But if it had fallen from space, it should be in an impact crater, not under a hill.

The ESA announced the geologists' findings to BBC Space and other news networks.

The next morning, President Darby told reporters in the White House, "The iron meteorite belongs to the United States since it is inside the U.S. protection zone. The American people will be the leaders in lunar mining."

President Zhu protested from the headquarters of the Chinese Lunar Settlement Agency. "A Chinese missile uncovered the iron deposit. It is logical that the iron belongs to China. I am ordering moon tanks to blockade the perimeter of the United States' illegal zone.

"I also warn the United States to keep its moon tanks away from the iron deposit. We will treat any attempt to put military personnel at the iron deposit as an act of war."

The U.S. moon tank at Apparition Hill withdrew to Moonbase Liberty. The Chinese victory was short-lived, though; the U.S. moon tanks drove to the protection zone's perimeter to follow the Chinese tanks.

At the late afternoon Mass, people filled every seat. After the Mass, he saw Mary sitting at the rear pew.

"It took only a day for China and the United States to threaten war over a chunk of iron," Wycliffe told her. "Perhaps the human race really is headed to Armageddon."

"I hope that's not the purpose of the rock," Mary said.

"Then what is its purpose? It's where Carla Delgada saw you. It's not ordinary iron, is it? Is it a Siren Stone?"

Mary smiled. "Perhaps it is."

"And it's an extremely strong one that's creating illusions of you and Jessica kilometers away from it," Wycliffe suggested.

"Are Jessica and I illusions?" Mary asked.

"Maybe. You and Jessica don't appear in photographs or video."

"Can God be photographed?"

"I don't know."

"You don't know for sure if God can be photographed. But just because you can't photograph Him, doesn't mean He isn't there. You don't doubt that Jesus and I exist either," Mary said.

She continued. "What you doubt is the purpose of this Siren Stone. Could this stone be how God lets my daughter and me come to you? Or could it be the catalyst that causes the death of the human race? That's something you need to decide on your own."

Mary rose from the pew and walked out of the church.

Father Wycliffe read the ESA geologists' report about the iron meteorite. By now, everyone was calling it "a meteorite" although it had been under a hill instead of an impact crater.

He scrolled through pages of test results and observations on his computer monitor. The geologists had conducted every test and recorded every observation normally done with meteorites.

However, he suspected this meteorite was not just ordinary iron. One more test might prove or disprove his suspicions. The geologists had not conducted that test, though. He didn't blame them; no geologist expects to find telepathic rocks.

He could ask the ESA geologists to return to the rock and search for electrochemical waves. However, he predicted they would refuse him. Who ever heard of a rock with brain waves? Why would they waste their time with such silliness?

He needed someone who had lived in deep space, someone who had seen unexplainable phenomenon there, someone who had opened her mind to ideas judged impossible by people on Earth.

Wycliffe closed the geologists' report file and opened his videophone program. He typed coordinates for a hotel in Dubai. After some beeping, the image of Amira Edip appeared on his computer monitor. She was wearing a white *hijab*, the headscarf for women, along with a chic blue jacket and white blouse.

"Mark!" she greeted him. "What a surprise to hear from you. How are you?"

"I am fine, Amira. Can we talk now, or are you busy?"

"I can talk now. I was at the Islamic Co-Existence Conference, but it has ended."

"How was the conference?" Wycliffe asked.

"Sometimes interesting, sometimes boring, but always important. A conference like this has never happened before," Amira replied. "Presidents, monarchs, and religious leaders are agreeing to stop Moslem-on-Moslem violence in their countries. They promise to pass tolerance laws and punish wrongdoers. Eventually, we will end centuries of feuding between Islamic sects."

"Christians call that ecumenicalism, the cooperation of Roman Catholics, Eastern Orthodox, Protestants, and their subdivisions. Christian denominations were far from peaceful with each other. It took Christians centuries to achieve ecumenicalism. Try not to make the same mistakes we did."

"We have already made all the same mistakes, for centuries. I guess it is human nature to repeat each other's mistakes."

"What are you doing after the conference?"

"I am going to visit India. I have never gone there before. I have another six months free time before I take a teaching position at Free University."

"Do you want to come to the Moon? Could you help me with some scientific research up here?"

"You want me? I have been back on Earth for only six months. I had not planned to return to space so soon. Can you not find other geologists there?"

"I want someone with deep space experience."

"The Moon is not deep space. The Moon is like a suburb of Earth."

"This project requires experience and knowledge gained in deep space. You've seen asteroids, meteors, and the moons of Mars."

"What is the research about?"

"The new meteorite just discovered at Apparition Hill. There's no impact crater, so nobody knows how long it's been buried there or how it got there."

"It is an interesting rock. How long will you need me?"

"One week, maybe less, is all I need from you. I'll get the ESA to cover your expenses. The ESA will pay for your flight, the hotel, the food, and any supplies and equipment you need," Wycliffe offered.

"Are you offering me a free trip to Timonium Base, the Dubai of the Moon?" Amira said excitedly. "Yes, I will do it."

"Wonderful. I'll have Dr. Schiller's secretary make travel arrangements for you."

"I look forward to seeing you and Timonium Base again," she said before signing off.

In addition to a geologist, Wycliffe needed another expert to help him. After closing the videophone program, he opened the on-line directory of the Timonium Base medical center. The medical center's staff list included many physicians, including the neurologist Dr. Thomas Hall, but there was no psychiatrist listed there.

He typed the coordinates of a Russian Orthodox monastery outside Paris. Father Alexei answered the videophone. He was wearing a simple black suit and an ornate pectoral cross of gold, rubies, and emeralds.

"Father Wycliffe," Alexei said. "This is an unexpected pleasure. How are things on the Moon?"

"Things are fine except for the possibility that World War Five will start here," Wycliffe said.

Alexei gave a small laugh. "So I see from the news. Yet pilgrims still go to that unauthorized shrine on Apparition Hill."

"The same happened at Medjugorje, a town in Herzegovina, in the twentieth century. Six teenagers saw apparitions of the Virgin Mary starting in 1981. Thousands of tourists and pilgrims went to the town each year. Twelve years after the first apparition, the ethnic groups of Bosnia and Herzegovina went to war against each other. The war lasted over three years and killed over one hundred thousand people. Yet throughout the war, pilgrims still traveled to Medjugorje."

"Such incredible devotion is happening again, again in dangerous times, and without your archbishop's ecclesiastical approval. You have a busy and complicated life, no doubt."

"It could be simpler. How about you?"

"I am very well. Thank you again for recommending that I retreat to a monastery when I returned to Earth. This monastery has refreshed me. Now I can ask for a church that needs a priest."

"Before you go to your next church, would you like to come to the Moon? Could you perform a psychiatric exam here?"

"A psychiatric exam? On whom?"

"Carla Delgada, the girl who claims she saw the Virgin Mary. I want to know if she's suffering from hallucinations or if she's mentally healthy or not."

"I am always willing to help you, but is there not a psychiatrist on the Moon already?"

"No. The medical center hasn't recruited one yet."

"I would like to help you, but the expense —"

"I'll get the ESA to pay for your travel. You can probably finish the examination in a day or two."

"It would be nice to see the Moon again, so long as I am not trapped there if a war breaks out," Alexei said. "Yes, I will come."

"Thank you, Alexei," Wycliffe said. "Dr. Schiller's secretary will make travel arrangements for you. Expect her call."

———

Father Wycliffe arrived at the Timonium Base medical center. The secretary took him to Dr. Thomas Hall's office.

Wycliffe looked at a framed newspaper photo of Dr. Hall and President

Darby. "You've been quite successful in politics in the short time since you returned from Mars."

"I got President Darby to take the motto 'In God We Trust' off the last U.S. coin," Thomas boasted. "He's the first avowed atheist elected as President of the United States. He's sympathetic to progressive views."

"And yet Pastor Crowberry and his End Timers love him."

Thomas grimaced.

"More correctly, they have a love-hate relationship with him," Wycliffe added. "They hate him because he's an atheist. But they love him because he's putting the military on the Moon. Maybe they think he's necessary to fulfill the prophecy of the *Book of Revelation*. Maybe they think his rise to power is prophesized in *Revelation*. Maybe they think he's the Anti-Christ."

Thomas shook his head. "No, no, the End Timers don't think President Darby is the Anti-Christ." He smirked. "They think the Pope is the Anti-Christ."

"We're used to that," Wycliffe said plainly. "But don't condemn the Pope too much. One of his Cardinals, the Archbishop of Paris, will pay you for your neurological services."

"Oh? What does the Church want from me?" Thomas said. He sounded intrigued.

"I need your help, scientist to scientist. Will you perform a neurological test on Carla Delgada?"

"Carla Delgada? The girl who says she saw the Virgin Mary walking on the Moon?"

"Yes, she's the one. Let her wear the brain scanner for a couple days. I want to know if there's anything unusual in her brain, anything that might make her see things that you or I don't see."

"Like the Virgin Mary? Yes, I'll do it. I'll be happy to debunk another vision of the Virgin Mary."

"You're not debunking or proving anything by your tests alone. Make your observations and conclusions fairly and without bias," Wycliffe said. "It's what I expect from a scientific colleague."

Both Imam Edip and Father Alexei arrived by space liner a week later. They moved into the last two residential rooms in the church. The next morning, the motley group gathered for breakfast in the church's kitchen: Mary, the Mother of God; Jessica, who was Jesus incarnated as a girl; a woman imam and geologist; a Russian Orthodox priest and psychiatrist; and a Roman Catholic priest and engineer.

Father Wycliffe introduced the residents to each other. His first introduction: "Mary, please meet Amira Edip, an imam from a Protestant Islamic mosque in Berlin."

Amira shook hands with Mary. "Nice to meet you," Mary said.

"I'm pleased to meet you too," Amira said. "What do you do? Are you with one of the scientific teams?"

"I'm a full-time mother. I'm the Mother of Jesus," Mary replied plainly.

The imam looked startled. "Oh." She paused for a moment. "I heard you were here on the Moon. I thought you would be at Apparition Hill, not here for breakfast." She paused again. "The Koran mentions you more times than the Bible does, and I have read only good things about you in both books. Uh, are you traveling alone?"

"No, my daughter is here."

"Daughter?"

Jessica stepped forward, smiled, and waved at Amira. "Hi, I'm Jessica. Some people call me the Savior, some call me the Messiah, and some call me Prince of Peace, but you can call me Jessica."

"Isa?" Amira muttered, calling Jesus by his Arabic name.

Father Alexei turned to Wycliffe and whispered, "Who are they? What do they want?"

"They just told us who they are. As for what they want, the girl wants to judge the living and the dead and end the world," Wycliffe said.

"What do you want us to do?"

"Convince her not to destroy the human race."

Mary sighed as she put a tray of toast on the table. "Let's eat first."

———

"You're the same Jessica from Space Station Troika?" Father Alexei asked. He stirred sugar into his coffee. "You claim to be Jesus?"

"Yes, that's me," Jessica said before drinking her orange juice.

"Is this a change in the Holy Trinity?" Alexei asked.

"Oh, no, stop before we go any further," Amira begged. "This is the most confusing part of Christianity to me. Somebody explain the Trinity to me."

Jessica laughed. "The Trinity is really mind-bending. That's its coolest, most awesome part. I'm a single God of three persons or *hypostases*, each distinct and co-equal and co-eternal, yet sharing the same divine essence, and each is God. The three persons are God the Father, God the Son, and God the Holy Spirit. We're all the same and yet not the same."

"So has the Trinity become a Tetrarchy of Father, Son, Holy Spirit, and Sacred Schoolgirl?" Wycliffe asked.

Jessica looked pensive. "Good question. I always assumed that I was Jesus, who is God the Son, but it's obvious that I'm not a boy anymore. However, I don't consider myself a fourth person in God either. Maybe this is the best way to explain things: I'm a second personality of God the Son. Therefore, the Trinity is four personalities in three persons in one God. Does that make sense?"

"This is like explaining how I got pregnant to my mother," Mary said.

"God is not a Trinity in Islam," Amira said. "This Trinity is so complicated."

"But not as complicated as the bubble theory of an infinite number of multiverses," Jessica replied. "Even to smart people, theoretical physics is more difficult to understand than theology about the Trinity."

"Jesus is male, not female," Father Alexei said. "If you are Jesus, why did you come back as a girl?"

"'God created man in His image, in the divine image He created him; male and female He created them,'" Jessica quoted from *Genesis*.

"Oh, I hadn't thought of that," Alexei said. He resumed drinking his coffee.

"Are you visiting the Moon for business or pleasure?" Amira asked.

"Business."

"What type of business?"

"I've come to judge the living and the dead and end the world."

"I have faith that the Last Judgment will come –- just not in my lifetime. If you really are Isa, should I try convincing you to postpone the Last Judgment?"

"Oh, no, I can't postpone it. The time has come. Besides, it won't be all doom and gloom. Good things will happen too."

"Like the dead will be resurrected, the righteous will be rewarded in Heaven, and the sinful will be punished in Hell?" Amira asked.

Jessica smiled. "I'm glad you see the bright side of the end of the world."

"Christian, Jewish, and Islamic beliefs about the Last Judgment are similar, but Moslems have a notable difference," Amira said. "Isa will accompany the Mahdi, the redeemer of Islam. The coming of the Mahdi will precede the second coming of Isa, and Isa will pray behind the Mahdi. Yet there is no one claiming to be the Mahdi.

"If you are Isa, in Christian theology, you can bring the End Times by yourself, but in Moslem theology, you cannot. A paradox."

"You're assuming that currently there is no Mahdi," Jessica replied. "But if the Mahdi were here, would he -- or she -- necessarily tell you? In Twelver Shia tradition, the Mahdi is already living among people, but people don't know him, just like Joseph's brothers did not know him until he introduced himself."

"Your pancakes are getting cold, dear," Mary said, interrupting her daughter. "Talk less and eat more."

Jessica nodded and began gobbling up a stack of pancakes.

Imam Amira Edip leaned to Father Wycliffe and whispered, "Am I dreaming? Am I having breakfast with Maryam and Isa? Or are they illusions created by a Siren Stone?"

"That's why I need you to check that meteorite," Wycliffe replied.

"I heard that," Jessica said. "You doubt me. Go check out the rock. It doesn't matter what you find. If it's an ordinary rock, my being God is the only explanation you have. If it's a telepathic rock putting my voice and image into your brain, that's how God shows Himself to you. Whatever you discover, I am who I am."

"Finish your breakfast, dear," Mary urged.

After breakfast, Jessica went to the commercial district, Mary went to a food store, Imam Edip went to the tourist information booth, and Father Alexei went to the medical center. Father Wycliffe went to Café Méliès to find Carla Delgada.

"Yes, I have the next two days off," said Carla. "Why do you ask?"

"Remember I mentioned neurological and psychiatric tests?" Wycliffe said. "A psychiatrist has come from Earth, and he can interview you. It won't last more than an hour, maybe two. I've also gotten a neurologist to monitor your brainwaves for a couple days. It requires you to wear a lightweight monitoring device on your head. It won't feel heavy or uncomfortable. It'll feel like a hat. You'll still be able to walk around and go places."

Carla shrugged. "I'll do it for my grandmother."

"Thank you. The psychiatrist is Father Alexei, and the neurologist is Dr. Thomas Hall. Meet me at the medical center tomorrow..."

Father Wycliffe waited in the reception area of the medical center. He heard the bell ring, signaling that someone was entering the room. Carla walked in, but she was not alone. To Wycliffe's surprise, Jessica walked in too.

The two young women held shopping bags.

"Carla knows all the fabulous shops," Jessica raved. "Look at this!" She pointed to her feet to show the black go-go boots that had replaced her flat black shoes. "Aren't these totally awesome?"

Jessica held out a bottle of perfume and sprayed into the air. The girls laughed.

"That is such a fantastic scent!" Carla said.

To Father Wycliffe, the perfume smelled like jellybeans.

Jessica and Carla pulled clothes out of their shopping bags: skirts, blouses, tops, shorts, pants, and belts. They recited the names of the famous designers whose boutiques sold the clothes. They must have spent hundreds of gold units.

Jessica held up a lacey red bra and giggled. "This is so skanky!" she squealed.

"You skank!" Carla cried.

"No, you're the skank!" Jessica accused.

Carla laughed and grabbed the bra away from Jessica. Jessica snatched the bra back and slapped Carla with it.

Father Wycliffe forced himself not to guess which girl would wear the bra. He would go to Hell for wondering and imagining.

Father Alexei, Dr. Hall, and a nurse came into the reception area.

"You again!" Dr. Hall cried.

Jessica smiled. "Oh, Dr. Hall, you're here too? The Moon's become the place where everyone hangs out."

Carla looked puzzled. "Do you two know each other?"

"Dr. Hall and I used to work on the same space station."

"You worked on a space station? What did you do?"

"I was the cook."

Wycliffe steered Carla away from Jessica. "Carla, this is Father Alexei, who is both a priest and a psychiatrist, and this is Dr. Thomas Hall, a neurologist," he said. "They will conduct the psychiatric and neurological tests. Gentlemen, this is Carla Delgada."

"Carla, I am very pleased to meet you," said Father Alexei.

He turned to the nurse and asked, "Have you set up the video recorder and the notepad?"

The nurse nodded. "It's all set up. I even recharged the notepad's batteries. We're ready."

"Thank you, Miss Hennessy." Father Alexei turned back to Carla. "Miss Hennessy and I will interview you for an hour. After that, Dr. Hall will give you a monitoring device, and you can go anywhere you wish. You won't be inconvenienced too much this weekend, I promise."

"Sounds okay to me," Carla said.

Alexei motioned for Carla to follow Hennessy to the room. Carla turned to Jessica and said, "See you in a couple hours at the food court, alright?"

"You got it!" Jessica replied as she put the clothes back into the shopping bags.

Hennessy led Carla away. Alexei went to Jessica and said, "I see you've been shopping."

"Totally. I haven't seen hot clothes like these since I was in Egypt. That was two thousand years ago. I liked Egyptian styles. The Egyptians were so more *haute couture* than Judeans."

"Humans can create such works of artistry, beauty, and creativity. But if you were to end our human race, you would never see such clothes again."

Jessica grinned. "I get to resurrect the dead. Some of them designed really hot clothes when they were alive. Like Coco Chanel and Gianni Versace. The Kingdom of God will rock!"

Alexei turned to Wycliffe. "Our attempts to convince Jesus to postpone the end of the world are not working. Pray that we are experiencing some form of mass hallucination, and that is all it is."

Alexei walked away to join Carla and Hennessy.

Humming "Havah Nagilah", Jessica carried the shopping bags to the door. Father Wycliffe and Dr. Hall silently watched her leave the medical center.

Dr. Hall said, "That's the girl who thinks she's Jesus. But she crashed the shuttlecraft into Mars. She's dead!"

"Haven't you heard about resurrection?" Wycliffe said. "She's a bit late this time. Instead of three days, she took three years."

"Be serious," Thomas insisted. "I don't know what she is, but she's not human. Is she an alien?"

"One who can turn invisible to our cameras? That teenaged girl is a space alien? That's highly speculative, if not preposterous," Wycliffe said.

"No more preposterous than a virgin woman getting impregnated by a ghost and giving birth to a god," Thomas rebutted. "At least it's scientifically plausible that Jessica could be an alien."

"Scientifically plausible? Does she look like an alien? Does she talk like an alien? Is it scientifically plausible that someone who looks and talks like a human is an alien? There's no proof that life exists beyond Earth, so how can you say Jessica is an alien?"

"It's theoretically possible..."

Wycliffe knew that Thomas would never accept that, perhaps, the Troika crew had lost the shuttlecraft. Spacer pride would not accept the blame.

The other alternative to blame was God, but for Thomas, God does not exist.

With neither humans nor God to blame, Thomas had to blame a hypothetical alien. To the fundamentalist atheist, a space alien was more plausible than God.

When Father Wycliffe returned to St. Dominic's Church, he found Jessica waiting for him. She sat surrounded by shopping bags.

"Where's your mother?" he asked.

"She went to check out the fashion boutiques."

"Speaking of which, where did you get the money to buy all that stuff?"

"I used my mother's money card," Jessica replied.

The answer only led to another mystery: how could Mary get a money card? The Holy Family could be so darned enigmatic.

He remembered that his son's ghost had a money card on Troika. Did everyone get a money card in heaven?

"Take me out to the surface," Jessica asked. "I want to walk on the Moon. I want to feel what it's like."

"So you want to go on a moonwalk?" Wycliffe said. "Okay, I'll take you. Maybe when you feel the Moon below your feet and see the bright lights and beautiful buildings that we have built here, you'll change your mind about the human race."

"No, not really. Biblical prophecy says the End Times will come sooner or later. I'm here to make it sooner.

"But I think it'll be amazing to go on a moonwalk before the End Times. I've walked on water, but I've never walked on the Moon. That's supreme procrastination, considering the Moon's been around for billions and billions of years, almost as old as God Himself."

―――――

Wycliffe and Jessica put on their spacesuits in the men's and women's change rooms respectively. After changing into their suits, they went to the airlock door. Dozens of other tourists, all in spacesuits, soon joined them.

Each suit bore the logo of Tranquility Tours, an American-owned company. Each suit also bore a number. Wycliffe's number was 10. Jessica's number was 26.

"How totally cool, I'm number twenty-six," Jessica bragged. "*Yod hey vah hey.*"

Yod hey vav hey are four Hebrew letters commonly transliterated to the Latin letters YHVH. They form the Tetragrammaton, the Sacred Name of God. In Jewish gematria or numerology, each letter has a numerical value. When the values of *yod hey vah hey* are added together, they add to twenty-six.

Is this a coincidence? Father Wycliffe wondered.

"And you're number ten. How appropriate for a lawgiver," Jessica observed.

She's referring to the Ten Commandments, Wycliffe mused. As a priest, he was a lawgiver.

Jessica examined her helmet. Like everyone else, she needed to wear a helmet outside. Wycliffe remembered the rumors about the ghosts of 20 521 Odette de Proust.

"The ghosts on the asteroid Odette de Proust didn't need to wear spacesuits in the space vacuum," Wycliffe said. "If they didn't need spacesuits, why do you?"

Jessica punched Wycliffe's arm. The punch did not hurt, but Wycliffe felt its force.

"Did that feel like a ghost?" Jessica asked.

"No."

"I'm not the Holy Spirit. I have a solid form. I'm an incarnation of Jesus who's both divine and human, so I'm a human being, made of flesh and blood, even though I'm made of the same substance as God. I need to breathe air just like everyone else. Just like Jesus did."

"But the ghosts on Odette de Proust felt solid too."

"Don't question everything. Just have faith, padre."

They put on their helmets. Wycliffe heard the other tourists talking over the helmet radio.

A woman walked into the area. "Welcome to Tranquility Tours' Moonwalk Experience," she said. "My name is Dawn Favreaux, President of Tranquility Tours. I'm also President of the American Chamber of Commerce on the Moon."

Wycliffe had seen Favreaux on the TV news recently. She had bemoaned that the military crisis would ruin the lunar tour companies. All tour companies had to cancel their moonbus tours into the U.S. protection zone. The ban on moonbus travel made the ESA install its teleporters, which became another threat to the tour bus industry. The American Chamber of Commerce on the Moon had protested to the U.S. Government, but this time, American business could not move its own government.

A technician walked from person to person, checking each spacesuit and helmet. Dawn Favreaux continued. "After we check each suit, you'll be ready for the Moonwalk Experience. Thank you for choosing Tranquility Tours."

The technician checked if Wycliffe's helmet was secured to the spacesuit. "Okay, you're connected now. Keep the radio tuned to 'general'," the technician told him. "We can talk to everyone on the general setting."

They entered the airlock and went out to the lunar surface. Some gathered around a tour guide who explained a Russian plaque on the ground. Other groups walked off to take photographs. Others wandered from place to place. Jessica jumped around like a child at play.

She bounced back to Father Wycliffe. "Where's Moonbase Liberty?" she asked.

Wycliffe pointed in the direction of the U.S. moonbase, which was too far away for them to see. "Somewhere over there."

"And Arcadia Base?"

"That way, inside the U.S. protection zone."

"And Apparition Hill?"

"I thought you would know that one. It's over there, also inside the U.S. protection zone."

A light shone down on the tourists. Their chattering grew louder. Wycliffe heard them talk about a shuttlecraft. He looked up and saw the shuttlecraft, a Tsiolkovsky model 3. It shone its lights down on tourists as it flew over them.

After the shuttlecraft had passed by, Wycliffe looked around again. He didn't see spacesuit number twenty-six.

"Jessica, where are you?" he said over the helmet radio. He heard only the other tourists talking to each other. Jessica did not reply.

He went from person to person, looking at their spacesuit numbers. None of them was number twenty-six.

YHVH had disappeared.

Colonel Rang Li, Commander of Yue 1, looked at the video monitors. They showed images of Moonbase Yue 1 from various security cameras. Unlike Timonium Base, most of Yue 1 was underground. The Chinese built Yue 1 before the invention of lightweight radiation shielding; living underground protected the crew from long exposure to space radiation. The crew did not spend too much time in the surface towers, which contained scientific sensors. Recent additions to the surface included grenade launchers.

The *Zhang Heng* sat on a launch pad. The large spacecraft should have been retired years ago. First used on the second Chinese expedition, she was the oldest spacecraft in use on the Moon. She had suffered all sorts of problems in recent years: shielding cracks, communications failure, landing gear damage, engine trouble. Her recent engine trouble nearly started a war when the Americans refused to let her land at Moonbase Liberty. Yet despite her problems, she could still fly, whereas younger spacecraft had already broken down completely. The Politburo kept her in use to show off her brilliant Chinese engineering, and Rang had to admit the ship was sleek and beautiful.

Except for a Chinese moon tank rumbling towards Yue 1, nothing else moved outside. Yue 1's population had decreased drastically. The civilian scientists had left when the military took over the base, and the workers had returned to China after building the missile silos. Only twenty soldiers remained...

...*with five political commissars*, Rang remembered. Although they had army officer ranks, the political commissars had only the most basic military training. They were useless in emergencies and warfare. Their job was to enforce the military's loyalty to the Communist Party.

The political commissars seldom mingled with the soldiers. Right now, they were in their own compound, on the other side of the base. They were studying the speeches of the last National Congress of the Communist Party. Undoubtedly, they would return in a few days and force Rang and his men to listen to lectures about the Party's new policies.

Satisfied that no intruders were outside, Colonel Rang went back to the table. Nine army officers sat there, all looking at calculations and graphs on their portable computers.

One of the officers, Captain Chu Shaozhu, sighed loudly and hit a key on his computer keyboard. Like Colonel Rang, Captain Chu wore the Rocket Engineering Corps badge on his green uniform. Chu looked haggard from the long days of work. He frowned as he scrolled down screens of mathematical calculations on his computer.

"It was stupid to send the Moon Punisher here without testing it on Earth," he complained. "Conducting development work on the Moon is ridiculous."

"It was the Politburo's idea, not the Army's," Colonel Rang reminded him. Since time immemorial, soldiers had commiserated about the silliness of their political masters. Officers could diffuse bad morale among their men by agreeing with their complaints about the politicians.

However, he could do that only to a limit. The Politburo was still the Politburo, and it had political commissars on the Moon.

"They felt it was necessary to give us the Moon Punisher immediately. We need to be the first country with a ballistic missile on the Moon," Rang explained.

The Chinese could have taken an existing missile, one they had tested and flown on Earth, and put it on the Moon. Instead, they designed a new missile, the first especially for lunar use. Outer space was weightless, but spaceships still had to fight gravity when lifting off and landing on either the Earth or the Moon. To reduce the weight for the spaceships carrying the missiles to the Moon, the Moon Punisher was lighter than Earth-based missiles.

The Politburo wanted to have the first ballistic missile on the Moon, so they rushed the Moon Punisher to the Moon without testing it. Now Colonel Rang, Captain Chu, and eight other rocketry engineers had to test the missile and make it work.

Their deadline was just two days away, the anniversary of the first Chinese landing on the Moon. The Politburo liked to announce propaganda news on anniversaries. Old Communist traditions lived on.

In their rush to the deadline, Rang's team had launched seven missiles in the same day. Each missile launch had a different combination of settings on variables such as fuel mix, pressure, temperature, and burn times. Each had failed and caused a diplomatic uproar.

"The politicians watch too many science fiction movies. They think engineers build spaceships by following easy instructions, as if they were building a model kit," Chu said. "How wrong they are. Rocketry is a subjective art, prone to trial and error and surprise."

Rang agreed. No computer simulation could recreate a real missile launch. Many things could go wrong: the mix of fuel and oxidizer, the temperature of the fuel, the time of the engines' ignition, the burn time, the pressure in the rocket, cracks in the shell of the missile...with so many variables, something was bound to go wrong.

At great expense, the Chinese had shipped nine missiles to the Moon. They had lost seven in unsuccessful tests. They had to keep one in reserve for an actual attack.

The eighth missile had to be successful. It was the last one they could test.

"We've got one shot left," Rang said.

"We need more missiles for testing," Chu declared. "On Earth, a new missile has at least twenty test launches before it succeeds. Here on the Moon, we're aiming for success within eight launches."

Videos of the missile crashes appeared on Chu's computer. Colonel Rang shook his head and walked to the door.

"In case anyone wants to see me, I'll be in the officers' mess," he said.

―――――

Despite its name, all ranks used the officers' mess. Yue 1 was originally a scientific research base, so it did not have separate officers', non-commissioned officers', and enlisted ranks' mess halls. It had a recreation room, which Rang ordered decorated like an officers' mess and opened to all ranks. With only twenty-five people on the base, separate mess halls would be a waste of space.

In practice, only twenty people used the officers' mess. The five political commissars stayed at their own mess hall in their compound.

Rang ran his hand through his black hair. It felt limp and greasy. He and his rocket engineers had spent many long days installing the missiles. Then they worked non-stop to plan and prepare the test launches. With all the work, he had not washed his hair in two weeks. Although he had not seen a mirror since yesterday, he knew he looked just as worn and haggard as the others did.

He took a can of beer from the refrigerator, opened it, and sipped it. He passed a picture of Zhang Heng, the Eastern Han astronomer, after whom the Chinese had named the spaceship.

Photos of the People's Liberation Army hung on another wall. He looked at a photograph of Chinese and American troops at Gwadar, a Pakistani port by the Arabian Sea. They were smiling, drinking, and eating around a table. The table held food from military supplies: biscuits, sardines, hamburger, beef, pork, noodles, applesauce, and fruit salad. A Chinese soldier, a woman, was playing a harmonica. Beside her, an American was uncorking a bottle of wine. At the table, Rang was pouring beer into an American's cup. The Chinese and U.S. flags hung on the back wall.

In the last Vernacular War, the Americans occupied Gwadar and camped in the downtown. It was a trap; the Purists returned and surrounded the Americans. They fought viciously in the streets.

In the battle's second week, the marines arrived: the People's Liberation Army Marines. They bombarded the port, overran it, and advanced into the city. Now the Chinese and Americans encircled the Purists. Fighting continued for another week before the Purists fell. The surviving allies celebrated in the ruins of the port.

The celebration at Gwadar was not long ago, Rang mused. The Americans had been our friends then. Now look at us, bickering on both the Earth and the Moon.

Another photo showed Chinese soldiers standing at the Tomb of Osama bin Laden. Black soot covered the tomb, and its dome had caved in. Bin Laden City lay in ruins behind the tomb.

Osama bin Laden, a Purist leader, started a war in the early twenty-first century. At first, he attacked Americans, Christians, and Jews. Five years after he started his war, he expanded his targets; he taped a speech denouncing the Chinese as "pagan Buddhists." The Chinese Communists were actually atheists, but the difference did not matter to Moslem rebels in China's Xinjiang Province. Buddhist or atheist, the Chinese were *kaffirs*, and bin Laden urged the rebels to fight them. Xinjiang would be in turmoil for over a century.

The Purists usually buried their dead in unmarked graves, the ultimate humility before God. However, Osama bin Laden was not a humble man; he considered himself Islam's greatest hero and craved attention in videotaped speeches. Before he died, he told his followers to build a tomb for him. They built a magnificent tomb of white marble with a glittering green dome. The tomb's pentagon shape celebrated bin Laden's attack on the Pentagon, the U.S. military's headquarters. Encircling the green dome were quotes from bin Laden's *fatwa* against Jews and Crusaders, inlaid in gold.

Now the dome was in ruins. China did what the United States wanted to do but wouldn't: drop a neutron bomb on Bin Laden City. U.S. military intelligence had discovered that Purist leaders would be meeting at the Tomb of Osama bin Laden. There was just one guaranteed way to kill them. The United States hesitated to drop a neutron bomb. Only China had the courage to drop the bomb.

The bombing stopped Purist Arabia from sending weapons to Xinjiang. It also cut supplies to Purists fighting Americans in the Middle East and Africa. Thus, the bombing saved countless American lives. The Americans owed so much to the Chinese.

Now the United States was threatening to attack China over a chunk of iron. The Americans were so ungrateful. How quickly they forgot.

Rang Li moved to a bookshelf that held twelve china sparrows. The birds came from a porcelain factory in Guangzhou, capital of Guangdong Province. His wife collected small porcelain animals and gave him the twelve sparrows to remind him of Earth. He wished he could return to Earth and watch real birds with his wife.

His pocket computer buzzed. Rang pulled it out and said, "This is Rang. What is it?"

"The moon tank has spotted an intruder about thirty meters from our base," Chu replied.

"I'm on my way," Rang said as he returned to the control room.

Back in the control room, Rang looked at the video monitors. Each showed a lonely lunar landscape. No intruder appeared anywhere.

The Chinese broadcast a recorded message on the frequency used by space helmet radios: "You are in Chinese territory. Stay away!" in Mandarin, English, Russian, French, German, and Arabic.

On one of the monitors, a single moon tank moved into view. It pointed towards Yue 1.

"The intruder is still moving towards the base," the tank captain reported.

"Negative, we do not see an intruder," Rang said.

"He is only about twenty meters from our base. Sir, permission to shoot him."

"No. Permission denied until I can see him." He did not want the tank shooting at someone he could not see. Without a visible target, the tank might hit one of the surface towers.

"But I see him clearly," the tank captain argued. "He is moving quickly."

"We have video cameras monitoring every centimeter of the base and the area around it, and we still cannot see him," Rang said.

"He is ten meters from airlock three."

"He is that close?"

"He is at the airlock."

Rang looked at the video monitors again. There was nobody at the exterior airlock door.

"There is nobody at airlock three," he argued.

"There is!" the tank commander yelled. "Darn, it is too late to shoot now. I would blow up the airlock too."

A message flashed on the computer monitors. Captain Chu read the message and looked up.

"Someone is opening airlock three," Chu reported.

"How can that be? Who can it be?" Rang asked, exasperated.

He looked at the video monitors again. Airlock three's exterior door remained closed. Yet his computer monitor showed a message saying that someone was entering the airlock.

"The procedures manual says we should alert the commanding political commissar," Chu said. "Should I tell Colonel Ming?"

"No!" Rang ordered. "Do not tell the political commissars. They will not understand how this security breach occurred. We will handle this situation by ourselves."

Chu nodded silently.

Rang pulled out his pocket computer and pressed the code for the secure communications channel to his security team. Only the security team would hear him; the political commissars would not.

"Security team, meet me at airlock three!" Rang ordered into his pocket computer.

He ran to the airlock, where two armed soldiers waited. The interior airlock door clicked as it unlocked. After a moment of silence, it swung open.

Someone in a spacesuit walked out of the airlock. The soldiers raised their guns and aimed at the intruder.

"Identify yourself!" Rang ordered.

The intruder raised her helmet visor and replied in Mandarin, "Number twenty-six."

"I can see that," Rang said, looking at the number on her spacesuit. "What is your name?"

"Jessica," the girl replied.

"What is your nationality?"

"That's a new one. I never had to answer that question before. I don't know. I was born in Judea, which was part of the Roman Empire, but I never got Roman citizenship."

"Judea? Roman Empire?"

"They're old countries. They don't belong to the United Nations."

Jessica unbuckled her helmet from her spacesuit, took off the helmet, and took a deep breath. "I'm so glad to breathe normal air again. You don't appreciate carbon dioxide until you can't get it. I'm so not used to breathing the pure oxygen inside a spacesuit."

She was wearing a tiara under her space helmet, Rang observed. *How strange.*

Jessica began shedding the rest of the spacesuit. The soldiers shouted, "Stop, stop!" Jessica looked at them sheepishly.

"Okay, I'll take off my spacesuit slowly so you can see that I'm not hiding anything," she said.

"Watch her from the front," Rang ordered as he moved behind Jessica. He examined the life-support backpack. It was a new unit, much smaller than the bulky packs worn up to five years ago. There was no timer, no extra part, nothing odd or suspicious that could be a bomb.

"You may remove the spacesuit, but do it slowly," he said.

Jessica unbuckled and unzipped the front of the spacesuit. Moments later, she squirmed out of the suit. She was wearing a schoolgirl uniform.

This is a very strange girl, Rang thought. She was not Chinese, but she knew Mandarin. She was a teenager, hardly old enough to be a spy or saboteur. She was wearing a schoolgirl uniform under her spacesuit; most people wore just a T-shirt and shorts.

"Why did you come here?" Rang demanded.

"To help you launch your missile," Jessica replied.

"I wish this base had a prison," Rang muttered. Since Yue 1 was originally a scientific research base, its designers had not foreseen a need to imprison people there.

"Take her to the officers' mess and hold her there for now," Rang told the soldiers.

The soldiers motioned for Jessica to march forward. She walked forward, leaving her spacesuit behind.

"Sit down," Rang ordered as he pulled a chair out from a table. Jessica obeyed quietly. The two soldiers hovered behind her.

Colonel Rang sat down opposite Jessica. "I'll ask you again. Why did you come here?"

"Like I said, to help you launch your missile," Jessica said. She sounded annoyed. "Why won't you believe me? Oh, nobody ever believes me!"

"Why should I believe you?" Rang asked. "You came here without permission. You have no identification or passport. You say you are a citizen of two dead countries. You say you are here to help us with secret weapons tests, yet you are not a citizen, scientist, or soldier of my country. You must admit that you seem highly suspicious."

"Okay, so I totally messed up in planning my trip here," Jessica admitted. "I didn't have time to get a visa from the Chinese Embassy, and anyway, neither the Kingdom of Judea nor the Roman Empire is around to give me a passport. But don't crucify me just because I didn't get a visa."

This girl is either an insane person or a master spy, Rang thought. If she were a spy, her style was unorthodox. Most spies would try to seem normal and inconspicuous, not strange and obvious. Either she was playing a psychological game or she was truly insane.

He decided to play her game -- assuming it was a game.

"What is your parents' telephone number?" he asked. "I'll tell them to come pick you up."

Jessica smiled. "Give me a pen and a piece of paper, and I'll write it down for you."

Why did she not simply say the number aloud? Colonel Rang decided to humor her. He left the table, went to the bar, and picked up a pen and paper. He put them in front of the girl.

Jessica furiously wrote several pages of notes. When she stopped, she smiled and handed the papers to Rang.

She had filled each page with writing: words, formulas, and calculations about fuel mix ratios, pressure build-up, velocity, trajectory, ignition sequences, burn times...

"These are calculations related to launching the missile," he said, awestruck. "How do you know them?"

"It's just rocket science," said Jessica. She smiled again. "You've been struggling with a large combination of variables that control an untested rocket. I've given you the best settings for the variables: the mix of fuel and liquid oxygen, the ignition timings, the burn times, the optimal pressure, and all other conditions and information on how to achieve them. Try these settings and conditions, and your launch will be successful."

The girl sounded confident. How could a teenager know so much about rocketry? Rang looked at the calculations again.

"Watch her. I'll be back," Rang told the soldiers as he walked out of the officers' mess.

He went to the control room and showed the papers to Captain Chu. "Take a look at these."

"Who gave these to you?" Chu asked as he studied the calculations. The other engineers crowded around him to look at the papers.

"The intruder," Rang said. Looks of surprise appeared on the engineers' faces.

"Run them through the computer model and forecast the flight using these settings."

———

Chu pointed at the flight data on the computer monitor. "The girl's settings and conditions work in the computer model. They produce the flight simulation with the highest chance of success."

"This is just a computer model simulation," Rang said. "Our other flights also looked good in the computer simulation."

"But those had smaller probabilities of success, ranging from twenty to fifty percent. The computer model forecasts that this flight will have a seventy percent probability of success, the highest so far."

Rang looked at his fellow rocket engineers. They looked back at him silently. He knew they expected a decision from him.

"Prepare the next missile using these suggestions," Rang ordered. "Be ready for launch tomorrow."

Chu looked at the calendar. "That will be a day before the deadline."

"I know, but if the eighth missile is going to fail, I do not want it to fail on the anniversary of the Moon landing."

———

Two days after Carla started her tests, Father Wycliffe, Father Alexei, and Dr. Hall met at the medical center.

Father Alexei looked at the notes on his pocket computer. "I interviewed Miss Delgada. She was also kind enough to give me permission to interview her family doctor in Canada, whom I interviewed by videophone. She also asked her doctor to send her medical records to me. She was very cooperative for her psychiatric assessment.

"She has no history of diagnosed mental illness. She has not suffered hysteria or hallucinations. She does not have any anxiety disorders, schizophrenia, paranoia, or any condition that might make her see things that others cannot perceive. Based on my interviews with her and her doctor and a review of her records, I cannot find any evidence of mental illness."

Father Alexei turned to Dr. Hall. "What does the medical imaging show?"

Thomas turned his computer to the two priests. "This is Carla's brain, scanned over two days."

A brain scan image appeared on the monitor. Like other brain scans, it showed different parts of the brain glowing and pulsating in red, green, and yellow. Unlike most brain scans, it showed a large red area pulsating in the left temporal lobe.

"That large red area is electrical activity in the left temporal lobe, also known as the God spot," Thomas explained.

"We're familiar with the nickname," Wycliffe said. It meant the left temporal lobe, but its implication depended on who used it. Some people used it to imply that God is just in people's imaginations. Other people used it to imply that God gave the left temporal lobe to humans so that they can experience Him.

Thomas resumed talking. "Note how large the red spot is. Carla's left temporal lobe is extremely active with electrochemical signals. I've seen scans like this before, on a crewmember of Troika when she saw Jessica."

"Carla says she went shopping with her again during those two days," Wycliffe said.

"She told me she was with Jessica for several hours each day but not for the whole day," Thomas said. "If she is seeing visions of Schoolgirl Jesus, I'm not surprised to see her God spot full of electrochemical signals -- while she is with Jesus.

"On most people, the electrical activity fluctuates. Even in religious mystics, their electrical activity increases when they experience mystical emotions, and it decreases when the emotions are over.

"But look at Carla's scan. It looked this red continuously throughout the whole two days, even when she didn't see Jessica. The electrochemical activity of her left frontal lobe never decreased, even when she was asleep.

"In other words, her God spot is always on," Thomas concluded.

"That's why she saw the Virgin Mary at Apparition Hill while nobody else did," Wycliffe realized. "She's highly sensitive to phenomenon that others can't see."

"But she is not a religious person," Alexei reminded him. "She has never attended Mass, and she has never prayed. She does not practice any religion."

"That makes her case even more remarkable," Wycliffe said. "I don't know what, if anything, it means, though. Do either of you have any idea?"

Both Alexei and Thomas shook their heads.

"She must be another one of God's mysteries," Wycliffe said.

Thomas grunted. "There you go again, mentioning God. What about me? I don't believe in God, and yet, I saw Jessica on Space Station Troika, and I see her again here. *Everybody* in Timonium has seen her by now, and we're not all faithheads."

Faithheads. Dr. Hall was zealously using pejorative words today. Was the doctor under stress?

"I'm well aware that not everybody in Timonium subscribes to religious belief, but perhaps that proves my theory of what's going on here," Wycliffe said. "Did you notice that we started seeing Jessica after the Chinese missile exposed the meteorite? Perhaps the meteorite is a Siren Stone, and now that it's in the open, it can reach all of us, not just Carla."

"That still doesn't explain the missing shuttlecraft at Troika," Thomas reminded him. "Whoever or whatever this person is, she has a physical presence. We know she's not human because she's invisible on video. Maybe she's an extraterrestrial."

"Seriously?" Alexei said.

"Well, you and your fellow priest aren't coming up with any good theories," Thomas argued, sounding aggravated. "At least mine is consistent and doesn't rely on blind faith and superstition."

"It isn't based on evidence either," Wycliffe retorted. "What verifiable, reproducible evidence could you publish?"

Thomas sighed in exasperation. "This is frustrating, not knowing the truth."

"What about Mary?" Alexei asked. "You saw her here before the meteorite got exposed."

Wycliffe shrugged. "I guess that's because I'm a faithhead."

―――――

The missile shot into the lunar sky. Rang anxiously watched the video images from surveillance satellites.

The rocket sped over the roads, moonbases, research stations, helium-3 mining plants, solar energy collectors, communications towers, and light beacons.

"It is passing over the inhabited side of the Moon, just like we planned,"

Rang said, relieved that the missile had not crashed into the inhabited area as the others had.

"The boost phase is over," Chu reported. "It's entering its suborbital flight."

On a large viewscreen, computer animation showed the missile flying to the uninhabited side of the Moon. Bright white dots flowed from the missile.

"The missile is releasing its chaff and decoys," Chu reported.

Although the missile carried no warhead, it carried warhead decoys and aluminum chaff. The bits of aluminum and the decoys could confuse the enemy about the missile's actual location. Rang nodded his head when he saw the decoys and chaff released. The other missiles had not gotten so far.

"The re-entry phase is starting," Chu said.

The animated flight path ended over the uninhabited side of the Moon. A starburst appeared on the viewscreen.

"That was the impact on the surface, and it was right on target," Chu reported. "The flight is over."

Flight data poured into the computer terminals. Chu looked up from his monitor. "A successful test. Hah, hah, eight is our lucky number!"

"We have the first operational ballistic missile on the Moon," Rang said.

Cheers and applause burst out in the control room. After his anxiety faded, Rang finally smiled.

A man in a colonel's uniform walked into the room. The soldiers suddenly became silent and saluted him. Rang turned around and looked at the colonel.

"Colonel Ming," Rang said, saluting the highest-ranking political commissar on the Moon.

Ming returned the salute and said, "I wanted a break from my work, so I went for a walk out of the political commissars' compound and came here. What do I see? I see that you have successfully launched a rocket, but you did not invite me to watch it."

"I'm sorry. As in any test launch, there is always a chance that it might not be successful. I did not want to interrupt your work in case the launch was not successful. I should have invited you."

"Oh, don't apologize. On the contrary, I am very happy that you finally launched a missile successfully. The Politburo will be very happy." Ming smiled. "Which one of your men solved your engineering problems?"

Nobody said anything.

"We did it together," Rang replied. "It was teamwork."

Ming's smile weakened. "Oh well, then I will have to nominate all of you for medals."

To Rang, Ming sounded disappointed that he would have to commend everyone instead of selecting one to be favored above the others.

"I'll return to the political commissars' compound and finish writing my lecture," Ming said. "Tomorrow, on the anniversary of our first landing on the Moon, I will tell you about the new economic and military policies of the Party."

"We are looking forward to it," Rang lied.

"Prepare the ninth missile for defensive operations, just in case we need it. See to it," Ming ordered as he left the room.

"We need an armed missile on standby," Rang said. "Put a nuclear warhead into the remaining missile."

Captain Chu went to the doorway and looked out. "Ming has gone." He turned to Colonel Rang. "What do we do with the prisoner?"

"Keep hiding her in the officers' mess," Rang said. "We are okay as long as the political commissars stay in their compound."

Father Wycliffe stared at the TV screen. After showing the launch of the Chinese missile, the TV news showed President Zhu of China, standing in front of the emblem of the People's Republic and between two red flags on staffs. The Chinese had obviously arranged the décor to show Zhu with the country's patriotic symbols.

"Now we have the power to protect our mining interests on the Moon," Zhu boasted. "We can protect our claim to the iron deposit and other mineral resources. China will not start a war on the Moon, but she will end it with the destruction of the enemy."

Mary walked into the room, threw her handbag on the couch, and sighed deeply.

"I still can't find her," she said. "She's been gone for two days. How can she disappear on a moonwalk with a bunch of tourists? Where could she be?"

"I don't know," Wycliffe said. "Has she run away from home before?"

"There was the time Jesus went into the desert for forty days."

The Devil tempted Jesus in the desert during those forty days, Wycliffe recalled. What could be happening now?

"To make matters worse, I just heard the news in the commercial district," Mary complained. She touched her crescent moon pendant. "The Chinese have an operational ballistic missile on the Moon. *My* Moon. They're spoiling my dominion."

Wycliffe glanced at a photo of Ingrid and Donald on his desk. "My family died during a missile attack by the Purists. The missile didn't kill them, but a suicide bomber did. I've had enough of war on Earth, and I don't want to be here for war on the Moon."

He sighed deeply. "Maybe Pastor Crowberry is right. These are the End Times. The *Revelation of John* is coming true. The human species is doomed."

"No, no," Mary said, shaking her head. "My daughter wouldn't do anything like that. I know she wants to destroy the world, but you know how teenagers are. If only we could talk to her! Where is she?"

I need to know more about the mysterious visitor, Rang kept telling himself as he walked back to the officers' mess. Although his engineers would take credit for the successful launch, he knew the credit really belonged to the foreign schoolgirl. Who was she?

In the officers' mess, he found Jessica sitting at a table and idly playing with her hair. She was singing a song in a language that Rang didn't recognize. However, he had heard similar songs on the radio, during a mission into the Middle East. It was on a pentatonic scale and maybe Persian, Arab, or Israeli.

The two soldiers silently watched over her, one behind her and one in front of her. Rang pulled out a chair and sat down opposite Jessica.

"So was the missile test successful?" she asked before he could speak.

The question startled Rang. He hadn't told her that he was going to test a missile.

"Yes, it was," he said. "Thank you."

"Oh, no problem, I'll do anything I can to be helpful."

"You've been very helpful to us. Still, I want to know more about you. Who are you? Why are you here?"

"If you must know, I've come to bring peace to the world."

"Which world? The Moon or the Earth?"

"Both."

"By helping us launch a ballistic missile? I agree missiles can preserve peace."

"I don't want peace. I want war."

"But you just said you want peace," Rang said suspiciously. "Who are you, really?"

"The Princess of Peace," Jessica replied. "It's been nice visiting here, but I have other places to go, other people to see."

She rose out of her chair. The soldiers raised their guns and aimed at her. She stopped and looked awkwardly at the soldiers and Colonel Rang.

"I've already given you what you need," she said. "Aren't you going to let me go?"

"Not yet."

Jessica shrugged. "Okay, I have to do that miracle again." She clapped her hands together.

Rang suddenly heard birds chirping. He looked at the bookcase behind him, at the porcelain sparrows that his wife had given him.

The twelve birds had come to life. They were chirping and flapping their wings.

"What?" Rang muttered.

Jessica yelled, "Sparrows be gone!"

The sparrows quickly flew from the bookcase and dove into the soldiers and Colonel Rang. The birds dashed into the men repeatedly, pecking at them and hitting them with their wings. Startled, the men flailed their arms to cast off the birds.

A pair of birds kept fluttering in front of Rang's face. He thrashed out with his fists to hit them, but they kept dodging him. He could see nothing but flapping wings and his own hands hitting the air.

Suddenly, the chirping ended, and the birds flew away. Rang looked at the bookcase. The sparrows were inanimate porcelain figures again.

"The girl is gone!" one of the soldiers shouted.

"Damn!" Rang said. He pulled out his pocket computer and spoke to Captain Chu. "Chu! This is Rang. The teenaged girl has escaped! Go find her. Don't let her get close to the political commissars' compound!"

———

"Stop! You are under arrest!" Captain Chu yelled as he ran towards the airlock.

The girl had put her spacesuit on again. After opening the interior airlock door, she waved at Captain Chu.

Chu drew his gun and aimed at the girl. At that moment, Colonel Rang and the two soldiers arrived.

"Hold your fire," Rang ordered. "No shooting in the station if we can avoid it."

The girl stepped into the airlock and slammed the door shut. Rang, Chu, and the soldiers rushed to the window and saw her run away.

"Shall I order the tanks to chase her?" Chu suggested.

Rang shook his head. "No, no. Just let her go. I don't want anyone to know that a foreign schoolgirl told us how to launch a missile. I don't want anyone to know that she made porcelain birds come to life. I don't know what happened, but it's best to let her go."

Chu pulled a piece of paper from his pocket. "This is the last page that she wrote. She wrote some symbols at the bottom. They have no meaning in rocketry. Do you know what they mean?"

Rang had never seen them before:

XP XP XP XP XP

Rang's pocket computer buzzed. He listened to it, looked at Chu, and sighed.

"That was Colonel Ming," Rang said. "He wants us to go to the political commissars' compound and listen to his lecture about the Party Congress."

Father Wycliffe and the Virgin Mary watched Jessica come back to St. Dominic's Church. The girl, smiling incessantly, pranced past them and went to the kitchen. They followed her there.

As Jessica sang "Havah Nagilah", she took a pitcher of water from the refrigerator and poured the water into a glass. The water turned into red wine as it filled the glass.

Mary grabbed the glass of wine and poured it down the sink. "You're too young to drink," she warned.

Jessica pouted. "Oh, Mommy, you're such a spoilsport," she whined. "It's not as if I was really born yesterday. You, of all people, should remember. I was born over two thousand years ago."

"You've been missing for two days. We've been worried about you," Father Wycliffe said. "Where have you been?"

"At Yue 1," Jessica replied. "Don't you think that's a dorky name for a moonbase? It means 'Moon one' in Chinese. What an unoriginal name."

"Oh, no, you were at the Chinese moonbase," Mary muttered. "Dear, what were you doing there?"

"I broke the fifth seal. I wonder if they noticed I signed my name five times?"

"The fifth seal from the *Revelation of John*," Father Wycliffe realized. "Oh my God."

"You got it, Father. I figured out how to launch their new missile. With a superpower ready to deliver death and destruction anywhere on the Moon, the time of tribulation and martyrdom is coming. Five down, two to go!"

"Young lady, you are grounded!" Mary scolded.

10 / THE BLACK STONE

AMIRA EDIP TELEPORTED to the apparition shrine. When she arrived, she put a *hijab* or headscarf loosely over her head. It was her custom on entering any house of worship, whether it was a mosque, church, synagogue, or temple.

Only a day after the successful Chinese missile launch, many tourists cancelled their trips to the Moon. Those were non-religious visitors, though; pilgrims still flocked to the shrine. She marveled at the people in the reception area. Father Wycliffe was right; it was like a crowded train station where nobody pushed or got rude.

Seldom had she heard so many languages all speaking about the same thing at the same time. She imagined that maybe the Hajj at Mecca had the same loud Babel of languages, but she didn't know from personal experience; since she was Protestant Moslem, the Purists had banned her from Mecca.

A young woman wearing a green *dirndl* brushed past her. Amira laughed to see the famous national dress of Bavaria. It was not the only national costume there. It was like a dress-up day at the United Nations. There was so much color here, unlike Mecca, where all the men wear white robes and all the women wear either white or black.

Along with the flags, rosaries, and statues, some people carried signs reading "PRAY FOR PEACE" and "ATOMS FOR PEACE". Father Wycliffe hadn't mentioned these signs; they could be new signs, undoubtedly in response to the increasing threats of war.

Someone tapped Amira on the shoulder. She turned around and saw a woman wearing a blue jumpsuit with an Austrian flag.

"Excuse me, but are you Imam Edip?" the woman asked in German.

Amira nodded. "Yes, I am. And who are you?"

"Roxanne von Gotha, teleporter operator."

"Ah, yes. Father Wycliffe said you would meet me here."

A handsome man approached them. He wore a uniform with a Belgian flag.

"Okay, Roxanne, I can take over the teleporter for a while," he said in English.

Roxanne leered at him. Her gaze did not hide her lascivious interest in the man.

"Thank you, Auguste. Father Wycliffe asked me to show this visitor around the shrine. I appreciate your helping me, I really do," she purred.

Auguste Peeters smirked at Roxanne. "Anything for you."

"I owe you a favor. If there is *anything* I can do for you, any favor I can perform for you, ask for it."

"I will. Do not worry, I will ask for something from you."

"Then go to Café Méliès tonight. Look for me there."

"I promise to be there," Auguste said as he went to the teleporter control panel.

The lustful banter between Roxanne and Auguste surprised Imam Edip. She hadn't expected to see and hear such things in a holy shrine. But she did not feel any disdain for them. She knew how it felt to be accused of unholy acts in a mosque, and she would not judge others so quickly.

Roxanne steered Amira out of the reception area. "That was Auguste Peeters, the hottest man on the Moon," Roxanne said.

"I see," Amira said, looking back at the teleporter.

"I have seen him at Café Méliès a few times, and I finally got the courage to go to him and talk to him last week. My friend Carla, who works at Café Méliès, thinks he is hot for me. She says she can see it in the way he looks at me."

Carla? Amira wondered if she was the same Carla Delgada who had seen the Virgin Mary, the same girl who went shopping with Jessica, the Schoolgirl Jesus.

They went to a room with a sign reading "ESA AND SHRINE MAINTENANCE CREW ONLY". Roxanne unlocked the door and led Amira in. Several spacesuits hung on the walls.

"Get into one of the spacesuits," Roxanne said. "Then I will show you to the airlock."

Carrying a sensor box, Imam Edip walked to the exposed meteorite. An outdoor light shone on the rock, and she saw that it was black yet shiny.

"It is good that neither the Chinese nor Americans have occupied this area and put barriers around the meteorite," Amira said.

"They both want to, I am sure," Roxanne replied over the helmet radio. "However, whoever does that will start a war. Both of them want to finish a war, but neither wants to start it."

Amira touched the rock. She gasped and pulled her hand away. Then she put her hand back on the rock.

Through the spacesuit glove, she felt a weak vibration. The rock was pulsating.

"What does the sensor say?" Roxanne asked over the helmet radio.

Amira looked at the sensor box. "Yes, it is iron, which I expected, but here is an odd observation. It is emitting strong electrochemical signals."

Electrochemical signals, like in the rumors about asteroid Odette de Proust and Space Station Troika: the meteorite was another Siren Stone.

"Amira, welcome to the Moon," a voice said from behind.

The voice startled her. It hadn't come over the helmet radio. It had come from behind. How could she hear a voice in a vacuum atmosphere? Amira turned around and gasped.

Her brother, Kemal, stood there. Instead of wearing a spacesuit, he wore a denim pants, a white shirt, and a green blazer.

"Kemal, is that you?" Amira asked.

"Yes, sister, it is me."

Shocked and terrified, Amira forced herself to breathe. She panted heavily, sucking in the oxygen in her spacesuit. In contrast, Kemal seemed to be breathing calmly in the airless atmosphere.

The light from the communications tower shone on Kemal at an angle, lighting half of his face and leaving the other half in shadow. His black hair covered his ears. That was too long for Kemal, who preferred his hair shorter. He had even made an appointment with a hair stylist.

But he had died before he could get his hair cut.

"Are you a ghost?" Amira asked.

Amira lectured on space geology at the Free University of Berlin when the Vernacular Movement began. The Vernacularists recited the Koran in languages other than Arabic at the Friday prayers.

Arabic speakers were a minority of the Moslems of the world, and many Moslems sat through the Koran readings without understanding them. According to the Vernacularists, vernacular languages would make Islam more accessible to Moslems born and raised in Europe; show their openness to the wider community; promote understanding of Islam by non-Moslems; and encourage conversions to Islam.

The Purists condemned the radical idea. The Koran came directly from God in Arabic, so it is true only in Arabic. All translations are only human interpretations. To read human interpretations instead of God's direct words is sacrilege. Any prayer leader who recites the Koran in a vernacular language is a heretic.

To incite more hatred against the Vernacularists, the Purists also accused the Vernacularists of being secret Christians. Christianity was the perverse religion that translated its Bible into hundreds of different languages and had no common Bible that all Christians used. Since the Vernacularists were doing the same to the Koran, could they be anything other than apostates working for the Crusaders?

Both heresy and apostasy carried the sentence of death in sharia law. The Purists promised death to the Vernacularists and the infidels who protected them.

Threats from the Purists did not stop the Free Mosque, a liberal mosque serving the university community. Elected by the Free Mosque's members, Amira became its first woman prayer leader. On her first day as an imam, she recited a *surah* of the Koran in German. The worshippers applauded.

Most mosques separated their men and women. Sometimes a partition separated the women from the men. Other mosques sent their women to another room. Often, the women could not see the imam as he spoke. At least those mosques allowed women to enter and pray; some mosques forbade women from entering.

Imam Edip tore down the burlap partition at the Free Mosque and put the women and men together on the same floor of the *musalla* or prayer hall. Men sat on the right side, and women sat on the left side. Although men and women did not sit together as in a Christian church, the women would be in the same room, and they could see the imam.

Edip also did not require the women to leave the mosque before the men. She never could understand why some mosques forbade their women to stay as long as the men. Hadn't God created women too, so are they not as much God's children as the men?

Despite these changes, she felt something was missing in the mosque. When her brother Kemal visited the mosque, he said, "It is too plain. Mosques are not supposed to be as gaudy as those Roman Catholic churches, but they are not supposed to be boring and barren of décor like this one. Redecorate it."

He was right. The mosque was all plain white walls and inspired nobody. Even the simple Protestant chapel at the university had more décor than the Free Mosque.

She redesigned the *mihrab*, the niche in the wall that shows the direction of qibla, the direction to Mecca. The original *mihrab* was a plain niche with the word "Mecca" painted in green Arabic calligraphy. Amira redecorated it with quotes from the Koran, in gold and green, and in Arabic written in the Diwani script of the Ottoman Turks. In the *mihrab*, she put an oak stand holding an old Turkish copy of the Koran.

Kemal, owner of a chocolate shop, donated the money for the new *mihrab*. "Make sure I get a tax receipt," he insisted.

Imam Edip also installed a *minbar* or pulpit, which had been sadly absent. Like most *minbars*, it was a small tower with stairs leading up to it. Unlike other *minbars*, which had one pointed roof, the Free Mosque's *minbar* had two pointed roofs to imitate the steeples of the Cologne Cathedral. By imitating the Cologne Cathedral in miniature, Amira hoped to show that her *masjid* was part of German society, not an alien society within society. Again, the money came from Kemal's chocolate shop.

Finally, Amira hired artists to paint flowing arabesques or repeating geometric forms on the walls of the *musalla*. The arabesques were black, gold, and red: the colors of Germany.

With a beautiful new *mihrab*, *minbar*, and *musalla*, how could anyone doubt that this mosque served the faithful and honored God? The mosque attracted visitors and new worshippers, both men and women, including many from outside the university.

One day, she saw a visitor enter and stand at the back of the *musalla* as she recited from *surah* ninety-five in German:

"We created man from the best fabric, then We brought him down to the lowest of the low, save those who believe and do right things, for theirs shall be a reward that fails not."

The visitor stormed up the center aisle, which separated the men and the women. Now Amira could see him more closely. He wore a blazer, pants, and shirt, all in black. He looked about thirty years old. His long, lean face, with a pointy black beard, looked like Satan.

"There is blasphemy all around us!" he shouted in German with an Arabic accent. "How dare you read the Holy Koran in an infidel language?"

Amira stepped down from the *minbar* and approached the man. "What is wrong with reading a translation of the Koran?"

"A translation is only an interpretation. Why read an interpretation when you can read the words that the Prophet received directly from God?" the man argued.

"Even the direct word of God needs interpretation," Amira said. "All humans are imperfect, so when we listen to God's words, we can never be certain if we know exactly what God means. For centuries, we have been using the *Hadith*, the Prophet's Companions, and theologians and experts to interpret the Koran. Religion is all about interpretation."

"You speak like a Christian," the man accused.

"This is a place of peace. Keep quiet or I will have to ask you to leave," she demanded.

"And look at this!" he shouted. "No wall between the men and the women! Why do you let the women tempt the men into acts of lust and sin? In my *masjid*, women are banned from the *musalla* and must listen in the basement!"

Amira stared at the man and forced herself to remain calm. "God made woman from Adam's rib, so a woman is not supposed to be behind a man, beneath him, or separated from him, but at his side."

"Bah!" The man began a speech about the corruption of Christians and Jews.

As the man kept shouting, Amira saw a male worshipper take out his pocket computer and whisper into it. She silently prayed that he was calling the university police.

A minute later, two university police officers ran into the mosque. *Thank God, the campus patrol reacted quickly*, Amira thought. They did not take off their shoes, but Amira silently forgave them for the breach of protocol and knew God would do so too.

A police officer pointed at the man. "Is this the man who disturbed the prayer service?"

Amira nodded. The officer turned to the man and ordered, "Show us your identification."

The man grumbled, took his I.D. card out of his wallet, and shoved it at the officer. The officer swiped the card through his pocket computer and read the man's information.

"Your surname is Al-Majuj, first name is Yosuf, correct?" the officer said. "You are a naturalized German citizen born in Amman, Jordan. You are not a student. You are a chemical engineer, educated at University of Toronto in Canada, now working for a Libyan food firm in Germany. You have no previous criminal convictions. Is this correct information about you?"

Al-Majuj grunted.

"Ah, but this is interesting," the police officer said. "Were you thrown out of a beer hall due to drunken conduct at Oktoberfest in Munich two years ago? Fortunately for you, the beer hall did not press charges."

Al-Majuj glared at the officer. "I have repented and found God. Have you?"

The officer ignored Al-Majuj and returned his I.D. card to him.

The second police officer held up his pocket computer and took a photo of Al-Majuj. Al-Majuj flinched at the camera flash. "I am just updating our files," the officer explained.

The officer turned to Amira. "We will ban him from the campus for trespassing," he said. "Do you also wish to press charges of disturbing the peace and uttering threats?"

"No, no," Amira said. "I just want this matter to end peacefully for everyone. I do not have time to go to court. Just escort him from the campus."

The police officer turned to Al-Majuj. "You are lucky that she is so forgiving to you."

Al-Majuj snickered. "You think keeping me away from your infidel university will save you from God's judgment?"

Grabbing Al-Majuj by his arms, the police hauled him out of the mosque. Amira returned to the *minbar* and resumed the prayers.

———

A year later, the Vernacular Wars came to Europe, where Purist terrorists killed scores of people. However, customers of Chocolatier Beau Spree saw no signs of war at the shop. As Christmas carols played softly on the sound system, chocolate angels rotated on a carousel in the store window. Wrapped in red and green aluminum foil, the chocolate angels added color to the dark winter night.

Beautiful Spree Chocolate Shop. For reasons that Amira never understood, Kemal had given a French name to his chocolate shop, named after the River Spree in Berlin. Despite the odd name, Chocolatier Beau Spree prospered by selling luxury chocolates from all over Europe.

Amira counted chocolate angels in the back room. Then she heard someone shouting from the front room.

Who was arguing with Kemal? She went to the doorway, looked out, and gasped.

As Kemal stood behind the cash register, a man thumped his fist against the counter.

He was Yosuf Al-Majuj.

"You call yourself a Moslem, but why do you not have a beard, my friend?" Al-Majuj demanded.

"The girls like me better clean shaven," Kemal retorted.

Al-Majuj grunted. "My friend, are they sisters or infidels?"

"What difference does it make to you?"

"Everything in our community is my business, my friend." Al-Majuj picked up a chocolate Saint Nicholas. "Look at you, selling *haram* chocolate to *kaffirs* for their holidays."

"This is Germany. I can sell *halal* chocolates, I can sell *haram* chocolates, and I can sell them to anyone. You can choose to buy either *halal* or *haram* chocolates. The choice is yours."

"With such infidel sympathies, my friend, no wonder you have never paid the *jihad* tax."

Amira shuddered when she heard Al-Majuj mention the *jihad* tax. To pay for their terrorism, the Purists extorted money from European Moslems. They murdered those who wouldn't pay.

A year ago, Al-Majuj had been simply an obnoxious pest, disruptive but harmless. Now he was a terrorist, eager to kill innocent people.

Still hiding behind the doorway, Amira punched the police emergency number into her handheld computer. "There is a terrorist robbing the shop Chocolatier Beau Spree," she said softly.

"I heard something," Al-Majuj said. "There is someone else here! Show yourself!"

Amira held her breath and did not move. She heard Al-Majuj moving to the doorway.

"Stop!" Kemal yelled. He darted at Al-Majuj and tackled him. The two men fell on a display table and scattered chocolates all over the floor.

They fell to the floor and fought. Grabbing and punching each other, they rolled on the floor. Kemal, on top of Al-Majuj, smashed his fist into Al-Majuj's nose. The terrorist howled in pain as blood gushed from his nose. Throwing his weight down, Kemal pinned the terrorist down.

With one hand, Al-Majuj pushed up Kemal's chin. With his other hand, Al-Majuj pulled a switchblade knife out of his pocket and flicked the blade out.

Al-Majuj shouted, *"Allahu Akbar!"* Howling like a demon, he stabbed the knife up into Kemal's throat.

Amira screamed and ran out. Al-Majuj rolled over Kemal, pulled his knife out of Kemal's throat, stood up, and stepped towards Amira. Covered with Kemal's blood, he pointed the knife at her.

Suddenly, police car sirens wailed from the street. Al-Majuj looked out the window and scowled. As the sirens grew louder, he ran from the shop.

Amira kneeled over Kemal and pressed her hands against the gash in his neck. He was still and silent and had stopped breathing.

His blood flowed over the chocolate angels scattered on the floor.

Al-Majuj fled from Germany and resurfaced in Jordan as Imam Yosuf, the Purist leader who fought against Queen Areej. When the Jordanians captured him, he begged the German Government to take him back and try him for crimes committed in Germany. Since Germany had no death penalty, the government realized that Al-Majuj was trying to escape the death sentence in Jordan. Germany asked Jordan to prosecute him for attempting to assassinate Queen Areej. After the Jordanians convicted him, they hanged him.

After Kemal's death, Amira cursed herself for not pressing charges against

Al-Majuj at the mosque. If only she had pressed charges, Al-Majuj could have gone to jail. Her brother had died for her act of forgiveness.

She found the mosque where Al-Majuj had worshipped. On a Friday morning, before the worshippers arrived for prayers, she nailed a piece of paper on the mosque's door. The paper listed twenty reforms she demanded from the mosque's imam.

Others followed her example by sending demands to radical imams, and a new Protestant movement started in Europe. Not since Martin Luther's time had so many Europeans demanded reforms from their religious leaders.

Nailing the demands to the mosque door did not end Amira's guilt and pain. Neither did the Protestant Reformation she started. Wishing to escape from Earth, she joined the ESA as a geologist and chaplain. Only after she had served three years on Mars did she feel enough peace to return to Earth.

Now on Earth's Moon, her dead brother was talking to her.

———

"Kemal, how can you be here?" she asked.

"I will always be alive in your heart and mind as long as you remember me," he replied.

Amira inhaled deeply. "Kemal, is God letting us talk one last time?"

"I do not know."

"Is there a heaven, a paradise?"

Kemal shook his head. "I am sorry, but mortal humans cannot know the answer to that question until they pass out of this life. Until then, rely on your faith to give you the answers."

"Of course," Amira said. "Such things must remain mysteries to human beings. Otherwise, we would be like gods."

Tears flowed down her cheeks. "Oh, Kemal, I would gladly give my life for yours! How I hate what I did to you! You must hate me too!"

"Stop crying, sister," Kemal said. "I do not feel any grudge against you. You are my sister; how can I hate you?"

"Oh, Kemal!" She ran to him and hugged him. He felt solid. Ghosts weren't supposed to feel solid, but Amira didn't care.

She felt his warmth. How could she feel the heat through her insulated spacesuit? Did it matter?

"I forgive you," Kemal said. "Do not feel the burden of guilt anymore."

As she sobbed, Amira muttered, "Thank, you, thank you, thank you..."

"The English have a saying about every cloud having a silver lining," Kemal said. "Look at our lives this way. Our tragedy got you to protest against the radical imams who oppressed the people. Others followed your example, and reforms started."

"Oh, do all good things require such a heavy price?" Amira asked.

"Sometimes the sacrifice must be great."

"I fear what sacrifices will be needed. Can there never be peace for our world? Even the Moon is in danger. The world is heading for another war because of this rock."

Kemal gently pushed himself away and looked at the meteorite. "Ah, the rock. Do you think it belongs here?"

"An interesting question," Amira said. "The geologists think it is a meteorite because iron is rare on the Moon, and the Moon has no iron deposits like this. But meteorites fall from space, so why is there no impact crater? Why is it under a hill instead? How did it get here? It is a mystery."

"Stones like this do not belong here. They belong in deep space."

"Like the Siren Stones?"

"You understand. Do you want my advice?"

"You gave me good advice about redecorating the mosque. Do not stop there. Give me more."

"Remember the story of the Prophet Mohammed and the Black Stone of the Kaaba?"

The Black Stone is Islam's most sacred relic, most probably a meteorite that fell in Arabia centuries ago. Moslems consider it a gift from God and proof of His existence. It sits in the Kaaba, a cube-shaped shrine built by the prophet Ibrahim in Mecca. Moslems do not worship it, but they venerate it. Each year, two million pilgrims visit the Kaaba and kiss the Black Stone.

"How does the story relate to this meteorite?" Amira asked.

Kemal told the story. "Remember, in Mohammed's time, the Kaaba housed the pagan idols that Arabs worshipped before they converted to Islam. After he received his revelation from God, he destroyed the idols in the Kaaba, but he left the Black Stone there. The Arabs already had it in the Kaaba for centuries before Mohammed was born. The Kaaba is a gift from God and reminds us of His existence.

"Even before Mohammed began his ministry, he was involved with the Black Stone. At one time, the Kaaba was a yard enclosed by a wall. The tribes around Mecca rebuilt it on the same foundation laid by Ibrahim, but with higher walls and a roof. During the construction, they removed their pagan idols and the Black Stone and put them aside. When they finished the building, they had to put the Black Stone back in its original corner.

"They argued over who should put the Black Stone back into the southeast corner. Each tribe thought it should have the honor. Violence nearly broke out until they agreed to wait for the next man who came through the gate. They would let that man make the decision.

"By chance, Mohammed came through the gate, and they asked him who should put the Black Stone in its place. Mohammed had not yet started his ministry, but he had already earned a reputation as being a wise man. He listened carefully to each tribe's claim to the honor.

"After listening to the tribes, he spread his cloak on the floor. Then he put the Black Stone on the cloak.

"He told the leaders of all the tribes to hold the cloak by its edge. They raised the Black Stone together and carried it to the corner.

"At the corner, Mohammed set the Stone in place. All the tribes were satisfied without bloodshed."

"I see," Amira said. "If we were to put the meteorite back where it belongs, if nobody could possess it, there will be no reason to fight."

Amira looked at the meteorite. A second later, she turned to look at Kemal, but he had disappeared.

———

"You were talking to someone, but I did not hear anyone else on the radio," Roxanne said as she helped Amira get out of her spacesuit.

Amira looked pensive. "I think I saw a ghost out there."

"A ghost?"

"Yes, a ghost."

"I have never heard of any ghost sightings on the Moon before," Roxanne said. "Forgive me for sounding skeptical, but this is difficult to believe."

"I do not blame you," Amira said. "As a scientist, I cannot say that it happened. I do not know if it actually happened. But I *feel* it happened."

11 / PERSONA NON GRATA

Father Wycliffe heard other people's confessions by videophone during his time around Mars. Since TV signals traveled instantly between the space stations, he could talk to people and give absolution to them in real-time. The sacrament of Reconciliation occurred like a conversation, as it should, even by videophone in Mars orbit.

The logistics of Father Wycliffe's own confession were much more difficult. Without another Catholic priest near Mars, Wycliffe had to confess by videophone to Cardinal Saint-Cloud on Earth. The TV signal took twenty-four minutes and twenty-four seconds to travel from Mars to Earth. Cardinal Saint-Cloud's reply would take just as long to go from Earth to Mars. Hence, the shortest dialogue took over forty-eight minutes. The sacrament of Reconciliation consisted of the confession and the absolution with no conversation between them. Fortunately, Father Wycliffe had no serious sins to confess around Mars.

Confessing to Cardinal Saint-Cloud from the Moon was easier; TV signals traveled instantly between Earth and the Moon. Like before, Wycliffe seldom had anything serious to confess, so the real-time dialogue did not matter too much to him.

Today, though, Father Wycliffe appreciated the real-time dialogue between Earth and the Moon. He and the Cardinal needed to talk; he was going to confess to a sin more painful than any he had committed around Mars.

"Bless me, Your Eminence, for I have sinned," Father Wycliffe said by videophone.

"How have you sinned?" Cardinal Saint-Cloud asked.

"I am losing my faith in God," replied Father Wycliffe.

Cardinal Saint-Cloud stared back at him by videophone. "This is an unusual confession. Please tell me more."

Wycliffe took a deep breath. "I used to think that God wants the human race to live. But now, I think He wants us to destroy ourselves. I cannot have faith in a God who wants our death."

"Why do you think that God will abandon us to our self-destruction?" Saint-Cloud asked.

"I lost my family in the Vernacular Wars. I saw many families lose their loved ones in the wars. A million people died like sacrifices. They weren't sacrifices to God — our God doesn't take human sacrifices — but rather, they were sacrifices for peace. When the wars ended, I thought we would get peace. After all, we sacrificed enough people, including my wife and son.

"Lunar colonization expanded after the Vernacular Wars. People did everything possible to guarantee peace on the Moon. We signed treaties banning weapons on the Moon. We built moonbases for scientific research and peaceful trade. We built churches and shrines on the Moon. Yet despite all these good works, we have weapons and countries ready to go to war. It'll be a war of annihilation; the human race might not recover this time.

"Everything that I do here is in vain. Every day, I tell the people at Mass that God and Jesus love us. Yet no amount of sacrifice and work can bring peace and love. Maybe God isn't a god of peace and love. Maybe He's a god of judgment and punishment. Maybe that's why everyone is obsessed with judging others and punishing them. The future is hopeless."

Cardinal Saint-Cloud looked pensive. "When hope dies, so does faith," he said. "Your loss of hope in humanity is destroying your faith in God.

"I know you saw much death and destruction in the wars. Sadly, your experience is not unique. Millions of people have lost their families. I am not saying that your loss is insignificant in any way; on the contrary, the personal losses are the worst. What I am saying is that human nature has caused your suffering.

"The human race is always challenging our capacity to hope. That is human nature and a symptom of our Original Sin. People have fought wars since civilization began: enough wars to end civilization long ago. We should have degenerated back to primitive cavemen without art, culture, or science. We have nearly fallen into total barbarism, especially when we created fascism in the twentieth century. Yet we have always recovered, and civilization keeps moving forward. When we try to destroy ourselves, God somehow redeems and saves us."

Wycliffe sighed softly. "No, God will let us destroy ourselves this time. He's unhappy with His creation."

"But we can never know that for sure, can we?" Saint-Cloud said.

"Jesus told me," Wycliffe said.

Cardinal Saint-Cloud looked puzzled. "He told you? You have seen him?"

"Yes, I've seen him, uh, her –- or an illusion of her, I don't know which," Wycliffe said. "A female Jesus appeared on the Moon, just like she appeared on Troika."

"I read the Troika crew's report and your report too. I am not convinced that the female Jesus actually is Jesus," Saint-Cloud said. "You too were skeptical that she was Jesus, were you not?"

"Yes, I was."

"And are you still skeptical?"

"Actually, I still am. I don't know what to make of her," Wycliffe admitted.

"Then do not believe things against your better judgment," Saint-Cloud advised. "You must keep your faith. Although there seems to be no tangible basis for faith, that is how faith is. Just believe it. As your superior, I urge you to think about your faith again."

Wycliffe nodded. "I'll try."

"Good, good," Saint-Cloud said. "The English have an expression: 'Hang in there.' The lunar colonists need you now more than ever. The Church needs you now more than ever. Keep the faith –- now more than ever."

"Thank you," Wycliffe said.

"Thank you for calling me," Saint-Cloud said. He smiled. "Remember what I said. *Au revoir et bonne chance.*"

"*Au revoir*, Your Eminence."

After Saint-Cloud ended the videophone call, Wycliffe realized that the Cardinal had not given him absolution for his sin. He remained unreconciled with God.

As the music pounded off the walls, the Moon's younger people partied at Café Méliès. It was a regular restaurant during the weekdays, but it became a wild dance club on weekends. Music blared from the speakers as people danced on the crowded floor. Laughing and shouting filled the air. Strobe lights flashed in the darkness.

The air reeked of perfume as women passed Father Wycliffe, Amira Edip, and Mary. The motley trio sat at a table and sipped their drinks.

Wycliffe had changed into a blue blazer and ordinary white shirt after the daily Mass. Although he was escorting the Virgin Mary and an imam tonight, he did not want to wear his black suit and shirt with the Roman collar. He could have worn his clerical garb to escort the two religious persons. However, clerical garb would attract too much attention on party night in this nightclub.

His companions did not look like religious figures either. Amira wore a shiny silvery dress that fell above her knees. A gold barrette decorated her hair. She sat in her chair and swayed with the music.

The Virgin Mary still wore the blue business suit that she had worn on Troika. Her crescent moon pendant flashed like lightning as it reflected the strobe lights.

Wycliffe looked at the bodies gyrating on the dance floor. Everywhere, people were dancing, drinking, and kissing.

"I haven't come to a club like this since I was in university," he said to Amira.

Amira smiled. "Neither have I. I am glad that I came here tonight. It makes me feel young again."

"It does? It makes me feel old," Wycliffe said.

"Well, you are a bit older than me," Amira chided him.

Wycliffe took another sip of his beer. "Don't remind me that you were the youngest chaplain in the ESA. You outran all us old guys in the treadmill competition."

"Oh, the girls are coming," Mary said as she put down her kosher red wine.

Carla and Jessica walked to their table. Instead of wearing her waitress uniform, Carla wore a pink tank top and matching shorts and high heels. Jessica wore her school uniform and the black go-go boots that she had bought in Timonium.

"Are you not working tonight?" Wycliffe asked Carla.

"No, I got the night off, so I'm partying!" Carla replied, jumping up and down.

Amira took a sip of her herbal tea and said, "You come back to your place of work to party?"

Carla nodded. "Sure, if it's the hottest nightclub on the Moon."

"It's the only nightclub on the Moon," Jessica added sardonically. She looked at Amira. "Wow, that's a smoking hot dress! So short and sassy and silvery and shiny! Where did you get it?"

Amira smiled and struck a pose, like a fashion model. "I got it at Angelo of Beverly Hills in the commercial district."

"Angelo of Beverly Hills?" Jessica said excitedly. "I saw the cutest bag there. I have to go back there and get it."

"No, dear, save your money. Why buy the bag if you're going to end the world next week?" Mary said.

"What's this about ending the world?" Carla asked.

"Oh, nothing," Jessica said. She rolled up her eyes. "This is so not cool. Why does my parental unit follow me on Saturday night?"

"Go have fun with your friends. I'll stay out of your way," Mary promised. "I'm here with friends too, so we'll just stay here."

Carla leaned towards Jessica and said, "I think your mother is hot! Is she here to pick up guys?" Carla giggled as Jessica moaned.

"Believe me, my mother is practically a virgin," Jessica said.

Carla laughed, grabbed Jessica's hand, and pulled her to the dance floor.

"If you grounded her, why is she roaming around the nightclub?" Wycliffe asked.

"She left her room," Mary lamented.

"I was at daily Mass and didn't see her leave. How did she leave?"

"She walked out the doorway."

"That's it? She simply walked out?"

"Yes. Isn't that the normal way to leave your room?"

"Why didn't you try to stop her?"

"She walks on water. She turns water into wine. She comes back from the dead. She takes after her father. How can I stop her from leaving her room?"

"So why are we here?" said Amira.

"To make sure she doesn't do anything rash –- like destroy the world," Mary said.

"As if we could stop God," Wycliffe said.

They watched Carla and Jessica dance with each other. Later, a young man and woman joined the girls on the dance floor. In the flashes of strobe light, Wycliffe saw that the woman wore a red bolero jacket and miniskirt and the man wore a green shirt and pants.

"They look familiar. Who are they?" Amira asked.

Wycliffe tried to see in the darkness lit by strobe light. "I think they're Roxanne von Gotha and Auguste Peeters. They're ESA teleporter operators."

"Oh, I met them at the apparition shrine. No wonder he is the Hottest Man on the Moon. He is dancing with three girls," Amira observed.

"Ah, but he's not going to get involved with Jessica," Mary said. "She may seem like a party girl, but she is made of the same substance as God."

———

Roxanne and Carla sauntered by, heading towards the washroom. As the ladies passed by, Wycliffe saw that Roxanne had unbuttoned her jacket, showing that she wore only a red bra underneath.

"I've seen that bra before," Wycliffe said.

"Yes, I brought it to the medical center after I went shopping with Carla," Jessica said.

Wycliffe turned around and saw Jessica standing at the table.

"Look at Roxanne," Jessica said. "Do you think she's hot?"

Wycliffe, Amira, and Mary nodded silently.

Jessica grinned. "I chose the bra, the jacket, and the skirt for her. Carla and I bought some new clothes for her because we want her to look hot for Auguste."

"So that's where my money card went," Mary said.

Jessica turned to Mary. "Mommy, can I borrow a gold unit?"

"Why?" Mary asked.

"I want to buy drinks and food for my friends," she said.

"You spent my whole money card in the commercial district," Mary reminded her. "Why don't you do what you did in Bethsaida? You fed five thousand people with five loaves of bread and two fishes."

"You always want me to show off that I can do miracles with alcoholic beverages and food. Okay, if you want me to do that again, I can. But I have to start with something, like one bottle of beer and a hot dog," Jessica said.

Mary looked at Wycliffe. "Father, can you give her five euros? That should be enough for one bottle of beer and a hot dog."

Father Wycliffe fished in his pockets and pulled out a money card. Its denomination was ten euros, but its counter panel read "5.00".

"This one still has five euros on it," he said as he passed the money card to Jessica.

"Thank you," Jessica said as she grabbed the card. She ran to the bar.

"She seems to be enjoying herself before the Apocalypse," Amira remarked. "She has made several new friends here."

"Every mother wants to see her child make friends, but I'm troubled that she's going to kill them in the Apocalypse," Mary said. "Why make friends if you're going to kill them a week later?"

After talking to the bartender, Jessica carried a tray of four bottles of beer and four hot dogs to the table where her friends sat. Wycliffe was sure that the money card had only five euros.

"It looks like she worked another miracle," Mary said.

"Either that or she sweet-talked the bartender into giving her extra hot dogs and beer," Wycliffe suggested.

"Hey, she looks too young to buy alcohol. Did the bartender check her identification card? Does she carry any identification?" Amira wondered.

They watched the young people eat and drink. Wycliffe looked wistfully at Roxanne and Auguste. Their laughing and bantering reminded him of his university days with Ingrid.

A short time later, Jessica, Carla, Roxanne, and Auguste returned to the dance floor.

"Oh, what are they doing?" Amira asked.

On the dance floor, Jessica pushed Auguste from behind as Carla did the same to Roxanne. They pushed Auguste and Roxanne together. Since Auguste was a couple inches taller than Roxanne, Jessica pushed Auguste's face down against Roxanne's. Auguste and Roxanne shared a long, lingering kiss while Jessica and Carla laughed and held them together.

"I think they are playing matchmaker," Amira said.

"Jesus is playing matchmaker. Everything is going to Hell here," Wycliffe mumbled.

"I'm a bit tired," he said as he rose from his chair. "I'm going home now. See you back at the church."

As he walked out of Café Méliès, he saw a TV behind one of the bars. U.S. President Darby was speaking from the White House again. With the loud music, Wycliffe could not hear the TV, but he saw the headline superimposed at the bottom of the screen: "DARBY ORDERS USE OF LETHAL FORCE ON VEHICLES ENTERING PROTECTION ZONE".

BBC Space news went to its next news item, and he recognized the people it showed. All over the world, the apostolic nuncios, the Vatican's diplomatic corps, were meeting with leaders and foreign ministers of many countries. He knew the archbishop visiting the foreign minister of Brazil. In Kinshasa, Cardinal Ferrata was talking to the Emperor of the Congo, an ally of China. In Paris, Cardinal Saint-Cloud was talking to the President of the European Commission. In the Vatican, Pope Christopher complained that the Chinese foreign minister would not phone him.

The headline superimposed on the screen was "VATICAN DIPLOMATS TRY TO PREVENT MOON WAR".

He looked back into the nightclub and saw Jesus dancing with her friends. This is how the world ends: God plays like an adolescent while the mortals work in futility.

———

Cardinal Saint-Cloud looked startled on the videophone. "Maybe there is a glitch in the transmission. What did you say?"

"I am asking for permission to leave the Moon and return to Earth," Father Wycliffe repeated.

"Well, this is a change," Cardinal Saint-Cloud remarked. "Two years ago, you wanted to stay away from Earth. Even the Moon was too close to Earth. Now you cannot wait to come back."

The videophone beeped. Saint-Cloud looked down at his message panel, and his eyes widened.

"We have a third person asking to join our call," he said. "You will want to see him."

The cardinal pressed a button, and the videophone image split in two: Cardinal Saint-Cloud from Paris on the left side of the screen, and Pope Christopher from the Vatican on the right side of the screen.

"Your Holiness!" Father Wycliffe said.

"Your Holiness, is your meeting over?" Cardinal Saint-Cloud asked.

The Pope frowned. "The Chinese sent a mere consulate information officer to meet me, and she had authority only to pick up written messages from me and give them to the consul. She works for the consul, not the ambassador. And she's a tourism information officer, not anyone working in foreign relations. I waited for her, and all for nothing."

"What an insult," Saint-Cloud said.

"Enough about the Chinese. On to other matters," the Pope said. "Father Wycliffe, I am sorry for interrupting your conversation with the Cardinal, but I wish to talk to both of you. I would have joined the call from the start had I not been waiting for the Ambassador of China. Has the Cardinal explained the importance of remaining on the Moon?"

"We had not gotten to discuss that yet," Saint-Cloud said. "Our conversation started on a different topic. Father Wycliffe has asked for permission to leave the Moon and return to Earth."

"Oh? Father, why do you want to leave?" Pope Christopher asked.

"The Moon is certainly doomed. There is no good that I can do here anymore. I would rather be on Earth now," Wycliffe said.

"And leave the parish of St. Dominic untended?"

"When war breaks out on the Moon, the parish is doomed. I can do nothing to save people here. It would be best if everyone left the Moon."

"No, you must stay on the Moon," the Pope urged. "We cannot retreat from space. That would be a great defeat to the human spirit. When the human spirit is defeated, hope dies, and so too does faith in God. As priests, we must fight against the loss of human spirit, hope, and faith."

"But is there anything we can really do?" Wycliffe asked.

"I know it seems grim," the Pope admitted. "China and the United States vetoed each other on the U.N. Security Council again. I've sent diplomats to China's African allies and the United States' Latin American allies to ask them to put pressure on their respective superpower friends. Our entire diplomatic corps is trying to prevent a war. I do not know how successful this effort will be.

"The last diplomatic frontier is the Moon. I have a mission for you."

Father Wycliffe felt as if his blood were freezing. "What is it?" he asked.

"The United States' strategy has been to blockade the U.S. protection zone. The Americans block and ram moonbuses, and they won't let spacecraft fly over the protection zone. They haven't killed anyone yet, though," the Pope said.

The Pope continued. "Last night, the President of the United States ordered Moonbase Liberty's commander to attack, with deadly force, any ground or sky vehicle that enters the protection zone. That is, the commander has orders to shoot to kill. You know how China will retaliate if the U.S. kills a Chinese citizen.

"The Cardinal Secretary of State has asked the U.S. State Department if you could visit Moonbase Liberty. The United States has agreed. President Darby is an atheist, but he doesn't want bad publicity from turning away my representative.

"Your mission is to visit the military commander of Moonbase Liberty and convince him not to destroy any vehicle that enters the protection zone. Instead, get him to capture the vehicles and their crews. Anything but kill them."

Wycliffe shook his head. "With all due respect, Your Holiness, that's impossible. American military officers are very well trained. Liberty's commander will follow orders. He will shoot down spacecraft."

"Not necessarily," the Pope said. "President Darby knows some vehicles cause more public relations trouble than others. He knows he could never explain shooting down a ship like an ambulance shuttlecraft. Therefore, he has given the commander the discretion to capture vehicles if extenuating circumstances justify so. For example, if a spacecraft sends a distress signal, will the Americans shoot it down? The commander could let the ship land and capture it and its crew.

"However, he will still be following orders if he shoots down the ship instead. Visit the American commander and convince him to always try to capture the vehicle rather than destroy it."

"We need you to try," Cardinal Saint-Cloud added. "You are the Holy See's only accredited diplomat on the Moon."

Not an apostolic nuncio, but a mere legate with no diplomatic training, Wycliffe thought. A heavy responsibility for someone unfit for it.

"We have the name of the commander of Moonbase Liberty," Saint-Cloud said. "His name is a military secret, but the U.S. State Department told us on condition that we keep it secret too. He is Colonel Michael Chang, a veteran of the Haiti Vernacular War. He was in deep space before coming here. I'm sorry we don't know much more about him."

"Michael Chang? Is he the same colonel who landed on asteroid Odette de Proust?" Wycliffe asked.

"Yes, it is the same person *rumored* to have gone to Odette de Proust," Saint-Cloud replied. "The incident is officially top secret despite the information leaks."

"How will I go to Moonbase Liberty?" Wycliffe asked. "I can't teleporter over there."

"You will have to fly there. It is the fastest way," Cardinal Saint-Cloud replied. "You are rated to fly shuttlecrafts, correct? Dr. Schiller will ask Mr. Layman to borrow a shuttlecraft from Timonium Base."

Great, I'll be flying over the Moon's most dangerous no-fly zone, Wycliffe thought.

A few hours later, Cardinal Ferrata called Father Wycliffe. The Cardinal Secretary of State looked tired.

"Forgive me for not joining the call with the Holy Father and Cardinal Saint-Cloud earlier," Ferrata said. "I was still meeting the Emperor or the Congo." He grimaced. "The Emperor is completely obedient to Zhu Biao after the Chinese paid for his coronation."

"Oh, yes, I remember that one," Wycliffe said. "The Pope did not attend because he would not put the crown on the Emperor, so the Chinese sent their Politburo-approved archbishop to do it."

"You can buy an entire country for twenty million euros, the cost of a coronation ceremony," Ferrata said. "But let us talk about your trip to Moonbase Liberty. I have arranged the visit with the U.S. Department of State.

"You will enter the U.S. protection zone between fifteen hundred and sixteen hundred hours tomorrow, standard lunar time. When you cross over the protection zone, give a password to Moonbase Liberty. The password is essential; if you do not give them the password, they will assume that you are hostile and shoot you down. I am sending the password by encrypted e-mail now."

Father Wycliffe heard a beep from his pocket computer. He looked at it and read the e-mail.

"I've got the password," he said.

"Good, you are ready to go," Ferrata said. "You are the only person with permission to fly over the U.S. protection zone. Good luck, Father."

"I'll need it," Wycliffe muttered.

The next day, he put on his clerical clothes and pinned his Vatican Observatory badge and British medal ribbons to his jacket. Perhaps he could build some goodwill with Colonel Chang by showing he had been a military chaplain.

He put his Vatican diplomatic passport in the inside breast pocket of his jacket. If the political crisis degraded further, he might need diplomatic immunity to stay out of a prison.

Someone knocked on his door. He opened it, and Mary came in.

"Good luck on your mission," Mary said.

"Take this cup away from me," said Wycliffe.

Mary looked intrigued. "You're quoting my daughter when she was a boy."

"I told you on Troika that I don't want a diplomatic job. I don't want to negotiate peace between nations. I'm not trained for international diplomacy. I'll be negotiating with a military commander who has no authority to negotiate for his country. This mission is doomed to failure," Wycliffe said sadly.

"No, have faith. Millions of people depend on you."

"That's the problem. Millions of people: that's an incredible burden for one man. If I fail, will the end of the human race be my fault?"

"When you fear failure, you are committing the sin of pride," Mary said. "It is pride that makes us fear failure; it is pride that stops us from doing the right thing. Sin no more; go out and do God's work."

"Isn't God out to destroy us?" Wycliffe asked.

"She is." Mary shrugged. "Do His work by doing the opposite. I know it's complicated, but have faith that you are doing the right thing."

"Thanks," said Father Wycliffe.

"Don't forget to wear this," Mary said as she picked a chain off Wycliffe's desk.

It was the chain holding the medal of Our Lady of Walsingham. Father Wycliffe had worn the medal throughout his career, from Walsingham, to the

Moon, to Mars, and now back to the Moon. He had worn it on his trip to Troika.

Mary put it in his palm and closed his hand. "Wear it and remember me," she said.

―――――

He climbed into the Tsiolkovsky service shuttlecraft borrowed from Timonium Base. He hung his jacket on a coat hook, retrieved his flight plan from the computer, and disconnected the shuttlecraft's airlock from the shuttlecraft dock. As Timonium's sky traffic controllers chattered on the radio, he prepared for flight.

As he lifted off and flew above the glittering buildings of Timonium, he wondered if his mission had any chance of success.

―――――

As he approached the U.S. protection zone, he heard the closet door creak open behind him. He was sure he had lowered the latch on the door. The door should not be open.

He looked back and saw Jessica leaving the small closet.

"What are you doing here?" he asked worriedly.

"I'm going to open the sixth seal," she replied as she sat down in the seat beside him.

The sixth of seven seals in the End Times in the *Book of Revelation*, Wycliffe realized.

"How are you going to do that?" he asked.

"You'll see," she said, her eyes full of mischief.

Wycliffe turned back to the shuttlecraft's controls. The coordinates panel lit up; the shuttlecraft flew into the U.S. protection zone.

"Excuse me. I have to identify myself to the Americans with a special password," he said.

"Not if a solar flare were to interrupt communications," Jessica said.

"What solar flare? Sunspot activity is low. No solar flares are forecast, are they?" Wycliffe said nervously.

"In my God the Father persona, I flooded the Earth and parted the Red Sea and created the Star of Bethlehem. You think I can't make a solar flare?"

Wycliffe opened a radio channel to Moonbase Liberty. A voice from Liberty said, "Foreign vessel, identify yourself."

"Moonbase Liberty, this is Timonium shuttlecraft, password Alpha ten..." he began.

Suddenly, a loud crackling noise came from the radio.

"I've lost contact with Liberty," Wycliffe said. "What have you done?"

"Like I said, I made a solar flare."

Wycliffe groaned. A burst of magnetic energy and radiation covered the Moon. It knocked out all communications on the Moon: between Earth and the Moon, between moonbases, between spacecraft, and between moonbases and spacecraft.

The shuttlecraft's shielding protected him from the radiation, but it wouldn't protect him from American missiles.

"If I don't give them the password, they'll shoot us down," Wycliffe said.

He saw a U.S. moon tank on the ground below. As he passed over the moon tank, the moon tank's coil gun shot a projectile up. The projectile exploded in front of the shuttlecraft, and bright flares lit up the sky until their oxidizer expired.

"I think that was a warning flare," Wycliffe said. He still heard only static from the radio. "The next one might be a serious."

"Don't worry, you'll be safe," Jessica assured him.

The shuttlecraft sped towards Moonbase Liberty. Liberty's famous towers appeared. Half of Liberty was underground, and the other half was above ground with lightweight radiation shielding.

He saw something new beside Moonbase Liberty: a long, wide metal tube pointing up a sloping earthwork.

"A mass driver," Wycliffe said. "The Americans are building a mass driver."

The mass driver was essentially a coil gun. Electromagnets within the long tube would activate in sequence, creating electromagnetic fields that propelled a magnetic payload through the tube and shot it out. This mass driver was much larger than the coil guns mounted on the moon tanks.

Another moon tank shot a projectile at the shuttlecraft. Again, it exploded in front of the shuttlecraft, but this time, the explosion's blast kicked the shuttlecraft. Father Wycliffe quickly shot some thrusters to stabilize the flight.

Flares flew into the sky. Another small rocket exploded beside the shuttlecraft. Crackling continued on the radio.

"I'm taking her down before they hit us," he said.

Without authorization from Liberty, he landed the shuttlecraft at the moonbase's spacecraft dock. As he docked the shuttlecraft, Jessica pulled a spacesuit out of the closet and quickly put it on.

"Don't tell anyone that I'm here, okay?" she said before putting the helmet on. She went into the closet and closed the door.

Wycliffe nodded silently and listened to the shuttlecraft's airlock connect to the spacecraft dock's airlock. He got out of his seat and took his jacket off its coat hook. As he put his jacket on, Wycliffe heard the metal airlock hatches opening.

"Hail, Mary, pray for me," he said before kissing the medal of Our Lady of Walsingham.

When the shuttlecraft's airlock door opened, a soldier rushed in and pointed a gun at Father Wycliffe.

"Put your hands up!" the soldier shouted.

Father Wycliffe raised his hands.

"Get against the wall, face the wall, hands against the wall," the soldier ordered.

Wycliffe obeyed. The soldier frisked him, looking for weapons.

"Clean," the soldier muttered, "but we haven't done a strip search yet."

"I'm a Vatican diplomat representing His Holiness Pope Christopher," Wycliffe protested.

"Yeah, padre," the solider said. "Okay, turn around, keep your hands above your head, and get out of the shuttlecraft."

As the soldier prodded him out of the shuttlecraft, another soldier went in.

"Search the shuttlecraft," the first soldier said to the other. "I'm taking the prisoner for interrogation."

As he left the shuttlecraft, Wycliffe wondered how Jessica would hide.

———

Colonel Matthew Chang listened to radio messages from Yue 1, recorded by a spy satellite. When China put its military on Yue 1, General Boyd transferred Colonel Chang from deep space to the Moon. Boyd thought Chang could provide valuable intelligence by listening to Chinese messages. But Chang, like many Chinese Americans, understood Cantonese, not Mandarin, which the Chinese soldiers spoke. To promote national unity, various Chinese regimes defined Cantonese and Mandarin as dialects of a single language.

However, they are actually distinct languages, so different as to be mutually incomprehensible.

He had to wait for intelligence interpreters on Earth to translate the messages and tell him if any had useful content. For now, other problems worried him.

He turned to Major John Hardy. "Have you figured out why the mass driver doesn't work?"

"We know why: the electromagnetic fields aren't strong enough," Hardy replied. "The mystery is why the electromagnetic fields aren't strong enough to propel the projectile."

Hardy pointed at plans and calculations on his computer monitor. "In theory, the system should work."

At Hardy's table, nine other Army engineers stared forlornly at their computers and scribbled notes. One of them yawned.

"The Chinese have their ballistic missile, so we're defenseless until we get that mass driver working," Chang said.

"Too bad those contractors had to leave," Hardy said. "They built the system. I wish they could stay until we got it operational."

"It was the cost overrun," Chang said. "Congress didn't want that twenty trillion dollar overrun to get any larger."

"But we cost nothing, so they ordered us to finish the project. Combat engineers and tank drivers working on magnetic physics: they're getting what they paid for," Hardy said.

President Darby wanted a weapon to destroy enemy moonbases without radiation; he considered nuclear weapons immoral. He saw no moral dilemma in hurling a heavy weight at another moonbase, though.

Defense contractors suggested a magnetism-based weapon. The contractors assured the President, his Cabinet, and Congress that magnetism-based weapons would be much cheaper than missiles, which use expensive and hazardous fuels. The U.S. moon tanks already had coil guns; the contractors could use the same principle for a super weapon. With funding from Congress, a consortium of contractors designed and built the mass driver. Nobody had ever built a mass driver as large and powerful as this one.

Far from being a cheap weapons system, the mass driver went twenty trillion dollars over budget, and it still wasn't working. Congress pulled the contractors off the Moon and told President Darby to get the military to finish it. The Army got the job simply because Liberty's commander was Army Colonel Chang.

It wouldn't have mattered if the Navy or Air Force had gotten the job. The U.S. military had only a few scientists of its own, and they all worked in procurement of equipment. The military relied on civilian contractors for research and development. The Army had ten engineers experienced in space duty, so they went to Moonbase Liberty. They could perform a wide variety of jobs, like build moonbases, alter the terrain, and lay mines. With help from other military engineers, they had built the sloping earthwork where the mass driver was mounted. But they were not magnetic physicists.

Chang feared that the size and scope of operations were stretching his troops dangerously thin. Major Hardy and nine other engineers worked continuously, if futilely, on the mass driver. Eleven tank drivers shadowed the Chinese tanks at the perimeter of the U.S. protection zone. One tank driver stayed close to Liberty. That left only him and two riflemen to keep watch for security within the base.

And a security *threat* had arisen: someone had flown a shuttlecraft into the protection zone and landed at Liberty.

Chang took his security risks seriously. Someone had slipped into his camp and planted the landmine that killed Ross in Haiti. The incident bothered him for years until he visited a mysterious asteroid and made peace with his past. Still, he vowed to secure his base as tightly as possible.

Chang's pocket computer buzzed. "This is Chang," he answered.

"I have a prisoner," a soldier said.

"How many people were on the shuttlecraft?" Chang asked.

"Just one, but we're searching the ship."

"Who is he?"

"He looks like a priest of some sort."

"A priest?"

"So he says. Where do you want to interrogate him?"

"Is he armed? Is he carrying anything suspicious?"

"He's clean on the outside, but do you want to strip search him?"

"No, not now. Let me interrogate him first. Bring him to my office," Chang said as he left the control room.

———

The rifleman opened the door of the shuttlecraft's storage closet. He saw a spacesuit in there. That did not surprise him. Shuttlecraft pilots stored their spacesuits in the closet.

But the spacesuit seemed to have bulk, as if it someone were in it. He pressed his hand against its chest.

Nothing resisted his pressure. He squeezed the sleeve; it was empty.

"Hacken, is there anything in the shuttlecraft?" Major Hardy said over the rifleman's headset.

"No, nothing here at all," Hacken replied.

"Good. Now I can go back to the joys of magnetic fields," Hardy said.

"You do that. For a civil engineer who built sewage systems, you're a mighty fine magnetism development physicist," Hacken joked.

"Don't remind me about it," Hardy said. "Go join the colonel and Cooper at the colonel's office. They're interrogating the prisoner there. They might need back-up in case the prisoner tries anything."

"Roger that, I copy," Hacken said as he left the shuttlecraft.

Father Wycliffe felt more annoyed than nervous as Riflemen Cooper and Hacken aimed their guns at him. Although Wycliffe stood beside a chair, Colonel Chang had not asked him to sit.

"Your arrival was unusual, unplanned, and unannounced," Chang said. "Who are you?"

"Mark Wycliffe, Papal legate representing His Holiness Pope Christopher," Wycliffe said.

"A Father Wycliffe was scheduled to visit us, but he hasn't arrived."

"That's me."

"He was supposed to give us a password before he landed. We heard no password from you."

"There was a solar flare. It knocked out communications."

Chang nodded. "Yes, there was."

"The password is Alpha ten Zulu sixteen Xray Papa," Wycliffe said.

Chang looked at his computer. "Yes, that's the password. Did you bring your credentials?"

Wycliffe reached inside his jacket, but Cooper raised his gun.

"Don't reach inside your pocket," Cooper warned.

"My Vatican diplomatic passport is in my inside breast pocket, left side," Wycliffe said.

With his free hand, Hacken opened Wycliffe's jacket and searched the breast pocket. He pulled his hand out and grunted.

"There's nothing in there," Hacken said.

"What do you mean?" Wycliffe said as he reached into his jacket.

"Keep your hands where I can see them!" Cooper yelled.

Wycliffe quickly pulled his hand out and patted his jacket from the outside. Where was the passport?

"It must be in there," he said, worried.

"Take off your jacket slowly," Chang said. He looked at Hacken. "You take it."

Wycliffe slipped off his jacket and handed it to Hacken.

"Lay it on my desk and search it again," Chang said.

Hacken laid the jacket on the desk, reached inside both breast pockets, and pulled them inside out. Nothing was in them. Then he pulled the two side pockets inside out. Nothing was in those pockets either. Finally, he picked up the jacket and shook it. Nothing fell out.

Wycliffe felt his blood freeze. Where was his passport?

The tank driver drove towards the mass driver. He saw someone in a spacesuit standing at the long tube.

"Hey, control room, this is Gomez. Is anyone working on the mass driver out here?" the tank driver asked over the radio.

"Negative," Major Hardy replied. "We're all working on the system design in here until we figure out how to make it work."

"There's someone standing out here by the tube."

A silence followed. Then Major Hardy said, "Negative. I'm looking at the mass driver from several video monitors, and I see nobody near the mass driver."

"But there is," Corporal Gomez insisted. "There is someone here."

"We don't see anyone," Hardy said. "We can see you driving towards the tube, though."

Darn, Gomez thought. With all the other tanks away at the perimeter, with the two riflemen guarding the prisoner, and with the engineers in the control room, only he could investigate the intruder immediately.

"I'm going closer," Gomez said.

The intruder faced the tube and put his or her hands on it. The intruder stood motionless in that position.

As Gomez drove closer to the figure, he opened the frequency for spacesuit radios. "You are trespassing on U.S. territory. Identify yourself," he said.

The intruder said nothing.

"Get your hands off the tube and back away from it," Gomez ordered.

The intruder did not move.

"I can't risk shooting and hitting the tube," Gomez muttered. "I'm going outside."

"Be careful out there," Hardy advised.

After putting on his spacesuit and going through the airlock, Gomez walked to the intruder. The intruder stayed still.

"Who are you?" he asked.

The intruder turned around. Gomez saw her face through the helmet visor. She was a teenaged girl.

"Don't bother me," she said. "I'm trying to fix your mass driver."

"Who are you?" Chang asked again.

"I told you, I'm Father Mark Wycliffe, a legate or diplomatic representative of the Pope," Wycliffe repeated. "Call anyone on Timonium Base. Call the Holy See's Ambassador to the United States. They'll confirm my identity."

Chang typed and sent a message on his computer. "I've asked the State Department to get information about you, if they have any."

"I know it's awkward that I lost my passport, but do I seem like a saboteur or a terrorist? Am I carrying any explosives or weapons?" Wycliffe said. "Colonel Chang, please believe that I'm the legate sent to meet you."

Chang looked startled. "You know my name. How do you know it?"

"Like I said, I'm supposed to meet you. Your State Department told me your name on condition that I keep it secret."

A beeping noise signaled a new message on Chang's computer. Since the computer faced away from Wycliffe, he could not see the message. He saw Chang reading the message intently.

"Okay, your photograph matches. Still, I prefer to see your passport." Chang motioned to the chair. "Sit down."

Wycliffe finally sat down on the chair. It was hard and uncomfortable, probably rejected from a military base on Earth.

"Why did you come here, Father Wycliffe?" Chang asked.

"I represent the Pope, so I bring his message to you," Wycliffe said. "President Darby has given you discretion to capture instead of shoot down vehicles that enter the protection zone. The Pope encourages you always to capture the vehicle and its crew alive."

Chang looked impassive. "You didn't have to come here to tell me that."

"The Pope encourages you to exercise your discretion — at all times," Wycliffe said.

"He probably means he wants non-lethal force used each and every time," Chang said. "Of course, that would be preferable, but it might not be practical in each case. There might be incidents where I have to bring down a vehicle."

"Perhaps not," Wycliffe said. "All ground and sky traffic on the Moon has been peaceful. There was no threat to your national security on the Moon before your country declared the protection zone."

"But the situation has changed. We have countries with competing interests and people sneaking into the protection zone and the shrine by teleporter," Chang said. "I'm sure you know about the ESA's teleporters."

Wycliffe nodded. He wondered if Chang knew he had set up the teleporters?

"It's ironic that the Europeans, who don't have any territorial interests, are the only people able to enter and leave the protection zone at will," Chang said. "They have some protection too; neither China nor the United States will attack Arcadia Base or Apparition Hill. That would certainly start a war.

"But the European presence bothers the President. He considers the Europeans to be a security risk. With so many security risks, we have to be careful." Chang paused for a moment. "I see from your ribbons that you served in the British military."

"Yes, I was an Air Force chaplain in the Vernacular Wars," Wycliffe said.

"Then I'm sure you understand the need for security and vigilance in times of war," Chang said.

"Yes, I do." Wycliffe wasn't winning the argument. He had to say something.

"You have to do everything possible to prevent an incident that can start a war," Wycliffe urged. "Do it for the sake of the Siren Stone."

"Siren Stone? What Siren Stone?" Chang said.

"The iron meteorite is a Siren Stone. You're probably familiar with them," Wycliffe said.

He waited for a reaction from Chang, but the colonel stayed silent and emotionless.

Wycliffe continued his ploy. "You know how mysterious they are. Nobody knows where they come from, nobody knows how they work, but we all know they do things with our minds. China and the United States are ready to fight over a Siren Stone. We don't know what mysterious power lies within it. Nobody can predict what will happen if the Siren Stone gets destroyed in a war."

Chang stayed silent and emotionless. Would Wycliffe's gambit work?

Gomez looked at the girl. "Who are you?" he demanded.

The girl turned away from him and put her hands on the tube again.

"Get your hands off the tube," Gomez ordered as he grabbed the girl's arms.

Gomez shrieked and suddenly pulled his hands back. The girl felt like fire. How could he have felt intense heat through his spacesuit?

"Gomez, what is it?" Hardy asked over the spacesuit helmet radio.

"The girl's hot, hot like a furnace!" Gomez said.

"What girl? I'm looking on the video monitor, and I see only you waving your arms around."

Gomez unclipped his police baton from his spacesuit and poked the girl. Still with her hands on the tube, the girl turned around.

"Oh my God!" Gomez yelled.

He did not see the girl's face through the helmet. Instead, a blinding white light shone from inside the helmet. The intruder shone as brightly as the sun.

Gomez backed away and looked to his side so he would not stare directly into the light. "Who are you?" he shouted.

The blinding white light did not answer.

"What are you doing?"

"Transfiguring," the light answered.

"Hey, what's going on?" Hardy said as he watched the magnetic field monitor.

Readings from the mass driver poured into the monitor. Throughout the mass driver, magnetic fields grew in strength.

"It's powering up the way we want it," Hardy said.

An engineer cheered. "It looks like we finally figured out how to fix it!"

"How did we do it?" another engineer asked.

"I hope the magnetic fields aren't going to go out of control," Hardy said. "Can we control their strength?"

An engineer typed commands to the mass driver. "I'm trying to bring the strength down. It should react to my commands."

Hardy looked at the monitor. "The magnetic fields are stabilizing."

"They're stabilizing at the levels I set for them," the engineer said. "The darned thing's finally working!"

Major Hardy looked at the monitor and shook his head.

"We finally did it, but I wish I knew what we did right," he said.

———

The intruder took her hands away from the tube, and the bright light disappeared. Gomez looked at her and saw the girl's face through the visor again.

"Your mass driver is fixed. Feel free to hurl weapons of mass destruction around the Moon," she said. "Have a good day."

As she walked away, Gomez chased after her and grabbed her. She spun around, and suddenly, the light burst out of her helmet again.

Gomez suddenly went blind. As he yelled and fell to the ground, he felt the girl slip out of his arms.

Twenty seconds later, he could see again. The girl was gone, nowhere to be seen.

He saw something shiny on the ground. He picked it up. It was a gold-colored card: a Vatican City State passport for Mark Wycliffe.

———

Colonel Chang swiped the passport through a card reader. As Chang waited for the passport's information to download onto his computer, Wycliffe looked around. Now Corporal Gomez had joined Riflemen Cooper and Hacken in Chang's office.

Chang looked at the computer. "Yes, you do have accredited diplomatic status. Fortunately, for you, that prevents me from detaining you."

Chang handed the passport back to Wycliffe, who shoved it into his jacket's breast pocket.

"Your passport was found near the mysterious girl. Perhaps she dropped it," Chang said. "I'm giving you one last chance. Who is she, and what is your association with her?"

"You wouldn't believe me if I told you," Wycliffe muttered.

"Try me, Father."

"She's Jesus."

"Who would name a girl Jesus? What's her last name?"

"Christ. Jesus Christ."

Cooper laughed softly. Chang glared at him, and he stopped.

"Do you really expect me to believe that?" Chang said.

"There are many mysterious, unbelievable things here and beyond," Wycliffe said. "There are people in deep space who say they've seen ghosts."

This time, Wycliffe saw a sudden glimmer in Chang's eyes.

"They're usually ghosts of people they knew," Wycliffe added.

Another brief spark appeared in Chang's eyes. Then he quickly looked impassive again.

"Continue," Chang said.

"If ghosts can appear on asteroids, then Jesus can appear on the Moon. After all, he's a Holy Ghost. Nobody can explain how these things happen, but they do," Wycliffe said.

Chang nodded. "Due to your unexplained association with an intruder, I will ask the State Department to declare you *persona non grata*. You'll never be allowed in the United States again."

"I don't care about that," Wycliffe said. "Just make sure that there still will be a United States –- and the rest of the world."

Chang looked at Gomez. "Corporal, take these two men and escort Father Wycliffe back to his shuttlecraft, and let him return to Timonium Base."

As the soldiers took Wycliffe away, he felt a sinking feeling of failure. Failing his Pope and Archbishop felt terrible. Failing the Virgin Mary felt awful too.

Failing the human race felt worst of all.

Some of the engineers cheered as the mass driver launched a magnetic projectile. The others watched silently, their faces showing both worry and anticipation.

Chang quietly watched the pictures from surveillance satellites. The shiny silver ball was the size of a truck and covered with gas nozzles. It kept rising into the sky.

The heavy ball, if it fell from the sky, could smash into a moonbase, demolish it, and kill its inhabitants. The ball's mass alone carried all that destructive energy; it did not need a nuclear bomb, although it could carry one.

"Okay, let's see if we can bring it down on target," Chang said. "The gas nozzles should activate soon."

Major Hardy looked at his computer monitor. "The nozzle thrusters are on," he reported.

The silver ball twisted and turned as its nozzles blasted out gaseous nitrogen. It descended slowly at first, then it fell faster and faster.

On a viewscreen showing a map of the Moon, a bright red star appeared on the uninhabited side of the Moon. The engineers cheered and applauded.

"Touchdown!" Hardy said, throwing his arms straight up into the air, the referee's signal for a touchdown in American football.

Chang looked at the map of the Moon. The big ball had reached its target as planned. It had hit the remains of the successful Moon Punisher rocket.

"Congratulations to you and your team, Major," Chang said.

Hardy nodded and smiled. "Thank you, sir."

"Now to look into the other event that occurred when I was busy with the priest," Chang said.

Colonel Chang watched the videos of Corporal Gomez at the mass driver. Gomez swung his arms in the air, backed away, ran, and fell on the ground — by himself. In addition, Gomez was talking to nobody.

"I don't see anyone else there," Chang said.

"I didn't either," Hardy said.

Gomez looked uneasy. "But I swear there was a girl there."

Chang smiled weakly at Gomez. "Corporal, I believe you."

Gomez's eyes lit up. Hardy looked puzzled.

"I think we have a freak phenomenon that doesn't appear on video," Chang said.

"Sir, is that possible?" Hardy said.

"What other explanation can there be?" Chang said. "In addition, the girl is obviously skilled in individual combat and maybe too much for one person to handle. If the girl returns, we should send an armed party to capture her."

"Uh, I can explain," Hardy said. "We were stretched so thin, and there was literally no visible threat —"

"No, let's not talk about it," Chang said, interrupting him. "I'm not blaming anyone, and I'm not going to put anyone on report. Let's just get on with our work. Is that okay, gentlemen?"

The two men nodded.

"Thank you. Dismissed."

After Hardy and Gomez left his office, Chang retrieved a photograph of asteroid Odette de Proust on his computer. He stared at the photograph and wondered how many other Siren Stones were out there.

Halfway on the flight back to Timonium Base, Father Wycliffe heard the closet door open. Jessica came out of the closet and sat beside him.

"They searched the shuttlecraft, didn't they?" Wycliffe asked.

Jessica nodded. "Uh huh."

"How did they not find you?"

"I used my Jesus power of telepathy. I made the soldier think that the spacesuit was empty."

"You can control minds with telepathy?"

"Well, actually, I don't really have the power. I channeled the electrochemical waves of the Siren Stone for my own use."

"And what did you do at the mass driver?" Wycliffe asked.

Before Jessica could answer, John Layman's voice came over the radio. "Timonium shuttlecraft six, this is John Layman. Timonium shuttlecraft six, come in please."

"John, this is Wycliffe aboard Timonium shuttlecraft six," Wycliffe said. "What is it?"

"Return to Timonium as soon as possible. I'm alerting all our spacecraft to get out of the sky."

"Why?"

"We just received news that the Americans have launched a test weapon from a new mass driver at Moonbase Liberty. They could be launching other test flights; we don't know for sure. As a precaution, keep a low altitude and return to Timonium as soon as possible. Do you copy?"

"Roger that, I copy. Out," Wycliffe said to end the call.

He turned to Jessica. "Was that your doing?"

"Yes. Wasn't it wonderful? I got the mass driver to work. I hadn't played with magnetic fields before," Jessica said.

"The end of the world can start anytime," Wycliffe said. "My diplomatic mission was a failure."

"Not totally. You did what I needed you to do."

"What was that?" Wycliffe asked, puzzled.

"I needed you to distract the soldiers while I worked on the mass driver. That's why I knocked out communications with the solar flare, and that's why I stole your passport from your jacket while you weren't watching. I figured they would suspect you of being a spy and hold you. While they were obsessing over you, I fixed their mass driver," Jessica explained.

She finished by saying, "Actually, one guy saw me, but I can deal with one person. I couldn't fight off the whole garrison, though. Thanks for keeping them busy."

Wycliffe groaned. "You used me to distract other people? How could you do that to me?"

"Don't be upset. I always work through my priests," Jessica assured him.

As he prepared to land the shuttlecraft, Wycliffe breathed deeply. Now he was sure that God had abandoned the human race.

12 / THE AGONY IN THE GARDEN

Father Alexei showed a wooden icon to Father Wycliffe. The wood was thin plywood, unlike the thicker, stronger wood of other icons. The image, however, was as beautiful as any icon in a church.

It reproduced Our Lady of Kazan, the most venerated icon in the Russian Orthodox Church. The icon, showing Mary and Jesus in Byzantine Greek clothes, originated in Constantinople in the thirteenth century. Someone brought it to Kazan, but it disappeared after the Tatars conquered Kazan in 1438. In 1579, the Blessed Virgin Mary told its location to a ten-year-old girl named Matrona. Matrona and her mother dug up the icon from their garden.

"It's beautiful," Wycliffe said, admiring the gold leaf and black and red tempera paint.

"Thank you, but it is just a rough practice painting," Alexei said.

"If this is just practice, I can't imagine how beautiful your paintings will be with more experience."

Alexei pushed the icon to Wycliffe. "Take this poor painting as a humble gift."

"Oh, no, I couldn't," Wycliffe said.

"No, please take it," Alexei said. "I wish to thank you for recommending that I go on a retreat to a monastery after returning to Earth. The monastery has a class in icon painting, and I discovered a new hobby. Please take this for now. When I become more skilled, I will give you a better icon."

"It can't get any better than this," Wycliffe said as he accepted the icon. "Thank you."

"Hang it up in your private office," Alexei suggested. "You will not be disobeying the Pope's iconoclasm rule by hanging it in private."

Iconoclasm in space would not last, Wycliffe mused. The Holy See could enforce the rule among the clergy, but it could not enforce it among the laity. On the Moon, the Catholics evaded the rule by building their own unauthorized shrine.

"I'll hang it where it will be venerated," Wycliffe promised.

Alexei closed his suitcase. "I am ready to go now."

The noisy crowd waited and watched the viewscreens at Timonium's spaceport. The list of departing flights filled the viewscreens. Fearful of war, people were fleeing from the Moon.

Father Wycliffe walked Father Alexei to the Air France counter. "Look at all the people," Wycliffe said.

Alexei looked at the viewscreen. "The number of departing flights has doubled, and the number of arriving flights has been cut in half."

"Who would want to come here now?" Wycliffe asked.

"Only foolhardy clergy like us," Alexei remarked. "I wish I could stay, but a church in France needs a priest, and my archbishop wants me to go there soon. Russian Orthodox priests are rare in France."

"I guess you're not renewing with the ESA," Wycliffe said. "Are you settling back to Earth?"

"Yes, I am. I had my adventure, I worked for both science and God on Mars, but I want an Earth parish again. I enjoyed deep space, but I missed some things from Earth. Regular parishioners, regular ceremonies like baptisms and weddings, movies in a real movie theater, and food that is not preserved and rehydrated. I missed those things," Alexei said. "What about you?"

"I don't know," Wycliffe admitted. "I feel like I can't do any more good here. But I don't feel that Earth has anything -- or anyone -- for me. Maybe I should stay here and minister to those who remain. But maybe they should leave too, in which case, I have no reason to stay. I don't know where I should go."

"Pray for guidance, that is the best any man can do," Alexei said. "Good luck, Mark, and I will see you later."

After leaving Alexei, Wycliffe walked through the spaceport. He saw familiar people in the Exodus: a group of Filipino pilgrims carried their national flag as they boarded a space liner; the Spanish pilgrims hummed a folk song as they marched through the spaceport; and the Mexican pilgrims Yolanda, Armando, and Manuel dragged their luggage across the floor.

The Mexicans saw Father Wycliffe and turned to meet him. Wycliffe braced himself for criticism of the Pope's iconoclasm in space, but the pilgrims smiled at him.

"Father, it is nice to see you again!" Armando said. "Thank you for saving our lives."

"Oh, think nothing of it," Wycliffe said.

"When I arrived at Timonium, I found out that I lost my pyx in the evacuation. I wonder what happened to it," Armando said.

"I don't know," Wycliffe lied.

"It is consecrated bread, so no harm will come to it."

Yolanda approached Father Wycliffe. "Father, thank you for all you have done for us. We are returning to Mexico, but we would like to come back to the Moon. Do you think the shrine will re-open?"

"I don't know. It depends on the political situation, I guess," Wycliffe said.

As war panic rose, the ESA stopped teleporter service to the apparition shrine. Although the ESA did not own or operate the shrine, the ESA controlled transportation to it. By shutting down the teleporter, the ESA effectively closed the shrine.

In any case, the shrine was unauthorized by Church authority. Despite the devotion he saw there, he could not encourage pilgrims to visit it. If any good came out of the war scare, it could be the closure of the shrine.

And that was really nothing to celebrate, he felt.

Wycliffe stopped at a coffee stand near the spaceport's gateway to Timonium's main street. He could have ordered a fresh-brewed Colombian coffee, but he bought an instant rehydrated spacer blend. In his time around Mars, he had developed a taste for spacer instant coffee. Rabbi Gabizon had joked that only the Catholic fondness for suffering could make anyone like spacer instant coffee.

He sat down at a stool and smelled the coffee. It had a weak smell, hardly an aroma, like the coffee at Space Station Exeter. It reminded him of the teamwork between the Martian spacers, of the enthusiasm of the Martian scientists, of the optimism of the Martian colonists.

It also reminded him of the Mars disaster. So much hope and so much despair followed people into space.

As he drank his coffee, a woman sat down on the stool beside him. He recognized her as Dawn Favreaux, President of Tranquility Tours and President of the American Chamber of Commerce on the Moon.

"Oh, Father Wycliffe, is it?" she asked after ordering her tea.

"Yes, that's right," Wycliffe answered.

"I knew it. I've seen you on the news about the Virgin Mary apparition," Favreaux said. "That's such a wonderful thing, don't you think? So many people came to visit the Moon because of it. We had our best season ever."

Wycliffe nodded. "I'm glad you appreciate it."

"Oh, excuse me, I haven't introduced myself," Favreaux apologized. "I'm Dawn Favreaux, owner of Tranquility Tours and President of the American Chamber of Commerce on the Moon."

"Yes, we've met before, but only briefly."

"Oh? Where was that?"

"I went on the Moonwalk Experience. I had a lot of fun," Wycliffe said. He didn't want to say that he actually hated the experience because Jessica ran away to Yue 1.

"Thanks for going on the Moonwalk Experience. I wish more people would go on it. I wish more people would come to the Moon," Favreaux lamented.

"I guess business is bad?" Wycliffe said.

"Very bad," Favreaux said. "It was bad enough when the bus tours couldn't go to the protection zone and the shrine. At least the pilgrims came and spent money at Timonium. They were good for business. Now, even the pilgrims are leaving, and nobody's coming for the other attractions. Nobody's staying in the hotels, going on moonwalks, taking shuttlecraft tours, or visiting the Soviet space museum. The commercial district is dying. There are no more tourists, pilgrims, or scientists."

"Eventually, there will be only fifty soldiers whose only job is to wait for the other side to attack, then strike back. Not exactly the most glorious vision of lunar settlement, is it?" Wycliffe said.

Wycliffe passed several closed shops as he walked through the commercial district. He saw only half the usual number of people on the street.

When he returned to St. Dominic's Church, he went to the corridor of residential rooms. Amira's door was open, and she was typing at her computer. After she finished typing, she pressed a button and the word "SEND" appeared on her monitor.

"That is it, I have finished writing my geological report about the iron rock and have sent it to you," Amira announced.

"Thank you, I'll read your report after Mass," Wycliffe said. "Amira, I guess you'll be going soon. I just came back from the spaceport, and hundreds of people are leaving. Book your flight soon; the departing flights are filling up."

"India can wait," Amira said. "I will stay a little longer if I am not imposing on you."

"Oh? No, you're not imposing. Why do you want to stay?" Wycliffe asked.

"That Siren Stone," Amira said. "I have an idea on what to do with it. Do you know the story of Mohammed and the Black Stone?"

"Mohammed and the Black Stone of the Kaaba? Is there a story about both of them?"

"Yes. Here is the story..."

"...and I think if we launch the Siren Stone into space, the U.S. and China will have nothing over which to fight," Amira proposed.

"Amira, do you really think this is possible or practical?" Wycliffe said. "Launch the Siren Stone into space? I wouldn't know how to start doing it."

"We don't have to do it. There are companies that blast asteroids out of the way," Amira suggested.

"Yes, but they destroy the asteroid in the process," Wycliffe said.

"There is a rumor that one company moved an asteroid instead of destroying it," Amira said. "It was the secret asteroid, Odette de Proust."

"Yes, Rock Blasters. That company moved Odette de Proust by changing its orbit, so the rumor goes," Wycliffe said. "It can be done –- once."

"If it can be done once, it can be done twice," Amira said. "How much do these asteroid demolition companies charge?"

"From what I heard, they're very well paid. Twenty million gold units, minimum," Wycliffe said.

"Neither of us has that much money, and the Free Mosque certainly does not," Amira said. "Hmmm, perhaps –- perhaps the Vatican can pay for it?"

Wycliffe laughed softly. "The Vatican doesn't have money. All the wealth of the Vatican is in old art and buildings. It doesn't carry much actual cash."

"It holds much more cash than the Free Mosque," Amira said. "It might not be as wealthy as either the United States or Chinese governments, but it is the largest church in the world. Twenty million gold units is a small price for peace to the Moon."

Wycliffe shook his head. "I doubt the Church will pay it."

He started for the door. "If you'll excuse me, I have to prepare for the daily Mass."

He left Amira's room and walked through the residential corridor. Mary came out of her room and approached him.

"Father, I think she has a brilliant idea. Call the Pope and ask for the money," Mary said.

"You were listening to us?" Father Wycliffe said, bewildered.

"Obviously," Mary admitted. "It's a great idea."

"But will it really change anything?" Wycliffe said. "Countries were already arguing on the Moon before we found a Siren Stone here. If they don't fight over the Siren Stone, they'll find something else to fight over."

"And they'll always be arguing and fighting, but you can remove the immediate danger and give them some more years," Mary said.

"No."

She touched the Our Lady of Walsingham medal around his neck. "You devoted your life to me. Don't leave me now."

"I don't think I can ask the Vatican for twenty million gold units just like that."

"You have to try. Don't give up. If you lose hope and faith now, the human race is doomed!"

"In a few minutes, I'm going to celebrate Mass for five people," Wycliffe said. "Five people. Three quarters of the Moon's population has gone back to Earth. Is there anything left to save here?"

"There is: the Moon. It's *my* Moon," Mary declared.

Her silver crescent moon pendant shone in the light.

Wycliffe sighed. "Okay, I'll call Cardinal Saint-Cloud after Mass and ask him what he thinks."

Father Wycliffe proposed the idea to Cardinal Saint-Cloud and Dr. Schiller by videophone. After he finished talking, both men looked blankly at him. They seemed unenthused by the idea.

"That is a nice story about Mohammed. It is engaging, exciting, and has a moral at the end," Cardinal Saint-Cloud said from the Vatican.

"You seem to be desperate for something nice to say," Wycliffe said softly.

Cardinal Saint-Cloud nodded silently.

"There is a critical difference between Mohammed's situation and ours," Dr. Schiller said from Paris. "In Mohammed's case, each tribe wanted the honor of putting the Black Stone in its place of honor, but no tribe claimed ownership of the stone. Once the Black Stone was back in its place, they could stop arguing.

"In our case, two countries claim ownership of the iron rock. Even if we put the iron rock where neither country could get it, both would still claim it as its own."

"And both countries would blame us –- the Holy See and the European Union –- for stealing its property," Saint-Cloud said.

"They'll be angry at us, but would they still go to war if neither could get the rock?" Wycliffe asked.

"Actually, they might not fight each other if neither could get the rock. And I doubt they would start a war against the Vatican City State or the European Union," Saint-Cloud said. "There would not be war, but there would not be peace either. The Holy See and the European countries would have a serious diplomatic crisis. The United States and China would certainly recall their ambassadors and ban our citizens from traveling to their countries."

"There could also be economic sanctions too," Schiller added. "The United

States and China could end their exports to us and prohibit their people from importing our goods."

"But Europe does so much trade with both the United States and China. We all need each other's markets; they're interconnected and dependent on each other. They would only be hurting themselves if they ended trade with us," Wycliffe said.

"They could expand their trade with their allies," Schiller said. "The United States has Latin America, and China has Africa. They could force Europe into economic isolation."

"Father, I am afraid that I do not support your proposal, so I will not take it to the Cardinal Secretary of State or the Pope," Cardinal Saint-Cloud said.

"The European Space Agency will not support it either," Dr. Schiller said. "I am sorry."

"I sympathize with you and support your desire for peace," Saint-Cloud said. "I want peace on the Moon and the Earth too. I just do not think this is the way to achieve it."

"I understand, Your Eminence," Wycliffe said.

"But do not be afraid to suggest other ideas," Saint-Cloud said. "We are desperate for them."

―――

After the videophone call ended, Wycliffe told Amira that both the Vatican and the ESA had rejected her idea. Looking dejected, she shrugged and left the church.

"I am going shopping," she said as she walked out the doorway. "There are plenty of bargains now. Sales in stores going out of business."

She returned two hours later with Dawn Favreaux. Why had she brought the President of the American Chamber of Commerce on the Moon to the church? Favreaux had never gone to Mass at St. Dominic's Church or any church.

"I believe you know each other," Amira said.

"Yes, we do," Wycliffe said. "Welcome, Ms. Favreaux. I think this is your first time at St. Dominic's Church."

"Yes, it is, but I hate to disappoint you, I'm not here for Mass," Favreaux said.

"Oh? So what brings you here? Do you wish to talk about something? Is something troubling you?"

"Yes, something is troubling me," she said as she handed a money card to him.

He looked at it. It was an anonymous card, and its display read "GU 20 000 000".

Twenty million gold units.

Puzzled, Wycliffe looked at her. "What is this for?"

"That's how much asteroid removal costs, is it?"

Shocked, Wycliffe looked at Amira. The imam grinned wickedly.

"You told her?" Wycliffe said.

Amira nodded. "I made lots of friends in the commercial district. I love it here. Remember how eagerly I accepted your invitation to Timonium Base?"

"Where did you get the money?"

"It's almost all that the American Chamber of Commerce has," Favreaux said.

"I can't accept it. Your organization will have nothing," Wycliffe said.

Favreaux laughed. "I'm all that's left of the American Chamber of Commerce on the Moon. There's no future for American-owned businesses on a European moonbase if war breaks out. All the other members have closed their businesses permanently and left for Earth. That is what's left after refunding their membership fees. I speak for the whole American Chamber of Commerce on the Moon now."

"I can't do it," Wycliffe said. "I would get in trouble with my superiors."

"We'll all be in trouble if we don't do anything," Favreaux said. "Popes, presidents, and emperors can't solve this crisis. It's up to us little people to do it."

"There will be political and diplomatic risks," Wycliffe warned. "Definitely some legal risks."

"We're not breaking any laws. We're not stealing anyone's property," Favreaux said. "Despite what two countries say, they do not own that rock, not according to the United Nations, not according to any other country, and not according to any treaty."

"Those two countries have stopped following international law for space, though," Amira reminded them. "For our own protection, we have to keep this operation secret."

"A secret operation," Wycliffe said. "It's like being in the Air Force again."

"Does that mean you'll help us?" Favreaux asked.

"Not really, but —"

At that moment, Mary came out of her room. Her sudden appearance startled them. Wycliffe had heard no noise from her room; he had thought she was somewhere else.

"Hi, everybody," she said. "We're lucky, my daughter's out shopping again." She shrugged. "I grounded her, but she still goes out anyway. Teenagers."

"Where does she get the money?" Amira asked.

"Uh, do I know you?" Favreaux asked nervously.

"Not yet," Mary said happily. "Hi, my name's Mary."

"Dawn Favreaux. I own a business in Timonium."

"Yes, I know, my daughter took one of your tours," Mary said. "Okay, we got the money. Now all we need are some trusted people to help us. And a plan."

Favreaux turned pale. "You've been listening to us?"

"She does that all the time," Wycliffe said. "Don't worry, she's on our side."

Mary turned to Wycliffe. "Father, you're ex-military. Can you plan a secret operation? Will you help us?"

"I was a chaplain, not a general," Wycliffe protested.

"For me," Mary said, touching the medal of Our Lady of Walsingham around his neck.

"Yes, Mary. I'll do it for you," Wycliffe agreed.

———

That evening, over dinner at the church, Wycliffe planned the operation with Amira and Favreaux.

"Alphonse and the Arcadia Base crew have evacuated to Timonium Base. It'll be easy to find him and talk to him," Wycliffe said. "He loves Arcadia Base and Apparition Hill, even though he isn't religious. He'll want to preserve both places."

"He will need someone to help him," Amira reminded him. "Someone to work the teleporter at the apparition shrine."

"I'll ask him if he can get Roxanne or Auguste," Wycliffe said. "They might do it for him."

Favreaux helped herself to another cup of coffee. "My company has landing rights at the spaceport. When the asteroid team arrives, they can land at Timonium. If anyone asks, I'll say I hired the ship to transport assets back to Earth."

"Don't forget the spacesuits," Wycliffe said.

"No, I haven't forgotten," Favreaux said. "I need to remove the company logo and I.D. numbers off my spacesuits."

"I'll paint over them," Amira offered. "Just get me the paint."

Wycliffe turned to Amira. "You have the ESA geologists' report and your own report about the iron rock. Convert both reports and any additional data to encrypted form. When we get the demolition team, we have to send them every measurement, mass estimate, drawing, photograph, and bit of data about the rock."

"We don't have an asteroid demolition company, much less one that'll agree to work on something like this," Favreaux said. "Unfortunately, I'm stumped. My business connections don't go into that business."

"I might have connections there," Wycliffe said. "I met several asteroid demolishers on Space Station Exeter. They often worked around Mars and in deep space."

"Do you know any we could trust with this type of job?" Amira asked. "Anyone who is willing to risk not getting a government contract again?"

"There's one company that might do it..."

Wycliffe read the message on the website of Rock Blasters, Inc.:

DEMOLITION OUR SPECIALTY

Large or small, we blast them all. Contact Rock Blasters, Inc., for all your space explosions. Specialists in clearing travel lanes of hazardous space debris, with a total of 47 years' experience working with asteroids and decommissioned hardware, Rock Blasters, Inc., can bring its expertise and equipment to your mining operation as well, offering on-site drilling and core blasting at competitive prices. With a flawless safety record and references on request, why go elsewhere? Contact Rock Blasters, Inc., today!

On a secure videophone line, Wycliffe typed the Rock Blasters contact number. Andrew Lundman appeared on the monitor. Judging by the scene around Andrew, Wycliffe guessed that Andrew was aboard a spaceship. Behind him, his colleagues George Hodding and Ed Benton checked the ship's controls.

"Mr. Lundman, do you remember me?" Wycliffe said. "My name's Mark Wycliffe. I was a priest on Space Station Exeter."

Andrew smiled. "Why, yes I remember you, Father. I haven't seen you for a long time, not since my crew and I stopped at Exeter. That was after we blasted that stray rock out of Space Station Carter's path."

"Oh, yes, the big silicate," Wycliffe remembered. "You did a good job on that one."

"Thanks. We're talking in real time, which means that you're not around Mars. I'm aboard the *Rocky Road* in Near-Earth Sector Three now. We just blasted another rock. You must be close to us, at the Moon or a near-Earth station."

"The Moon."

"Why are you still there? I thought almost everyone was leaving."

"Almost everyone has left, but a few of us have stayed. Did you say you just blasted another rock? Does that mean you're free for another job?"

"Yes, we have a month before the next job. Why do you ask?"

"Mr. Lundman, I have a job for you and your crew."

"You're hiring us? This is unusual, the first time a priest has asked us to do a job."

"I'm asking you because you have experience in this type of job. I need to move a rock off the Moon. Not destroy it, but move it."

"Move it off the Moon? Is it on the lunar surface?"

"Yes. I can send you the coordinates."

Andrew eyed Wycliffe suspiciously. "Is it that iron meteorite that the U.S. and China are fighting over?"

"Yes," Wycliffe replied.

"That rock isn't my type of assignment," Andrew said. "First, it's a political problem, and I don't want to get mixed up in international politics or start a war. Secondly, it's sitting immobile on the Moon; it's not in anyone's path. Why do you want us to remove it?"

"It's a Siren Stone, and I hear you know how to move them," Wycliffe said.

Andrew looked startled. George Hodding and Ed Benton stopped looking at the ship's controls and turned to look at Wycliffe via videophone.

"What do you know about Siren Stones?" Andrew demanded.

"I heard the rumors about Odette de Proust, and I had my own experience with a Siren Stone on Space Station Troika," Wycliffe said.

George Hodding nodded. "I heard a rumor about a girl ghost on Troika."

Another rumor? Deep space was full of rumors, Wycliffe realized.

"You saw a ghost on Troika?" Ed Benton asked.

"Yes, I did," Wycliffe said. "Troika is carved out of a Siren Stone."

The crew murmured, "There's another one."

"You want us to move the Siren Stone off the Moon?" Andrew asked.

"Take it off the surface of the Moon, move it into space, away from Earth," Wycliffe replied.

"Why?" asked Andrew. "It may be a Siren Stone, but it's not in anyone's way."

"It's the object of dispute between two countries. If war breaks out, it could get destroyed," Wycliffe said. "We can't let a Siren Stone get destroyed."

"No, of course not," Andrew agreed.

———

Five days later, the *Rocky Road* landed at Timonium Base's spaceport. Immigration officers ushered the crew to an office, where an officer swiped their passports through a card reader. Their personal information appeared on the monitor.

"I didn't think we needed passports to enter Timonium Base," Andrew said.

The immigration officer stared impassively at the information on the monitor. "We started three days ago," he said in a German accent. "Your country requires us to get passports and visas to visit its moonbases. We need passports and visas to go into the protection zone, which the U.N. says belongs to everybody. However, Americans could enter ESA moonbases without passports, whenever they wished. We have fixed the imbalance.

"Look on the bright side. We do not require you to get a visa from any European country in advance. And if a ship is in distress, we will let her land even if the crew and passengers have no passports."

The passport issue, the *Zhang Heng* crisis, the U.N. Rescue Agreement, the U.S. protection zone: all these crises had shoved the Moon closer to war. Now the Siren Stone made war inevitable. It was only a matter of time. Would civilization survive a world war fought on both Earth and space? Andrew wasn't sure.

"Who hired you?" asked the immigration officer.

"Tranquility Tours," Andrew replied.

"Do you have any proof of that?"

Andrew gave a memory card to the immigration officer. "This is the work order and contract from our client."

The officer swiped the card and read the work order and contract.

"What is the purpose of your contract?" asked the officer.

"To transport the client's equipment and assets back to Earth," Andrew replied, knowing that the officer could read the information from the work order. Immigration officers often asked redundant questions, hoping to find a contradiction.

"Another one is leaving," the officer said. He returned the passports to the men. "Everything is fine. You may go."

Andrew, George, and Ed left for the Tranquility Tours office to meet Dawn Favreaux. Later that day, the Rock Blasters quietly moved some crates to Tranquility Tours' storage room. The large room filled with drills, digging equipment, and rockets.

―――

Alphonse Bangolo went to Timonium's teleporter booth. At its control console, he sent a radio signal to the apparition shrine's teleporter booth.

"The shrine's teleporter booth is active now," he said, reading the messages appearing on the control console.

Auguste Peeters, wearing casual clothes without the ESA logo or a national flag, stepped into the teleporter booth.

"*Bonne chance,*" Alphonse said as he adjusted the controls.

"*Je suis prêt,*" Auguste said. "*Pour l'avenir de notre lune.*"

For the future of our Moon, Alphonse thought as he teleported Auguste to the apparition shrine.

A half hour later, a transport cart, loaded with crates, arrived at the teleporter booth. The Rock Blasters used transport robots to move their crates into the teleporter booth. One by one, Alphonse sent the crates to the apparition shrine.

Ed Benton and George Hodding drove the transport cart back to Tranquility Tours, picked up more crates, and returned to the teleporter booth.

They repeated the round trips until they had brought all their equipment. Alphonse sent it all to the apparition shrine.

Finally, only the three Rock Blasters remained.

"I've never traveled this way before," George said.

Ed looked warily at the teleporter booth. "All our equipment went in there, but is it rated for humans?"

"The European Union says it's safe, right?" Andrew asked as he stepped into the teleporter booth.

"Completely safe. We teleported hundreds of people without problem," Alphonse reassured them.

Ed and George joined Andrew in the teleporter booth. They turned into energy and rematerialized at the apparition shrine.

Auguste greeted them when they arrived. "That was not so bad, was it?" he said with a smile.

"No, not at all," Andrew said. He looked around in disbelief. "This is incredible."

A transport robot rolled up beside Auguste. "I have put your equipment in various rooms of the shrine," he said. "I will show you where they are."

Instead of their company spacesuits, the Rock Blasters brought spacesuits with Tranquility Tours logos and numbers painted over in white. Dawn Favreaux had given them to the crew.

Andrew looked out the shrine's window. "Does that communications tower have a video camera?"

"Yes, that is how we first saw the meteorite," Auguste said.

"Darn, a hole in the plan," Andrew realized. "If we go outside, we'll show up on video. Someone will come and stop us."

"We can disable the camera," Ed suggested.

"But someone will notice and come and repair it," George said.

"This is a flaw in the plan, but we have a lucky coincidence," Auguste said.

"Oh?" said Andrew.

Auguste explained. "The ESA put up that communications tower, so ESA Arcadia Base repairs it. Alphonse, as director of Arcadia Base, assigned me to repair this tower when needed. If anyone wants the communications tower fixed, I get to fix it."

They laughed and put on their spacesuits. Then they went into the airlock. As the Rock Blasters waited in the airlock, Auguste went outside.

He walked down to the communications tower, climbed up its ladder, and pulled the memory card out of the camera's BF-36 antenna.

"It is okay to come out now," Auguste said over the helmet radio.

Andrew, George, and Ed dug openings under the meteorite and planted four small rocket thrusters on the meteorite's underbelly. They had to drill through the rock and attach the rocket engines to the rock. Mounting the four engines took four long days.

Next, they attached a complicated mix of cables, a box, and a joystick to the meteorite's top.

"That box is the control mechanism from a Bumblebee, a small shuttlecraft used as a training vehicle," Andrew explained to Auguste. "We're turning the meteorite into a self-propelled spacecraft."

"How ingenious. Someone will fly it out into space," Auguste said.

"Someone could, but nobody will need to," Andrew said. He pointed at a device like a large box with buttons, a joystick, and a keyboard. "We can use that remote control device to send signals to the control box, which in turn will control the rocket thrusters, also from a Bumblebee."

George walked to them. "I'm tired. Let's take a break," he said.

"Alright, let's go back into the shrine," Andrew said.

Ed looked at the iron meteorite. "Father Wycliffe says this is a Siren Stone. But have you noticed that we're alone? We haven't seen any ghosts."

"You're right, we haven't seen any late friends or relatives," George said. "Is this really a Siren Stone?"

"Maybe the stone wants to get out of here, so it isn't sending ghosts to distract us," Andrew suggested.

Colonel Matthew Chang looked at John Layman and Alphonse Bangolo via videophone. The colonel looked worried.

"The security camera has been malfunctioning for a week," Chang said. "When will you get it fixed?"

Sitting in Layman's office, Layman and Alphonse looked at each other and shrugged.

"The malfunction is quite complicated," Alphonse said. "We ran a diagnostic and replaced a few parts. We are still looking into it."

"Either fix it or replace the whole unit," Chang demanded. "Whatever you do, do it immediately."

"Why are you so interested in our security camera? It's on our communications tower, not yours," Layman said.

"The camera looks over the iron rock," Chang said. "When the camera works, it provides continuous surveillance of the rock."

"*We*, not you, get to watch the feed from that camera," Alphonse said.

"You should watch the rock all the time," Chang said. "Fix the camera."

Alphonse said, "We are not interested in the iron rock. Only you and the Chinese are interested in the rock."

"Take a look at this," Chang said.

He replaced his own image with an aerial video of Apparition Hill.

"A U.S. surveillance satellite flew over Apparition Hill yesterday," Chang said. "I'm going to zoom in on the rock."

The picture zoomed in on the iron meteorite. Four persons in spacesuits walked around it. Drilling and digging equipment, transport robots, and opened crates lay around the meteorite.

"Somebody is working on the meteorite," Chang concluded.

"What on Earth? Who are they?" Layman asked, surprised.

"They have covered their spacesuit insignia, so we can't identify them," Chang said. "Are they from the ESA?"

"No, they are not," Layman declared. "The European Union and the ESA have no interest in the rock."

"What are they doing?" Chang asked.

Alphonse replied, "I do not know what they are doing."

"That looks like digging equipment and a rock drill," Layman observed. "However, I don't know what they're doing."

"Are they your people?" Alphonse asked.

"Of course not," Chang snapped. "Do you think I would be asking you about them if they are Americans?"

"Just a thought," Alphonse said. "Perhaps they are from China?"

Chang glared at Alphonse and Layman. "We monitor vehicular traffic in the protection zone very closely. No land or flying vehicle has entered the protection zone. The only other way to go there is by teleporter. Only the ESA has teleporters on the Moon. How do you explain these people?"

"I have no obligation to explain anything to you, much less something in which I have no involvement," Layman insisted.

"The camera is the ESA's, so this is the ESA's security problem," Chang said. "Fix your camera immediately."

"Is your surveillance satellite not working?" Alphonse asked. "Use it to watch the rock, if you wish."

"The surveillance satellite orbits the Moon and isn't always over the rock," Chang said. "However, your security camera can monitor the rock all the time. Fix your camera, find out who these trespassers are, and watch that rock."

"You can't give us orders!" Layman retorted.

"If the trespassers harm the rock, the United States will hold the European Union responsible," Chang threatened. "Watch the rock!"

"It's your protection zone. You protect it!" Layman argued.

Chang banged his fist against his desk. "I just might!"

Chang abruptly ended the videophone call. Layman and Alphonse sank back in their chairs.

"Do you think he's finally going to order his troops to surround the rock?" Alphonse asked.

"No, the Americans are still afraid that if they send their tanks in, the Chinese will too, and fighting will start," Layman said. "Neither side wants to be the one who ends the stalemate."

"And now, an unknown third side has entered the dispute," Alphonse remarked.

"I heard a rumor in the commercial district," Layman said. "An asteroid demolition crew landed here, ostensibly to carry a tenant's equipment to Earth."

"Is that so?" Alphonse said, playing innocent.

"So I hear," Layman said. "Isn't it odd that a rock blasting company is doing transport work?"

Alphonse nodded. "It is legal, though."

"I suppose," Layman said. "I don't know who's at the rock, but I wouldn't mind if they got rid of it. That rock is causing so many problems. I wish it would go away."

Layman's computer beeped, and the message "INCOMING VIDEOPHONE CALL" appeared.

"Oh, who is it this time?" he grumbled as he opened the call.

Colonel Rang Li's face appeared by videophone. The colonel looked worried.

"Colonel Rang, what a surprise," Layman greeted. "We almost never hear from you. What can we do for you?"

"Do you know when your security camera will be fixed?" Rang asked, frowning.

Alphonse shook his head. "No. It is very complicated."

Colonel Rang frowned. "Still not repaired? Then look at this image from our surveillance satellite."

Rang replaced his own image with an aerial video of Apparition Hill. The scene looked familiar to Alphonse. He heard Layman sigh softly.

"Here we go again," Layman muttered.

———

Father Wycliffe sat on a bar stool in the Devil's Pitchfork. When pilgrims came to Timonium, the British pub served fish and chips on Fridays. It still served fish and chips but no longer advertised it as a Christian special. Without the pilgrims, the Devil's Pitchfork needed another gimmick.

This Friday afternoon, the pub was holding its "Wormwood Naming Party", really a "happy hour" of discounted drink prices. The Wormwood Naming Party supposedly celebrated the naming of an asteroid.

Wycliffe watched the TV screen. BBC Space was showing the General Assembly of the International Astronomical Union in Tokyo.

The President of the IAU announced, "I have the pleasure of naming this asteroid 10 000 149 Wormwood..."

Asteroid 10 000 149 Wormwood appeared on TV. The white, jagged, irregular rock rotated as it flew through space.

"Wormwood is the most radioactive asteroid in Near-Earth Sector Three. About seventy percent of it is radioactive isotope aluminum-26," the announcer said. "Aluminum-26 has a half-life of only seven hundred thousand years..."

A photograph of the late Arthur Wormwood appeared. Wormwood was the first editor of *The Spacer's Encyclopedia*. The photo showed a seventy-five year old man wearing glasses and a sweet smile.

"...*The Spacer's Encyclopedia* is the most popular general reference work off Earth," the IAU President continued. "The IAU is honored to name this asteroid after Arthur Wormwood."

At a corner of the pub, a few people clapped. Despite the happy hour, only ten people came to the Devil's Pitchfork. In the boom times, a hundred and fifty people often packed into the pub.

"Hello, Father," Jessica said from behind.

Wycliffe spun around on his bar stool and saw Jessica and Carla standing there. The two girls held shopping bags.

"This place is rather homely," Carla said. "Look at it: all the wood paneling, paintings of people's dogs and houses, a pool table, a dart board, and a fake medieval shield on the wall. It's based on the places where the working class people drink after work."

"Ewww, look at that deer's head on the wall," Jessica squealed.

"What brings you two here?" Wycliffe asked. "I thought Café Méliès was more your style."

"It totally is, but Carla told me the drinks are half price in the Devil's Pitchfork this afternoon," Jessica said.

"Come on, let's take advantage of happy hour. My treat," Carla said.

Jessica squealed, jumped up, hugged Carla, and kissed her on the cheek. "We're Best Friends Forever! You're my best friend since Magdalena!"

Magdalena, wondered Wycliffe. *Could that be Mary Magdalene?*

"Carla, you so have to try this wine," Jessica urged, pointing at the drink menu.

"That wine?"

"It's a really sweet red wine that Jews drink. It's like grape juice with alcohol."

The bartender took the Carla's and Jessica's orders. They sat down at a table and drank their sweet kosher wine. The bartender brought a basket of bread buns to them. Jessica broke off a piece of bread and put it into Carla's mouth.

"Show me that cool skirt you bought!" Jessica urged.

Carla pulled the skirt out of a shopping bag, and the two girls chattered about it. They continued comparing the clothes, electronic gadgets, candies, cosmetics, and other things they had bought.

Carla did not know that her Best Friend Forever was planning the Apocalypse secretly. Wycliffe wondered what Carla would think if she knew.

Would she be angry? Would she be sad? Would she feel betrayed? Would she be happy? Would she accept the End of the World?

At least the wine was kosher for Passover. Some things were sacred.

———

The words "BREAKING NEWS" appeared on TV. Beside a computer graphic of the U.S. and Chinese flags, the BBC Space announcer said, "Both the United States and China have denied that it has sent unidentified people to the iron meteorite..."

Wycliffe suddenly snapped to attention. *Was the secret out?*

The news unfolded: surveillance satellites had recorded videos of mysterious people on a mysterious mission at the mysterious rock. The satellite images appeared.

In Washington, the Secretary of State said, "We vehemently deny that these people are Americans. The Chinese must stop making such accusations, which impede a peaceful settlement. These accusations offend us. Effective immediately, the United States bans the import of electronic goods made in China. If the Chinese government does not apologize for the accusations, we will impose more trade sanctions on China."

In Beijing, the Minister of Foreign Affairs lashed out. "We are outraged by the ban on Chinese electronic goods. In response, China will not import American wheat. Since we have shared our agricultural expertise with our allies, several African countries can supply wheat to us."

Holy Mary, Mother of God, what have I done? Wycliffe silently asked himself. He had started an economic war. He put his beer down as he felt his stomach turn queasy.

The BBC Space announcer said, "Earlier today, both China and the United States wanted to send its moon tanks to Apparition Hill to evict the unidentified people. However, both countries threatened war if the other sent its moon tanks to the hill. Consequently, neither country is acting against the mysterious intruders. The military standoff continues."

A military standoff could not last forever, Wycliffe knew. As political tensions rose, eventually, someone would attack first.

Jessica came to sit beside Wycliffe. She looked frantic and shook slightly.

"I just saw a news item on TV," said Jessica. "I'm traumatized."

Wycliffe felt fear crawl down his spine.

"There's something going on with the rock," she said.

"So it seems," Wycliffe said.

"Do you think those guys want to blow up the rock?" asked Jessica.

"I don't know," Wycliffe lied.

"If they wanted to blow up the rock, they would already have done it. It doesn't take that long to plant some bombs and blow it up," Jessica reasoned.

Wycliffe nodded.

"I think those people are trying to move the rock. They're stealing the rock!" Jessica said.

"Don't jump to conclusions," said Wycliffe.

"Of course they are!" Jessica cried. "I need the rock there. I need countries to fight over it! It's useless anywhere else!"

Carla came to the bar. "Hey, Jessica, what's wrong?"

"Oh, nothing," Jessica replied, calming down. "Come on, let's go."

Wycliffe watched the two girls strut out of the Devil's Pitchfork. What would Jessica do now?

―――

In the evening, Wycliffe and Amira ate dinner in the church's kitchen. In the corner, a TV showed the opera *Götterdämmerung* by Richard Wagner. Images of valkyries, Norse gods, Germanic heroes, and fire appeared on the screen.

The orchestra played Siegfried's Funeral Music as Siegfried's vassals took their hero's body up a hill. After the war of the gods, Valhalla caught fire, and the gods burned to death. Then the curtain fell, ending the Toronto Opera Company's abridged TV version of *Götterdämmerung*.

"That was wonderful," Amira said. "I grew up with stories from Norse and German mythology. I feel as much a part of that culture as anything else."

"What's on next?" Wycliffe asked.

Amira looked at the TV schedule on her pocket computer. "The news, followed by the movie *On the Beach*, from the British Film Institute Archives. It is a twentieth-century film about nuclear fallout drifting to Australia and fatally poisoning the population." She put her pocket computer down. "The BBC is obsessed with the end of the world."

"Do you blame it?"

A spinning Moon, the logo of BBC Space, appeared on the TV. The news show started.

"In Near-Earth Sector 3, the asteroid 10 000 149 Wormwood exploded less than a day after the International Astronomical Union named it," the announcer reported. "These pictures from a probe show the asteroid exploding."

The probe's video showed Wormwood exploding into seven chunks, each flying in a different direction.

"The U.N. Committee on Asteroids and Meteor Collisions thinks that Wormwood's high content of radioactive isotope aluminium-26, which generates heat as it decays, caused the asteroid to overheat and explode," the announcer said.

The church doorbell rang. Wycliffe went to the door and let Andrew, George, Ed, and Auguste into the church.

"Come, I'm finishing dinner. Do you want some food or a drink?" Wycliffe asked.

"Yes, thank you, we've had a long day," Andrew said as the Rock Blasters followed Wycliffe into the kitchen.

Amira dished out chicken stew to the exhausted men. They began eating it ravenously. As Wycliffe poured coffee for them, Andrew looked down and sighed.

"I'm sorry, but we have to leave right away," Andrew said.

"Why? Have you blasted the Siren Stone back to space?" Wycliffe asked.

"No, we don't have time. We just got a message from the U.N. An asteroid called Wormwood split apart, and one of its chunks is heading to Earth. It's large enough to damage a city."

"*Gott in Himmel*," Amira said.

Wycliffe stared in shocked silence at the Rock Blasters. The day's events were too suspicious to be coincidental.

"Are there other asteroid demolishers the U.N. could use?" Amira asked.

"Not as close to the Wormwood fragment as we are," Andrew said.

Ed washed down his dinner with coffee. "We just got the remote control working, and then we got the call from the U.N."

"Can you launch the rock before you go?" Wycliffe asked.

"We've got to check all the flight schedules first," George said. "We'll be sending the rock high and far enough that we risk hitting something if we control it from the ground. We need to find a window of opportunity first."

"Thanks for dinner," Andrew said as he stood up. "We've got no choice but to go after the Wormwood fragment first. After we eliminate the

Wormwood fragment, we'll come back and send the Siren Stone on its way."

After some rushed goodbyes, the Rock Blasters left for their spaceship.

"They are in a rush to leave. They already put all their equipment back aboard their ship before we came here," Auguste said. "They estimate it will take a month to destroy the Wormwood fragment and return."

Wycliffe frowned. "One month. Can the two countries hold off on war for another month?"

"I do not know, but the economic sanctions cannot help," Amira said.

Auguste headed for the door. "I will go now. I have to visit a jewelry store in the commercial district before I leave."

"You're leaving?" Wycliffe asked.

"Why see the Apocalypse on the Moon when you can see it on Earth?" Auguste asked as he left the church.

―――

Wormwood, thought Wycliffe. The name seemed familiar, and not just as the editor of *The Spacer's Encyclopedia*.

He went to his computer and opened an electronic Bible. He searched for the word "Wormwood" and found *Revelation*, chapter eight, verses ten and eleven:

When the third angel blew his trumpet, a large star burning like a torch fell from the sky. It fell on a third of the rivers and on the springs of water. The star was called "Wormwood," and a third of all the water turned to wormwood. Many people died from the water, because it was made bitter.

He heard footsteps outside. He went out and saw Jessica coming into the residential corridor.

Wycliffe asked the obvious. "Did you have anything to do with the Wormwood asteroid?"

Jessica nodded. "I wanted those asteroid movers to leave the iron rock alone. Now they'll go chasing after Wormwood and leave us in peace."

"You mean on the brink of war," Wycliffe said.

"I have a feeling that you're not happy," Jessica said plainly.

Wycliffe shook his head in silence.

"I know that you hired those asteroid movers," Jessica said. She talked in a flat, emotionless voice, but her face looked stern.

"I do what I have to do to save lives. I'm a priest of God," Wycliffe replied.

Jessica's face softened a bit.

"Don't worry, I'm not angry with you, and I'm not going to strike you dead or turn you into a pillar of salt," she said. "I'm not angry. Just disappointed."

"Your mother and I want the best for you and the human species, God's greatest creation."

"You're not going to stop me. You *can't* stop me. I take after my father. I am what I am."

She went into her room and quietly closed the door. Wycliffe returned into his room, sat on his bed, and stared sadly at the Biblical text on his computer.

Someone knocked on his door. He looked to see Mary standing in his doorway.

"May I come in?" Mary asked.

"Sure, come on in," said Wycliffe.

Mary sat down beside him on the bed. She looked worried and sad, not angry and excited.

"I think I'm getting resigned to the idea that the End Times are coming," Mary admitted. "But still, I don't want to give up.

"Her father is a God of law and judgment, but He is also the God who taught us love and forgiveness. She's supposed to be the Prince of Peace on Earth and goodwill towards men." Mary smiled. "That's what an angel told me when I gave birth to him."

"I'm a priest of God. I believed in a God that loves His children, a god that wouldn't kill their entire species. What has happened to my God?" Wycliffe asked.

"Go talk some sense into her," Mary said.

Now they were like parents trying to deal with an errant teenager, Wycliffe realized.

"You go talk to her," Wycliffe replied.

"Why should I talk to her?"

"You're her mother."

"But she's your God."

"I suppose she is," Wycliffe said, "but does that mean I have to be the one who talks her out of ending the world? In case you haven't noticed, my diplomacy skills are nil."

"You're an ordinary human being, one who will live and die, not one who will be resurrected or be assumed into heaven. You need her, and she needs you," Mary said.

"Why would God need me?" Wycliffe asked.

"Gods and their people need each other. People need their gods to define who they are. Without gods, people have no civilization; every aspect of a civilization derives from something worshipped or idolized," Mary explained.

She continued. "Just as people need gods, gods need people too. Gods need people to believe in them; when belief in a god dies, the god dies too.

"It's a mutual symbiotic relationship. If there's anyone that she'll listen to, it'll be you. Go talk to her."

Since his only child never grew into his teen years, he had no real experience with teenagers. He imagined this is how fathers have talked to their wayward teenagers since time immemorial.

Wycliffe knocked on Jessica's door. "Come in, the door's unlocked," came the reply.

He entered her room and gawked at the scene. The room was full of flowers and plants. Scores of pots and vases lined the floor along the walls. The plants came in every color, including red, yellow, green, blue, purple, pink, black, and white. A vase of red roses and tropical greens sat on her table.

"Do you like the redecorating I did?" Jessica asked. "Carla took me to a flower shop, and we bought all these plants and flowers. I like plants and flowers. I used to hang out with my friends at a garden."

Wycliffe knew of the garden: the garden that Jesus visited before his crucifixion, the garden where Jesus felt his agony, the garden where Judas betrayed him.

Jessica was sitting at her table. She was looking at 3-D photographs of her, Carla, Roxanne, and Auguste.

"Don't these look so incredible?" she asked him, seemingly no longer disappointed at him.

Wycliffe took the photos from her. They were photographs taken in an instant photo booth in Café Méliès. They showed Auguste and Roxanne hugging and kissing. They showed Carla and Jessica together, making faces for the camera. How typical; teenagers and young adults had been posing like this since the twentieth century.

"Such memories, such friends," Wycliffe said as he handed them back to Jessica. "You'll keep these photos forever, I expect."

Jessica grinned. "Oh, totally, forever and ever. I've had so much fun with Carla, going to the nightclubs and fashion boutiques and movies with her, hanging around with her. I haven't had this much fun since Magdalena was around. Carla and I are Best Friends Forever."

"Except the world — at least the world where you and your friends can hang around in photo booths, nightclubs, fashion boutiques, and movie theaters — won't last forever, will it?" Wycliffe said.

Jessica's grin faded. "Oh, yeah, that," she said as she turned away from him.

She stood up, walked to a mirror, and looked at herself. Her face turned grim.

She turned back to face him. "I have to do it. It's my job to judge the living and the dead. It's God's will. He'll be really pissed off if I don't do it," she declared.

"What will happen if you don't do it? What then?" Wycliffe asked.

"How should I know?" Jessica sighed loudly in exasperation. "Do you think I know everything? Who do you think I am, God?"

Wycliffe nodded.

"Uh, yeah, I suppose I am," Jessica said, "but I'm only one of three persons in a single God. I don't always know what the other two are thinking, even if I have co-existed with them since eternity."

She dropped to her knees and sobbed. "Oh, I wish He would take this cup away from me!" she cried. "The only thing more painful than sacrificing yourself is to sacrifice your friends!"

Her sobs grew into a torrent of tears. Wycliffe knelt down beside her and put his hands on her shoulders, but she brushed him off.

For the first time, Wycliffe felt sorry for Jessica. The mental torment she felt now must be more agonizing than in the Garden of Gethsemane.

"Is there anything I can do to help?" he asked.

Jessica shook her head and continued crying.

Wycliffe stood up and saw Mary standing in the doorway. She had that agonized face of a mother seeing her child in pain.

The Mother of God took a deep breath, went to her daughter, knelt down, and hugged her.

Wycliffe quietly walked out of the room. *Tonight, nobody will betray you,* he thought.

Jessica cried for an hour until Mary coaxed her into bed.

After the girl fell asleep, Wycliffe asked, "Is she okay?"

"As much as any teenaged girl with the weight of God and the universe on her shoulders," Mary said. "Yeah, it's not easy being a teenager, especially this teenager."

"I don't know what to do," Wycliffe said.

"Pray for us all," Mary said. "She told me when the Apocalypse will happen."

Wycliffe felt cold fear.

"One standard Earth month from now, and there's nothing we can do to stop it."

13 / APOCALYPSE WHEN?

Father Alexei was right when he said only foolhardy clergy would come to the Moon now. As people left the Moon, a familiar face arrived on Timonium Base. Father Wycliffe did not know why Rabbi Joseph Gabizon had come. He went to meet his fellow Mars chaplain at a former bookstore.

Gabizon had put a large silver metal storage box against the far wall. It used to store equipment and had two doors. The storage box stood upright so that the doors swung open towards anyone standing in front of the box. The doors were open, and a cloth hung behind them.

The cloth was black velvet with symbols embroidered in metallic threads and brocade. It showed two gold heraldic lions *rampant* holding a gold menorah between them. Above the menorah was a silver Moon. Silver heraldic crowns were in the four corners.

Wycliffe realized that Gabizon was using the storage box as an ark, the cabinet to hold the Torah scrolls. He recognized the cloth as a *parokhet*, a curtain hanging on the ark to protect the Torah scrolls within. As per an old Spanish Jewish custom, Gabizon put the *parokhet* behind the doors of the ark.

A framed illustration of the two tablets of the Ten Commandments hung on a wall. At another wall hung a painting of Noah's Ark on Mount Ararat, with a rainbow in the sky.

Wycliffe was looking at the painting of Noah's Ark when Gabizon approached him.

"Do you like it?" Gabizon asked. "It is a reproduction of an illuminated manuscript from Spain in the Middle Ages."

"It's beautiful. Sephardic art at its best," Wycliffe commented.

Wycliffe looked at the chairs in the room. He imagined people sitting in the chairs. "Why are you building a synagogue now?" he asked.

"The Jewish National Fund wants to establish the first Jewish temple in space," Gabizon answered. "Since I have space experience, they asked me to go to the Moon."

"The Jewish National Fund? That explains the potted trees," Wycliffe said, pointing at two short trees in the corner. "Those trees won't grow to their natural height in pots or anywhere on a moonbase. I'm afraid that forestry will be limited to potted plants up here."

Gabizon laughed. "The JNF knows it cannot turn the Moon into a large forest. Those two Lebanon cedar trees are bonsai trees, artificially kept at their small height. They are here to remind us of the Holy Land.

"The JNF wants to build a temple for Jewish visitors, like what you have for Roman Catholics."

"An honorable goal, but why now? Do you really expect to find a *minyan* while people are leaving?" Wycliffe asked, referring to the minimum of ten persons needed for communal prayers.

"The troubles will pass, and the people will come back. When they come, the temple will be ready for them," Gabizon said.

Wycliffe walked through the new temple, looking at the décor and the furnishings. As he walked past the ark again, he saw a light flick on. He looked up and noticed an electric light bulb on top of the ark.

"Every synagogue or temple has an eternal light," Gabizon explained. "It symbolizes our eternal covenant with God."

"You have plenty of faith that people will come back here," Wycliffe said. "That's difficult in these times."

"We Jews are used to living in troubled times," Gabizon said.

———

As Timonium's population dwindled, those who stayed continued life as normal. Some wanted to show that nothing could interrupt their normal routine. Others carried on as usual as a way of coping with the inevitable. Still others were in denial of the future.

Father Wycliffe celebrated Mass each day, even if only one person came. Rabbi Gabizon posted the sign for Mount Ararat Temple. Carla served food and drink to decreasing numbers of people at Café Méliès. Amira planned her vacation to India. Alphonse Bangolo catalogued ESA research reports and transmitted them to Earth. Roxanne and Auguste worked on vehicle and equipment maintenance on Timonium. Dawn Favreaux gave tours of Timonium Base to reporters writing about its decline.

On weekends, Café Méliès still turned into a noisy dance club. The club attracted only a quarter of the clientele as before, so the dance floor had many open areas. Nonetheless, the club kept the music playing and the lights flashing on Friday and Saturday evenings.

Back on Earth, the United States and China continued their diplomatic and trade war. They recalled their ambassadors from each other. They imposed more trade sanctions on the each other. They forced their respective allies to end trade with the other country. On the Moon, the U.S. and Chinese garrisons waited for orders. Each side waited for the other to approach Apparition Hill.

The U.N. Security Council remained deadlocked. European and Vatican diplomats could not negotiate anything between the opposing countries.

BBC Space reported that an asteroid demolition team was chasing a fragment of asteroid Wormwood, thus confirming media rumors that the U.N. had ordered the fragment's destruction. The BBC said that the rock was in the path of a new exploration probe. Wycliffe guessed that the U.N. did not want to reveal the true reason for the mission. The world was nervous enough already.

At Apparition Hill, the pilgrims no longer came, but the iron meteorite remained, with rocket thrusters and control equipment attached to it.

Wycliffe and the others saw Jessica and Mary throughout the month. The Holy Mother and Daughter continued living at the church. Their daily routine turned into a repeating weekend: visiting the Soviet Museum again because the other museums had closed; watching TV and going to the sole remaining movie theater; eating at a few remaining restaurants; and shopping at stores that decreased in number and wares each day.

Wycliffe noticed that Jessica showed no emotion unless she joined Carla,

Roxanne, and Auguste. Then she would revert to the laughing, jumping, playful teenager again.

Occasionally, Wycliffe heard Mary quietly ask Jessica if she could postpone the Apocalypse, at least until Jessica could guarantee forgiveness to the majority of the human race. Each time, Jessica said no and left the room.

Then the month ended. On the night before Apocalypse, Mary went to Father Wycliffe and Amira.

"Jessica is inviting us for dinner tonight," Mary said.

"Is this the last supper?" Wycliffe asked.

"I think it is," Mary said.

"I guess this is an honor," Amira said. "We get to have dinner with Isa before the end of the world."

Mary, Wycliffe, Amira, Roxanne, and Auguste sat around a table at Café Méliès. Carla, wearing her Café Méliès costume, came and took their orders. She looked at her friends and shrugged.

"I'm really sorry I can't be eating with you tonight, but I'm one of only three waitresses left," she said. "There's nobody to take my shift."

"Don't worry, we'll catch up with you later," Roxanne said.

It was the dullest Saturday night in the history of Café Méliès. Despite the upbeat music, nobody danced. Only a few tables had customers.

Carla brought their food. Wycliffe had the sirloin steak; he guessed this might be his last meal, so it might as well be steak. Amira had the chicken cacciatore, a dish her mother used to cook; Wycliffe guessed she longed for comfort food from her childhood.

Roxanne had her Café Méliès favorite, the lamb with mint sauce. Auguste had the filet mignon. Mary opted for a salad and latkes, the fried potato pancakes.

Jessica ordered grilled salmon in a tomato sauce. *Fish again; how typically Messianic*, Wycliffe thought.

The adults — Wycliffe, Amira, and Mary — said little at dinner. However, Jessica and her friends gossiped, joked, and laughed. Carla joined in the fun when she wasn't busy, which was frequent; she had few customers.

Carla gave a small, flat object to Jessica. It was wrapped in colorful paper. "For you, my dear," Carla said.

Jessica's eyes gleamed. "What is it?" she asked as she tore the paper apart. She held up a plastic card. "What is it?"

"It's a Montreal metro pass," Carla said.

"Metro pass?" Jessica asked, seemingly not knowing what it was.

"Yes, for the metro," Carla explained. "You know, for the subway, the train that runs underground in Montreal."

"Oh, that!" Jessica said. "You got one for me? Why?"

"Because I'm going back to Montreal next year, and I'm inviting you to visit me," Carla said. "You'll love it there. Montreal is such a spectacular city. It has the most beautiful clothes, and it has the hottest nightclubs on Rue St. Catherine."

"Next year, eh?" Jessica said.

"See, you're even faking the Canadian accent!" Carla said.

Jessica gave a small smile. "Thank you, Carla, I really appreciate it."

"Hey, no problem. We're Best Friends Forever, right?"

"Uh, yes, right," Jessica said. "Uh, I might not get to Montreal next year."

"Oh? Why?" Carla asked.

"Uh, nothing, I just, uh, have some things to do," Jessica said uncertainly. "Next year, next year, oh, dear -- "

Mary smiled and reached across the table and touched Jessica's hand. "Go to Montreal, dear. You're not grounded anymore."

Jessica laughed, and a tear fell down her cheek. Wycliffe sensed the laugh was bitter, and the tear one of sadness.

Jessica looked up at Carla. "Thank you. I haven't had a gift like this for a long time."

"If we are giving gifts, I have a presentation to make," Auguste announced.

He got off his chair, kneeled down beside Roxanne, and pulled a small box out of his pocket. He opened the box to show a diamond ring.

"*Fräulein von Gotha, heiraten sie mich?*" he proposed.

"*Ja! Ja! Ja!*" Roxanne screamed. She threw her arms around him, pulled him up, and gave him a long, passionate kiss.

Carla, Wycliffe, Amira, Mary, and Jessica clapped and cheered as Auguste slipped the ring on Roxanne's finger.

"I'm going to get some champagne," Carla said as she walked away.

Auguste pulled Roxanne to the dance floor. They were the only couple dancing.

"Wow, that was a short courtship," Wycliffe said.

"At least they had a courtship," Mary said. "In my day, marriages were arranged."

Jessica stared blankly in front of her. "I can't do this."

"What's wrong, dear?" Mary asked.

"I love my friends. I love people. I love all people, both the virtuous and the sinful," Jessica said. "I don't want them to die. If I have to judge the living and the dead, I want to forgive all of them."

Jessica got up and ran away. She ran past Carla, who was carrying a bottle of champagne. Wycliffe saw the surprised look on Carla's face.

Carla ran out the door and into Timonium's empty street.

———

Rabbi Gabizon stared at the ark. What a dilemma: no yeshiva full of scholars could answer this question.

The ark should always be on the wall closest to Jerusalem. On Earth, that wall is easy to find. On the Moon, it was impossible. Not only did the Moon rotate on its own axis, but it also orbited the Earth. Jerusalem's position constantly changed relative to Timonium Base. To make matters more complicated, he wasn't sure if Timonium's side of the Moon *ever* faced Jerusalem.

He heard someone panting for her breath, as if she had been running. He turned around to see who had come.

A teenaged girl, wearing a Catholic schoolgirl uniform and a tiara, stumbled into Mount Ararat Temple. Gabizon was perplexed. Why was a Catholic school student hanging around Timonium Base?

As she approached him, he saw the gold Star of David hanging around her neck. He had heard stories about Space Station Troika. Could this be Jesus?

The girl raised her arms in front of the ark. "Oh, I'm finally with my own tribe again!" she cried.

"Well, there is just you and me here," Gabizon said.

The girl looked into Gabizon's eyes and said, "I've got a problem, rabbi. If I end the world tomorrow, can I go shopping and partying in Montreal next year?"

Oh, God, this is their Messiah? he thought. *No wonder we Jews are still waiting for ours.*

He stayed calm and asked, "What is wrong? Do you wish to talk about your problem?"

"I'm supposed to bring the Apocalypse. I'm supposed to end the world. Then I get to judge the living and the dead. This is God's will," she said.

"Why would God do this to us?" Gabizon asked.

"The human race has completely spazzed out," the girl said. "War, violence, intolerance, cruelty, oppression, starvation, slavery — you name it, the human race has done it. God wants to start over again. He's created the Martians to replace us."

"The Martians?" Gabizon asked in disbelief.

"Yes, Martians. They're evolving as we speak."

"We know what your Father has asked you to do, but tell me, do *you* want to end the human race?"

The girl shook her head. "Oh, no, no, no. I love human beings too much. I *am* a human being."

She screamed in anguish. "What am I supposed to do? This is all prophesized! How can I disobey my Father?"

"Are you sure that God really wants to destroy the human race? That is just one interpretation of the New Testament, but there are other interpretations," Gabizon said.

He added, "I am not as learned as my Christian friends in interpreting the New Testament, but I do know the original book of the Lord. Let me show you something. Follow me, please."

He led the girl to the painting of Noah's Ark on Mount Ararat. "You are familiar with the story of Noah, I presume," he said.

"Humanity had become so sinful and corrupt that God flooded the Earth to kill all mortal creatures except Noah and those he saved on the Ark," she said.

"Good, you remember our people's history with God," said Gabizon.

He went to the ark and pulled the *parokhet* aside. A *tik* or Torah case stood inside the ark. A shiny silver crown topped the blue wooden cylinder.

The rabbi lifted the Torah case out of the ark and carried it to a table covered with a red cloth.

"You must excuse me, but this table will have to serve as our *bimah*," he said, referring to the raised platform from which the reader recites the Torah. "We cannot build a true, raised *bimah* here yet."

He opened the *tik*, raised the Torah scroll out of its case, and held it up. Then he placed it on the table and unrolled it.

He picked up a silver pointer and said, "Come here."

The girl came to the table, and Gabizon used the pointer to point at the sacred text.

"I will translate from *Genesis*," he said:

"*Then Noah built an altar to the Lord, and choosing from every clean animal and every clean bird, he offered holocausts on the altar. When the Lord smelled the sweet odor, he said to himself: Never again will I doom the earth because of man, since the desires of man's heart are evil from the start; nor will I ever again strike down all living beings, as I have done.*

As long as the earth lasts, seedtime and harvest, cold and heat, summer and winter, and day and night shall not cease."

The girl's eyes widened and shone, and she smiled. "That's right, my Father did say that!"

"In this case, His meaning is very clear, I think," Gabizon said.

Laughing, she jumped up and down and danced across the floor. "Yes, yes, yes, yes!" she chanted.

She surprised Gabizon by dancing to him and hugging him.

"Thank you, you've told me what I need to know, what everyone needs to know," she said.

"Always glad to be of assistance," he said as he gently pushed her away.

"Now I can go to Montreal. Now I can go to Roxanne's and Auguste's wedding," she said.

"A trip to Montreal. A wedding. No more apocalyptic thoughts?" Gabizon asked.

"None! Thank you, again! *Shalom.*"

Wycliffe saw Jessica return to Café Méliès and walk to their table. She strutted confidently, like a princess again.

"She's coming back," he said.

"She looks happy again," Amira noticed.

"We'll see."

Jessica sat down at her seat, smiled, picked up her fork, and resumed eating her grilled salmon.

"We were worried about you, dear," Mary said. "Are you okay?"

"Why did you run out? Where did you go?" Roxanne asked.

"Are you in any sort of trouble?" asked Auguste. "Is there anything we can do to help you?"

Carla stopped at the table. "You're back. Is everything okay?"

Jessica drank some kosher red wine and smiled. "Yes, everything is fine. I just let the international politics stuff get to me for a moment.

"But look at us. We have so much to celebrate. I'm going to Montreal next year with Carla." She looked up at Carla and smiled.

She looked at Roxanne and Auguste. "You're getting married!"

Then she looked at Amira, Wycliffe, and Mary. "I don't care what the stupid politicians say. Let's celebrate! The Apocalypse is postponed indefinitely!"

Wycliffe looked at his watch. It was six minutes after midnight. The day of the Apocalypse had come, and nothing apocalyptic was happening.

Amira and Mary, who had Wycliffe sitting between them, both leaned over and kissed him on the cheek. Wycliffe laughed and smiled at Jessica.

When Carla brought the desert, Wycliffe looked at a TV screen in the nightclub. BBC Space showed a familiar spaceship. Was she the *Rocky Road*?

"Excuse me," he said as he left the table and went to the TV. The TV showed a rock exploding into small fragments in space.

"The U.N. Committee on Asteroid and Meteor Collisions announced that a stray fragment of asteroid Wormwood was successfully destroyed today," the news announcer said. "It no longer poses any danger to any spacecraft."

The signs of the Apocalypse were disappearing, Wycliffe concluded. He felt a great relief.

The image of Zhu Biao, President of China, appeared on TV. What was Zhu Biao doing now?

BBC Space showed a Chinese spaceship landing at Yue 1. President Zhu walked through Yue 1 with his Presidential Guard, who wore green parade uniforms with gold braid and glittering medals. Colonel Ming and his political commissars, also dressed in parade uniforms but with Party badges, walked behind the Presidential Guard. Colonel Rang and his soldiers, dressed in ordinary service uniforms, lined up for inspection by their President.

"President Zhu of China arrived at Yue 1 to visit the troops stationed there," the BBC announcer said. "He intends his trip to boost morale for the Chinese garrison."

President Zhu spoke to the soldiers. "The Motherland expects you to defend her if war breaks out. This is your duty, and I know you will fight bravely. Be prepared at all times. The battle can start at any time."

The Siren Stone remained on the Moon. The dispute between the United States and China remained.

President Zhu was taking a large risk. With the current crisis, the Moon was no place for a head of state.

Maybe the Apocalypse could proceed without Jesus.

———

In the early morning, at six hundred hours, standard lunar time, Zhu Biao boarded the spaceship *Zhang Heng*. The *Zhang Heng* lifted off from Yue 1 and took President Zhu, his secretary, three members of the Politburo, and the Presidential Guard on a flying tour of the Moon.

Colonel Rang watched the ship head towards the horizon. "I will not relax until they return," he said to Captain Chu.

"You warned them about the ship," Chu said. "We should retire the ship and turn it into a museum, like the British did with *H.M.S. Victory*."

"I agree, but the President cannot resist the chance to fly aboard our most famous spaceship," Rang said.

14 / THE SEVENTH SEAL

Father Wycliffe was making breakfast in the church's kitchen when a map of the U.S. protection zone appeared on TV.

"Chinese authorities report that the spaceship *Zhang Heng*, carrying President Zhu Biao and three members of the Chinese Communist Politburo, has been missing for two hours," the announcer said. "*Yue 1* lost contact with the ship at seven hundred hours, standard lunar time, when she was flying along the perimeter of the U.S. protection zone."

The TV showed Chinese moon tanks moving along the perimeter of the protection zone. In the distance, within the protection zone, U.S. moon tanks waited.

"We're getting conflicting information by the minute," the announcer said. "At first, we heard that the commander of Moonbase Liberty will allow the Chinese to enter the protection zone to search for the missing spaceship. Now we hear that President Darby has countermanded the order."

Amira walked into the kitchen. "What's going on?" she asked, pointing at the TV.

"The President of China is missing, possibly inside the U.S. protection zone," Wycliffe said.

"Oh, may God protect us," Amira prayed.

"Why did the Chinese have to fly that spaceship?" Wycliffe said. "They must have known she was falling apart."

"Can't someone's surveillance satellite spot the ship?" Amira asked.

"Sometimes yes, sometimes no," Wycliffe said. "First, a satellite has to pass over the area, and not every area is covered all the time. Secondly, the Americans can jam some satellites."

The TV image changed to Washington, D.C., where President Darby sat in the Oval Office. He looked tired and frustrated. He held a piece of paper, obviously a speech he had written.

"I don't have a long speech, but it's an important one," Darby said, reading from the paper. "Under no circumstances will I allow U.S. territorial integrity to be compromised. My Executive Order prohibits all non-American vehicles from entering into or flying over the U.S. protection zone on the Moon. The Executive Order supersedes any previous orders or permissions that U.S. authorities, military or civil, may have granted. Thank you, and have a good day."

As Wycliffe and Amira watched, the situation degenerated quickly. The United States would not search for the missing spacecraft because all its moon tanks were busy watching the Chinese tanks. China accused the United States of shooting down the *Zhang Heng*. The United States accused China of spying with the *Zhang Heng*. China demanded that the United States return the crew and passengers. The United States said it didn't have any of the crew or passengers, but if the U.S. found them, the U.S. would arrest them for espionage and trespassing. Both the ESA and the United Arab Emirates Space Department offered to send search parties; the United States rejected both neutral agencies. By ten hundred hours, standard lunar time, both the United States and China had put their military forces on high alert.

In Beijing, Premier Xia surrounded himself with the remaining members of the Politburo and the Chairman of the Central Military Commission. Visibly distraught, Xia spoke to the TV cameras.

"This is the worst violation of every international treaty about outer space," Xia said. "Our beloved President, members of the Politburo, his secretary, and many senior officials may be dying, if not already dead, due to American apathy.

"As acting head of state, and upon the advice of the Politburo and the Central Military Commission, I ask the United States to return the passengers and crew of the *Zhang Heng* to Moonbase Yue 1 by thirteen hundred hours, standard lunar time.

"If the passengers and crew are not returned by that time, China will retaliate on Moonbase Liberty. We have nothing else to say."

Wycliffe gasped. The Apocalypse was just three hours away.

Jessica and Mary came into the kitchen. Jessica hummed a song and helped herself to some orange juice.

"That was a great dinner last night, wasn't it?" she said before drinking the orange juice.

Mary smiled. "Yes, it was, dear. I'm very proud of you."

They were happy, oblivious to the events unfolding.

Jessica pointed at the TV. "What's that all about?"

"A Chinese spaceship has disappeared in the U.S. protection zone, and the Chinese will attack Moonbase Liberty unless they get the ship's passengers and crew back in three hours," Wycliffe told her.

Jessica's jaw dropped in surprise. She looked up at the ceiling and yelled, "Father, I changed my mind! I don't want the Apocalypse now!"

She looked back at the TV and stayed perfectly still and silent.

Mary approached Jessica. "Dear, I thought you postponed the Apocalypse. What's going on?"

Instead of responding, Jessica continued gawking at the TV, as if entranced by it.

"I think she's getting a message from God," Amira said.

"Dear?" Mary said.

"This isn't my doing," Jessica said, snapping out of her trance. "This isn't prophesized, and it's not God's will."

"Then what is it?" Wycliffe asked.

Jessica sighed. "It's *you*. Do you think that humans are puppets controlled by God? Do you think that God has scripted all your actions in advance? No, I don't think so, and you don't think so either. For centuries, your theologians have insisted that God gave free will to the human race. You do whatever you want, whether God likes it or not."

She pointed at the TV. "This is free will. This is not Biblical prophecy. This is not the will of God. This is not the Second Coming of Jesus. This is totally human-made."

Amira groaned. "So we do to ourselves what God won't do to us."

"My Moon and my shrine will be destroyed," Mary said sadly.

My shrine. Wycliffe thought about Apparition Hill and its shrine. The Siren Stone was there too — rigged as a self-propelled spacecraft.

"I've got an idea," Wycliffe said. "The Chinese will probably attack

Moonbase Liberty with a missile. What if something were to hit the missile in flight?"

"Do you think the Americans have interceptor missiles?" Amira asked.

"I don't think they do; they put all their money and effort into a mass driver intended to hit Yue 1," Wycliffe said, "but we've got a missile we can launch against the Chinese missile."

"The Vatican has a missile?" Mary asked skeptically.

"No, not the Vatican, but us, here on the Moon," Wycliffe said. "We've got the Siren Stone wired up as a self-propelled spacecraft.

"If the Chinese launch their missile, we can send the Siren Stone to intercept the missile. The missile will explode high enough that nobody will die on the ground."

"Wait a minute, I see a problem with the idea," Amira said. "Your idea would destroy the Siren Stone. Do you really want to do that after all your trouble to protect it?"

"I don't want to destroy it, but I want to save lives too. I don't see another choice. Does anyone have another choice?" Wycliffe asked.

They looked at each other in silence.

"Alright, we don't have another choice," Wycliffe declared.

"Then destroying the Siren Stone is a necessary sacrifice," Amira said.

"Sacrifices, it's all about sacrifices," Mary commented.

"Wait, I thought of another problem," Amira said. "Will the Rock Blasters be back in time to launch the rock?"

Amira had found the vital gap in the plan, Wycliffe realized. Only the Rock Blasters had experience in moving a large rock.

"I better call them," Wycliffe said. He knew the answer already, though. The *Rocky Road* needed at least five days to return from where her crew had destroyed the Wormwood fragment.

Amira looked at her watch. "Oh, Mark, I don't know about this. It's less than three hours until the deadline."

———

It took two hours to contact the *Rocky Road*. For some reason, all communications frequencies on the Moon were overloaded. It must have been the war crisis.

Andrew Lundman, aboard the *Rocky Road*, shook his head via videophone. "No, it'll be at least five days before we can get to the Moon."

"But the deadline is an hour from now," Wycliffe said desperately. "Is there nothing we can do except sit and wait?"

"There's one possibility," Andrew suggested. "You can try to launch and fly the Siren Stone by yourself. It can fly by remote control, so you don't have to be on the rock. But you will have to work the remote control."

"What type of control system does it have?"

"Both the controls and the thrusters are from a Bumblebee. Do you know that spacecraft?"

"I trained on one, and I'm rated to fly shuttlecrafts," Wycliffe said.

"I guess you're elected, Father," Andrew said. "Good luck, and we should meet up again -- assuming there will be a place where we can meet."

"I know that we do not have anyone else who can do it, but what chance do we have? None of us has experience with moving a big meteorite, much less intercepting a missile with one," Amira said. "Also, this sounds dangerous."

"Not at all," Wycliffe said. "The rock is rigged to launch by remote control. I'll be on the ground all the time."

"So *you're* volunteering for this mission?" Mary asked.

"I might as well," said Wycliffe.

He turned to Jessica. "Until last night, I wasn't sure if you were on my side. Now I know, and I'm ready to devote myself to your mother and you again. I'll save your mother's shrine."

Jessica smiled. "Glad to have you back on board, padre."

Wycliffe took out his pocket computer. "I'm going to call Alphonse and get him to teleport me to the apparition shrine."

"I'll come along too," Jessica offered. "A little bit of divine help never hurt."

They arrived in the apparition shrine's teleporter booth. The shrine was eerily quiet without the pilgrims. Instead of pilgrims, odd items littered the floor: crates abandoned by the Rock Blasters; empty food packages, also left by the Rock Blasters; and small tools used by geologists.

"That's one of the pickaxes that Alphonse bought with souvenir sales at Arcadia," Wycliffe said, pointing at the floor.

"So Mommy's fans paid for it," Jessica said, picking up the small pickaxe. "What's it doing here?"

"Alphonse and some geologists came back briefly to get some rock samples. They must have forgotten it."

They found the anonymous spacesuits and put them on. Before they put on their helmets, Wycliffe adjusted their helmet radios.

"I'm setting them on a frequency so we can hear each other and Amira back at Timonium Base," Wycliffe explained.

After putting on their helmets, they went outside and climbed down to the Siren Stone. Wycliffe looked at the control box and the thrusters. He recognized the components, all from the Bumblebee. He marveled at the Rock Blasters' ingenuity in using shuttlecraft parts to turn a rock into a spaceship.

Then he remembered that thirteen hundred hours was only half an hour away. Time to stop admiring their work, he told himself.

He looked at the ground. There was nothing, not even litter, near the Siren Stone. The Rock Blasters had cleaned their site thoroughly before leaving.

"Where's the remote control?" he asked.

Jessica shrugged.

"Are you missing something?" Amira said over the helmet radio.

"Yes, the remote control box," Wycliffe said.

"It's not there?"

"No."

"Is it in the shrine?"

"Not there either. I didn't see anything that resembled a remote control in there."

"I'm going to call the *Rocky Road*," Amira said. "There's got to be a frequency or channel I can use."

———

After a few long minutes, he heard a familiar voice: "This is *Rocky Road*. Wycliffe, come in please."

"*Rocky Road*, this is Wycliffe. Is that you, Andrew?"

"Yeah, it is."

Andrew didn't sound very enthused to hear from him, Wycliffe thought.

"Andrew, I'm looking for the remote control," Wycliffe said. "Where did you put it?"

An awkward silence followed. Finally, Andrew cleared his throat.

"The remote control is aboard the *Rocky Road*. I'm sorry," Andrew said.

"It's where?" Wycliffe cried in disbelief.

"It's aboard the *Rocky Road*," Andrew repeated. "We were in a hurry to pack up and leave, and we took back more than we should. We didn't intend to take it with us. It was an error."

Wycliffe looked at the Siren Stone again. It had Bumblebee shuttlecraft controls. Was there another way to launch the rock without sitting at its controls?

He remembered the Tsiolkovsky shuttlecraft that crashed on Mars. His theory was that the Troika crew had put the shuttlecraft on autopilot and sent it to Mars.

"I got an idea," Wycliffe said. "Each shuttlecraft has an autopilot feature."

"Autopilot will be difficult to use," Andrew said. "You can input a flight plan and send the shuttlecraft away. You can point the shuttlecraft in a direction and send it away. Unfortunately, you have a moving target to hit. You don't know where the missile will fly, so you have to guide the rock during its flight. Autopilot won't do that for you."

Wycliffe's heart sank in disappointment. "Yeah, I should have known that," he agreed. "I got excited and didn't think things through."

"This is Amira. Mark, come back. There's nothing you can do."

"Roger that, Amira," Wycliffe said sadly.

Wycliffe looked at the Siren Stone. It had the joystick and controls of a Bumblebee rigged to it. A pilot could sit or lie at the controls and fly it. It would be very difficult to hold onto the Siren Stone, but it was not impossible.

It would be a suicide mission. Whoever flew the Siren Stone into the Moon Punisher would not come back alive.

His life was a life of sacrifices, some deliberate, some not. What was one more sacrifice?

Wycliffe sighed. "I guess there's no choice. I'm going to fly the Siren Stone."

"No!" Amira yelled over the radio.

"What did you say?" Andrew asked.

Jessica ran to him. "No, I'll fly the rock!"

"You? You're a kid, and you don't have a shuttlecraft pilot's license," Wycliffe said.

"I'm over two thousand years old, and I flew a shuttlecraft to Mars," Jessica protested.

As Wycliffe walked towards the Siren Stone, Jessica chased and grabbed him. He kept brushing her away.

"Let me do it," she urged. "You've done enough for me and Mommy already!"

He grabbed her and looked into her eyes. "I devoted my life to serving God. I sacrificed my family."

"That was an accident!"

"And it was my free will that sent them into the bomb shelter, so I sacrificed them, even if unintentionally. Now I have nobody with whom to live. Is it so bad that I sacrifice myself now?"

As Wycliffe climbed onto the Siren Stone, Jessica grabbed his back and tugged him, sending him stumbling back to the ground. Regaining his footing, he climbed back on the Siren Stone. Jessica scrambled after him and pushed him.

"Padre, listen to me," Jessica urged. "I'm Jesus. I'm eternally begotten of the Father, God from God, Light from Light, true God from true God. I crashed a shuttlecraft on Mars, and I came back. If I crash the Siren Stone into the missile, I'll come back again."

"If you fly the Siren Stone, you will die and stay dead. Let me do it."

Wycliffe challenged her. "But what if you're really an illusion caused by the Siren Stone? If you're an illusion, letting you fly the rock means the rock won't fly. As for me, I'm real, regardless of whether you're Jesus or an illusion. Choosing me has a one hundred percent chance that the rock will fly."

"Whoa, you're good," Jessica said. "Those Jesuits trained you well."

"I'm not a Jesuit. Not all the smart priests are Jesuits," Wycliffe said. "Now get out of my way."

He climbed on the Siren Stone and kneeled beside the control box. After raising the lid on the keyboard, he typed commands for the pre-launch sequence.

"Oh my God, the Chinese have launched their missile!" Amira screamed over the radio.

Wycliffe looked at his watch: 13:00.

"Amira, how do you know?" Wycliffe asked.

"It's on TV!" Amira shouted.

He felt a tug at his back, and suddenly, he felt oxygen seep out of his spacesuit.

"What have you done?" he yelled, gasping for air.

Jessica yanked on his back again, harder than before. Then she skipped in front of him and held up an air hose.

"I pulled the air hose that connects your backpack to your spacesuit. In other words, I disconnected your oxygen supply," she said.

Wycliffe saw Jessica grin. She pulled a suit repair bandage from an external pocket of her spacesuit and went behind him. He felt the oxygen seepage stop. He breathed deeply and turned around to face Jessica.

Jessica said, "I've just bandaged your suit, so you'll keep the oxygen that remains in the suit. However, you're not getting any new oxygen, so you'll be breathing your own carbon dioxide soon."

"Great, thanks," Wycliffe said sardonically.

"My pleasure," Jessica said. "You don't have enough oxygen to fly the rock on its flight to destiny, but you do have enough oxygen to go back into the shrine. You better go back now; you'll run out of oxygen soon if you keep hyperventilating like that."

"No!" Wycliffe protested.

"It's my job to die for your salvation. Let me do it."

She pushed him, and he stumbled and fell off the Siren Stone. As he stood back up, he saw her hacking at the Siren Stone with Alphonse's small pickaxe. She threw the blows down furiously.

A small chunk of iron flew from the Siren Stone. She grabbed it and tossed it at Wycliffe.

"A souvenir for you," she said. "Remember."

Wycliffe caught the iron chunk and looked back at Jessica.

"Go, you don't want to be near the thrusters when the bird launches," she said.

Jessica lay belly down on the Siren Stone, grasped the joystick in one hand, and pressed controls with her other hand. The rocket thrusters ignited and blasted clouds of lunar soil outward.

Wycliffe turned and scrambled up the hill. His heart beat quickly, he panted for breath, and he felt sweat all over his body. He felt terribly hot. Was he breathing more carbon dioxide than oxygen now?

He reached the airlock and looked down the hill. The Siren Stone launched into the sky. It shot straight up until he could not see it.

He returned inside the shrine, took off his spacesuit, and found a TV. As he checked each channel, he saw TV networks pulling images from every surveillance satellite in the sky. Images of Moonbase Liberty and Yue 1 flashed on the TV. The airwaves filled with the voices of reporters, military officers, politicians, and scientists. He settled on BBC Space, as usual.

"Surveillance satellites are trying to find the missile, unseen since its launch. The new jamming technology has made getting a picture more difficult. In addition, nobody is certain of the missile's path," the BBC Space news announcer said. She suddenly looked surprised. "Wait, we got a picture from a TV satellite."

The Moon Punisher missile appeared on TV, caught on video by a shaky satellite camera. The missile climbed steadily into the sky.

The missile reached its maximum height and started its descent. Suddenly, a black object shot up and smashed into the missile. The missile exploded, and its fragments shot in many different directions.

"This incredible!" the news announcer cried. "Something has intercepted the missile and destroyed it!"

Wycliffe gasped. Jessica had done it.

"Wait, there's more coming. Is this confirmed?" the news announcer asked. She checked her messages and looked back at the camera. "It isn't over yet. We're receiving reports that something has hit Moonbase Liberty."

What could it be? Jessica destroyed the missile, Wycliffe thought. *What else remained?*

"An ESA satellite in high orbit snapped this photograph of Moonbase Liberty before the Americans jammed the signal," the BBC Space announcer said.

An aerial photo of Moonbase Liberty appeared on TV. The mass driver lay in ruins around a crater. The earthworks were flattened, and the pieces of the tube lay everywhere.

Something had hit the mass driver and carved out the crater.

Suddenly, the ground shook, and the TV image turned into static.

Wycliffe went to the window and looked out. He couldn't see the communications tower. Instead, a crater sat where the tower had been. Shards of metal were scattered over the hill's base.

He tried calling Amira on his pocket computer, but he couldn't get a signal. Without the communications tower, the TV and the pocket computer would have to search for another tower to receive signals. With all the chatter about the war, all communications systems were overloaded. He might have to wait for a while.

Like his first moments in Troika, he was alone with nobody with whom to talk.

Well, not completely alone...

Wycliffe walked into the chapel, kneeled in front of the altar and the crucifix, and prayed, "Dear God, thank you for sparing us from destruction despite our violent ways..."

After half an hour had passed, the TV signal returned. The BBC announcer smiled as she read her report. "In an amazing and bizarre series of events, a rocky iron object collided with the Chinese missile and destroyed it. Fragments of the iron rock then fell on the mass driver at Moonbase Liberty. U.S. officials will not confirm if the mass driver was destroyed, but the U.S. has not launched its own attack with it.

"We don't have any other confirmed reports of damage from falling debris, but some may have hit a communications tower at Apparition Hill. All contact with that communications tower ended thirty minutes ago. Since the tower's video camera malfunctioned several weeks ago, we can't get video of what happened there."

The silence had lasted thirty minutes. That length of time seemed familiar. Wycliffe opened the electronic Bible on his pocket computer and searched the *Book of Revelation*.

He found chapter eight, verse one:

"*When he broke open the seventh seal, there was silence in heaven for about half an hour.*"

He sighed in relief and looked out the window. The Lamb had opened the seventh seal, and the world still lived.

PART 5
PAX

15 / THE CRESCENT MOON

When a large chunk of iron smashed the mass driver, Colonel Chang ordered his moon tanks to return and protect Moonbase Liberty. When the Chinese saw the Americans leave, they drove their moon tanks into the zone but didn't chase the Americans. In the only battle of the war, both armies retreated from each other.

Instead of attacking Moonbase Liberty, the Chinese tanks searched for the *Zhang Heng*. They found her sitting in the protection zone. After suffering both communications and engine trouble, she had landed, intact but unable to send a distress signal. All the crew and passengers survived unharmed, much to their country's relief. After a week of repairs, the Chinese flew the *Zhang Heng* back to Yue 1, grounded her, and turned her into a museum.

The United States ignored the Chinese during the week they repaired the *Zhang Heng*. President Darby did not issue any stern warnings, threats, or ultimatums. In response, the Chinese ignored the Americans. The war ended as abruptly as it had started.

Despite President Darby's insistence, the United States Congress voted against construction of another mass driver on the Moon. When Darby proposed a ballistic missile system, Congress rejected it too. The mass driver had gone twenty trillion dollars over budget, and the United States had simply run out of money for arming the Moon.

Likewise, China did not send more ballistic missiles to the Moon. Although the Chinese lunar military budget was secret, defense experts estimated it in the hundreds of trillions of gold units. Combined with losses in international trade, China also ran out of money for arming the Moon.

Finally, the European Union got the two countries to negotiate at summit conferences in Berlin. The United States abolished the protection zone and returned it to international use. China agreed to dismantle its missile silos. Both countries signed the U.N. Rescue Agreement again. Both countries returned their moonbases to civilian scientific control.

Pope Christopher declared the first Galactic Day of Prayer for Peace in Space. Father Wycliffe and priests from Rome to Mars prayed for all countries to uphold the international space treaties.

"By the way, does the Pope realize that the human race lives only in this solar system? We're not spread out across the galaxy," Father Wycliffe told Cardinal Saint-Cloud.

"He knows that, but he chose the name 'Galactic Day' anyway. He is planning for future expansion," the Cardinal explained.

"Don't misunderstand me, I'm glad the Apocalypse didn't happen," Michael Crowberry said after returning to the United States. "I could use the time to save more people and turn them to Jesus before the End.

"*Revelation*, chapter seven, says there will be one hundred and forty-four thousand people who will be saved from destruction. I've recruited only twelve thousand of them. I need to recruit some more."

Cardinal Saint-Cloud closed the electronic file of Wycliffe's report and looked back at him via videophone. "Thank you for your report," said Saint-Cloud.

"You're welcome, Your Eminence," Wycliffe replied.

"I agree with you that we should not authenticate the apparition seen by Carla Delgada," Saint-Cloud said. "I will declare it unworthy of veneration on doctrinal grounds. That is, the apparition did not promote a specific Church teaching."

"I'm glad that you agree that's the best way to deal with it," Wycliffe said.

"I also agree with your recommendation to not comment on whether the apparition was a hoax or hallucination," Saint-Cloud said. "I will say that we did not need to investigate a potential hoax or hallucination after rejecting the apparition on doctrinal grounds. Like you, I do not wish to create any trouble for Miss Delgada."

"I'm sure she will appreciate our silence on the matter," Wycliffe said. "I don't want people to think that she's dishonest or mentally disturbed. Rather, she's one of the sanest, most honest people I have met."

"Good, let us not draw any more attention to her," Cardinal Saint-Cloud said. "I will release the report to the public next week. By the way, you will not believe who has asked me to authenticate the apparition."

"Who? The pilgrims? Were they from Mexico?" Wycliffe asked.

The Cardinal laughed. "Not the pilgrims. I got messages from John Layman, Alphonse Bangolo, and Dawn Favreaux, urging me to declare the apparition to be authentic and worthy of veneration. Marian shrines are good for business. They think the tourist business will drop if the Church rejects the apparition."

Wycliffe shook his head. "I kept telling them that the Church does not spread fairy tales and ghost stories."

Saint-Cloud stopped laughing and looked serious again. "Ah, speaking of ghost stories, I also read your *secret* report for Church authorities only, not for public release."

"Forgive me, I realize that a secret report is unusual," Wycliffe said. "I needed to tell you about some findings even if the public is not ready for them."

"Thank you for telling me about them, and I agree, the public is not ready for the more bizarre findings," Saint-Cloud reassured him. "It is too bad that the public report must conceal the truth about your research. For example, you conducted psychiatric and psychological tests on Miss Delgada. I am pleased that you did that. We need scientific rigor in investigating apparitions.

"And you think that the apparition's peace message, its only message, supports the Church's teaching. I agree that it does."

Wycliffe nodded. "I found reasons both in favor and against approval, but the deciding question was whether the apparition was supernatural, due to unnatural forces. Due to the Siren Stone, it was possible that the apparition had natural causes."

"And yet Siren Stones are not scientifically-proven either," Saint-Cloud commented. "There has not been any independent verification or repetition of any observations or data about them. If we mentioned them in our report, scientists would criticize us for basing our conclusion on unproven science."

"I'm glad you understand the purpose of the secret report," Wycliffe said.

"I am intrigued by the Siren Stones, though," Saint-Cloud admitted. "Assuming that they really are telepathic rocks that work on our brains, could God have created them so people like the Apostles could see Jesus after his Resurrection? Or are they simply godless telepathic rocks that create illusions? Did God give us frontal lobes so we could see Jesus and angels? Or does the frontal lobe create the illusions that we want to see? There is so much that we do not know."

"There is so much that we have to learn," Wycliffe said. "I should be preparing for Mass soon. Is there anything more to discuss?"

"Ah, yes," Saint-Cloud said. "Let us talk about the Siren Stone that flew off and hit the Chinese missile."

Wycliffe felt uneasy. "Yes, sir?"

"The ESA's space crash investigators found Bumblebee shuttlecraft parts on the ground: rocket thrusters and control mechanisms. They did not find any human remains, though. The investigators are certain that someone rigged the Siren Stone with rocket thrusters and controls.

"However, they are not certain how the Siren Stone launched into flight. They speculate that someone put it on autopilot and sent it up. Without human remains, that is the best theory they have."

"Interesting," said Wycliffe. He did not want to talk about the Siren Stone's collision with a ballistic missile.

Saint-Cloud stared intently at Wycliffe. "Did you have anything to do with launching the Siren Stone?"

"No," Wycliffe lied.

He still had doubts that Jessica really was Jesus. She could have been an illusion.

He still wondered if he had imagined Jessica pushing him away and riding the Siren Stone. Did a real person actually ride the Siren Stone? Or did he suffer an illusion, and it was actually he who sent the Siren Stone up on autopilot? He had suspected the Troika crew of crashing a shuttlecraft by autopilot, so could he have done it too?

"What an incredible stroke of luck for whoever did it," Saint-Cloud said. "It is impossible for a shuttlecraft on autopilot to hit a ballistic missile. It is a miracle that the Siren Stone hit its target."

"Indeed, a miracle," Wycliffe said.

"Do you remember the mysterious people who appeared and worked on the Siren Stone before it flew off?" Saint-Cloud asked. "They were obviously the people who rigged the Siren Stone with rockets."

Saint-Cloud looked suspiciously at Wycliffe. "Did you have anything to do with that?"

"No, sir," Wycliffe lied again.

Saint-Cloud stared silently at him for a moment. Then he said, "Thank you for talking to me. Remember, if you need to confess your sins, you can always call me."

Father Wycliffe built a side altar to the Virgin Mary at St. Dominic's Church. It had a statue of Our Lady of Walsingham. Gold leaf decorated the wall behind the statue, and a row of red votive candles burned in front of it. On one side of the side altar, he hung pictures of Our Lady of Fatima, Our Lady of Guadalupe, and Our Lady of Lourdes. On the other side of the altar, he hung Father Alexei's icon of Our Lady of Kazan and other Orthodox icons. Now the Moon had an approved Marian shrine.

He installed statues of saints along the walls. Behind the altar, he replaced the empty cross with a crucifix.

"What are you doing?" Saint-Cloud asked him. "The Pope forbids conspicuous displays of devotion in space. He does not want to provoke the fundamentalist atheists."

"That's why people spent more time at the unauthorized shrine instead of St. Dominic's Church," Wycliffe argued. "We took something away from them, and they built it by themselves. You would not believe the devotion I saw at the unauthorized shrine. If only we could recapture such enthusiasm in our church.

"As for the atheist fundamentalists, they aren't going to accept us because we have boring décor. They simply don't want us out here at all. How we decorate our church is irrelevant."

"I come from Paris, city of Notre Dame de Paris and great cathedrals and churches," Saint-Cloud said. "I admit that I sympathize with you."

"Pilgrims are returning to the Moon because they have a folk belief in Carla Delgada's apparition. We can never stamp it out," Wycliffe said. "If they must see a Marian shrine, let's attract them back to *our* church. Let's give Mary back to them."

"I will discuss the matter with the Holy Father, if he has time," Saint-Cloud said. "In the meantime, you may carry on with the redecoration.

"However, do not slip too much into our past. Keep the Mass in vernacular, please. If you celebrate a Mass in Latin, celebrate one in French or English too. Speak facing the people, not facing away from them. Provide Communion in the hand to those who desire it; do not force them to accept it from your hand to their mouths. I do not want to see a reversion to pre-Vatican II times. The Pope will certainly make time to talk about that."

Wycliffe laughed. "Don't worry. I won't take us back to the nineteenth century."

One day, Wycliffe received a parcel from France. He opened it and took out an icon. He marveled at the brilliant colors and shiny gold leaf.

It showed a young brunette girl wearing a white blouse, a green school tie, and a silver tiara. She had a gold halo.

The note in the box read:

Dear Mark,

I hope that my icon painting skills have improved. Please accept this icon of our friend Jessica as a token of our friendship. I know that her status in the Trinity is highly debatable, yet I feel that she has enriched us with her presence.

Alexei

P.S. Do not hang this icon in the Church.

Father Wycliffe watched the people walk through the commercial district. Shops, restaurants, and other businesses had reopened, and Moon colonists and tourists swarmed through the Timonium Base again.

He walked past the Tranquility Tours office, where Dawn Favreaux talked to tourists about the bus tour to the Soviet Museum. He stopped for lunch at Café Méliès, where Carla and the other waitresses carried food and drink to customers. When he passed the Devil's Pitchfork, he smelled the aroma of steak and kidney pie and roast beef again.

After lunch, he visited Mount Ararat Temple and watched Rabbi Gabizon lead a *minyan*. Gabizon could always get a *minyan*, although sometimes he cheated by inviting Father Wycliffe and Imam Edip to fill the ten positions. Today, the rabbi would not need his colleagues' help.

After returning to St. Dominic's Roman Catholic Church, he polished a gold crown. To lure pilgrims away from Apparition Hill, he staged coronations for a statue of Our Lady of Fatima at St. Dominic's Church. Pilgrims and tourists packed the church for these ceremonies. Cardinal Saint-Cloud turned a blind eye to these events.

Life returned to normal at Timonium Base.

———

A month after the war, Auguste Peeters married Roxanne von Gotha in St. Dominic's Church. It was the first wedding on the Moon.

The groom bought his black tuxedo from the most elegant men's clothier in Timonium Base. His bow tie, blue with small ESA symbols, was a gift from Alphonse Bangolo.

The bride looked gorgeous in her white dress from a fashion house in Timonium. It fell just below her knees; Roxanne joked that it was the first time she had worn a dress that went below her knees. In the new style, it had no train, but it did have white floral patterns embroidered on it.

Father Wycliffe did not mind that only Roxanne was Catholic. He performed the ceremony and gave his blessing to the couple. As the couple walked out, recorded sounds of church bells blared from the sound system.

At the wedding dinner at Café Méliès, Father Wycliffe sat beside Carla Delgada. Between the salad and the soup, Carla asked about her missing friends.

"It's too bad that Jessica and Mary can't be here," Carla said.

"Yes, it's too bad. I'm sure they would have loved to see Roxanne and Auguste get married," Wycliffe agreed.

Nobody had seen Jessica or Mary since the Siren Stone smashed into the missile.

"Did they ever say why they had to leave so quickly?" Carla asked.

"It was some sort of family matter. They didn't tell me what it was," Wycliffe said. It was a necessary lie.

"Do you know their address on Earth?" Carla asked.

Wycliffe had to invent a story. "No, I don't," he said. "They showed up as pilgrims one day, but the hotel made an error with their reservation, and they had no place to stay. I offered to house them at the church for a while, and they offered to do some of the household chores. Then they just stayed until they left, but they never gave me their Earth address. I guess they never thought they would stay so long."

Carla took a sip of wine. "I wish they had given me their forwarding address or contact information."

"Yes, I wish they had too." Wycliffe said. That was not a lie.

"I miss Jessica," Carla moaned. "I thought she was my Best Friend Forever. Why doesn't she come back?"

Wycliffe sighed and smiled. "Just have faith. When you least expect her, she might come back."

———

Roxanne von Gotha stood on a chair, turned her back on all the single women, and tossed her bouquet into the air. It soared in an arc. Dozens of women reached out for it. Jumping into the air, Carla caught it. Amidst moans from the single women and cheers from the other guests, she held the bouquet above her head.

Next, Auguste pulled up Roxanne's dress and pulled a garter down one of her legs. Carla had bought the lacey blue garter at a sexy lingerie store for Roxanne. As Auguste held up the garter and hooted, all the single men gathered around him. Watching the ritual with amusement, Wycliffe sat at his table and drank his coffee.

Auguste turned his back on the men and tossed the garter into the air. The men raised their arms and jumped to catch it, but it flew over their heads...

...and landed in front of Father Wycliffe.

He held it up and smiled sheepishly. Everyone broke out laughing. None of the single men seemed disappointed to miss the garter.

"Father, are you getting married?" Amira asked.

Wycliffe laughed and tossed the garter back onto the table. "No, of course not! I'm a Catholic priest!"

"But you were not always one, were you?" Amira teased him.

———

A year after the war, Father Wycliffe's term at St. Dominic's Church ended. Rather than renewing his term, he chose to return to Earth.

"I'm getting old," he told Cardinal Saint-Cloud and Dr. Schiller. "I think it's time I went back to England."

"We would love to have you back here," Dr. Schiller said. "I'll arrange to send a new priest."

"You are a pioneer," Saint-Cloud said. "I think the Pope may give you a Papal knighthood, like the Order of St. Gregory the Great."

"A decoration or medal would be nice, but what I really want is to see grass and trees again," Wycliffe said. "I ran away from Earth once, but now I want to come back."

"Ah, the prodigal son returns," Dr. Schiller joked.

As Wycliffe packed his luggage, someone rang the doorbell. When he opened the door, he saw Dr. Thomas Hall.

Wycliffe had not expected the fundamentalist atheist to visit him. "Thomas, will you come in?" he asked.

"Thank you, Father," Thomas said. "May I ask a question about Jessica?"

"Yes. What is it?"

"You doubted that Jessica was really Jesus. You thought she could be an illusion, correct?"

"Yes, you know I had my doubts."

"And I suspect you never considered if she was an alien."

"That's right. I didn't consider that possibility."

"If you doubted she was a real person, human or alien or divine, why did you interact with her? You talked to her, you walked with her, you had dinner with her. Why did you treat her as a real person?"

"Have you heard of Pascal's wager?"

"No. What's that?"

"Pascal said that it is not certain that everything is certain," Wycliffe explained. "Nobody can prove if God exists or does not exist. Therefore, you have two options in believing about Him, which lead to three potential outcomes. If God exists, and you believe in Him, He will reward you. If God exists, and you don't believe in Him, He will punish you. If God does not exist, then regardless of whether you believe in Him or not, you get nothing.

"Therefore, if there is a chance that God exists, it is safer to believe in God because He will reward you if he exists. The potential gain by believing in God is always better than the potential gain of not believing in Him.

"I had a dilemma with Jessica. Do I interact with her or ignore her as an illusion? Her invisibility on videos plus my scientific background led me to dismiss her as a Siren Stone illusion. But due to Pascal's wager, I decided to treat Jessica as if she was both real and Jesus. I had nothing to lose by doing so.

"As to whether she really was Jesus, I'm still not sure. Pascal's wager is only about the expected gains of belief and non-belief; it does not actually assess the probability of the existence of God. Whether you believe God exists is a matter of faith -- or lack of it."

Thomas looked pensive and nodded his head. "Hmmm, interesting. If I think long enough, I'm sure I can find flaws in the argument."

"Oh, you don't have to think for too long. Philosophers and theologians have already thought of plenty of criticisms of Pascal's wager," Wycliffe said. "Thinking of arguments for and against Pascal's wager is like a sport in philosophy classes."

Thomas laughed, held out his hand, and said, "Good luck, Father."

"Thank you, it was actually a pleasure to work with you," Wycliffe said as he shook hands with Thomas. "Visit me if you're ever in Walsingham."

"I've still got a few years left here, but I'm sure I'll get the urge to return to Earth sometime, like you do," Thomas said. "I'll be sure to look you up. We actually have more in common than you think."

"Oh?"

"Jessica. Whatever she was, we both cared for her and wanted to protect her and keep her out of harm."

"Yes, we both did, didn't we?" Wycliffe said.

Wycliffe sat in the spaceport bar and waited for his flight. He looked suspiciously as a U.S. Army officer entered the bar and walked towards him. Colonel Michael Chang sat down beside him.

"Father Wycliffe, I want you to know something," Chang said.

"Yes, Colonel?" Wycliffe said, putting down his cup of coffee.

"I didn't have you declared *persona non grata*. You're free to enter the United States," Chang said.

"Wow, this is a wonderful surprise," Wycliffe said. "Why did you change your mind?"

"Two reasons. First, you were wearing a Vatican Observatory badge. I know the Vatican Observatory has an observatory in Tucson, Arizona. I didn't want to prevent a fellow spacer from conducting scientific research there."

"Secondly, we both have experiences with Siren Stones. It's something we share with other people. I don't know what Siren Stones are, but I'm hoping that you, a scientist, will find out. You have to be free to travel for your research."

"Thank you for considering these things," Wycliffe said.

"I ask for just one thing, Father. When you find the secret of the Siren Stones, tell me," Chang said.

After returning to Montreal, Carla invited her friend Amira Edip to visit her. After the end of the winter semester at Free University, Amira went to Montreal and saw Carla again.

They reminisced about the Moon, looked at photos of Auguste and Roxanne and their baby, joked about how Father Wycliffe had caught the garter, and talked about Amira's trip to India. Inevitably, they talked about absent friends.

"I wish Jessica and Mary would call us," Carla said sadly. "I miss Jessica very much."

Amira hugged her. "I am sure when the time is right, she will come back. I have faith that she will."

Carla, the incurable shopper, took Amira shopping in her favorite stores. As they walked downtown, they saw a grandiose church. It had a soaring green dome, statues of Jesus and the twelve Apostles along its roof, and ornate masonry.

"What is that?" Amira asked.

"The Cathedral-Basilica of Mary Queen of the World," Carla answered.

"It is large. Is it pretty inside?"

"I confess that I've never gone inside it."

"Then let us go inside," Amira suggested.

They discovered that the church was a scaled-down replica of St. Peter's Basilica in Rome. It epitomized Roman Catholic gaudiness: side altars, shrines, statues, votive candles, chapels, paintings, and stained glass everywhere.

They stopped at a statue of the Virgin Mary, attached to a marble wall. According to the tourist brochure, Canadian sculptor Sylvia Daoust carved the wooden statue. It showed Mary wearing a crown. Behind her, on the wall, twelve four-pointed stars and a crescent moon surrounded her.

They looked at the sole crescent moon.

"That reminds me of someone," Carla said, remembering the crescent moon pendant that Jessica's mother, Mary, wore.

16 / THE GODDESS

According to legend, the Virgin Mary visited Lady Richeldis de Faverches, a Saxon noblewoman of Norfolk, in 1061. The Virgin took Lady Richeldis in spirit to Nazareth three times and showed her the house where Mary had lived and received the Annunciation of Christ's coming birth. After these visions ended, Lady Richeldis built a stone chapel containing a wooden replica of the Holy House. Later, a towering gothic Augustinian priory was built beside the Holy House and its chapel. Over the centuries, other buildings were added to the shrine complex, including the Slipper Chapel, a mile away from the Holy House. Pilgrims would take off their shoes at the Slipper Chapel and walk barefoot on the last mile of their pilgrimage to Mary, Our Lady of Walsingham.

The Holy House of Walsingham became the most popular pilgrimage site in England. For centuries, pilgrims both rich and poor visited the shrine. In the Holy House, they prayed to a statue of Mary and Jesus. The statue showed Mary, dressed in blue and white robes, sitting on a throne and holding the baby Jesus on her lap. The medieval clergy called the statue a "throne of wisdom", not for the throne upon which Mary sat, but for the mother on whose lap Jesus sat.

The Holy House smelled of sweet incense, and only candles lit its darkness. On its altar, gifts of gold, silver, and gemstones glistened in the candlelight. The ancient pagan customs had survived: pilgrims still gave offerings to their gods –- or goddesses.

In Christian theology, Mary is Mother of God, but she is not a goddess or a form of God. Yet people insisted on praying to her, asking her to mediate between them and God. For fifteen centuries, Christians venerated the Virgin Mary as enthusiastically as ancient pagans had worshipped their goddesses.

In May, when life returns to the land after winter, pagan Europeans had celebrated a spring festival. Celts, Greeks, and Romans carried statues of their fertility goddesses in processions. Christians turned May into Mary's month, and they continued the processions, now with Mary's statue. The statues often showed Mary standing atop a crescent Moon, like Diana the Moon Goddess.

Mary moved into the pagan goddess temples. In Ephesus, a major center of Diana worship, the people built a church in Mary's honor over the ruins of a temple of Diana. In Chartres, a Marian cathedral arose where the Celtic Druids had worshipped "la Virgo Paritura", a virgin who gave birth. In Enna in Sicily, the people used an ancient statue of Demeter and her daughter Kore as a statue of Mary and Jesus until Pope Pius IX discovered and removed it.

In the sixteenth century, Western Christendom split in two factions, the Roman Church and the Protestant Reformers. The Reformers believed in a personal relationship to God, one without priests and saints as intermediaries. Marian devotion, with its prayers and statues and processions in honor of a human woman, seemed like pagan idol worship. The Mother was taking attention away from her Son.

But the Roman Church's devotion to Mary grew stronger under the Protestant onslaught. To the Reformers, Marian devotion was the most visible sign of Roman vice. Protestant Europe was about to dethrone another female deity.

The Protestants stopped chanting the Rosary, the series of prayers to Mary. They stopped carrying her in processions. They stripped their churches of statues and pictures of Mary and burned them.

King Henry VIII of England separated the Church of England from the Roman Church, thus putting England in the Protestant camp. In 1538, the King and Church of England dissolved the Walsingham shrine. They tore down the priory, pillaged the chapel for its stones, destroyed the Holy House, and turned the Slipper Chapel into a barn for animals. They took the statue of Mary and Jesus to London and burned it. Walsingham fell into obscurity.

In 1896, a wealthy Anglican woman, Charlotte Boyd, bought the Slipper Chapel. She hoped to restore it, but she converted to Roman Catholicism and donated the chapel to Downside Abbey, a Catholic monastery that had survived three centuries in an Anglican country. Downside Abbey's monks restored Slipper Chapel.

In 1897, the local Catholic clergy led a procession to Slipper Chapel, the first public devotion to Mary, Our Lady of Walsingham, in over three hundred years.

Some Anglicans, called High Church Anglicans or Anglo-Catholics, had kept statues of Mary and continued to pray their own version of the Rosary. In the 1920's, Father Hope Patten, Anglican Vicar of Walsingham, recreated the medieval shrine to Mary for the Church of England. Walsingham's Anglicans resumed their pilgrimages and processions in honor of Our Lady of Walsingham.

Two shrines, one Anglican and one Roman Catholic, were dedicated to the Virgin. Just like in the medieval era, Walsingham became a major place of pilgrimage and tourism.

———

Father Wycliffe went home after a day at the Roman Catholic National Shrine of Our Lady of Walsingham. As always, he had dinner alone, watched the TV news alone, read the newspaper alone, and went to his bedroom alone.

He looked out the window, and a full Moon shone in the sky. As he looked at the Moon, he remembered a souvenir of his time there. Suddenly, he felt a need to hold it again.

He opened his dresser drawer and pulled out a small chunk of black iron: the rock that Jessica had hacked off the Siren Stone and tossed to him.

He felt the cold, hard, metallic rock. Despite the growth of space tourism, few people owned a Moon rock. He knew he had a rare gem.

"Mark, why hold that cold, hard rock when you can hold me?" a voice said behind him.

He turned around and saw Ingrid.

Ingrid, his late wife.

"Ingrid," he muttered in disbelief.

He was almost sixty years old, aged from years in space, with white hair. She was twenty-one years old, with blonde hair. She wore the short yellow sundress that she had worn when he saw her reading a book about Héloïse and Abélard.

He stared silently at her.

"You look like you've seen a ghost," she joked. "Say something, will you?"

"Ingrid, are you a ghost?" he asked.

Ingrid giggled. "Can a ghost do this?"

She walked to him, picked the Siren Stone fragment out of his hands, and put it on the dresser.

Then she took him in her arms, and gave him a long, wet kiss.

"It's the Siren Stone, isn't it?" Wycliffe asked. "You're an illusion caused by that rock I brought back."

She looked deep into his eyes and put the palm of her hand on his left chest. "Our love was no illusion. I've always been alive in your heart."

"In my heart, you never died. Oh, Ingrid, I've missed you for so long. I tried running away, but it didn't help," Wycliffe said.

"I'm giving you a reason to stay on Earth," she said before kissing him again.

———

Father Mark Wycliffe settled into a new routine. After a day at the Shrine, he went home and ate dinner with Ingrid, watched the TV news with Ingrid, read the newspaper with Ingrid, and went to bed with Ingrid.

She appeared to him only when he was alone at home. When visitors came, she disappeared. When he left his home, she didn't follow him outside.

One night, as they lay in bed, Mark asked, "Are you an illusion in my mind?"

Ingrid smiled. "Mark, we've talked about this before. Can an illusion make love the way we just did?"

Mark snickered. "Probably not, but I never see you when visitors come, and I never see you outside the house. That's why I wonder if you're only in my mind."

"I don't appear for visitors, and I don't go outside for a very good reason," Ingrid said. "What would people think if they saw an old priest like you snogging with a sexy young girl like me?"

Mark embraced her in his arms and kissed her. "Enough talking. I prefer snogging."

———

A year after Ingrid's return, Mark Wycliffe asked the new Anglican Archbishop of Norfolk if he could convert back to Anglicanism.

When he came home that night, Ingrid asked, "Mark, what's gotten into you? You love the Roman Catholic shrine. Why are you leaving?"

"In case you haven't noticed, one thing about the Catholic Church hasn't changed in centuries. Its priests can't get married," Mark said.

He continued. "We've been together again for a year, and I feel like I've been sinning behind the Pope's back. If I became Anglican again, I could marry again without problems."

Ingrid put her arms around him. "Oh, Mark, you know we can't really get married," she said sadly.

Mark nodded. "I don't care if you're an illusion caused by a Siren Stone, and I don't care if you're a ghost that God has sent to me. I know that we can't have a wedding ceremony, but as long as you're with me, I feel we're married."

"I love you, dear, even after 'til death do us part," Ingrid said.

———

Father Mark Wycliffe, priest of the Roman Catholic National Shrine of Our Lady of Walsingham, past Roman Catholic chaplain of Space Station Exeter, past parish priest of St. Dominic's Roman Catholic Church, and Knight of the Order of St. Gregory the Great, returned to the Church of England.

Never before had a Roman Catholic priest converted to Anglicanism with the blessings of the Roman Catholic Church. Cardinal Saint-Cloud and Pope Christopher wrote letters to the Archbishop of Norfolk to praise Father Wycliffe for his evangelization of Mars and the Moon. They asked the Anglican community to protect him always.

———

On a hot afternoon in July, the doorbell rang. Father Wycliffe opened the door. Carla Delgada, holding a tourist map of Walsingham, stood in the doorway.

"Father Wycliffe, I finally tracked you down!" Carla said.

"Carla, what a surprise!" Mark said. "Come in. Why didn't you tell me you were coming?"

"I wanted to, but I couldn't find you," Carla said. "I searched the Roman Catholic Shrine website, but I didn't find your name. I called the Shrine, but they said you had left the Roman Catholic Church. I asked them for your videophone number, but they said they couldn't tell me. They have a policy of protecting personal information."

"So how did you find me?" Mark asked as he led Carla into the living room.

"I went to the Anglican Shrine and bribed a secretary with some Moon rocks," Carla said.

Carla shoved the map back into her pocket. "I'm here for the summer on a student exchange program with the University of London. Amira and Rabbi Gabizon are both on Earth, and they say they can meet us anywhere in Europe. Maybe I can find out what Roxanne and Auguste and little Albert are doing. Do you want to have a Timonium Base reunion?"

"That would be splendid," Mark said.

Ingrid came into the living room. "Mark, are you going to introduce me to your friend?" she said.

Carla gave a puzzled look to Mark. "Hey, Father, who's that?" she whispered.

Carla could see Ingrid, Mark realized. Ingrid put her arms around Mark and smiled.

"Do you remember when I caught the garter at the wedding?" Mark said.

17 / THE POOL OF LIFE

The Greeneye Tribe's Chief dug the dirt away with his bare claws. He saw more of the tarnished metal plaque. Grasping it firmly, he pulled it out of the ground. He grunted in triumph as he held it up for all to see. His scales turned orange in excitement. As his youngest hatchling ran in front of him, his female carried their newest egg behind him. The tribe grunted and sang as he carried the metal plaque through the crowd.

The tribe walked around the Pool of Life. Each tribe made the pilgrimage every two to six years. Sometimes as many as ten tribes converged on the Pool at the same time. Since the beginning of time, the God-talkers had taught that life began at this Pool. Despite their differences, all the tribes agreed the Pool was sacred, so sacred that warring tribes lived in peace while camped around it.

Occasionally, someone found an object of unknown purpose by the Pool. Nobody knew what these objects were, but they knew the Sacrifice Gods had used them. The relics brought immense prestige to a tribe. Tribes with relics could camp closest to the Pool, where the mud was softest and warmest.

The Chief showed the metal plaque to the tribe's God-talker. The God-talker's tail wagged excitedly as he examined the plaque. As he felt the plaque, his scales turned orange.

It was a thick, metal, rectangular plaque. Like relics owned by other tribes, it had mysterious symbols of unknown meaning:

REDSANDS BASE

When the God-talker had visited the Bluetail Tribe, they had shown him another metal plaque. Reaching into his bag, he pulled out his sketch of the other plaque:

MARTIAN HABITAT
PROTECTED AREA
ENTRY PROHIBITED

The God-talker said that the symbols were the same as on the Bluetails' relic. He bared his fangs in happiness and declared the object to be a relic of the Sacrifice Gods.

The tribe's grunting sounded over the Pool. Now the Greeneye Tribe could camp in the most comfortable mud.

That night, as fires flickered in the mud flats, the God-talker felt the metal plaque. The plaque was tarnished, and corroded in places, but it was still in one piece. Its raised symbols had worn over the centuries, but they were still visible. The Sacrifice Gods were talented metalworkers.

Who were the Sacrifice Gods?

Like anyone else, God-talker had never seen a Sacrifice God, but he knew the stories that his people had told since time began. The Sacrifice Gods came from another world and threw themselves into the Pool of Life. Their physical bodies died and sank to the mud at the bottom of the Pool. Their remains mixed with the mud and became the first people. After creating the people, the Sacrifice Gods' spirits flew back to their home world. In ancient legends, they returned and left again.

Mars had three moons. Tonight, the God-talker could see the brightest one. Two of the moons had existed since the beginning of time. The third moon, the brightest one, was younger. The Sacrifice Gods created it somewhere else and moved it here.

A female ghost sat in the third moon and watched the world. Some tribes believed that the Sacrifice Gods made her; other tribes believed that *she* made the Sacrifice Gods. Sometime in the future, she would come down and visit the people.

God-watcher stared at the third moon and wondered when the ghost would come down.

AUTHOR'S AFTERWORD

Science fiction writers, fans, and scholars often discuss how accurately science fiction predicts the future. There is a paradox here; science fiction writers supposedly write about the future, but the stories are usually about today's issues. The future is science fiction's space for examining the present. Nonetheless, the writer has to create a credible future.

Science fiction writers, through extrapolation of current affairs or sheer imagination or both, have created futures with varying degrees of success. Sometimes, a successful prediction is cause for celebration, as with the Moon landing in 1969. Apollo 11 fulfilled the promise of countless stories dating back to Jules Verne's From the Earth to the Moon. At other times, a successful prediction is a sombre event, as with the Al-Qaida attacks of September 11, 2001. 9/11 was reminiscent of Tom Clancy's 1994 novel *Debt of Honor*, in which a Japanese pilot crashes his plane into the U.S. Capitol (However, *Debt of Honor*'s future war between the United States and Japan, with China and India aiding Japan, has not occurred. Indeed, Japan, China, and India are anything but allies now.).

I didn't accurately predict how Osama bin Laden would die, but I did better in extrapolating the Vernacular Wars. When I wrote *The Moon Under Her Feet* between 2005 and 2007, the West thought its arch enemies were Al-Qaida and other Islamist terrorist organizations. These organizations were deadly, but they had to work in secret and lacked the infrastructure of a state, the traditional form of the enemy in war. *The Moon Under Her Feet* has two countries, Purist Arabia and Sudan, forming the Holy Alliance for Monotheism, an authoritarian power with armies, weapons, land, and the entire natural, industrial, and human resources of its member states. In 2013, such a state emerged: the Islamic State of Iraq and the Levant (ISIL), also known as ISIS or Daesh. In the opinion of many Westerners, ISIL has replaced Al-Qaida as the major Islamist threat. The international community does not recognize the ISIL as a state, but it functions like one. It controls land and oil resources, has its own army, collects taxes, and runs social services, public utilities, public works, and law enforcement, albeit at a rudimentary level. ISIL is not merely a terrorist organization; it's a country.

In *The Moon Under Her Feet*, a series of wars between rival Moslem groups spreads into the Western countries. In 2007, these fictional conflicts must have seemed absurd to some readers; many Westerners perceived (and still perceive) the "War on Terror" as a war strictly between Islam and the West.

However, despite urging by Islamist extremists, the Moslem world has not united against the West. Instead, by 2016, most Middle Eastern conflicts are between Moslems: Sunni versus Shiite, liberals versus conservatives, rebels versus dictators, Saudi Arabia versus Iran, Turks versus Kurds, Kurds versus ISIL, ISIL versus everybody. It's true that Islamist terrorists have attacked Europe and North America; however, the majority of Islamist violence has targeted other Moslems in the Middle East. Until recently, the worst clash of civilizations was between Sunni and Shiite. That conflict hasn't ended, but now, rival Sunni groups are fighting each other, making the War on Terror more complicated, like in my novel.

Many Americans and Europeans do not realize — or are in denial — that Islam, like Christianity, is split into numerous diverse denominations. Some, like the Ahmadiyyah and the Ismailis, have no grudges against non-Moslems and are considered heretics by ultra-conservative sects like the Wahhabis. In *The Moon Under Her Feet*, the Holy Alliance for Monotheism isn't really interested in destroying Christianity of Western civilization. Instead, it wants to destroy other Moslems. However, the West, as the traditional defender of individualism and religious freedom, unwillingly gets in the way.

In *The Moon Under Her Feet*, Islamic Purists kill other Moslems in Europe for personal "sins" such as wearing a miniskirt or shaving a beard. As of 2015, Europe and North America have not experienced a widespread, violent morality campaign by Moslems against Moslems. However, the same cannot be said of Indonesia, Malaysia, and Brunei. These countries used to be relatively liberal and relaxed in personal freedoms, but in recent years, they have become more conservative. Local sharia law officials now publicly flog people whom they judge to have behaved immodestly. Such punishments were unknown only a few years ago. I predicted the shift to hardline restrictions on personal freedoms, though I didn't set it in the right countries.

When I wrote *The Moon Under Her Feet*, many North Americans thought terrorism was primarily committed by organized groups of foreigners entering the country. In my novel, a new type of terrorist appears: an individual working alone, undetected by his neighbours, attacking his own country. One such character blows up Mark Wycliffe's wife and son. A few years after *The Moon Under Her Feet* was published, the number of so-called "homegrown" and "self-radicalized" terrorists increased. Now Americans and Europeans worry about "homegrown and self-radicalized" terrorists as much, if not more, than they do about organized foreign terrorist groups.

Back in 2007, terrorists tended to attack targets important to the government, military, and economic infrastructure of their enemies: the World Trade Center, the Pentagon, the U.S.S. *Cole*, government offices and embassies, and transportation systems (such as the London subway bombings of 2005). Islamist terrorists rarely wasted their efforts on mundane, everyday places. However, Europe had a history of terrorism on both strategic and mundane targets, thanks to groups such as the Provisional Irish Republican Army and the Baader-Meinhof Gang. Also, in 2002, violent Islamists bombed a tourist district in Bali, a place with no military or governmental importance (though it was important to Bali's tourism industry). Mundane places were always at risk but people didn't think of them as the most likely targets.

In *The Moon Under Her Feet*, terrorists attack the most mundane targets, such as a menorah in a Las Vegas shopping plaza. Shopping malls and other religions' temples become regular targets in my novel. No target is too small for the Holy Alliance for Monotheism.

Sadly, reality has mirrored fiction. Attacks on mundane and non-strategic place have increased in number and casualties since *The Moon Under Her Feet* was published: Mumbai in 2008, Nairobi in 2013, and Paris and San Bernardino in 2015. Even a small Cambodian restaurant in Paris can be a target now.

When I wrote *The Moon Under Her Feet*, China rigidly abstained from military intervention overseas. Although China seemed willing to fight its neighbours over territorial and maritime disputes, China would never think of sending its military to another continent, except for U.N. peacekeeping missions.

That was in 2007. After *The Moon Her Feet* was published, China started its first military operations far beyond its borders. In 2008, the People's Liberation Army Navy began fighting the Somali pirates in the Gulf of Aden, the first time any Chinese warships had fought so far away from China's coastal waters and maritime claims. In 2015, China negotiated with Djibouti to build a naval base there, the first Chinese military base overseas. Later that year, China passed an anti-terrorism law that, for the first time, allows the Chinese military to engage in counter-terrorism operations overseas. In late 2015, the Russian media reported that China would send troops to join the Russians fighting ISIL in Syria. I predicted that China would fight wars abroad, and now it seems that China is ready and willing to do so.

What did I not predict correctly? As of 2016, Saudi Arabia has not turned into Purist Arabia – for now. However, the Kingdom has no shortage of extremists eager to overthrow the House of Saud and establish a more conservative regime, so a Purist Arabia is by no means impossible.

Somalia, despite its remarkable record of piracy, has not turned into a naval power. The ISIL does not have a navy and is unlikely to gain one. For now, the extreme Islamists lack sea power. I hope they never gain it.

How will the War on Terror and the Islamic Wars end? In *The Moon Under Her Feet*, China ends the Vernacular Wars by dropping a neutron bomb on Purist Arabia. That may seem like a desperate act, but when countries have been fighting for over a decade with no sign of an end to the war, they can resort to desperate measures. Hopefully, the real-life Vernacular Wars will end by other means. Only time will tell.

Derwin Mak
Toronto, January 5, 2016

ABOUT THE AUTHOR

Derwin Mak wearing the Medal of the Grand Associates of Brother André. Photo by Kent Wong.

Derwin Mak lives in Toronto, Canada. His short story *Transubstantiation* won the 2006 Aurora Award for Best Short Form-Work in English. He and Eric Choi co-edited *The Dragon and the Stars*, an anthology of science fiction and fantasy by ethnic Chinese outside China, which won the 2011 Aurora Award for Best Related Work in English. His first novel, *The Moon Under Her Feet*, was a finalist for the 2008 Aurora Award for Best Long-Form Work in English. His second novel, *The Shrine of the Siren Stone*, is another novel in the Siren Stone universe. Another story in the Siren Stone universe, "Mecha-Jesus", was a finalist for the 2015 Aurora Award for Best Short Fiction. Derwin also writes articles about East Asian pop culture and anime for *Parsec* and *Ricepaper* magazines.

Derwin is a chartered professional accountant with Master's degrees in accounting (University of Waterloo) and military studies (American Military University). He is a member of the Royal Canadian Military Institute, a vice-chair of its Library Committee, and an Officer of the Most Venerable Order of the Hospital of St. John of Jerusalem.

His website is www.derwinmaksf.com.

Made in the USA
Middletown, DE
09 April 2023